A Note From The Author

To the faithful followers of the chronicles of Darkover, whose greatest delight seems to be discovering even the most minute inconsistencies from book to book:

This book tells a story which a great many of the friends of Darkover have asked me to tell—the story of the early life of Regis Hastur, and of the Sharra rising, and of Lew Alton's first encounter with Marjorie Scott and the man who called himself Kadarin.

The faithful followers mentioned above will discover a very few minute inconsistencies between the account herein, and the story as Lew Alton told it later. I make no apology for these. The only explanation I can make is that in the years which elapsed between the events in this book, and the later novel dealing with the final destruction of the Sharra matrix, Lew's memories of these events may have altered his perceptions. Or, as I myself believe, the telepaths of the Arilinn Tower may have mercifully blurred his memories, to save his reason.

MARION ZIMMER BRADLEY

THE HERITAGE OF HASTUR

MARION
ZIMMER
BRADLEY

DAW BOOKS, INC.

DONALD A. WOLLHEIM, PUBLISHER

1633 Broadway, New York, NY 10019

FIRST PRINTING, AUGUST 1975

8 9 10 11 12 13 14

 DAW TRADEMARK REGISTERED
U.S. PAT. OFF. MARCA
REGISTRADA. HECHO EN U.S.A.

PRINTED IN U.S.A.

DEDICATION

for

Jacqueline Lichtenberg

Who convinced me that
this book could and
should be written, and
kept after me until
(and while)
I wrote it.

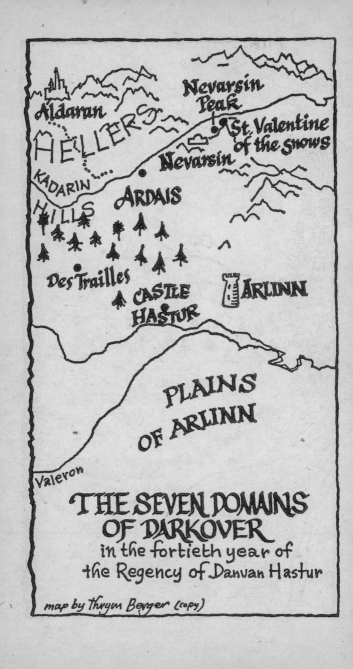

THE SEVEN DOMAINS
OF DARKOVER
in the fortieth year of
the Regency of Danvan Hastur

map by Thrym Berger (copy)

THE
HERITAGE
OF
HASTUR

Chapter ONE

As the riders came up over the pass which led down into Thendara, they could see beyond the old city to the Terran spaceport. Huge and sprawling, ugly and unfamiliar to their eyes, it spread like some strange growth below them. And all around it, ringing it like a scab, were the tightly clustered buildings of the Trade City which had grown between old Thendara and the spaceport.

Regis Hastur, riding slowly between his escorts, thought that it was not as ugly as they had told him in Nevarsin. It had its own beauty, an austere beauty of steel towers and stark white buildings, each for some alien and unknown purpose. It was not a cancer on the face of Darkover, but a strange and not unbeautiful garment.

The central tower of the new headquarters building faced the Comyn Castle, which stood across the valley, with an unfortunate aspect. It appeared to Regis that the tall skyscraper and the old stone castle were squared off and facing one another like two giants armed for combat.

But he knew that was ridiculous. There had been peace between the Terran Empire and the Domains all of his lifetime. The Hasturs made sure of it.

But the thought brought him no comfort. He was not much of a Hastur, he considered, but he was the last. They would make the best of him even though he was a damned poor substitute for his father, and everyone knew it. They'd never let him forget it for a minute.

His father had died fifteen years ago, just a month before Regis had been born. Rafael Hastur had at thirty-five already shown signs of being a strong statesman and leader, deeply loved by his people, respected even by the Terrans. And he had been blown to bits in the Kilghard Hills, killed by contraband weapons smuggled from the Terran Empire. Cut off in the full strength of his youth and promise, he had left only an eleven-year-old daughter and a fragile, pregnant wife. Alanna Elhalyn-Hastur had nearly died of the shock of his death. She had clung fitfully to life only because she knew she was carrying the last of the Hasturs, the longed-for son of Rafael. She had lived, racked with grief, just long enough for Regis to be born alive; then, almost with relief, she had laid her life down.

And after losing his father, after all his mother went through, Regis thought, all they got was him, not the son they would have chosen. He was strong enough physically, even good-looking, but curiously handicapped for a son of the telepathic caste of the Domains, the Comyn. A nontelepath. At fifteen, if he had inherited laran power, he would have shown signs of it.

Behind him, he heard his bodyguards talking in low tones.

"I see they've finished their headquarters building. Hell of a place to put it, within a stone's throw of Comyn Castle."

"Well, they started to build it back in the Hellers, at Caer Donn. It was old Istvan Hastur, in my grandsire's time, who made them move the spaceport to Thendara. He must have had his reasons."

"Should have left it there, away from decent folk!"

"Oh, the Terrans aren't all bad. My brother keeps a shop in the Trade City. Anyway, would you want the *Terranan* back in the hills, where those mountain bandits and the damned Aldarans could deal with them behind our backs?"

"Damned savages," the second man said. "They don't even observe the Compact back there. You see them in the Hellers, wearing their filthy cowards' weapons."

"What would you expect of the Aldarans?" They lowered their voices, and Regis sighed. He was used to it. He put constraint on everyone, just by being what he was: Comyn and Hastur. They probably thought he could read their minds. Most Comyn could.

"Lord Regis," said one of his guards, "there's a party of riders coming down the northward road carrying banners. They must be the party from Armida, with Lord Alton. Shall we wait for them and ride together?"

Regis had no particular desire to join another party of Comyn lords, but it would have been an unthinkable breach of manners to say so. At Council season all the Domains met together at Thendara; Regis was bound by the custom of generations to treat them all as kinsmen and brothers. And the Altons *were* his kinsmen.

They slackened pace and waited for the other riders.

They were still high on the slopes, and he could see past Thendara to the spread-out spaceport itself. A great distant sound, like a faraway waterfall, made the ground vibrate like thunder, even where he stood. A tiny toylike form began to rise far out on the spaceport, slowly at first, then faster and faster. The sound peaked to a faint scream; the shape was a faraway streak, a dot, was gone.

Regis let his breath go. A starship of the Empire, outward bound for distant worlds, distant suns.... Regis realized his fists had clenched so tightly on the reins that his horse tossed its head, protesting. He slackened them and gave the horse an absentminded, apologetic pat on the neck. His eyes were still riveted on the spot in the sky where the starship had vanished.

Outward bound, free for the immeasurable immensities of space, the ship was headed to worlds whose wonders he, chained down here, could never guess. His throat felt tight. He wished he were not too old to cry, but the heir to Hastur could not make any display of unmanly emotion in public. He wondered why he was getting so worked up about this, but he knew the answer: that ship was going where he could never go.

The riders from the pass were nearer now; Regis could identify some of them. Next to his bannerman rode Kennard, Lord Alton, a stooped, heavy-set man with red hair going gray. Except for Danvan Hastur, Regent of the Comyn, Kennard was probably the most powerful man in the Seven Domains. Regis had known Kennard all his life; as a child, he had called him uncle. Behind him, among a whole assembly of kinsmen, servants, bodyguards and poor relations, he saw the banner of the Ardais Domain, so Lord Dyan must be with them.

One of Regis' guards said in an undertone, "I see the old buzzard has both his bastards with him. Wonder how he has the face?"

"Old Kennard can face anything, and make Hastur like it," returned the other man in a prison-yard mutter. "Anyway, young Lew's not a bastard; Kennard got him legitimated so he could work in the Arilinn Tower. The younger one—"

The guard saw Regis glance his way and he stiffened; the expression slid off his face as if a sponge had wiped it blank.

Damn it, Regis thought irritably, I can't read your mind, man, I've just got good, normal ears. But in any case, he realized, he had overheard an insolent remark about a Comyn lord, and the guard would have been embarrassed about that. There was an old proverb: *The mouse in the walls may look at a cat, but he is wise not to squeak about it.*

Regis, of course, knew the old story. Kennard had done a shocking, even a shameful thing: he had taken, in honorable marriage, a half-Terran woman, kin to the renegade Domain of Aldaran. Comyn Council had never accepted the marriage or the sons. Not even for Kennard's sake.

Kennard rode toward Regis. "Greetings, Lord Regis. Are you riding to Council?"

Regis felt exasperated at the obviousness of the question—where else would he be going, on this road, at this season?—until he realized that the formal words implied recognition as an adult. He replied, with equally formal courtesy, "Yes, kinsman, my grandsire has requested that I attend Council this year."

"Have you been all these years in the monastery at Nevarsin, kinsman?"

Kennard knew perfectly well where he had been, Regis reflected; when his grandfather couldn't think of any other way to get Regis off his hands, he packed him away to Saint-Valentine-of-the-Snows. But it would have been a fearful breach of manners to mention this before the assembly so he merely said, "Yes, he entrusted my education to the *cristoforos;* I have been there three years."

"Well, that was a hell of a way to treat the heir to Hastur," said a harsh, musical voice. Regis looked up and recognized Lord Dyan Ardais, a pale, tall, hawk-faced man he had seen making brief visits to the monastery. Regis bowed and greeted him. "Lord Dyan."

Dyan's eyes, keen and almost colorless—there was said to be *chieri* blood in the Ardais—rested on Regis. "I told Hastur that only a fool would send a boy to be brought up in that place. But I gathered that he was much occupied with affairs of state, such as settling all the troubles the *Terranan* have brought to our world. I offered to have you fostered at Ardais; my sister Elorie bore no living child and would have welcomed a kinsman to rear. But your grandsire, I gather, thought me no fit guardian for a boy your age." He gave a faint, sarcastic smile. "Well, you seem to have survived three years at the hands of the *cristoforos*. How was it in Nevarsin, Regis?"

"Cold." Regis hoped that settled that.

"How well I remember," Dyan said, laughing. "I was brought up by the brothers, too, you know. My father still had his wits then—or enough of them to keep me well out of sight of his various excesses. I spent the whole five years shivering."

Kennard lifted a gray eyebrow. "I don't remember that it was so cold."

"But you were warm in the guesthouse," Dyan said with a smile. "They keep fires there all year, and you could have had someone to warm your bed if you chose. The students' dormitory at Nevarsin—I give you my solemn word—is the coldest place on Darkover. Haven't you watched those poor brats shivering their way through the offices? Have they made a *cristoforo* of you, Regis?"

Regis said briefly, "No, I serve the Lord of Light, as is proper for a son of Hastur."

Kennard gestured to two lads in the Alton colors, and they rode forward a little way. "Lord Regis," he said formally, "I ask leave to present my sons: Lewis-Kennard Montray-Alton; Marius Montray-Lanart."

Regis felt briefly at a loss. Kennard's sons were not accepted by Council, but if Regis greeted them as kinsman and equals, he would give them Hastur recognition. If not, he would affront his kinsman. He was angry at Kennard for making this choice necessary, especially when there was nothing about Comyn etiquette or diplomacy that Kennard did not know.

Lew Alton was a tall, sturdy young man, five or six years older than Regis. He said with a wry smile, "It's all right, Lord Regis, I was legitimated and formally designated heir a couple of years ago. It's quite permissible for you to be polite to me."

Regis felt his face flaming with embarrassment. He said, "Grandfather wrote me the news; I had forgotten. Greetings, cousin, have you been long on the road?"

"A few days," Lew said. "The road is peaceful, although my brother, I think, found it a long ride. He's very young for such a journey. You remember Marius, don't you?"

Regis realized with relief that Marius, called Montray-Lanart instead of Alton because he had not yet been accepted as a legitimate son, was only twelve years old—too young in any case for a formal greeting. The question could be sidestepped by treating him as a child. He said, "You've grown since I last saw you, Marius. I don't suppose you remember me at all. You're old enough now to ride a horse, at least. Do you still have the little gray pony you used to ride at Armida?"

Marius answered politely, "Yes, but he's out at pasture; he's old and lame, too old for such a trip."

Kennard looked annoyed. Diplomacy indeed! His grandfather would be proud of him, Regis considered, even if he was not proud of himself for the art of double tongues. Fortunately, Marius was not old enough to know he'd been snubbed. It occurred to Regis how ridiculous it was for boys their own age to address one another so formally anyway. Lew and he used to be close friends. The years at Armida, before Regis went to the monastery, they were as close as brothers. And now Lew was calling him Lord Regis! It was stupid!

Kennard looked at the sky. "Shall we ride on? It's near sunset and sure to rain. It would be a nuisance to have to stop and pack away the banners. And your grandfather will be eager to see you, Regis."

"My grandfather has been spared my presence for three years," Regis said dryly. "I am sure he can endure another hour or so. But it would be better not to ride in the dark."

Protocol said that Regis should ride beside Kennard and Lord Dyan, but instead he dropped back to ride beside Lew Alton. Marius was riding with a boy about Regis' own age, who looked so familiar that Regis frowned, trying to recall where they'd met.

While the entourage was getting into line, Regis sent his banner-bearer to ride at the head of the column with those of Ardais and Alton. He watched the man ride ahead with the silver-and-blue fir-tree emblem of Hastur and the *casta* slogan, *Permanedál. I shall remain,* he translated wearily, yes, I shall stay here and be a Hastur whether I like it or not.

Then rebellion gripped him again. Kennard hadn't stayed. He was educated on Terra itself, and by the will of the Council. Maybe there was hope for Regis too, Hastur or no.

He felt queerly lonely. Kennard's maneuvering for proper respect for his sons had irritated him, but it had touched him too. If his own father had lived, he wondered, would he have been so solicitous? Would he have schemed and intrigued to keep his son from feeling inferior?

Lew's face was grim, lonely and sullen. Regis couldn't tell if he felt slighted, ill-treated or just lonely, knowing himself different.

Lew said, "Are you coming to take a seat in Council, Lord Regis?"

The formality irritated Regis again. Was it a snub in return for the one he had given Marius? Suddenly he was tired of this. "You used to call me cousin, Lew. Are we too old to be friends?"

A quick smile lighted Lew's face. He was handsome without the sullen, withdrawn look. "Of course not, cousin. But I've had it rubbed into me, in the cadets and elsewhere, that you are Regis-Rafael, Lord Hastur, and I'm ... well, I'm *nedestro* heir to Alton. They only accepted me because my father has no proper Darkovan sons. I decided that it was up to you whether or not you cared to claim kin."

Regis' mouth stretched in a grimace. He shrugged. "Well, they may have to accept me, but I might as well be a bastard. I haven't inherited *laran*."

Lew looked shocked. "But certainly, you—I was sure—" He broke off. "Just the same, you'll have a seat in Council, cousin. There *is* no other Hastur heir."

"I'm all too well aware of that. I've heard nothing else since the day I was born," Regis said. "Although, since Javanne married Gabriel Lanart, she's having sons like kittens. One of them may very well displace me some day."

"Still, you are in the direct line of male descent. A *laran* gift does skip a generation now and then. All your sons could inherit it."

Regis said with impulsive bitterness, "Do you think that helps—to know that I'm of no value for myself, but only for the sons I may have?"

A thin, fine drizzle of rain was beginning to fall. Lew drew his hood up over his shoulders and the insignia of the City Guard showed on his cloak. So he's taking the regular duties of a Comyn heir, Regis thought. He may be a bastard, but he's more useful than I am.

Lew said aloud, as if picking up his thoughts, "I expect you'll be going into the cadet corps of the Guard this season, won't you? Or are the Hasturs exempt?"

"It's all planned out for us, isn't it, Lew? Ten years old, fire-watch duty. Thirteen or fourteen, the cadet corps. Take my turn as an officer. Take a seat in Council at the proper time. Marry the right woman, if they can find one from a family that's old enough and important enough and, above all, with *laran*. Father a lot of sons, and a lot of daughters to marry other Comyn sons. They've got our lives all planned, and all we have to do is go through the motions, ride their road whether we want to or not."

Lew looked uneasy, but he didn't answer. Obediently, like a proper prince, Regis drew a little ahead, to ride through the city gates in his proper place beside Kennard and Lord Dyan. His head was getting wet but, he thought sourly, it was his duty to be seen, to be put on display. A little thing like a soaking wasn't supposed to bother a Hastur.

He forced himself to smile and wave graciously at the crowds lining the streets. But far away, through the very ground, he could hear again the dull vibration, like a waterfall. The starships were still there, he told himself, and the stars beyond them. No matter how deep they cut the track, I'll find a way to break loose somehow. Someday.

Chapter TWO

(Lewis-Kennard Montray-Alton's narrative)

I hadn't wanted to attend Council this year. To be exact, I never wanted to attend Council at all. That's putting it mildly. I'm not popular with my father's equals in the Seven Domains.

At Armida, nothing bothers me. The house-folk know who I am and the horses don't care. And at Arilinn nobody inquires about your family, your pedigree or your legitimacy. The only thing that matters in a Tower is your ability to manipulate a matrix and key into the energon rings and relay screens. If you're competent, no one cares whether you were born between silk sheets in a great house or in a ditch beside the road; and if you're not competent, you don't come there at all.

You may ask why, if I was good at managing the estate at Armida, and more than adequate in the matrix relays at Arilinn, Father had this flea in his brain about forcing me on the Council. You may ask, but you'll have to ask someone else. I have no idea.

Whatever his reasons, he had managed to force me on the Council as his heir. They hadn't liked it, but they'd had to allow me the legitimate privileges of a Comyn heir and the duties that went with them. Which meant that at fourteen I had gone into the cadets and, after serving as a junior officer, was now a captain in the City Guard. It was a privilege I could have done without. The Council lords might be forced to accept me. But making the younger sons, lesser nobles and so forth who served in the cadets accept me—that was another song!

Bastardy, of course, is no special disgrace. Plenty of

21

Comyn lords have half a dozen. If one of them turns out to have *laran*—which is what every woman who bears a child to a Comyn lord hopes for—nothing is easier than having the child acknowledged and given privileges and duties somewhere in the Domains. But to make one of them the heir-designate to the Domain, *that* was unprecedented, and every unacknowledged son of a minor line made me feel how little I merited this special treatment.

I couldn't help knowing why they felt that way—I had what every one of them wanted, felt he merited as much as I did. But understanding only made things worse. It must be comfortable never to know *why* you're disliked. Maybe then you can believe you don't deserve it.

Just the same, I've made sure none of them could complain about me. I've done a little of everything, as Comyn heirs in the cadets are supposed to: I've supervised street patrols, organizing everything from grain supplies for the pack animals to escorts for Comyn ladies; I've assisted the armsmaster at his job, and made sure that the man who cleaned the barracks knew *his* job. I disliked serving in the cadets and didn't enjoy command duty in the Guard. But what could I do? It was a mountain I could neither cross nor go around. Father needed me and wanted me, and I could not let him stand alone.

As I rode at Regis Hastur's side, I wondered if his choosing to ride beside me had been a mark of friendship or a shrewd attempt to get on the good side of my father. Three years ago I'd have said friendship, certainly. But boys change in three years, and Regis had changed more than most.

He'd spent a few winters at Armida before he went to the monastery, before I went to Arilinn. I'd never thought about him being heir to Hastur. They said his health was frail; old Hastur thought that country living and company would do him good. He'd mostly been left to me to look after. I'd taken him riding and hawking, and he'd gone with me up into the plateaus when the great herds of wild horses were caught and brought down to be broken. I remembered him best as an undersized youngster, following me around, wearing my outgrown breeches and shirts because he kept growing out of his own; playing with the puppies and newborn foals, bending solemnly over the clumsy stitches he was learning to set in hawking-hoods, learning swordplay from Father and practicing with me. During the terrible spring of his twelfth year, when the Kilghard Hills had gone up in forest fires and every able-bodied man between ten and eighty was commandeered into the fire-lines, we'd gone together, working side by side by day, eating from one bowl and sharing blankets at night. We'd been afraid Armida itself would go up in the holocaust; some of the outbuildings were lost in the backfire. We'd been closer than brothers. When he went to Nevarsin, I'd missed him terribly. It was difficult to reconcile my memories of that almost-brother with this self-possessed, solemn young prince. Maybe he'd learned, in the interval, that friendship with Kennard's *nedestro* heir was not quite the thing for a Hastur.

I could have found out, of course, and he'd never have known. But that's not even a temptation for a telepath, after the first few months. You learn not to pry.

But he didn't *feel* unfriendly, and presently asked me outright why I hadn't called him by name; caught off guard by the blunt question, I gave him a straight answer instead of a diplomatic one and then, of course, we were all right again.

Once we were inside the gates, the ride to the castle was not long, just long enough to get thoroughly drenched. I could tell that Father was aching with the damp and cold—he's been lame ever since I could remember, but the last few winters have been worse—and that Marius was wet and wretched. When we came into the lee of the castle it was already dark, and though the nightly rain rarely turns to snow at this season, there were sharp slashes of sleet in it. I slid from my horse and went quickly to help Father dismount, but Lord Dyan had already helped him down and given him his arm.

I withdrew. From my first year in the cadets, I'd made it a habit not to get any closer to Lord Dyan than I could possibly help. Preferably well out of reach.

There's a custom in the Guards for first-year cadets. We're trained in unarmed combat and we're supposed to cultivate a habit of being watchful at all times; so during our first season, in the guardroom and armory, anyone superior to us in the Guards is allowed to take us by surprise, if he can, and throw us. It's good training. After a few weeks of being grabbed unexpectedly from behind and dumped hard on a stone floor, you develop something like eyes in the back of your head. Usually it's fairly good-natured, and although it's a rough game and you collect plenty of bruises, no one really minds.

Dyan, we all agreed, enjoyed it entirely too much. He was an expert wrestler and could have made his point without doing much harm, but he was unbelievably rough and never missed a chance to hurt somebody. Especially me. Once he somehow managed to dislocate my elbow, which I wore in a sling for the rest of that season. He said it was an accident, but I'm a telepath and he didn't even bother to conceal how much he had enjoyed doing it. I wasn't the only cadet who had that experience. During cadet training, there are times when you hate all your officers. But Dyan was the only one we really feared.

I left Father to him and went back to Regis. "Someone's looking for you," I told him, pointing out a man in Hastur livery, sheltering in a doorway and looking wet and miserable, as if he'd been out in the weather, waiting, for some time. Regis turned eagerly to hear the message.

"The Regent's compliments, Lord Regis. He has been urgently called into the city. He asks you to make yourself comfortable and to see him in the morning."

Regis made some formal answer and turned to me with a humorless smile. "So much for the eager welcome of my loving grandsire."

One hell of a welcome, indeed, I thought. No one could expect the Regent of Comyn to stand out in the rain and wait, but he could have sent more than a servant's message! I said quickly, "You'll come to us, of course. Send a message with your grandfather's man and come along for some dry clothing and some supper!"

Regis nodded without speaking. His lips were blue with cold, his hair lying soaked on his forehead. He gave appropriate orders, and I went back to my own task: making sure that all of Father's entourage, servants, bodyguards, Guardsmen, banner-bearers and poor relations, found their way to their appointed places.

Things gradually got themselves sorted out. The Guardsmen went off to their own quarters. The servants mostly knew what to do. Someone had sent word ahead to have fires lighted and the rooms ready for occupancy. The rest of us found our way through the labyrinth of halls and corridors to the quarters reserved, for the last dozen generations, to the Alton lords. Before long no one was left in the main hall of our quarters except Father, Marius and myself, Regis, Lord Dyan, our personal servants and half a dozen others. Regis was standing before the fire warming his hands. I remembered the night when Father had broken the news that he was to leave us and spend the next three years at Nevarsin. He and I had been sitting before the fire in the great hall at Armida, cracking nuts and throwing the shells into the fire; after Father finished speaking he had gone to the fire and stood there just like that, quenched and shivering, his face turned away from us all.

Damn the old man! Was there no friend, no kinswoman, he could send to welcome Regis home?

Father came to the fire. He was limping badly. He looked at Marius' riding companion and said, "Danilo, I had your things sent directly to the cadet barracks. Shall I send a man to show you the way, or do you think you can find it?"

"There's no need to send anyone, Lord Alton." Danilo Syrtis came away from the fire and bowed courteously. He was a slender, bright-eyed boy of fourteen or so, wearing shabby garments which I vaguely recognized as once having been my brother's or mine, long outgrown. That was like Father; he'd make sure that any protégé of his started with the proper outfit for a cadet. Father laid a hand on his shoulder. "You're sure? Well, then, run along, my lad, and good luck go with you."

Danilo, with a polite formula murmured vaguely at all of us, withdrew. Dyan Ardais, warming his hands at the fire, looked after him, eyebrows lifted. "Nice looking youngster. Another of your *nedestro* sons, Kennard?"

"Dani? Zandru's hells, no! I'd be proud enough to claim him, but truly he's none of mine. The family has Comyn blood, a few generations back, but they're poor as miser's mice; old Dom Felix couldn't give him a good start in life, so I got him a cadet commission."

Regis turned away from the fire and said, "Danilo! I knew I should have recognized him; he was at the monastery one year. I truly couldn't remember his name, Uncle. I should have greeted him!"

The word he used for *uncle* was the *casta* term slightly more intimate than *kinsman*: I knew he had been speaking to my father, but Dyan chose to take it as addressed to himself. "You'll see him in the cadets, surely. And I haven't greeted you properly, either." He came and took Regis in a kinsman's

embrace, pressing his cheek, to which Regis submitted, a little flustered; then, holding him at arm's length, Dyan looked
closely at him. "Does your sister hate you for being the
beauty of the family, Regis?"

Regis looked startled and a little embarrassed. He said,
laughing nervously, "Not that she ever told me. I suspect
Javanne thinks I should be running around in a pinafore."

"Which proves what I have always said, that women are no
judge of beauty." My father gave him a black scowl and said,
"Damn it, Dyan, don't tease him."

Dyan would have said more—damn the man, was he start-
ing that again, after all the trouble last year—but a servant
in Hastur livery came in quickly and said, "Lord Alton, a
message from the Regent."

Father tore the letter open, began to swear volubly in
three languages. He told the messenger to wait while he got
into some dry clothes, disappeared into his room, and then I
heard him shouting to Andres. Soon he came out, tucking a
dry shirt into dry breeches, and scowling angrily.

"Father, what is it?"

"The usual," he said grimly, "trouble in the city. Hastur's
summoned every available Council elder and sending two extra patrols. Evidently a crisis of some sort."

Damn, I thought. After the long ride from Armida and a
soaking, to call him out at night . . . "Will you need me, Father?"

He shook his head. "No. Not necessary, son. Don't wait
up, I'll probably be out all night." As he went out, Dyan said,
"I expect a similar summons awaits me in my own rooms; I
had better go and find out. Good night, lads. I envy you
your good night's sleep." He added, with a nod to Regis,
"These others will never appreciate a proper bed. Only we
who have slept on stone know how to do that." He managed
to make a deep formal bow to Regis and simultaneously ignore me completely—it wasn't easy when we were standing
side by side—and went away.

I looked around to see what remained to be settled. I sent
Marius to change out of his drenched clothes—too old for a
nanny and too young for an aide-de-camp, he's left to me
much of the time. Then I arranged to have a room made
ready for Regis. "Have you a man to dress you, Regis? Or
shall I have father's body-servant wait on you tonight?"

"I learned to look after myself at Nevarsin," Regis said.

He looked warmer now, less tense. "If the Regent is sending for all the Council, I suspect it's really serious and not just that Grandfather has forgotten me again. That makes me feel better."

Now I was free to get out of my own wet things. "When you've changed, Regis, we'll have dinner here in front of the fire. I'm not officially on duty till tomorrow morning."

I went and changed quickly into indoor clothing, slid my feet into fur-lined ankle-boots and looked briefly in on Marius; I found him sitting up in bed, eating hot soup and already half asleep. It was a long ride for a boy his age. I wondered again why Father had subjected him to it.

The servants had set up a hot meal before the fire, in front of the old stone seats there. The lights in our part of the castle are the old ones, luminous rock from deep caves which charge with light all day and give off a soft glow all night. Not enough for reading or fine needlework, but plenty for a quiet meal and a comfortable talk by firelight. Regis came back, in dry garments and indoor boots, and I gestured the old steward away. "Go and get your own supper; Lord Regis and I can wait on ourselves."

I took the covers off the dishes. They had sent in a fried fowl and some vegetable stew. I helped him, saying, "Not very festive, but probably the best they could do at short notice."

"It's better than we got on the fire-lines," Regis said and I grinned. "So you remember that too?"

"How could I forget it? Armida was like home to me. Does Kennard still break his own horses, Lew?"

"No, he's far too lame," I said, and wondered again how Father would manage in the coming season. Selfishly, I hoped he would be able to continue in command. It's hereditary to the Altons, and I was next in line for it. They had learned to tolerate me as his deputy, holding captain's rank. As commander, I'd have all those battles to fight again.

We talked for a little while about Armida, about horses and hawks, while Regis finished the stew in his bowl. He picked up an apple and went to the fireplace, where a pair of antique swords, used only in the sword-dance now, hung over the mantel. He touched the hilt of one and I asked, "Have you forgotten all your fencing in the monastery, Regis?"

"No, there were some of us who weren't to be monks, so

Father Master gave us leave to practice an hour every day,
and an arms-master came to give us lessons."

Over wine we discussed the state of the roads from Nevarsin.

"Surely you didn't ride in one day from the monastery?"

"Oh, no. I broke my journey at Edelweiss."

That was on Alton lands. When Javanne Hastur married
Gabriel Lanart, ten years ago, my father had leased them the
estate. "Your sister is well, I hope?"

"Well enough, but extremely pregnant just now," Regis
said, "and Javanne's done a ridiculous thing. It made sense to
call their first son Rafael, after her father and mine. And the
second, of course, is the younger Gabriel. But when she
named the third Mikhail, she made the whole thing absurd. I
believe she's praying frantically for a girl this time!"

I laughed. By all accounts the "Lanart angels" should be
named for the archfiends, not the archangels; and why should
a Hastur seek names from *cristoforo* mythology? "Well, she
and Gabriel have sons enough."

"True. I am sure my grandfather is annoyed that she
should have so many sons, and cannot give them Domain-
right in Hastur. And I should have told Kennard; her husband will be here in a few days to take his place in the
Guard. He would have ridden with me, but with Javanne so
near to her time, he got leave to remain with her till she is
delivered."

I nodded; of course he would stay. Gabriel Lanart was a
minor noble of the Alton Domain, a kinsman of our own,
and a telepath. Of course he would follow the custom of the
Domains, that a man shares with his child's mother the ordeal
of birth, staying in rapport with her until the child is born
and all is well. Well, we could spare him for a few days. A
good man, Gabriel.

"Dyan seemed to take it for granted that you would be in
the cadets this year," I said.

"I don't know if I'll have a choice. Did you?"

I hadn't, of course. But that the heir to Hastur, of all people, should question it—that made me uneasy.

Regis sat on the stone bench, restlessly scuffing his felt ankle-boots on the floor. "Lew, you're part Terran and yet
you're Comyn. Do you feel as if you belonged to us? Or to
the Terrans?"

A disturbing question, an outrageous question, and one I

had never dared ask myself. I felt angry at him for speaking it, as if taunting me with what I was. Here I was an alien; among the Terrans, a freak, a mutant, a telepath. I said at last, bitterly, "I've never belonged anywhere. Except, perhaps, at Arilinn."

Regis raised his face, and I was startled at the sudden anguish there. "Lew, what does it feel like to have *laran?*"

I stared at him, disconcerted. The question touched off another memory. That summer at Armida, in his twelfth year. Because of his age, and because there was no one else, it had fallen to me to answer certain questions usually left to fathers or elder brothers, to instruct him in certain facts proper to adolescents. He had blurted those questions out, too, with the same kind of half-embarrassed urgency, and I'd found it just as difficult to answer them. There are some things it's almost impossible to discuss with someone who hasn't shared the experience. I said at last, slowly, "I hardly know how to answer. I've had it so long, it would be harder to imagine what it feels like *not* to have *laran.*"

"Were you born with it, then?"

"No, no, of course not. But when I was ten, or eleven, I began to be aware of what people were feeling. Or thinking. Later my father found out—proved to them—that I had the Alton gift, and that's rare even—" I set my teeth and said it, "even in legitimate sons. After that, they couldn't deny me Comyn rights."

"Does it always come so early? Ten, eleven?"

"Have you never been tested? I was almost certain . . ." I felt a little confused. At least once during the shared fears of that last season together, on the fire-lines, I had touched his mind, sensed that he had the gift of our caste. But he had been very young then. And the Alton gift is forced rapport, even with non-telepaths.

"Once," said Regis, "about three years ago. The *leronis* said I had the potential, as far as she could tell, but she could not reach it."

I wondered if that was why the Regent had sent him to Nevarsin: either hoping that discipline, silence and isolation would develop his *laran,* which sometimes happened, or trying to conceal his disappointment in his heir.

"You're a licensed matrix mechanic, aren't you, Lew? What's that like?"

This I could answer. "You know what a matrix is: a jewel stone that amplifies the resonances of the brain and transmutes psi power into energy. For handling major forces, it demands a group of linked minds, usually in a tower circle."

"I know what a matrix is," he said. "They gave me one when I was tested." He showed it to me, hung, as most of us carried them, in a small silk-lined leather bag about his neck. "I've never used it, or even looked at it again. In the old days, I know, they made these mind-links through the Keepers. They don't have Keepers any more, do they?"

"Not in the old sense," I said, "although the woman who works centerpolar in the matrix circles is still called a Keeper. In my father's time they discovered that a Keeper could function, except at the very highest levels, without all the old taboos and terrible training, the sacrifice, isolation, special cloistering. His foster-sister Cleindori was the first to break the tradition, and they don't train Keepers in the old way any more. It's too difficult and dangerous, and it's not fair to ask anyone to give up their whole lives to it any more. Now everyone spends three years or less at Arilinn, and then spends the same amount of time outside, so that they can learn to live normal lives." I was silent, thinking of my circle at Arilinn, now scattered to their homes and estates. I had been happy there, useful, accepted. Competent. Some day I would go back to this work again, in the relays.

"What it's like," I continued, "it's—it's intimate. You're completely open to the members of your circle. Your thoughts, your very feelings affect them, and you're wholly vulnerable to theirs. It's more than the closeness of blood kin. It's not exactly love. It's not sexual desire. It's like—like living with your skin off. Twice as tender to everything. It's not like anything else."

His eyes were rapt. I said harshly, "Don't romanticize it. It can be wonderful, yes. But it can be sheer hell. Or both at once. You learn to keep your distance, just to survive."

Through the haze of his feelings I could pick up just a fraction of his thoughts. I was trying to keep my awareness of him as low as possible. He was, damn it, too vulnerable. He was feeling forgotten, rejected, alone. I couldn't help picking it up. But a boy his age would think it prying.

"Lew, the Alton gift is the ability to force rapport. If I do have *laran*, could you open it up, make it function?"

I looked at him in dismay. "You fool. Don't you know I could kill you that way?"

"Without *laran*, my life doesn't amount to much." He was as taut as a strung bow. Try as I might, I could not shut out the terrible hunger in him to be part of the only world he knew, not to be so desperately deprived of his heritage.

It was my own hunger. I had felt it, it seemed, since my birth. Yet nine months before my birth, my father had made it impossible for me to belong wholly to his world and mine.

I faced the torture of knowing that, deeply as I loved my father, I hated him, too. Hated him for making me bastard, half-caste, alien, belonging nowhere. I clenched my fists, looking away from Regis. He had what I could never have. He belonged, full Comyn, by blood and law, legitimate—

And yet he was suffering, as much as I was. Would I give up *laran* to be legitimate, accepted, belonging?

"Lew, will you try at least?"

"Regis, if I killed you, I'd be guilty of murder." His face turned white. "Frightened? Good. It's an insane idea. Give it up, Regis. Only a catalyst telepath can ever do it safely and I'm not one. As far as I know, there are no catalyst telepaths alive now. Let well enough alone."

Regis shook his head. He said, forcing the words through a dry mouth, "Lew, when I was twelve years old you called me *bredu*. There is no one else, no one I can ask for this. I don't care if it kills me. I have heard"—he swallowed hard—"that *bredin* have an obligation, one to the other. Was it only an idle word, Lew?"

"It was no idle word, *bredu*," I muttered, wrung with his pain, "but we were children then. And this is no child's play, Regis, it's your life."

"Do you think I don't know that?" He was stammering. "It *is* my life. At least it can make the difference in what my life will be." His voice broke. "*Bredu* . . ." he said again and was silent, and I knew it was because he could not go on without weeping.

The appeal left me defenseless to him. Try as I might to stay aloof, that helpless, choked "*Bredu* . . ." had broken my last defense. I knew I was going to do what he wanted. "I can't do what was done to me," I told him. "That's a specific test for the Alton gift—forcing rapport—and only a full Alton can live through it. My father tried it, just once, with my full knowledge that it might very well kill me, and only for about thirty seconds. If the gift hadn't bred true, I'd have died. The fact that I didn't die was the ,only way he could think of to prove to Council that they could not refuse to accept me." My voice wavered. Even after almost ten years, I didn't like thinking about it. "Your blood, or your paternity, isn't in question. You don't need to take that kind of risk."

"*You* were willing to take it."

I had been. Time slid out of focus, and once again I stood before my father, his hands touching my temples, living again that memory of terror, that searing agony. I had been willing because I had shared my father's anguish, the terrible need in him to know I was his true son—the knowledge that if he could not force Council to accept me as his son, life alone was worth nothing. I would rather have died, just then, than live to face the knowledge of failure.

Memory receded. I looked into Regis' eyes.

"I'll do what I can. I can test you, as I was tested at Arilinn. But don't expect too much. I'm not a *leronis*, only a technician."

I drew a long breath. "Show me your matrix."

He fumbled with the strings at the neck, tipped the stone out in his palm, held it out to me. That told me as much as I needed to know. The lights in the small jewel were dim, inactive. If he had worn it for three years and his *laran* was active, he would have rough-keyed it even without knowing it. The first test had failed, then.

As a final test, with excruciating care, I laid a fingertip against the stone; he did not flinch. I signaled to him to put it away, loosened the neck of the case of my own. I laid my matrix, still wrapped in the insulating silk, in the palm of my hand, then bared it carefully.

"Look into this. No, don't touch it," I warned, with a drawn breath. "Never touch a keyed matrix; you could throw me into shock. Just look into it."

Regis bent, focused with motionless intensity on the tiny ribbons of moving light inside the jewel. At last he looked away. Another bad sign. Even a latent telepath should have had enough energon patterns disrupted inside his brain to show *some* reaction: sickness, nausea, causeless euphoria. I asked cautiously, not wanting to suggest anything to him, "How do you feel?"

"I'm not sure," he said uneasily. "It hurt my eyes."

Then he had at least latent *laran*. Arousing it, though,

might be a difficult and painful business. Perhaps a catalyst telepath could have roused it. They had been bred for that work, in the days when Comyn did complex and life-shattering work in the higher-level matrices. I'd never known one. Perhaps the set of genes was extinct.

Just the same, as a latent, he deserved further testing. I knew he had the potential. I had known it when he was twelve years old.

"Did the *leronis* test you with *kirian*?" I asked.

"She gave me a little. A few drops."

"What happened?"

"It made me sick," Regis said, "dizzy. Flashing colors in front of my eyes. She said I was probably too young for much reaction, that in some people, *laran* developed later."

I thought that over. *Kirian* is used to lower the resistance against telepathic contact; it's used in treating empaths and other psi technicians who, without much natural telepathic gift, must work directly with other telepaths. It can sometimes ease fear or deliberate resistance to telepathic contact. It can also be used, with great care, to treat threshold sickness—that curious psychic upheaval which often seizes on young telepaths at adolescence.

Well, Regis seemed young for his age. He might simply be developing the gift late. But it rarely came as late as this. Damn it, I'd been positive. Had some event at Nevarsin, some emotional shock, made him block awareness of it?

"I could try that again," I said tentatively. The *kirian* might actually trigger latent telepathy; or perhaps, under its influence, I could reach his mind, without hurting him too much, and find out if he was deliberately blocking awareness of *laran*. It did happen, sometimes.

I didn't like using *kirian*. But a small dose couldn't do much worse than make him sick, or leave him with a bad hangover. And I had the distinct and not very pleasant feeling that if I cut off his hopes now, he might do something desperate. I didn't like the way he was looking at me, taut as a bowstring, and shaking, not much, but from head to foot. His voice cracked a little as he said, "I'll try." All too clearly, what I heard was, *I'll try anything.*

I went to my room for it, already berating myself for agreeing to this lunatic experiment. It simply meant too much to him. I weighed the possibility of giving him a sedative dose, one that would knock him out or keep him safely

drugged and drowsy till morning. But *kirian* is too unpredict-
able. The dose which puts one person to sleep like a baby at
the breast may turn another into a frenzied berserker, raging
and hallucinating. Anyway, I'd promised; I wouldn't deceive
him now. I'd play it safe though, give him the same cautious
minimal dose we used with strange psi technicians at Arilinn.
This much *kirian* couldn't hurt him.

I measured him a careful few drops in a wineglass. He
swallowed it, grimacing at the taste, and sat down on one of
the stone benches. After a minute he covered his eyes. I
watched carefully. One of the first signs was the dilation of
the pupils of the eyes. After a few minutes he began to tremble, leaning against the back of the seat as if he feared he
might fall. His hands were icy cold. I took his wrist lightly in
my fingers. Normally I hate touching people; telepaths do,
except in close intimacy. At the touch he looked up and whispered, "Why are you angry, Lew?"

Angry? Did he interpret my fear for him as anger? I said,
"Not angry, only worried about you. *Kirian* isn't anything to
play with. I'm going to try and touch you now. Don't fight
me if you can help it."

I gently reached for contact with his mind. I wouldn't use
the matrix for this; under *kirian* I might probe too far and
damage him. I first sensed sickness and confusion—that was
the drug, no more—then a deathly weariness and physical
tension, probably from the long ride, and finally an overwhelming sense of desolation and loneliness, which made me
want to turn away from his despair. Hesitantly, I risked a
somewhat deeper contact.

And met a perfect, locked defense, a blank wall. After a
moment, I probed sharply. The Alton gift was forced rapport, even with nontelepaths. He wanted this, and if I could
give it to him, then he could probably endure being hurt. He
moaned and moved his head as if I was hurting him. Probably I was. The emotions were still blurring everything. Yes,
he had *laran* potential. But he'd blocked it. Completely.

I waited a moment and considered. It's not so uncommon;
some telepaths live all their lives that way. There's no reason
they shouldn't. Telepathy, as I told him, is far from an un-
mixed blessing. But occasionally it yielded to a slow, patient
unraveling. I retreated to the outer layer of his consciousness
again and asked, not in words, *What is it you're afraid to
know, Regis? Don't block it. Try to remember what it is you*

couldn't bear to know. There was a time when you could do
this knowingly. Try to remember. . . .

It was the wrong thing. He had received my thought; I felt
the response to it—a clamshell snapping rigidly shut, a sensitive plant closing its leaves. He wrenched his hands roughly
from mine, covering his eyes again. He muttered, "My head
hurts. I'm sick, I'm so sick. . . ."

I had to withdraw. He had effectively shut me out. Possibly a skilled, highly-trained Keeper could have forced her
way through the resistance without killing him. But I couldn't
force it. I might have battered down the barrier, forced him
to face whatever it was he'd buried, but he might very well
crack completely, and whether he could ever be put together
again was a very doubtful point.

I wondered if he understood that he had done this to himself. Facing that kind of knowledge was a terribly painful
process. At the time, building that barrier must have seemed
the only way to save his sanity, even if it meant paying the
agonizing price of cutting off his entire psi potential with it.
My own Keeper had once explained it to me with the example of the creature who, helplessly caught in a trap, gnaws off
the trapped foot, choosing maiming to death. Sometimes
there were layers and layers of such barricades.

The barrier, or inhibition, might some day dissolve of itself, releasing his potential. Time and maturity could do a lot.
It might be that some day, in the deep intimacy of love, he
would find himself free of it. Or—I faced this too—it might
be that this barrier was genuinely necessary to his life and
sanity, in which case it would endure forever, or, if it were
somehow broken down, there would not be enough left of
him to go on living.

A catalyst telepath probably could have reached him. But
in these days, due to inbreeding, indiscriminate marriages
with nontelepaths and the disappearance of the old means of
stimulating these gifts, the various Comyn psi powers no longer bred true. I was living proof that the Alton gift did sometimes appear in pure form. But as a general thing, no one
could sort out the tangle of gifts. The Hastur gift, whatever
that was—even at Arilinn they didn't tell me—is just as likely
to appear in the Aillard or Elhalyn Domains. Catalyst telepathy was once an Ardais gift. Dyan certainly wasn't one! As
far as I knew, there were none left alive.

It seemed a long time later that Regis stirred again, rub-

bing his forehead; then he opened his eyes, still with that terrible eagerness. The drug was still in his system—it wouldn't
wear off completely for hours—but he was beginning to have
brief intervals free of it. His unspoken question was perfectly
clear. I had to shake my head, regretfully.

"I'm sorry, Regis."

I hope I never again see such despair in a young face. If
he had been twelve years old, I would have taken him in my
arms and tried to comfort him. But he was not a child now,
and neither was I. His taut, desperate face kept me at arm's
length.

"Regis, listen to me," I said quietly. "For what it's worth,
the *laran* is there. You have the potential, which means, at
the very least, you're carrying the gene, your children will
have it." I hesitated, not wanting to hurt him further, by telling him straightforwardly that he had made the barrier himself. Why hurt him that way?

I said, "I did my best, *bredu*. But I couldn't reach it, the
barriers were too strong. *Bredu*, don't look at me like that," I
pleaded, "I can't bear it, to see you looking at me that way."

His voice was almost inaudible. "I know. You did your
best."

Had I really? I was struck with doubt. I felt sick with the
force of his misery. I tried to take his hands again, forcing
myself to meet his pain head-on, not flinch from it. But he
pulled away from me, and I let it go.

"Regis, listen to me. It doesn't matter. Perhaps in the days
of the Keepers, it was a terrible tragedy for a Hastur to be
without *laran*. But the world is changing. The Comyn is
changing. You'll find other strengths."

I felt the futility of the words even as I spoke them. What
must it be like, to live without *laran*? Like being without
sight, hearing ... but, never having known it, he must not be
allowed to suffer its loss.

"Regis, you have so much else to give. To your family, to
the Domains, to our world. And your children will have it—"
I took his hands again in mine, trying to comfort him, but he
cracked.

"Zandru's hells, *stop* it," he said, and wrenched his hands
roughly away again. He caught up his cloak, which lay on
the stone seat, and ran out of the room.

I stood frozen in the shock of his violence, then, in horror,
ran after him. *Gods!* Drugged, sick, desperate, he couldn't be

allowed to run off that way! He needed to be watched, cared for, comforted—but I wasn't in time. When I reached the stairs, he had already disappeared into the labyrinthine corridors of that wing, and I lost him.

I called and hunted for hours before, reeling with fatigue since I, too, had been riding for days. I gave up finally and went back to my rooms. I couldn't spend the whole night storming all over Comyn Castle, shouting his name! I couldn't force my way into the Regent's suite and demand to know if he was there! There were limits to what Kennard Alton's bastard son could do. I suspected I'd already exceeded them. I could only hope desperately that the *kirian* would make him sleepy, or wear off with fatigue, and he would come back to rest or make his way to the Hastur apartments and sleep there.

I waited for hours and saw the sun rise, blood-red in the mists hanging over the Terran spaceport, before, cramped and cold, I fell asleep on the stone bench by the fireplace.

But Regis did not return.

Chapter THREE

Regis ran down the corridor, dazed and confused, the small points of color still flashing behind his eyes, racked with the interior crawling nausea. One thought was tearing at him:

Failed. I've failed. Even Lew, tower-trained and with all his skill, couldn't help me. There's nothing there. When he said what he did about potential, he was humoring me, comforting a child.

He reeled, feeling sick again, clung momentarily to the wall and ran on.

The Comyn castle was a labyrinth, and Regis had not been inside it in years. Before long, in his wild rush to get away from the scene of his humiliation, he was well and truly lost. His senses, *kirian*-blurred, retained vague memories of stone cul-de-sacs, blind corners, archways, endless stairs up which he toiled and down which he blundered and sometimes fell, courtyards filled with rushing wind and blinding rain, hour after hour. To the end of his life he retained an impression of the Comyn Castle which he could summon at will to overlay his real memories of it: a vast stone maze, a trap through which he wandered alone for centuries, with no human form to be seen. Once, around a corner, he heard Lew calling his name. He flattened himself in a niche and hid for a few thousand years until, long after, the sound was gone.

After an indeterminate time of wandering and stumbling and hallucinating, he became aware that it had been a long time since he had fallen down a flight of stairs; that the corridors were long, but not miles and miles long; and that they were no longer filled with uncanny crawling colors and silent sounds. When he came out at last on to a high balcony at the uppermost level, he knew where he was.

Dawn was breaking over the city below him. Once before, during the night, he had stood against a high parapet like this, thinking that his life was no good to anyone, not to the Hasturs, not to himself, that he should throw himself down and be done with it. This time the thought was remote, nightmarish, like one of those terrible real dreams which wakes you shaking and crying out, but a few seconds later is gone in dissolving fragments.

He drew a long, weary sigh. Now what?

He should go and make himself presentable for his grandfather, who would certainly send for him soon. He should get some food and sleep; *kirian,* he'd been told, expended so much physical and nervous energy that it was essential to compensate with extra food and rest. He should go back and apologize to Lew Alton, who had only very reluctantly done what Regis himself had begged him to do.... But he was sick to death of hearing what he should do!

He looked across the city that lay spread out below him. Thendara, the old town, the Trade City, the Terran headquarters and the spaceport. And the great ships, waiting, ready to take off for some unguessable destination. All he really wanted to do now was go to the spaceport and watch, at close range, one of those great ships.

Quickly he hardened his resolve. He was not dressed for out-of-doors at all, still wearing felt-soled indoor boots, but in his present mood it mattered less than nothing. He was unarmed. So what? Terrans carried no sidearms. He went down long flights of stairs, losing his way, but knowing, now that he had his wits about him, that all he had to do was keep going down till he reached ground level. Comyn Castle was no fortress. Built for ceremony rather than defense, the building had many gates, and it was easy to slip out one of them unobserved.

He found himself in a dim, dawnlit street leading downhill through closely packed houses. He was keyed up, having had no sleep after his hard ride yesterday, but the energizing effect of the *kirian* had not worn off yet, and he felt no drowsiness. Hunger was something else, but there were coins in his pockets, and he was sure that soon he would pass some kind of eating-house where workmen ate before their day's business.

The thought excited him with a delicious forbiddenness. He could not remember ever having been completely alone in his entire life. There had always been others ready at hand to look after him, protect him, gratify his every wish: nurses

and nannies when he was small, servants and carefully select-
ed companions when he was older. Later, there were the
brothers of the monastery, though they were more likely to
thwart his wishes than carry them out. This would be an ad-
venture.

He found a place next to a blacksmith's shop and went in.
It was dimly lit with resin-candles, but there was a good
smell of food. He was briefly afraid of being recognized, but
after all, what could they do to him? He was old enough to
be out alone. Besides, if anyone noticed the blue-and-silver
cloak with the Hastur badge, they would only think he was a
Hastur servant.

The men seated at the table were blacksmiths and stable
hands, drinking hot ale or *jaco* or boiled milk, eating foods
Regis had never seen or smelled. A woman came to take
Regis' order. She did not look at him. He ordered fried nut
porridge and hot milk with spices in it. His grandfather, he
thought with definite satisfaction, would have a fit.

He paid for the food and ate it slowly, at first feeling the
residual queasiness of the drug which wore off as he ate.
When he went out, feeling better, the light was spreading, although the sun had not risen. As he went downhill he found
himself among unfamiliar houses, built in strange shapes of
strange materials. He had obviously crossed the line into the
Trade City. He could hear, in the distance, that strange
waterfall sound which had excited him so intensely. He must
be near the spaceport.

He had been told a little about the spaceport on Darkover.
Darkover, which did almost no trading with the Empire, was
in a unique location, between the upper and lower spiral
arms of the galaxy, unusually well suited as a crossroads stop
for much of the interstellar traffic. In spite of the self-chosen
isolation of Darkover, therefore, enormous numbers of ships
came for rerouting, bearing passengers, personnel and freight
bound elsewhere. They also came for repairs and reprovision-
ing and for rest leaves in the Trade City. Most of the Terrans
scrupulously kept the agreement limiting them to their own
areas. There had been a few intermarriages, a little trade,
some small—very small—importation of Terran machinery
and technology. This was strictly limited by the Darkovans,
each item studied by Council before permission was given. A
few licensed matrix technicians were set up in the cities; a few
had even gone out into the Empire. The Terrans, he had

heard, were intrigued by Darkovan matrix technology and in the old days had laid intricate plots to uncover some of its secrets. He didn't know details, but Kennard had told him some stories.

He started, realizing that the street directly before him was blocked by two very large men in unfamiliar black leather uniforms. At their belts hung strangely shaped weapons which, Regis realized with a prickle of horror, must be blasters or nerve guns. Such weapons had been outlawed on Darkover since the Ages of Chaos, and Regis had literally never seen one before, except for antiques in a museum. These were no museum pieces. They looked deadly.

One of the men said, "You're violating curfew, sonny. Until the trouble's over, all women and children are supposed to be off the streets from an hour before sunset until an hour after sunrise."

Women and children! Regis' hand strayed to his knife-hilt. "I am no child. Shall I call challenge and prove it?"

"You're in the Terran Zone, son. Save yourself trouble."

"I demand—"

"Oh hell, one of *those*," said the second man in disgust. "Look here, kiddie, we're not allowed to fight duels, on duty anyhow. You come along and talk to the officer."

Regis was about to make an angry protest—ask a Comyn heir to give an account of himself in Council season?—when it occurred to him that the headquarters building was right on the spaceport, where he was going anyway. With a secret grin he went along.

After they had passed through the spaceport gates, he realized that he had actually had a better view yesterday from the mountainside. Here the ships were invisible behind fences and barricades. The spaceforce patrolmen led him inside a building where a young officer, not in black leather but in ordinary Terran clothing, was dealing with assorted curfew violators. As they came in he was saying, "This man's all right; he was looking for a midwife and took the wrong turn. Send someone to show him back to the town." He looked up at Regis, standing between the officers. "Another one? I'd hoped we'd be through for the night. Well, kid, what's your story?"

Regis threw his head back arrogantly. "Who are you? By what right did you have me brought here?"

"My name's Dan Lawton," the man said. He spoke the same language in which Regis had addressed him, and spoke it well. That wasn't common. He said, "I am an assistant to the Legate and just now I'm handling curfew duty. Which you were violating, young man."

One of the spaceforce men said, "We brought him straight to you, Dan. He wanted to fight a duel with us, for God's sake! Can you handle this one?"

"We don't fight duels in the Terran Zone," Lawton said. "Are you new to Thendara? The curfew regulations are posted everywhere. If you can't read, I suggest you ask someone to read them to you."

Regis retorted, "I recognize no laws but those of the Children of Hastur!"

A strange look passed over Lawton's face. Regis thought for a moment that the young Terran was laughing at him, but face and voice were alike noncommittal. "A praiseworthy objective, sir, but not particularly suitable here. The Hasturs themselves made and recognized those boundaries and agreed to assist us in enforcing our laws within them. Do you refuse to recognize the authority of Comyn Council? Who are you to refuse?"

Regis drew himself to his full height. He knew that between the giant spaceforce men he still looked childishly small.

"I am Regis-Rafael Felix Alar Hastur y Elhalyn," he stated proudly.

Lawton's eyes reflected amazement. "Then what, in the name of all your own gods, are you doing roaming around alone at this hour. Where is your escort? Yes, you look like a Hastur," he said as he pulled an intercom toward him, speaking urgently in Terran Standard. Regis had learned it at Nevarsin. "Have the Comyn Elders left yet?" He listened a moment, then turned back to Regis. "A dozen of your kinfolk left here about half an hour ago. Were you sent with a message for them? If so, you came too late."

"No," Regis confessed, "I came on my own. I simply had a fancy to see the starships take off." It sounded, here in this office, like a childish whim. Lawton looked startled.

"That's easily enough arranged. If you'd sent in a formal request a few days ago, we'd gladly have arranged a tour for any of your kinsmen. At short notice like this, there's nothing spectacular going on, but there's a cargo transport about to take off for Vega in a few minutes, and I'll take you up to one of the viewing platforms. Meanwhile, could I offer you some coffee?" He hesitated, then said, "You couldn't be Lord Hastur; that must be your father?"

"Grandfather. For me the proper address is Lord Regis."

He accepted the proffered Terran drink, finding it bitter but rather pleasant. Dan Lawton led him into a tall shaft which rose upward at alarming speed, opening on a glass-enclosed viewing terrace. Below him an enormous cargo ship was in the final stages of readying for takeoff, with refueling cranes being moved away, scaffoldings and loading platforms being wheeled like toys to a distance. The process was quick and efficient. He heard again the waterfall sound, rising to a roar, a scream. The great ship lifted slowly, then more swiftly and finally was gone . . . out, beyond the stars.

Regis remained motionless, staring at the spot in the sky where the starship had vanished. He knew there were tears in his eyes again but he didn't care. After a little while Lawton guided him down the elevator shaft. Regis went as if sleepwalking. Resolve had suddenly crystallized inside him.

Somewhere in the Empire, somewhere away from the Domains which had no place for him, there must be a world for him. A world where he could be free of the tremendous burden laid on the Comyn, a world where he could be himself, more than simply heir to his Domain, his life laid out in preordained duties from birth to grave. The Domain? Let Javanne's sons have it! He felt almost intoxicated by the smell of freedom. Freedom from a burden he'd been born to—and born unfit to bear!

Lawton had not noticed his preoccupation. He said, "I'll arrange an escort for you back to Comyn Castle, Lord Regis. You can't go alone, put it out of your mind. Impossible."

"I came here alone, and I'm not a child."

"Certainly not," Lawton said, straight-faced, "but with the situation in the city now, anything might happen. And if an accident occurred, I would be personally responsible."

He had used the *casta* phrase implying personal honor. Regis lifted his eyebrows and congratulated him on his command of the language.

"As a matter of fact, Lord Regis, it is my native tongue. My mother never spoke anything else to me. It was Terran I learned as a foreign language."

"You are Darkovan?"

"My mother was, and kin to Comyn. Lord Ardais is my

mother's cousin, though I doubt he'd care to acknowledge the relationship."

Regis thought about that as Lawton arranged his escort. Relatives far more distant than that were often seated in Comyn Council. This Terran officer—half-Terran—might have chosen to be Darkovan. He had as much right to a Comyn seat as Lew Alton, for instance. Lew could have chosen to be Terran, as Regis was about to choose his own future. He spent the uneventful journey across the city thinking how he would break the news to his grandfather.

In the Hastur apartments, a servant told him that Danvan Hastur was awaiting him. As he changed his clothes—the thought of presenting himself before the Regent of Comyn in house clothes and felt slippers was not even to be contemplated—he wondered grimly if Lew had said anything to his grandfather. It occurred to him, hours too late, that if anything had happened to him, Hastur might well have held Lew responsible. A poor return for Lew's friendship!

When he had made himself presentable, in a sky-blue dyed-leather tunic and high boots, he went up to his grandfather's audience room.

Inside he found Danvan Hastur of Hastur, Regent of the Seven Domains, talking to Kennard Alton. As he opened the door, Hastur raised his eyebrows and gestured to him to sit down. "One moment, my lad, I'll talk to you later." He turned back to Kennard and said in a tone of endless patience, "Kennard, my friend, my dear kinsman, what you ask is simply impossible. I let you force Lew on us—"

"Have you regretted it?" Kennard demanded angrily. "They tell me at Arilinn that he is a strong telepath, one of their best. In the Guard he is a competent officer. What right have you to assume Marius would bring disgrace on the Comyn?"

"Who spoke of disgrace, kinsman?" Hastur was standing before his writing table, a strongly built old man, not as tall as Kennard, with hair that had once been silver-gilt and was now nearly all gray. He spoke with a slow, considered mildness. "I let you force Lew on us and I've had no reason to regret it. But there is more to it than that. Lew does not look Comyn, no more than you, but there is no question in anyone's mind that he is Darkovan and your son. But Marius? Impossible."

Kennard's mouth thinned and tightened. "Are you questioning the paternity of an acknowledged Alton son?" Standing quietly in a corner, Regis was glad Kennard's rage was not turned on *him*.

"By no means. But he has his mother's blood, his mother's face, his mother's eyes. My friend, you know what the first-year cadets go through in the Guards. . . ."

"He's my son and no coward. Why do you think he would be incompetent to take his place, the place to which he is legally entitled—"

"Legally, no. I won't quibble with you, Ken, but we never recognized your marriage to Elaine. Marius is *legally,* as regards inheritance and Domain-right, entitled to nothing whatever. We *gave* Lew that right. Not by birth entitlement, but by Council action, because he was Alton, telepath, with full *laran.* Marius has received no such rights from Council." He sighed. "How can I make you understand? I'm sure the boy is brave, trustworthy, honest—that he has all the virtues we Comyn demand of our sons. Any lad you reared would have those qualities. Who knows better than I? But Marius *looks* Terran. The other lads would tear him to pieces. I know what Lew went through. I pitied him, even while I admired his courage. They've accepted him, after a fashion. They would never accept Marius. Never. Why put him through that misery for nothing?"

Kennard clenched his fists, striding angrily up and down the room. His voice choked with rage, he said, "You mean that I can get a cadet commission for some poor relation, or for my bastard son by a whore or an idiot, sooner than for my own legitimately born younger son!"

"Kennard, if it were up to me, I'd give the lad his chance. But my hands are tied. There has been enough trouble in Council over citizenship for those of mixed blood. Dyan—"

"I know all too well how Dyan feels. He's made it abundantly clear."

"Dyan has a great deal of support in Council. And Marius' mother was not only Terran but half-Aldaran. If you had hunted over Darkover for a generation, you could not have found a woman less likely to be accepted as the mother of your legitimate sons."

Kennard said in a low voice, "It was your own father who had me sent to Terra, by the will of Council, when I was fourteen years old. Elaine was reared and schooled on Terra, but she thought of herself as Darkovan. I did not even know of her Terran blood at first. But it made no difference. Even had she been all Terran ..." He broke off. "Enough of that. It is long past and she is dead. As for me, I think my record and reputation, my years commanding the Guard, my ten years at Arilinn, prove abundantly what I am." He paced the floor, his uneven step and distraught face betraying the emotion he tried to keep out of his voice. "You are not a telepath, Hastur. It was easy for you to do what your caste required of you. The Gods know I tried to love Caitlin. It wasn't her fault. But I did love Elaine, and she *was* mother to my sons."

"Kennard, I'm sorry. I cannot fight the whole Council for Marius, unless—has he *laran*?"

"I have no idea. Does it matter so much?"

"If he had the Alton gift, it might be possible, not easy but possible, to establish some rights for him. There are precedents. With *laran*, even a distant kinsman can be adopted into the Domains. Without it ... no, Kennard. Don't ask. Lew is accepted now, even respected. Don't ask more."

Kennard said, his head bent, "I didn't want to test Lew for the Alton gift. Even with all my care, it came near to killing him. Hastur, I cannot risk that again! Would you, for your youngest son?"

"My only son is dead," Hastur said and sighed. "If I can do anything else for the boy—"

Kennard answered, "The only thing I want for him is his right, and that is the one thing you will not give. I should have taken them both to Terra. You made me feel I was needed here."

"You are, Ken, and you know it as well as I." Hastur's smile was very sweet and troubled. "Some day, perhaps, you may see why I can't do what you wish." His eyes moved to Regis, fidgeting on the bench. He said, "If you will excuse me, Kennard ... ?"

It was a courteous but definite dismissal. Kennard withdrew, but his face was grim and he omitted any formal leave-taking. Hastur looked tired. He sighed and said, "Come here, Regis. Where have you been? Haven't I trouble enough without worrying that you've run away like a silly brat, to look at the spaceships or something like that?"

"The last time I gave you too much trouble, Grandfather, you sent me into a monastery. Isn't it too bad you can't do it again, sir?"

"Don't be insolent, you young pup," Hastur growled. "Do you want me to apologize for having no welcome last night? Very well, I apologize. It wasn't my choice." He came and took Regis in his arms, pressing his withered cheeks one after another to the boy's. "I've been up all night, or I'd think of some better way to welcome you now." He held him off at arm's length, blinking with weariness. "You've grown, child. You are very like your father. He would have been proud, I think, to see you coming home a man."

Against his own will, Regis was moved. The old man looked so weary. "What crisis kept you up all night, Grandfather?"

Hastur sank down heavily on the bench. "The usual thing. I expect it's known on every planet where the Empire builds a big spaceport, but we're not used to it here. People coming and going from all corners of the Empire. Travelers, transients, spacemen on leave and the sector which caters to them. Bars, amusement places, gambling halls, houses of . . . er . . ."

"I'm old enough to know what a brothel is, sir."

"At your age? Anyway, drunken men are disorderly, and Terrans on leave carry weapons. By agreement, no weapons can be carried into the old city, but people do stray across the line—there's no way of preventing it, short of building a wall across the city. There have been brawls, duels, knife fights and sometimes even killings, and it isn't always clear whether the City Guard or the Terran spaceforce should properly handle the offenders. Our codes are so different that it's hard to know how to compromise. Last night there was a brawl and a Terran knifed one of the Guardsmen. The Terran offered as his defense that the Guardsman had made him what he called an indecent proposition. Must I explain?"

"Of course not. But are you trying to tell me, seriously, that this was offered as a legal defense for murder?"

"Seriously. Evidently the Terrans take it even more seriously than the *cristoforos.* He insisted his attack on the Guardsman was justifiable. Now the Guardsman's brother has filed an intent-to-murder on the Terran. The Terrans aren't subject to our laws, so he refused to accept it and instead filed charges against the Guardsman's brother for attempted murder. What a tangle! I never thought I'd see the day when Council had to sit on a knife fight! Damn the Terrans anyhow!"

"So how did you finally settle it?"

Hastur shrugged. "Compromise, as usual. The Terran was deported and the Guardsman's brother was held in the brig until the Terran was off-planet; so nobody gets any peace except the dead man. Unsatisfactory for everyone. But enough of them. Tell me about yourself, Regis."

"Well, I'll have to talk about the Terrans again," Regis said. This wasn't the best time, but his grandfather might not have time to talk with him again for days. "Grandfather, I'm not needed here. You probably know I don't have *laran*, and I found out in Nevarsin that I'm not interested in politics. I've decided what I want to do with my life: I want to go into the Terran Empire Space Service."

Hastur's jaw dropped. He scowled and demanded, "Is this a joke? Or another silly prank?"

"Neither, Grandfather. I mean it, and I'm of age."

"But you can't do that! Certainly they'd never accept you without my consent."

"I hope to have that, sir. But by Darkovan law, which you were quoting at Kennard, I am of legal age to dispose of myself. I can marry, fight a duel, acknowledge a son, stand responsible for a murder—"

"The Terrans wouldn't think so. Kennard was declared of age before he went. But on Terra he was sent to school and required, legally forced, mind you, to obey a stipulated guardian until he was past twenty. You'd hate that."

"No doubt I would. But I learned one thing at Nevarsin, sir—you can live with the things you hate."

"Regis, is this your revenge for my sending you to Nevarsin? Were you so unhappy? What can I say? I wanted you to have the best education possible and I thought it better for you to be properly cared for, there, than neglected at home."

"No, sir," Regis said, not quite sure. "It's simply that I want to go, and I'm not needed here."

"You don't speak Terran languages."

"I understand Terran Standard. I learned to read and write at Nevarsin. As you pointed out, I am excellently well educated. Learning a new language is no great matter."

"You say you are of age," Hastur said coldly, "so let me quote some law back to you. The law provides that before you, who are heir to a Domain, undertake any such risky task as going offworld, you must provide an heir to your Domain. Have you a son, Regis?"

Regis looked sullenly at the floor. Hastur knew, of course,

that he had not. "What does that matter? It's been generations since the Hastur gift has appeared full strength in the line. As for ordinary *laran*, that's just as likely to appear at random anywhere in the Domains as it is in the direct male line of descent. Pick any heir at random, he couldn't be less fit for the Domain than I am. I suspect the gene's a recessive, bred out, extinct like the catalyst telepath trait. And Javanne has sons; one of them is as likely to have it as any son of mine, if I had any. Which I don't," he added rebelliously, "or am likely to. Now or ever."

"Where do you get these ideas?" Hastur asked, shocked and bewildered. "You're not, by any chance, an *ombredin*?"

"In a *cristoforo* monastery? Not likely. No, sir, not even for pastime. And certainly not as a way of life."

"Then why should you say such a thing?"

"Because," Regis burst out angrily, "I belong to myself, not to the Comyn! Better to let the line die with me than to go on for generations, calling ourselves Hastur, without our gift, without *laran*, political figureheads being used by Terra to keep the people quiet!"

"Is that how you see me, Regis? I took the Regency when Stefan Elhalyn died, because Derik was only five, too young to be crowned even as a puppet king. It's been my ill-fortune to rule over a period of change, but I think I've been more than just a figurehead for Terra."

"I know some Empire history, sir. The Empire will finally take over here too. It always does."

"Don't you think I know that? I've lived with the inevitable for three reigns now. But if I live long enough, it will be a slow change, one our people can live with. As for *laran*, it wakens late in Hastur men. Give yourself time."

"Time!" Regis put all his dissatisfaction into the word.

"I haven't *laran* either, Regis. But even so, I think I've served my people well. Couldn't you resign yourself to that?" He looked into Regis' stubborn face and sighed. "Well, I'll bargain with you. I don't want you to go as a child, subject to a court-appointed guardian under Terran law. That would disgrace all of us. You're the age when a Comyn heir should be serving in the cadet corps. Take your regular turn in the Guards, three cadet seasons. After that, if you still want to go, we'll think of a way to get you offworld without going through all the motions of their bureaucracy. You'd hate it—I've had fifty years of it and I still hate it. But don't walk

out on the Comyn before you give it a fair try. Three years
isn't that long. Will you bargain?"

Three years. It had seemed an eternity at Nevarsin. But
did he have a choice? None, except outright defiance. He
could run away, seek aid from the Terrans themselves. But if
he was legally a child by their laws, they would simply hand
him over again to his guardians. That would indeed be a disgrace.

"Three cadet seasons," he said at last. "But only if you
give me your word of honor that if I choose to go, you won't
oppose it after that."

"If after three years you still want to go," said Hastur, "I
promise to find some honorable way."

Regis listened, weighing the words for diplomatic evasions
and half-truths. But the old man's eyes were level and the
word of Hastur was proverbial. Even the Terrans knew that.

At last he said, "A bargain. Three years in the cadets, for
your word." He added bitterly, "I have no choice, do I?"

"If you wanted a choice," said Hastur, and his blue eyes
flashed fire though his voice was as old and weary as ever,
"you should have arranged to be born elsewhere, to other
parents. I did not choose to be chief councillor to Stefan Elhalyn, nor Regent to Prince Derik. Rafael—sound may he
sleep!—did not choose his own life, nor even his death. None
of us has ever been free to choose, not in my lifetime." His
voice wavered, and Regis realized that the old man was on
the edge of exhaustion or collapse.

Against his will, Regis was moved again. He bit his lip,
knowing that if he spoke he would break down, beg his
grandfather's pardon, promise unconditional obedience. Perhaps it was only the last remnant of the *kirian*, but he knew,
suddenly and agonizingly, that his grandfather did not meet
his eyes because the Regent of the Seven Domains could not
weep, not even before his own grandson, not even for the
memory of his only son's terrible and untimely death.

When Hastur finally spoke again his voice was hard and
crisp, like a man accustomed to dealing with one unremitting
crisis after another. "The first call-over of cadets is later this
morning. I have sent word to the cadet-master to expect you
among them." He rose and embraced Regis again in dismissal. "I shall see you again soon. At least we are not now separated by three days' ride and a range of mountains."

So he'd already sent word to the cadet-master. That was

how sure he was, Regis realized. He had been manipulated, neatly mouse-trapped into doing just exactly what was expected of a Hastur. And he had maneuvered himself into promising three years of it!

Chapter FOUR

(Lew Alton's narrative)

The room was bright with daylight. I had slept for hours on the stone seat by the fireplace, cold and cramped. Marius, barefoot and in his nightshirt, was shaking me. He said, "I heard something on the stairs. Listen!" He ran toward the door; I followed more slowly, as the door was flung open and a pair of Guards carried my father into the room. One of them caught sight of me and said, "Where can we take him, Captain?"

I said, "Bring him in here," and helped Andres lay him on his own bed. "What happened?" I demanded, staring in dread at his pale, unconscious face.

"He fell down the stone stairs near the Guard hall," one of the men said. "I've been trying to get those stairs fixed all winter; your father could have broken his neck. So could any of us."

Marius came to the bedside, white and terrified. "Is he dead?"

"Nothing like it, sonny," said the Guardsman. "I think the Commander's broken a couple of ribs and done something to his arm and shoulder, but unless he starts vomiting blood later he'll be all right. I wanted Master Raimon to attend to him down there, but he made us carry him up here."

Between anger and relief, I bent over him. What a time for him to be hurt. The very first day of Council season! As if my tumbling thoughts could reach him—and perhaps they could—he groaned and opened his eyes. His mouth contracted in a spasm of pain.

"Lew?"

"I'm here, Father."

"You must take call-over in my place. . . ."

"Father, no. There are a dozen others with better right."

His face hardened. I could see, and feel, that he was struggling against intense pain. "Damn you, you'll go! I've fought ... whole Council ... for years. You're not going to throw away all my work ... because I take a damn silly tumble. You have a right to deputize for me and, damn you, you're going to!"

His pain tore at me; I was wide open to it. Through the clawing pain I could feel his emotions, fury and a fierce determination, thrusting his will on me. "You *will*!"

I'm not Alton for nothing. Swiftly I thrust back, fighting his attempt to *force* agreement. "There's no need for that, Father. I'm not your puppet!"

"But you're my son," he said violently, and it was like a storm, as his will pressed hard on me. "My son and my second in command, and no one, *no one* is going to question that!"

His agitation was growing so great that I realized I could not argue further without harming him seriously.

I had to calm him somehow. I met his enraged eyes squarely and said, "There's no reason to shout at me. I'll do what you like, for now at least. We'll argue it out later."

His eyes fell shut, whether with exhaustion or pain I could not tell. Master Raimon, the hospital-officer of the Guards, came into the room, moving swiftly to his side. I made room for him. Anger, fatigue and loss of sleep made my head pound. Damn him! Father knew perfectly well how I felt! And he didn't give a damn!

Marius was still standing, frozen, watching in horror as Master Raimon began to cut away my father's shirt. I saw great, purple, blood-darkened bruises before I drew Marius firmly away. "There's nothing much wrong with him," I said. "He couldn't shout that loud if he was dying. Go get dressed, and keep out of the way."

The child went obediently and I stood in the outer room, rubbing my fists over my face in dismay and confusion. What time was it? How long had I slept? Where was Regis? Where had he gone? In the state he'd been in when he left me, he could have done something desperate! Conflicting loyalties and obligations held me paralyzed. Andres came out of my father's room and said, "Lew, if you're going to take call-over you'd better get moving," and I realized I'd been standing as if my feet had frozen to the floor.

My father had laid a task on me. Yet if Regis had run away, in a mood of suicidal despair, shouldn't I go after him, too? In any case I would have been on duty this morning. Now it seemed I was to handle it on my own. There were sure to be those who'd question it. Well, it was Father's right to choose his own deputy, but I was the one who'd have to face their hostility.

I turned to Andres. "Have someone get me something to eat," I said, "and see if you can find where Father put the staff lists and the roll call, but don't disturb him. I should bathe and change. Have I time?"

Andres regarded me calmly. "Don't lose your head. You have what time you need. If you're in command, they can't start till you get there. Take the time to make yourself presentable. You ought to *look* ready to command, even if you don't feel it."

He was right, of course; I knew it even while I resented his tone. Andres has a habit of being right. He had been the *coridom*, chief steward, at Armida since I could remember. He was a Terran and had once been in Spaceforce. I've never known where he met my father, or why he left the Empire. My father's servants had told me the story, that one day he came to Armida and said he was sick of space and Spaceforce, and my father had said, "Throw your blaster away and pledge me to keep the Compact, and I've work for you at Armida as long as you like." At first he had been Father's private secretary, then his personal assistant, finally in charge of his whole household, from my father's horses and dogs to his sons and foster-daughter. There were times when I felt Andres was the only person alive who completely accepted me for what I was. Bastard, half-caste, it made no difference to Andres.

He added now, "Better for discipline to turn up late than to turn up in a mess and not knowing what you're doing. Get yourself in order, Lew, and I don't just mean your uniform. Nothing's to be gained by rushing off in several directions at once."

I went off to bathe, eat a hasty breakfast and dress myself suitably to be stared at by a hundred or more officers and Guardsmen, each one of whom would be ready to find fault. Well, let them.

Andres found the staff lists and Guard roster among my father's belongings; I took them and went down to the Guard hall.

The main Guard hall in Comyn Castle is on one of the lowest levels; behind it lie barracks, stables, armory and parade ground, and before it a barricaded gateway leads down into Thendara. The rest of Comyn Castle leaves me unmoved, but I never looked up at the great fan-lighted windows without a curious swelling in my throat.

I had been fourteen years old, and already aware that because of what I was my life was fragmented and insecure, when my father had first brought me here. Before sending me to my peers, or what he hoped would be my peers—they'd had other ideas—he'd told me of a few of the Altons who had come before us here. For the first and almost the last time, I'd felt a sense of belonging to those old Altons whose names were a roll call of Darkovan history: My grandfather Valdir, who had organized the first fire-beacon system in the Kilghard Hills. Dom Esteban Lanart, who a hundred years ago had driven the catmen from the caves of Corresanti. Rafael Lanart-Alton, who had ruled as Regent when Stefan Hastur the Ninth was crowned in his cradle, in the days before the Elhalyn were kings in Thendara.

The Guard hall was an enormous stone-floored, stone-arched room, cobblestones half worn away by the feet of centuries of Guardsmen. The light came curiously, multicolored and splintered, through windows set in before the art of rolling glass was known.

I drew the lists Andres had given me from a pocket and studied them. On the topmost sheet were the names of the first-year cadets. The name of Regis Hastur was at the bottom, evidently added somewhat later than the rest. Damn it, where *was* Regis? I checked the list of second-year cadets. The name of Octavien Vallonde had been dropped from the rolls. I hadn't expected to see his name, but it would have relieved my mind.

On the staff list Father had crossed out his own name as commander and written in mine, evidently with his right hand, and with great difficulty. I wished he had saved himself the trouble. Gabriel Lanart-Hastur, Javanne's husband and my cousin, had replaced me as second-in-command. He should have had the command post. I was no soldier, only a matrix technician, and I fully intended to return to Arilinn at the end of the three-year interval required now by law. Gabriel, though, was a career Guardsman, liked it and was competent. He was an Alton too, and seated on Council. Most Comyn felt he should have been designated Kennard's heir. Yet we were friends, after a fashion, and I wished he were here today, instead of at Edelweiss waiting for the birth of Javanne's child.

Father evidently saw no discrepancy. He had been psi technician in Arilinn for over ten years, back in the old days of tower isolation, yet he had been able afterward to return and take command of the Guards without any terrible sense of dissonance. My own inner conflicts evidently were not important, or even comprehensible, to him.

Arms-master again was old Domenic di Asturien, who had been a captain when my father was a cadet of fourteen. He had been my own cadet-master, my first year and was almost the only officer in the Guard who had ever been fair to me.

Cadet-master—I rubbed my eyes and stared at the lists; I must have read it wrong. The words obstinately stayed the same. *Cadet-master: Dyan-Gabriel, Lord Ardais.*

I groaned aloud. Oh, hell, this had to be one of Father's perverse jokes. He's no fool, and only a fool would put a man like Dyan in charge of half-grown boys. Not after the scandal last year. We had managed to keep the scandal from reaching Lord Hastur, and I had believed that even Dyan knew he had gone too far.

Let me be clear about one thing: I don't like Dyan and he doesn't approve of me, but he is a brave man and a good soldier, probably the best and most competent officer in the Guards. As for his personal life, no one dares to comment on a Comyn lord's private amusements.

I learned, long ago, not to listen to gossip. My own birth had been a major scandal for years. But this had been more than gossip. Personally, I think Father had been unwise to hustle the Vallonde boy away home without question or investigation. Part of what he said was true. Octavien *was* disturbed, unstable, he'd never belonged in the Guards and it was our mistake for ever accepting him as a cadet. But Father had said that the sooner it was hushed up, the quicker the unsavory story would die down. The rumors had never died of course, probably never would.

The room was beginning to fill up with uniformed men.

Dyan came to the dais where the officers were collecting, gave me an unfriendly scowl. No doubt *he* had expected to be named as Father's deputy. Even that would have been better than making him cadet-master.

Damn it, I *couldn't* go along with that. Father's choice or not.

Dyan's private life was no one's affair but his own and I wouldn't care if he chose to love men, women or goats. He could have as many concubines as a Dry-Towner, and most people would gossip no more and no less. But more scandal in the Guards? Damn it, no! This touched the honor of the Guards, and of the Altons who were in charge of it.

Father had put me in command. This was going to be my first command decision, then.

I signaled for Assembly. One or two late-comers dashed into their places. The seasoned men took their ranks. The cadets, as they had been briefed, stayed in a corner.

Regis wasn't among the cadets. I resented bitterly that I was tied here, but there was no help for it.

I looked them all over and felt them returning the favor. I shut down my telepathic sensitivity as much as I could—it wasn't easy in this crowd—but I was aware of their surprise, curiosity, disgust, annoyance. It all added up, more or less, to *Where the hell is the Commander?* Or, worse, *What's old Kennard's bastard doing up there with the staff?*

Finally I got their attention and told them of Kennard's misfortune. It caused a small flurry of whispers, mutters, comments, most of which I knew it would be unwise to hear. I let them get through most of it, then called them to order again and began the traditional first-day ceremony of call-over.

One by one I read out the name of every Guardsman. Each came forward, repeated a brief formula of loyalty to Comyn and informed me—a serious obligation three hundred years ago, a mere customary formality now—of how many men, trained, armed and outfitted according to custom, he was prepared to put into the field in the event of war. It was a long business. There was a disturbance halfway through it and, escorted by half a dozen servants in Hastur livery, Regis made an entrance. One of the servants gave me a message from Hastur himself, with some kind of excuse or explanation for his lateness.

I realized that I was blisteringly angry. I'd seen Regis des-

perate, suicidal, ill, prostrated, suffering some unforeseen af-
tereffect of *kirian*, even dead—and he walked in casually, upsetting call-over ceremony and discipline. I told him
brusquely, "Take your place, cadet," and dismissed the servants.

He could not have resembled less the boy who had sat by
my fire last night, eating stew and pouring out his bitterness.
He was wearing full Comyn regalia, badges, high boots, a
sky-blue tunic of an elaborate cut. He walked to his place
among the cadets, his head held stiffly high. I could sense the
fear and shyness in him, but I knew the other cadets would
regard it as Comyn arrogance, and he would suffer for it. He
looked tired, almost ill, behind the façade of arrogant control. What had happened to him last night? Damn him, I recalled myself with a start, why was I worrying about the heir
to Hastur? He hadn't worried about me, or the fact that if
he'd come to harm, I'd have been in trouble!

I finished the parade of loyalty oaths. Dyan leaned toward
me and said, "I was in the city with the Council last night.
Hastur asked me to explain the situation to the Guards; have
I your permission to speak, Captain Montray-Lanart?"

Dyan had never given me my proper title, in or out of the
Guard hall. I grimly told myself that the last thing I wanted
was his approval. I nodded and he walked to the center of
the dais. He looks no more like a typical Comyn lord than I
do; his hair is dark, not the traditional red of Comyn, and he
is tall, lean, with the six-fingered hands which sometimes turn
up in the Ardais and Aillard clans. There is said to be nonhuman blood in the Ardais line. Dyan looks it.

"City Guardsmen of Thendara," he rapped out, "your commander, Lord Alton, has asked me to review the situation."
His contemptuous look said more plainly than words that I
might play at being in command, but he was the one who
could explain what was going on.

There seemed, as nearly as I could tell from Dyan's words,
to be a high level of tension in the city, mostly between the
Terran Spaceforce and the City Guard. He asked every
Guardsman to avoid incidents and to honor the curfew, to
remember that the Trade City area had been ceded to the
Empire by diplomatic treaty. He reminded us that it was our
duty to deal with Darkovan offenders, and to turn Terran
ones over to the Empire authorities at once. Well, that was

fair enough. Two police forces in one city had to reach some agreements and compromises in living together.

I had to admit Dyan was a good speaker. He managed, however, to convey the impression that the Terrans were so much our natural inferiors, honoring neither the Compact nor the codes of personal honor, that we must take responsbility for them, as all superiors do; that, while we would naturally prefer to treat them with a just contempt, we would be doing Lord Hastur a personal favor by keeping the peace, even against our better judgment. I doubted whether that little speech would really lessen the friction between Terrans and Guardsmen.

I wondered if our opposite numbers in the Trade City, the Legate and his deputies, were laying the law down to Spaceforce this morning. Somehow I doubted it.

Dyan returned to his place and I called the cadets to stand forward. I called the roll of the dozen third-year cadets and the eleven second-year men, wondering if Council meant to fill Octavien Vallonde's empty place. Then I addressed myself to the first-year cadets, calling them into the center of the room. I decided to skip the usual speech about the proud and ancient organization into which it was a pleasure to welcome them. I'm not Dyan's equal as a speaker, and I wasn't going to compete. Father could give them that one when he was well again, or the cadet-master, whoever he was. Not Dyan. Over my dead body.

I confined myself to giving basic facts. After today there would be a full assembly and review every morning after breakfast. The cadets would be kept apart in their own barracks and given instructions until intense drill in basics had made them soldierly enough to take their place in formations and duties. Castle Guard would be set day and night and they would take it in turns from oldest to youngest, recalling that Castle Guard was not menial sentry duty but a privilege claimed by nobles from time out of mind, to guard the Sons of Hastur. And so on.

The final formality—I was glad to reach it, for it was hot in the crowded room by now and the youngest cadets were beginning to fidget—was a formal roll call of first-year cadets. Only Regis and Father's young protégé Danilo were personally known to me, but some were the younger brothers or sons of men I knew in the Guards. The last name I called was Regis-Rafael, cadet Hastur.

There was a confused silence, just too long. Then down the line of cadets there was a small scuffle and an audible whispered "That's *you*, blockhead!" as Danilo poked Regis in the ribs. Regis' confused voice said "Oh—" Another pause. "Here."

Damn Regis anyhow. I had begun to hope that *this* year we would get through call-over without having to play this particular humiliating charade. Some cadet, not always a first-year man, invariably forgot to answer properly to his name at call-over. There was a procedure for such occasions which probably went back three dozen generations. From the way in which the other Guardsmen, from veterans to older cadets, were waiting, expectant snickers breaking out, they'd all been waiting—yes, damn them all, and hoping—for this ritual hazing.

Left to myself, I'd have said harshly, "Next time, answer to your name, cadet," and had a word with him later in private. But if I tried to cheat them all of their fun, they'd probably take it out on Regis anyway. He'd already made himself conspicuous by coming in late and dressed like a prince. I might as well get on with it. Regis would have to get used to worse things than this in the next few weeks.

"Cadet Hastur," I said with a sigh, "suppose you step forward where we can get a good look at you. Then if you forget your name again, we can all be ready to remind you."

Regis stepped forward, staring blankly. "You know my name."

There was a chorus of snickers. Zandru's hells, was he confused enough to make it worse? I kept my voice cold and even. "It's my business to know it, cadet, and yours to answer any question put to you by an officer. What is your name, cadet?"

He said, rapid and furious, "Regis-Rafael Felix Alar Hastur-Elhalyn!"

"Well, Regis-Rafael This-that-and-the-other, your name in the Guard hall is *cadet Hastur*, and I suggest you memorize your name and the proper response to your name, unless you prefer to be addressed as *That's you, blockhead*." Danilo giggled; I glared at him and he subsided. "Cadet Hastur, nobody's going to call you *Lord Regis* down here. How old are you, cadet Hastur?"

"Fifteen," Regis said. Mentally, I swore again. If he had made the proper response this time—but how could he? No

one had warned him—I could have dismissed him. Now I
had to play out this farce to the very end. The look of hilari-
ous expectancy on the faces around us infuriated me. But
two hundred years of Guardsman tradition were behind it.
"Fifteen *what*, cadet?"

"Fifteen *years*," said Regis, biting on the old bait for the
unwary. I sighed. Well, the other cadets had a right to their
fun. Generations had conditioned them to demand it, and I
gave it to them. I said wearily, "Suppose, men, you all tell
cadet Hastur how old he is?"

"Fifteen, *sir*," they chorused all together, at the top of
their voices. The expected uproar of laughter finally broke
loose. I signaled Regis to go back to his place. The murderous glance he sent me could have killed. I didn't blame him.
For days, in fact, until somebody else did something out-
standingly stupid, he'd be the butt of the barracks. I knew. I
remembered a day several years ago when the name of the
unlucky cadet had been Lewis-Kennard, cadet Montray, and
I had, perhaps, a better excuse—never having heard my
name in that form before. I haven't heard it since either, because my father had demanded I be allowed to bear his
name, Montray-Alton. As usual, he got what he wanted. That
was while they were still arguing about my legitimacy. But he
used the argument that it was unseemly for a cadet to bear a
Terran name in the Guard, even though a bastard legally
uses his mother's name.

Finally the ceremony was over. I should turn the cadets
over to the cadet-master and let him take command. No,
damn it, I couldn't do it. Not until I had urged Father to
reconsider. I hadn't wanted to command the Guards, but he
had insisted and now, for better or worse, all the Guards,
from the youngest cadet to the oldest veteran, were in my
care. I was bound to do my best for them and, damn it, my
best didn't include Dyan Ardais as cadet-master!

I beckoned to old Domenic di Asturien. He was an experienced officer, completely trustworthy, exactly the sort of man
to be in charge of the young. He had retired from active
duty years ago—he was certainly in his eighties—but no one
could complain of him. His family was so old that the
Comyn themselves were upstarts to him. There was a joke,
told in whispers, that he had once spoken to the Hasturs as
"the new nobility."

"Master, the Commander met with an accident this morning, and he has not yet informed me about his choice for cadet-master." I crushed the staff lists in my hand as if the old man could see Dyan's name written there and give me the lie direct. "I respectfully request you to take charge of them until he makes his wishes known."

As I returned to my place, Dyan started to his feet. "You damned young pup, didn't Kennard tell—" He saw curious eyes on us and dropped his voice. "Why didn't you speak to me privately about this?"

Damn it. He knew. And I recalled that he was said to be a strong telepath, though he had been refused entry to the towers for unknown reasons, so he knew that I knew. I blanked my mind to him. There are few who can read an Alton when he's warned. It was a severe breach of courtesy and Comyn ethics that Dyan had done so uninvited. Or was it meant to convey that he didn't think I deserved Comyn immunity? I said frigidly, trying to be civil, "After I have consulted the Commander, Captain Ardais, I shall make his wishes known to you."

"Damn you, the Commander has made his wishes known, and you know it," Dyan said, his mouth hardening into a tight line. There was still time. I could pretend to discover his name on the lists. But eat dirt before the filthy he-whore from the Hellers? I turned away and said to di Asturien, "When you please, Master, you may dismiss your charges."

"You insolent bastard, I'll have your hide for this!"

"Bastard I may be," I said, keeping my voice low, "but I consider it no edifying sight for two captains to quarrel in the hearing of cadets, Captain Ardais."

He swallowed that. He was soldier enough to know it was true. As I dismissed the men, I reflected on the powerful enemy I had made. Before this, he had disliked me, but he was my father's friend and anything belonging to a friend he would tolerate, provided it stayed in its place. Now I had gone a long way beyond his rather narrow concept of that place and he would never forgive it.

Well, I could live without his approval. But I had better lose no time in talking to Father. Dyan wouldn't.

I found him awake and restive, swathed in bandages, his lame leg propped up. He looked haggard and flushed, and I wished I need not trouble him.

"Did the call-over go well?"

"Well enough. Danilo made a good appearance," I said, knowing he'd want to know.

"Regis was added at the last moment. Was he there?"

I nodded, and Father asked, "Did Dyan turn up to take charge? He had a sleepless night too, but said he'd be there."

I stared at him in outrage, finally bursting out, "Father! You can't be serious! I thought it was a joke! Dyan, as cadet-master?"

"I don't joke about the Guards," Father said, his face hard, "and why not Dyan?"

I hesitated, then said, "Must I spell it out for you in full? Have you forgotten last year and the Vallonde youngster?"

"Hysterics," my father said with a shrug. "You took it more seriously than it deserved. When it came to the point, Octavien refused to undergo *laran* interrogation."

"That only proves he was afraid of you," I stormed, "nothing more! I've known grown men, hardened veterans, break down, accept any punishment, rather than face that ordeal! How many mature adults can undergo telepathic examination at the hands of an Alton? Octavien was fifteen!"

"You're missing the point, Lew. The fact it, since he did *not* substantiate the charge, I am not officially required to take notice of it."

"Did you happen to notice that Dyan never denied it either? He didn't have the courage to face an Alton and lie, did he?"

Kennard sighed and tried to hoist himself up in bed. I said, "Let me help you," but he waved me away. "Sit down, Lew, don't stand over me like a statue of an avenging god! What makes you think he would stoop to lie, or that I have any right to ask for any details of his private life? Is your own life so pure and perfect—"

"Father, whatever I may have done for amusement before I was a grown man is completely beside the point," I said. "I have never abused authority—"

He said coldly, "It seems you abused it when you ignored my written orders." His voice hardened. "I told you to sit down! Lew, I don't owe you any explanations, but since you seem to be upset about this, I'll make it clear. The world is made as it's made, not as you or I would like it. Dyan may not be the ideal cadet-master, but he's asked for this post and I'm not going to refuse him."

"Why not?" I was more outraged than ever. "Just because

he is Lord Ardais, must he be allowed a free hand for any kind of debauchery, corruption, anything he pleases? I don't care what he does, but does he have to have license to do it in the Guards?" I demanded. "Why?"

"Lew, listen to me. It's easy to use hard words about anyone who's less than perfect. They have one for you, or have you forgotten? I've listened to it for fifteen years, because I needed you. We need Lord Ardais on Council because he's a strong man and a strong supporter of Hastur. Have you become so involved with your private world at Arilinn that you don't remember the real political situation?" I grimaced, but he said, very patient now, "One faction on Council would like to plunge us into war with the Terrans. That's so unthinkable I needn't take it seriously, unless this small faction gains support. Another faction wants us to join the Terrans completely, give up our old ways and traditions, give up the Compact, become an Empire colony. That faction's bigger, and a lot more dangerous to Comyn. I feel that Hastur's solution, slow change, compromise, above all *time,* is the only reasonable answer. Dyan is one of the very few men who are willing to throw their weight behind Hastur. Why should we refuse him a position he wants, in return?"

"Then we're filthy and corrupt," I raged. "Just to get his support for your political ambitions, you're willing to bribe a man like Dyan by putting him in charge of half-grown boys?"

My father's quick rage flared. It had never been turned full on me before. "Do you honestly believe it's my personal ambition I'm furthering? I ask you, which is more important— the personal ethics of the cadet-master or the future of Darkover and the very survival of the Comyn? No, damn it, you sit there and listen to me! When we need Dyan's support so badly in Council do you think I'd quarrel with him over his private behavior?"

I flung back, equally furious, "I wouldn't give a damn if it *was* his private behavior! But if there's another scandal in the Guards, don't you think the Comyn will suffer? I didn't ask to command the Guards. I told you I'd rather not. But you wouldn't listen to my refusal and now you refuse to listen to my best judgment! I tell you, I won't have Dyan as cadet-master! Not if I'm in command!"

"Oh, yes you will," said my father in a low and vicious voice. "Do you think I am going to let you defy me?"

"Then, damn it, Father, get someone else to command the

Guards! Offer Dyan the command—wouldn't *that* satisfy his ambition?"

"But it wouldn't satisfy me," he said harshly. "I've worked for years to put you in this position. If you think I'm going to let you destroy the Domain of Alton by some childish scruples, you're mistaken. I'm still lord of the Domain and you are oath-bound to take my orders without question! The post of cadet-master is powerful enough to satisfy Dyan, but I'm not going to endanger the rights of the Altons to command. I'm doing it for you, Lew."

"I wish you'd save your trouble! I don't want it!"

"You're in no position to know what you want. Now do as I tell you: go and give Dyan his appointment as cadet-master, or"—he struggled again, ignoring the pain—"I'll get out of bed and do it myself."

His anger I could face; his suffering was something else. I struggled between rage and a deadly misgiving. "Father, I have never disobeyed you. But I beg you, I *beg* you," I repeated, "to reconsider. You know that no good will come of this."

He was gentle again. "Lew, you're still very young. Some day you'll learn that we all have compromises to make, and we make them with the best grace we can. You have to do the best you can within a situation. You can't eat nuts without cracking some shells." He stretched out his hand to me. "You're my main support, Lew. Don't force me to fight you too. I need you at my side."

I clasped his hand between my fingers; it felt swollen and feverish. How could I add to his troubles? He trusted me. What right had I to set up my judgment against his? He was my father, my commander, the lord of my Domain. My only duty was to obey.

Out of his sight, my rage flared again. Who would have believed Father would compromise the honor of the Guards? And how quickly he had maneuvered me again, like a puppet-master pulling strings of love, loyalty, ambition, my own need for his recognition!

I will probably never forget the interview with Dyan Ardais. Oh, he was civil enough. He even commended me on my caution. I kept myself barriered and was scrupulously polite, but I am sure he knew how I felt like a farmer who had just set a wolf to guard the fowl-house.

There was only one grain of comfort in the situation: *I* was no longer a cadet!

Chapter FIVE

As the cadets walked toward the barracks, Regis among them, he heard little of their chatter and horseplay. His face was burning. He could cheerfully have murdered Lew Alton.

Then a tardy fairness came back to him. Everybody there obviously knew what was going to happen, so it was evidently something that went on now and then. He was just the one who stumbled into it. It could have been anyone.

Suddenly he felt better. For the first time in his life he was being treated exactly like anybody else. No deference. No special treatment. He brightened and began to listen to what they were saying.

"Where the hell were you brought up, cadet, not to answer to your name?"

"I was educated at Nevarsin," Regis said, provoking more jeers and laughter.

"Hey, we have a monk among us! Were you too busy at your prayers to hear your name?"

"No, it was the hour of Great Silence and the bell hadn't rung for speech!"

Regis listened with an amiable and rather witless grin, which was the best thing he could possibly have done. A third-year cadet, superior and highly polished in his green and black uniform, conveyed them into a barracks room at the far end of the courtyard. "First-year men in here."

"Hey," someone asked, "what happened to the Commander?"

The junior officer in charge said, "Wash your ears next time. He broke some bones in a fall. We all heard."

Someone said, carefully not loud enough for the officer to hear, "Are we going to be stuck with the bastard all season?"

"Shut up," said Julian MacAran, "Lanart-Alton's not a bad sort. He's got a temper if you set him off, but nothing like the old man in a rage. Anyway, it could be worse," he added, with a wary glance at the cadet who was out of range for the moment. "Lew's fair and he keeps his hands to himself, which is more than you can say for *some* people."

Danilo asked, "Who's really going to be cadet-master? Di Asturien's been retired for years. He served with my grandfather!"

Damon MacAnndra said with a careful look at the officer, "I heard it was going to be you-know-who. Captain Ardais."

Julian said, "I hope you're joking. Last night I was down in the armory and . . ." His voice fell to a whisper. Regis was too far away, but the lads crowded around him reacted with nervous, high-pitched giggles. Damon said, "That's nothing. Listen, did you hear about my cousin Octavien Vallonde? Last year—"

"Chill it," a strange cadet said, just loud enough for Regis to hear. "You know what happened to him for gossiping about a Comyn heir. Have you forgotten there's one in the barracks now?"

Silence abruptly fell over the knot of cadets. They separated and began to drift around the barracks room. To Regis it was like a slap in the face. One minute they were laughing and joking, including him in their jokes; suddenly he was an outsider, a threat. It was worse because he had not really caught the drift of what they were saying.

He drifted toward Danilo, who was at least a familiar face. "What happens now?"

"I guess we wait for someone to tell us. I didn't mean to attract attention and get you in trouble, Lord Regis."

"You too, Dani?" That formal *Lord Regis* seemed a symbol of the distance they were all keeping. He managed to laugh. "Didn't you just hear Lew Alton remind me very forcibly that nobody would call me Lord Regis down here?"

Dani gave him a quick, spontaneous grin. "Right." He looked around the barracks room. It was bleak, cold and comfortless. A dozen hard, narrow camp-beds were ranged in two rows along the wall. All but one had been made up. Danilo gestured to the only one still unchosen and said, "Most of us were down here last night and picked beds. I guess that one will have to be yours. It's next to mine, anyhow."

Regis shrugged. "They haven't left me much choice." It was, of course, the least desirable location, in a corner under a high window, which would probably be drafty. Well, it couldn't be worse than the student dormitory at Nevarsin. Or colder.

The third-year cadet said, "Men, you can have the rest of the morning to make up your beds and put away your clothing. No food in barracks at any time; anything left lying on the floor will be confiscated." He glanced around at the boys waiting quietly for his orders. He said, "Uniforms will be given out tomorrow. MacAnndra—"

Damon said, "Sir?"

"Get a haircut from the barber; you're not at a dancing class. Hair below the collarbone is officially out of uniform. Your mother may have loved those curls, but the officers won't."

Damon turned as red as an apple and ducked his head.

Regis examined the bed, which was made of rough planking, with a straw mattress covered with coarse, clean ticking. Folded at the foot were a couple of thick dark gray blankets. They looked scratchy. The other lads were making up the beds with their own sheets. Regis began making a mental list of the things he should fetch from his grandfather's rooms. It began with bed linens and a pillow. At the head of each bed was a narrow wooden shelf on which each cadet had already placed his personal possessions. At the foot of the bed was a rough wooden box, each lid scarred with knife-marks, intertwined initials and hacked or lightly burned-in crests, the marks of generations of restless boys. It struck Regis that years ago his father must have been a cadet in this very room, on a hard bed like this, his possessions reduced, whatever his rank or riches, to what he could keep on a narrow shelf a hand-span wide. Danilo was arranging on his shelf a plain wooden comb, a hairbrush, a battered cup and plate and a small box carved with silver, from which he reverently took the small *cristoforo* statue of the Bearer of Burdens, carrying his weight of the world's sorrows.

Below the shelf were pegs for his sword and dagger. Danilo's looked very old. Heirlooms in his family?

All of them were there because their forefathers had been, Regis thought with the old resentment. He swore he would never walk the trail carved out for a Hastur heir, yet here he was.

The cadet officer was walking along the room, making some kind of final check. At the far end of the room was an open space with a couple of heavy benches and a much-

scarred wooden table. There was an open fireplace, but no fire
was burning at present. The windows were high and narrow,
unglazed, covered with slatted wood shutters, which could be
closed in the worst weather at the price of shutting out most
of the light. The cadet officer said, "Each of you will be sent
for some time today and tested by an arms-master." He saw
Regis sitting on the end of his bed and walked down the row
of beds to him.

"You came in late. Did anyone give you a copy of the
arms-manual?"

"No, sir."

The officer gave him a battered booklet. "I heard you were
educated at Nevarsin; I suppose you can read. Any questions?"

"I didn't—my grandfather didn't—no one sent my things
down. May I send for them?"

The older lad said, not unkindly, "There's no one to fetch
and carry for you down here, cadet. Tomorrow after dinner
you'll have some off-duty time and you can go and fetch what
you need for yourself. Meanwhile, you'll just have to make
out with the clothes on your back." He looked Regis over, and
Regis imagined a veiled sneer at the elaborate garments he
had put on to present himself to his grandfather this morning.
"You're the nameless wonder, aren't you? Remembered your
name yet?"

"Cadet Hastur, sir," Regis said, his face burning again, and
the officer nodded, said, "Very good, cadet," and went away.

And that was obviously why they did it, Regis thought.
Probably nobody ever forgot twice.

Danilo, who had been listening, said, "Didn't anyone tell
you to bring down everything you'd need the night before?
That's why Lord Alton sent me down early."

"No, no one told me." He wished he had thought to ask
Lew, while they could speak together as friends and not as
cadet and commander, what he would need in barracks.

Danilo said diffidently, "Those are your best clothes, aren't
they? I could lend you an ordinary shirt to put on; you're
about my size."

"Thank you, Dani. I'd be grateful. This outfit isn't very
suitable, is it?"

Danilo was kneeling in front of his wooden chest, brought
out a clean but very shabby linen shirt, much patched around
the elbows. Regis pulled off the dyed-leather tunic and the

fine frilled shirt under it and slid into the patched one. It was a little large. Danilo apologized. "It's big for me too. It used to belong to Lew—Captain Alton, I mean. Lord Kennard gave me some of his outgrown clothes, so that I'd have a decent outfit for the cadets. He gave me a good horse too. He's been very kind to me."

Regis laughed. "I used to wear Lew's outgrown clothes the years I was there. I kept growing out of mine, and with the fire-watch called every few days, no one had time to make me any new ones or send to town." He laced up the cords at the neck. Danilo said, "It's hard to imagine *you* wearing outgrown clothes."

"I didn't mind wearing Lew's. I hated wearing my sister's outgrown nightgowns, though. Her governess taught her needlework by having her cut them down to size for me. Whenever she was cross about it, she used to pinch or prick me with her pins while she was trying them on. She's never liked sewing." He thought of his sister as he had last seen her heavy-footed, swollen in pregnancy. Poor Javanne. She was caught too, with nothing ahead of her except bearing children for the house of Hastur.

"Regis, is something wrong?"

Regis was startled at Danilo's look of concern. "Not really. I was thinking of my sister, wondering if her child had been born."

Danilo said gently, "I'm sure they'd have sent word if anything was wrong. The old saying is that good news crawls on its belly; bad news has wings."

Damon MacAnndra came toward them. "Have you been tested yet by the arms-master?"

"No," said Dani, "they didn't get to me yesterday. What happens?"

Damon shrugged. "The arms-master hands you a standard Guardsmen sword and asks you to demonstrate the basic positions for defense. If you don't know which end of it to take 'hold by, he puts you down for beginners' lessons and you get to practice about three hours a day. In your off-duty time, of course. If you know the basics, he or one of his assistants will test you. When I went up last night, Lord Dyan was there watching. I tell you, I sweat blood! I made a damn fool of myself, my foot slipped and he put me down for lessons every other day. Who could do anything with that one staring at you?"

"Yes," Julian said from the cot beyond, where he was trying to get a spot of rust off his knife. "My brother told me he likes to sit and watch the cadets training. He seems to enjoy seeing them get rattled and do stupid things. He's a mean one."

"I studied swordplay at Nevarsin," Danilo said. "I'm not worried about the arms-master."

"Well, you'd better worry about Lord Dyan. You're just young enough and pretty enough—"

"Shut your mouth," Danilo said. "You shouldn't talk that way about a Comyn lord."

Damon snickered. "I forgot. You're Lord Alton's protégé, aren't you? Strange, I never heard that *he* had any special liking for pretty boys."

Danilo flared, his face burning. "You shut your filthy mouth! You're not fit to wipe Lord Kennard's boots! If you say anything like that again—"

"Well, it seems we have a whole cloister of monks back here." Julian joined in the laughter. "Do you recite the Creed of Chastity when you ride into battle, Dani?"

"It wouldn't hurt any of you dirty-mouths to say something decent," Danilo said and turned his back on them, burying himself in the arms-manual.

Regis had also been shocked by the accusation they had made and by their language. But he realized he could not expect ordinary young men to behave and talk like novice monks, and he knew they would quickly make his life unbearable if he showed any sign of his distaste. He held his peace. That sort of thing must be common enough here to be a joke.

Yet it had touched off a murder and near-riot in the Terran Zone. Could grown men actually take such things seriously enough to kill? Terrans, perhaps. They must have very strange customs, if they were even stricter than the *cristoforos*.

He suddenly recalled, as something that might have taken place years ago, that only this morning he had stood beside young Lawton in the Terran Zone, watching the starship break free from the planet and make its way to the stars. He wondered if Dan Lawton knew which end of a sword to take hold by, and if he cared. He had a strange sense of shuttling, rapidly and painfully, between worlds.

Three years. Three years to study swordplay while the Terran ships came and went less than a bowshot away.

Was this the kind of awareness his grandfather carried night and day, a constant reminder of two worlds rubbing shoulders, with violently opposed histories, habits, manners, moralities? How did Hastur live with the contrast?

The day wore on. He was sent for, and an orderly measured him for his uniform. When the sun was high, a junior officer came to show them the way to the mess hall, where the cadets ate at separate tables. The food was coarse and plain, but Regis had eaten worse at Nevarsin and he made a good meal, though some of the cadets grumbled loudly about the fare.

"It's not so bad," he said in an undertone to Danilo, and the younger boy's eyes glinted with mischief. "Maybe they want to make sure we know they're used to something better! Even if we're not."

Regis, aware of Danilo's patched shirt on his back, remembered how desperately poor the boy's family must be. Yet they had had him well educated at Nevarsin. "I'd thought you were to be a monk, Dani."

"I couldn't be," Dani said. "I'm my father's only son now, and it wouldn't be lawful. My half-brother was killed fifteen years ago, before I was born." As they left the mess hall, he added, "Father had me taught to read and write and keep accounts so that someday I'd be fit to manage his estate. He's growing too old to farm Syrtis alone. He didn't want me to go into the Guards, but when Lord Alton made such a kind offer, he couldn't refuse. I *hate* to hear them gossip about him," he said vehemently. "He's not like that! He's good and kind and decent!"

"I'm sure he doesn't listen," Regis said. "I lived in his house too, you know. And one of his favorite sayings used to be, if you listen to dogs barking, you'll go deaf without learning much. Are the Syrtis people under the Alton Domain, Danilo?"

"No, we have always been under Hastur wardship. My father was hawk-master to yours, and my half-brother his paxman."

And something Regis had always known, an old story which had been part of his childhood·but which he had never associated with living people, fell into place in his mind. He said excitedly, "Dani! Your brother—was his name Rafael-Felix Syrtis of Syrtis?"

"Yes, that was his name. He was killed before I was born, in the same year Stefan Fourth died—"

"So was my father," said Regis, with a surge of unfamiliar emotion. "All my life I have known the story, known your brother's name. Dani, your brother was my father's personal guard, they were killed at the same instant—he died trying to shield my father with his body. Did you know they are buried side by side, in one grave, on the field of Kilghairlie?"

He remembered, but did not say, what an old servant had told him, that they were blown to bits, buried together where they fell, since no living man could tell which bits were his father's, which Dani's brother's.

"I didn't know," Danilo whispered, his eyes wide. Regis, caught in the grip of a strange emotion, said, "It must be horrible to die like that, but not so horrible if your last thought is to shield someone else...."

Danilo's voice was not entirely steady. "They were both named Rafael and they had sworn to one another, and they fought together and died and were buried in one grave—" As if he hardly knew what he was doing, he reached out to Regis and clasped his hands. He said, "I'd like to die like that. Wouldn't you?"

Regis nodded wordlessly. For an instant it seemed to him that something had reached deep down inside him, an almost painful awareness and emotion. It was almost a physical touch, although Danilo's fingers were only resting lightly in his own. Suddenly, abashed by the intensity of his own feelings, he let go of Danilo's hand, and the surge of emotion receded. One of the cadet officers came up and said, "Dani, the arms-master has sent for you." Danilo caught up his shabby leather tunic, pulled it quickly over his shirt and went.

Regis, remembering that he had been up all night, stretched out on the bare straw ticking of his cot. He was too restless to sleep, but he fell at last into an uneasy doze, mingled with the unfamiliar sounds of the Guard hall the metallic clinking from the armory where someone was mending a shield, men's voices, very different from the muted speech of the monastery. Half asleep, he began to see a nightmarish sequence of faces: Lew Alton looking sad and angry when he told Regis he had no *laran*, Kennard pleading for Marius, his grandfather struggling not to betray exhaustion or grief. As

he drifted deeper into the neutral country on the edge of
sleep, he remembered Danilo, handling the wooden practice
swords at Nevarsin. Someone whose face Regis could not see
was standing close behind him; Danilo moved abruptly away,
and he heard through the dream a harsh, shrill laugh, raucous as the scream of a hawk. And then he had a sudden
mental picture of Danilo, his face turned away, huddled
against the wall, sobbing heartbrokenly. And through the
dreamlike sobs Regis felt a shocking overtone of fear, disgust
and a consuming shame. . . .

Someone laid a careful hand on his shoulder, shook him
lightly. The barracks room was filled with the dimness of sunset. Danilo said, "Regis? I'm sorry to wake you, but the
cadet-master wants to see you. Do you know the way?"

Regis sat up, still a little dazed by the sharp edges of nightmare. For a moment he thought that Danilo's face, bent over
him in the dim light, was actually red and flushed, as if he
had been crying, like in the dream. No, that was ridiculous.
Dani looked hot and sweaty, as if he'd been running hard or
exercising. Probably they'd tested his swordplay. Regis tried
to throw off the remnants of dream. He went into the stone-
floored washroom and latrine, sluiced his face with the par-
alyzingly cold water from the pump. Back in the barracks,
tugging his leather tunic over Dani's patched shirt, he saw
Danilo slumped on his cot, his head in his hands. He must
have done badly at his arms-test and he's upset about it, he
decided, and left without disturbing his friend.

Inside the armory there was a second-year cadet with long
lists in his hands, another officer writing at a table and Dyan
Ardais, seated behind an old worm-eaten desk. Because the
afternoon had turned warm, his collar was undone, his coarse
dark hair clinging damply around his high forehead. He
glanced up, and Regis felt that in one swift feral glance Dyan
had learned everything he wanted to know about him.

"Cadet Hastur. Getting along all right so far?"

"Yes, Lord Dyan."

"Just Captain Ardais in the Guard hall, Regis." Dyan
looked him over again, a slow evaluating stare that made
Regis uncomfortable. "At least they taught you to stand
straight at Nevarsin. You should see the way some of the
lads stand!" He consulted a long sheet on his desk. "Regis-
Rafael Felix Alar Hastur-Elhalyn. You prefer Regis-Rafael?"

"Simply Regis, sir."

"As you wish. Although it seems a great pity to let the name of Rafael Hastur be lost. It is an honored name."

Damn it, Regis thought, I know I'm not my father! He knew he sounded curt and almost impolite as he said, "My sister's son has been named Rafael, Captain. I prefer not to share my father's honor before I have earned it."

"An admirable objective," Dyan said slowly. "I think every man wants a name for himself, rather than resting on the past. I can understand that, Regis." After a moment, with an odd impulsive grin, he said, "It must be a pleasant thing to have a father's honor to cherish, a father who did not outlive his moment of glory. You know, I suppose, that *my* father has been mad these twenty years, without wits enough to know his son's face?"

Regis had only heard rumors of old Kyril Ardais, who had not been seen by anyone outside Castle Ardais for so long that most people in the Domains had long forgotten his existence, or that Dyan was not Lord Ardais, but only Lord Dyan. Abruptly, Dyan spoke in an entirely different tone.

"How tall are you?"

"Five feet ten."

The eyebrows went up in amused inquiry. "Already? Yes, I believe you are at that. Do you drink?"

"Only at dinner, sir."

"Well, don't start. There are too many young sots around. Turn up drunk on duty and you'll be booted, no excuses or explanations accepted. You are also forbidden to gamble. I don't mean wagering pennies on card games or dice, of course, but gambling substantial sums is against the rules. Did they give you a manual of arms? Good, read it tonight. After tomorrow you're responsible for everything in it. A few more things. Duels are absolutely forbidden, and drawing your sword or knife on a fellow Guardsman will break you. So keep your temper, whatever happens. You're not married, I suppose. Handfasted?"

"Not that I've heard, sir."

Dyan made an odd derisive sound. "Well, make the best of it; your grandfather will probably have you married off before the year's out. Let me see. What you do in off-duty time is your own affair, but don't get yourself talked about. There's a rule about causing scandalous talk by scandalous behavior.

I don't have to tell you that the heir to a Domain is expected to set an example, do I?"

"No, Captain, you don't have to tell me that." Regis had had his nose rubbed in that all his life and he supposed Dyan had too.

Dyan's eyes met his again, amused, sympathetic. "It's unfair, isn't it, kinsman? Not allowed to claim any Comyn privileges, but still expected to set an example because of what we are." With another swift change of mood, he was back to the remote officer. "In general, keep out of the Terran Zone for your . . . amusements."

Regis was thinking of the young Terran officer who, before they parted, had again offered to show him more of the spaceport whenever he wished. "Is it forbidden to go into the Terran Zone at all?"

"By no means. The prohibition doesn't apply to sightseeing, shopping or eating there if you have a taste for exotic foods. But Terran customs differ enough from ours that getting entangled with Terran prostitutes, or making any sexual advances to them, is likely to be a risky business. So keep out of trouble. To put it bluntly—you're supposed to be grown up now—if you have a taste for such adventures, find them on the Darkovan side of the line. Zandru's hells, my boy, aren't you too old to blush? Or hasn't the monastery worn off you yet?" He laughed. "I suppose, brought up at Nevarsin, you don't know a damn thing about arms, either?"

Regis welcomed the change of subject this time. He said he had had lessons, and Dyan's nostrils flared in contempt. "Some broken-down old soldier earning a few coins teaching the basic positions?"

"Kennard Alton taught me when I was a child, sir."

"Well, we'll see." He motioned to one of the junior officers. "Hjalmar, give him a practice sword."

Hjalmar handed Regis one of the wood and leather swords used for training. Regis balanced it in his hand. "Sir, I'm very badly out of practice."

"Never mind," Hjalmar said, bored. "We'll see what kind of training you've had."

Regis raised his sword in salute. He saw Hjalmar lift an eyebrow as he dropped into the defensive stance Kennard had taught him years ago. The moment Hjalmar lowered his weapon Regis noted the weak point in his defense; he feinted, sidestepped and touched Hjalmar almost instantly on the thigh. They reengaged. For a moment there was no sound but the scuffle of feet as they circled one another, then Hjalmar made a swift pass which Regis parried. He disengaged and touched him on the shoulder.

"Enough." Dyan threw off his vest, standing in shirtsleeves. "Give me the sword, Hjalmar."

Regis knew, as soon as Dyan raised the wooden blade, that this was no amateur. Hjalmar, evidently, was used for testing cadets who were shy or completely unskilled, perhaps handling weapons for the first time. Dyan was another matter. Regis felt a tightness in his throat, recalling the gossip of the cadets: Dyan liked to see people get rattled and do something stupid.

He managed to counter the first stroke and the second, but on the third his parry slid awkwardly along Dyan's casually turned blade and he felt the wooden tip thump his ribs hard. Dyan nodded to him to go on, then beat him back step by step, finally touched him again, again, three times in rapid succession. Regis flushed and lowered his sword.

Then he felt the older man's hand gripping his shoulder hard. "So you're out of practice?"

"Very badly, Captain."

"Stop bragging, *chiyu*. You made me sweat, and not even the arms-master can always do that. Kennard taught you well. I'd halfway expected, with that pretty face of yours, you'd have learned nothing but courtly dances. Well, lad, you can be excused from regular lessons, but you'd better turn out for practice every day. If, that is, we can find anyone to match you. If not, I'll have to work out with you myself."

"I would be honored, Captain," Regis said, but hoped Dyan would not hold him to this. Something about the older man's intense stare and teasing compliments made him feel awkward and very young. Dyan's hand on his shoulder was hard, almost a painful grip. He turned Regis gently around to look at him. He said, "Since you already have some skill at swordplay, kinsman, perhaps, if you like the idea, I could ask to have you assigned as my aide. Among other things, it would mean you need not sleep in the barracks."

Regis said quickly, "I'd rather not, sir." He fumbled for an acceptable excuse. "Sir, that is a post for an—an experienced cadet. If I am assigned at once to a post of honor, it will look as if I am taking advantage of my rank, to be excused from what the other cadets have to do. Thank you for the honor, Captain, but I don't think I—I ought to accept."

Dyan threw back his head and laughed, and it seemed to Regis that the raucous laughter sounded a little like the feral cry of a hawk, that there was something nightmarish about it. Regis was caught in the grip of a strange *déjà vu*, feeling that this had happened before.

It vanished as swiftly as it had come. Dyan released his grip on Regis' shoulder.

"I honor you for that decision, kinsman, and I dare say you are right. And in training already to be a statesman, I see. I can find no fault with your answer."

Again the wild, hawklike laugh.

"You can go, cadet. Tell young MacAran I want to see him."

Chapter SIX

(Lew Alton's narrative)

Father was bedridden during the first several days of Council season, and I was too busy and beset to have much time for the cadets. I had to attend Council meetings, which at this particular time were mostly concerned with some dreary business of trade agreements with the Dry Towns. One thing I did find time for was having that staircase fixed before someone else broke his leg, or his neck. This was troublesome too: I had to deal with architects and builders, we had stonemasons underfoot for days, the cadets coughed from morning to night with the choking dust and the veterans grumbled constantly about having to go the long way round and use the other stairs.

A long time before I thought he was well enough, Father insisted on returning to his Council seat, which I was glad to be out of. Far too soon after that, he returned to the Guards, his arm still in a sling, looking dreadfully pale and worn. I suspected he shared some of my uneasiness about how well the cadets would fare this season, but he said nothing about it to me. It nagged at me ceaselessly; I resented it as much for my father's sake as my own. If my father had *chosen* to trust Dyan Ardais, I might not have been quite so disturbed. But I felt that he, too, had been *compelled,* and that Dyan had enjoyed having the power to do so.

A few days after that, Gabriel Lanart-Hastur returned from Edelweiss with news that Javanne had borne twin girls, whom she named Ariel and Liriel. With Gabriel at hand, my father sent me back into the hills on a mission to set up a new system of fire-watch beacons, to inspect the fire-watch stations which had been established in my grandfather's day and to instruct the Rangers in new fire-fighting techniques. This kind of mission demands tact and some Comyn author-.ty, to persuade men separated by family feuds and rivalries, sometimes for generations, to work together peacefully. Fire-truce is the oldest tradition on Darkover but, in districts which have been lucky enough to escape forest fires for centuries, it's hard to persuade anyone that the fire-truce should be extended to the upkeep of the stations and beacons.

I had my father's full authority, though, and that helped. The law of the Comyn transcends, or is supposed to transcend, personal feuds and family rivalries. I had a dozen Guardsmen with me for the physical work, but I had to do the talking, the persuading and the temper-smoothing when old struggles flared out of control. It took a lot of tact and thought; it also demanded knowledge of the various families, their hereditary loyalties, intermarriages and interactions for the last seven or eight generations. It was high summer before I rode back to Thendara, but I felt I'd accomplished a great deal. Every step against the constant menace of forest fire on Darkover impresses me more than all the political accomplishments of the last hundred years. That's something we've actually gained from the presence of the Terran Empire: a great increase in knowledge of fire-control and an exchange of information with other heavily wooded Empire planets about new methods of surveillance and protection.

And back in the hills the Comyn name meant something. Nearer to the Trade Cities, the influence of Terra has eroded the old habit of turning to the Comyn for leadership. But back there, the potency of the very name of Comyn was immense. The people neither knew nor cared that I was a half-Terran bastard. I was the son of Kennard Alton, and that was all that really mattered. For the first time I carried the full authority of a Comyn heir.

I even settled a blood-feud which had run three generations by suggesting that the eldest son of one house marry the only daughter of another and the disputed land be settled on their children. Only a Comyn lord could have suggested this without becoming himself entangled in the feud, but they accepted it. When I thought of the lives it would save, I was glad of the chance.

I rode into Thendara one morning in midsummer. I've heard offworlders say our planet has no summer, but there had been no snow for three days, even in the pre-dawn hours, and that was summer enough for me. The sun was dim and cloud-hidden, but as we rode down from the pass it broke through the layers of fog, throwing deep crimson lights on the city lying below us. Old people and children gathered inside the city gates to watch us, and I found I was grinning to myself. Part of it, of course, was the thought of being able to sleep for two nights in the same bed. But part of it was pure pleasure at knowing I'd done a good job. It seemed, for the first time in my life, that this was *my* city, that I was coming home. I had not chosen this duty—I had been born into it—but I no longer resented it so much.

Riding into the stable court of the Guards, I saw a brace of cadets on watch at the gates and more going out from the mess hall. They seemed a soldierly lot, not the straggle of awkward children they had been that first day. Dyan had done well enough, evidently. Well, it had never been his competence I questioned, but even so, I felt better. I turned my horse over to the grooms and went to make my report to my father.

He was out of bandages now, with his arm free of the sling, but he still looked pale, his lameness more pronounced than ever. He was in Council regalia, not uniform. He waved away my proffered report.

"No time for that now. And I'm sure you did as well as I could have done myself. But there's trouble here. Are you very tired?"

"No, not really. What's wrong, Father? More riots?"

"Not this time. A meeting of Council with the Terran Legate this morning. In the city, at Terran headquarters."

"Why doesn't he wait on you in the Council Chamber?" Comyn lords did not come and go at the bidding of the Terranan!

He caught the thought and shook his head. "It was Hastur himself who requested this meeting. It's more important than you can possibly imagine. That's why I want you to handle this for me. We need an honor guard, and I want you to choose the members very carefully. It would be disastrous if this became a subject of gossip in the Guards—or elsewhere."

"Surely, Father, any Guardsman would be honor-bound—"

"In theory, yes," he said dryly, "but in practice, some of them are more trustworthy than others. You know the younger men better than I do." It was the first time he had ever admitted so much. He had missed me, needed me. I felt warmed and welcomed, even though all he said was, "Choose Guardsmen or cadets who are blood-kin to Comyn if you can, or the trustiest. You know best which of them have tongues that rattle at both ends."

Gabriel Lanart, I thought, as I went down to the Guard hall, an Alton kinsman, married into the Hasturs. Lerrys Ridenow, the younger brother of the lord of his Domain. Old di Asturien, whose loyalty was as firm as the foundations of Comyn Castle itself. I left him to choose the veterans who would escort us through the streets—they would not go into the meeting rooms, so their choice was not so critical—and went off to cadet barracks.

It was the slack time between breakfast and morning drill. The first-year cadets were making their beds, two of them sweeping the floor and cleaning out the fireplaces. Regis was sitting on the corner cot, mending a broken bootlace. Was it meekness or good nature which had let them crowd him into the drafty spot under the window? He sprang up and came to attention as I stopped at the foot of his bed.

I motioned him to relax. "The Commander has sent me to choose an honor guard detail," I said. "This is Comyn business; it goes without saying that no word of what you may hear is to go outside Council rooms. Do you understand me, Regis?"

"Yes, Captain." He was formal, but I caught curiosity and excitement in his lifted face. He looked older, not quite so childish, not nearly so shy. Well, as I knew from my own first tormented cadet season, one of two things happened in the first few days. You grew up fast . . . or you crawled back home, beaten, to your family. I've often thought that was why cadets were required to serve a few terms in the Guard. No one could ever tell in advance which ones would survive.

I asked, "How are you getting along?"

He smiled. "Well enough." He started to say something else, but at that moment Danilo Syrtis, covered in dust, crawled out from under his bed. "Got it!" he said. "It evidently slipped down this morning when I—" He saw me, broke off and came to attention.

"Captain."

"Relax, cadet," I said, "but you'd better get that dirt off your knees before you go out to inspection." He was father's protégé, and his family had been Hastur men for gener-

ations. "You join the honor guard too, cadet. Did you hear
what I said to Regis, Dani?"

He nodded, coloring, and his eyes brightened. He said,
with such formality that it sounded stiff, "I am deeply honored, Captain." But through the formal words, I caught the
touch of excitement, apprehension, curiosity, unmistakable
pleasure at the honor.

Unmistakable. This was not the random sensing of emotions which I pick up in any group, but a definite touch.

Laran. The boy had *laran*, was certainly a telepath, probably had one of the other gifts. Well, it was not much of a
surprise. Father had told me they had Comyn blood a few
generations back. Regis was kneeling before his chest, searching for the leather tabard of his dress uniform. As Danilo
was about to follow suit, I stepped to his side and said, "A
word, kinsman. Not now—there is no urgency—but some
time, when you are free of other duties, go to my father, or
to Lord Dyan if you prefer, and ask to be tested by a *leronis*.
They will know what you mean. Say that it was I who told
you this." I turned away. "Both of you join the detail at the
gates as soon as you can."

The Comyn lords were waiting in the court as the detail of
Guards was forming. Lord Hastur, in sky-blue cloak with the
silver fir tree badge. My father, giving low-voiced directions
to old di Asturien. Prince Derik was not present. Hastur
would have had to speak for him as Regent in any case, but
Derik at sixteen should certainly have been old enough, and
interested enough, to attend such an important meeting.

Edric Ridenow was there, the thickset, red-bearded lord of
Serrais. There was also a woman, pale and slender, folded in
a thin gray hooded cloak which shielded her from curious
eyes. I did not recognize her, but she was evidently *comynara*; she must be an Aillard or an Elhalyn, since only those
two Domains give independent Council right to their women.
Dyan Ardais, in the crimson and gray of his Domain, strode
to his place; he gave a brief glance to the honor guard,
stopped briefly beside Danilo and spoke in a low voice. The
boy blushed and looked straight ahead. I'd already noticed that
he still colored like a child if you spoke to him. I wondered
what small fault the cadet-master had found in his appearance and bearing. I had found none, but it's a cadet-master's
business to take note of trivialities,

As we moved through the streets of Thendara, we drew

surprised glances. Damn the Terrans anyway! It lessened
Comyn dignity, that they beckoned and we came at a run!

The Regent seemed conscious of no loss of dignity. He
moved between his escort with the energy of a man half his
years, his face stern and composed. Just the same I was glad
when we reached the spaceport gates. Leaving the escort outside, we were conducted, Comyn lords and honor guard, into
the building to a large room on the first floor.

As custom decreed, I stepped inside first, drawn sword in
hand. It was small for a council chamber, but contained a
large, round table and many seats. A number of Terrans
were seated on the far side of the table, mostly in some sort
of uniform. Some of them wore a great number of medals,
and I surmised they intended to do the Comyn honor.

Some of them showed considerable unease when I stepped
inside with my drawn sword, but the gray-haired man at
their center—the one with the most medals—said quickly, "It
is customary, their honor guard. You come for the Regent of
Comyn, officer?"

He had spoken *cahuenga*, the mountain dialect which has
become a common tongue all over Darkover, from the Hellers to the Dry Towns. I brought my sword up to salute and
replied, "Captain Montray-Alton, at your service, sir." Since
I saw no weapons visible anywhere in the room, I forebore
any further search and sheathed the sword. I ushered in the
rest of the honor guard, placing them around the room, mo-
tioning Regis to take a position directly behind the Regent,
stationing Gabriel at the doorway, then ushering in the members of the Council and announcing their names one by one.

"Danvan-Valentine, Lord Hastur, Warden of Elhalyn, Regent of the Crown of the Seven Domains."

The gray-haired man—I surmised that he was the Terran
Legate—rose to his feet and bowed. Not deeply enough, but
more than I'd expected of a Terran. "We are honored, Lord
Regent."

"Kennard-Gwynn Alton, Lord Alton, Commander of the
City Guard." He limped heavily to his place.

"Lord Dyan-Gabriel, Regent of Ardais." Whatever my personal feelings about him, I had to admit he looked impres-
sive. "Edric, Lord Serrais. And—" I hesitated a moment as
the gray-cloaked woman entered, realized I did not know her
name. She smiled almost imperceptibly and murmured under

her breath, "For shame, kinsman! Don't you recognize me? I am Callina Aillard."

I felt like an utter fool. Of course I knew her.

"Callina, Lady Aillard—" I hesitated again momentarily; I could not remember in which of the towers she was serving as Keeper. Well, the Terrans would never know the difference. She supplied it telepathically, with an amused smile behind her hood, and I concluded, "*leronis* of Neskaya."

She walked with quiet composure to the remaining seat. She kept the hood of her cloak about her face, as was proper for an unwedded woman among strangers. I saw with some relief that the Legate, at least, had been informed of the polite custom among valley Darkovans and had briefed his men not to look directly at her. I too kept my eyes politely averted; she was my kinswoman, but we were among strangers. I had seen only that she was very slight, with pale solemn features.

When everyone was in his appointed place, I drew my sword again, saluted Hastur and then the Legate and took my place behind my father. One of the Terrans said, "Now that all *that*'s over, can we come to business?"

"Just a moment, Meredith," the Legate said, checking his unseemly impatience. "Noble lords, my lady, you lend us grace. Allow me to present myself. My name is Donnell Ramsay; I am privileged to serve the Empire as Legate for Terra. It is my pleasure to welcome you. These"—he indicated the men beside him at the table—"are my personal assistants: Laurens Meredith, Reade Andrusson. If there are any among you, my lords, who do not speak *cahuenga*, our liaison man, Daniel Lawton, will be honored to translate for you into the *casta*. If we may serve you otherwise, you have only to speak of it. And if you wish, Lord Hastur," he added, with a bow, "that this meeting should be conducted according to formal protocol in the *casta* language, we are ready to accede."

I was glad to note that he knew the rudiments of courtesy. Hastur said, "By your leave, sir, we will dispense with the translator, unless some misunderstanding should arise which he can settle. He is, however, most welcome to remain.

Young Lawton bowed. He had flaming red hair and a look of the Comyn about him. I remembered hearing that his mother had been a woman of the Ardais clan. I wondered if Dyan recognized his kinsman and what he thought about it.

It was strange to think that young Lawton might well have been standing here among the honor guard. My thoughts were wandering; I commanded them back as Hastur spoke.

"I have come to you, Legate, to draw your attention to a grave breach of the Compact on Darkover. It has been brought to my notice that, back in the mountains near Aldaran, a variety of contraband weapons is being openly bought and sold. Not only within the Trade City boundaries there, where your agreement with us allows your citizens to carry what weapons they will, but in the old city of Caer Donn, where Terrans walk the streets as they wish, carrying pistols and blasters and neural disrupters. I have also been told that it is possible to purchase these weapons in that city, and that they have been sold upon occasion to Darkovan citizens. My informant purchased one without difficulty. It should not be necessary to remind you that this is a very serious breach of Compact."

It took all my self-control to keep the impassive face suitable for an honor guard, whose perfect model is a child's carved toy soldier, neither hearing nor seeing. Would even the Terrans dare to breach the Compact?

I knew now why my father had wanted to be certain no hint of gossip got out. Since the Ages of Chaos, the Darkovan Compact has banned any weapon operating beyond the hand's reach of the man wielding it. This was a fundamental law: the man who would kill must himself come within reach of death. News that the Compact was being violated would shake Darkover to the roots, create public disorder and distrust, damage the confidence of the people in their rulers.

The Legate's face betrayed nothing, yet something, some infinitesimal thightening of his eyes and mouth, told me this was no news to him.

"It is not our business to enforce the Compact on Darkover, Lord Hastur. The policy of the Empire is to maintain a completely neutral posture in regard to local disputes. Our dealings in Caer Donn and the Trade City there are with Lord Kermiac of Aldaran. It was made very clear to us that the Comyn have no jurisdiction in the mountains near Aldaran. Have I been misinformed? Is the territory of Aldaran subject to the laws of Comyn, Lord Hastur?"

Hastur said with a snap of his jaw, "Aldaran has not been a Comyn Domain for many years, Mr. Ramsay. Nevertheless, the Compact can hardly be called a local decision. While Aldaran is not under our law—"

"So I myself believed, sir," the Legate said, "and there-fore—"

"Forgive me, Mr. Ramsay, I had not yet finished." Hastur was angry. I tried to keep myself barriered, as any telepath would in a crowd this size, but I couldn't shut out everything. Hastur's calm, stern face did not alter a muscle, but his anger was like the distant glow of a forest fire against the horizon. Not yet a danger, but a faraway menace. He said, "Correct me if I am wrong, Mr. Ramsay, but is it not true that when the Empire negotiated to have Darkover given status as a Class D Closed World"—the technical language sounded strange on his tongue, and he seemed to speak it with dis-taste—"that one condition of the use and lease of the spaceport and the establishment of the cities of Port Chicago, Caer Donn and Thendara as Trade Cities, was complete en-forcement of Compact outside the Trade Cities and control of contraband weapons? Mindful of that agreement, can you truthfully state that it is not your business to enforce the Compact on Darkover, sir?"

Ramsay said, "We did and we do enforce it in the Comyn Domains and under Comyn law, my lord, at considerable trouble and expense to ourselves. Need I remind you that one of our men was threatened with murder, not long ago, be-cause he was unweaponed and defenseless in a society which expects every man to fight and protect himself?"

Dyan Ardais said harshly, "The episode you mention was unnecessary. It is necessary to remind you that the man who was threatened with murder had himself murdered one of our Guardsman, in a quarrel so trivial that a Darkovan boy of twelve would have been ashamed to make more of it than a joke! Then this Terran murderer hid behind his celebrated *weaponless* status"—even a Terran could not escape that sneer—"to refuse a lawful challenge by the murdered man's brother! If your men choose to go weaponless, sir, they alone are responsible for their acts."

Reade Andrusson said, "They do not *choose* to go weapon-less, Lord Ardais. We are forced by the Compact to deprive them of their accustomed weapons."

Dyan said, "They are allowed by our laws to carry what-ever ethical weapons they choose. They cannot complain of a defenselessness which is their own choice."

The Legate, turning his eyes consideringly on Dyan, said, "Their defenselessness, Lord Ardais, is in obedience to *our* laws. We have a very distinct bias, which our laws reflect, against carving people up with swords and knives."

Hastur said harshly, "Is it your contention, sir, that a man is somehow less dead if he is shot down from a safe distance without visible bloodshed? Is death cleaner when it comes to you from a killer safely out of reach of his own death?" Even through my own barriers, his pain was so violent, so palpable that it was like a long wail of anguish; I knew he was thinking of his own son, blown to fragments by smuggled contraband weapons, killed by a man whose face he never saw! So intense was that cry of agony that I saw Danilo, impassive behind Lord Edric, flinch and tighten his hands into white-knuckled fists at his sides; my father looked white and shaken; Regis' mouth moved and he blinked rapidly, and I wondered how even the Terrans could be unaware of so much pain. But Hastur's voice was steady, betraying nothing to the aliens. "We banned such coward's weapons to insure that any man who would kill must see his victim's blood flow and come into some danger of losing his own, if not at the hands of his victim, at least at the hands of his victim's family or friends."

The Legate said, "That episode was settled long ago, Lord Regent, but I remind you we stood ready to prosecute our man for the killing of your Guardsman. We could not, however, expose him to challenges from the dead man's family one after another, especially when it was abundantly clear that the Guardsman had first provoked the quarrel."

"Any man who found provocation in such a trivial occurrence should expect to be challenged," said Dyan, "but your men hide behind your laws and surrender their own personal responsibility! Murder is a private affair and nothing for the laws!"

The Legate surveyed him with what would have been open dislike, had he been a little less controlled. "Our laws are made by agreement and consensus, and whether you approve of them or not, Lord Ardais, they are unlikely to be amended to make murder a matter of private vendetta and individual duels. But this is not the matter at issue."

I admire his control, the firm way in which he cut Dyan off. My own barriers, thinned by the assault of Hastur's anguish, were down almost to nothing; I could feel Dyan's contempt like an audible sneer.

I got my barriers together a little while Hastur silenced Dyan again and reminded him that the incident in question had been settled long since. "Not settled," Dyan half snarled, "hidden from," but Hastur firmly cut him off, insisting that there was a more important matter to be settled. By the time I caught up with the discussion again, the Legate was saying:

"Lord Hastur, this is an ethical question, not a legal one at all. We enforce Comyn laws within the jurisdiction of the Comyn. In Caer Donn and the Hellers, where the laws are made by Lord Aldaran, we enforce what laws *he* requires. If he cannot be bothered to enforce the Compact you value so highly, it is not our business to police it for him—or, my lord, for you."

Callina Aillard said in her quiet clear voice, "Mr. Ramsay, the Compact is not a law, in your sense, at all. I do not believe either of us quite understands what the other means by *law*. The Compact has been the ethical basis of Darkovan culture and history for hundreds of years; neither Kermiac of Aldaran nor any other man on Darkover has any right to disregard or disobey it."

Ramsay said, "You must debate that point with Aldaran himself, my lady. He is not an Empire subject and I have no authority over him. If you want him to keep the Compact, you'll have to make him keep it."

Edric Ridenow spoke up for the first time. He said, "It is your responsibility, Ramsay, to enforce the substance of your agreement on our world. Are you intending to shirk that duty because of a quibble?"

"I am not shirking any responsibility which comes properly within the scope of my duties, Lord Serrais," he said, "but neither is it my duty to settle your disagreements with Aldaran. It seems to me that would be to infringe on the responsibility of the Comyn."

Dyan opened his mouth again, but Hastur gestured him to silence. "You need not teach me my responsibilities, Mr. Ramsay. The Empire's agreement with Darkover, and the status of the spaceport, was determined with the Comyn, not with Kermiac of Aldaran. One stipulation of that agreement was enforcement of the Compact; and we intended enforcement, not only in the Domains, but all over Darkover. I dislike using threats, sir, but if you insist upon your right to violate your own agreement, I would be within my authority in closing the spaceport until such time as the agreement is kept in every detail."

The Legate said, "This, sir, is unreasonable. You have said yourself that the Compact is not a law but an ethical preference. I also dislike using threats, but if you take that course, I am certain that my next orders from the Administrative Center would be to negotiate a new agreement with Kermiac of Aldaran and move the Empire headquarters to Caer Donn Trade City, where we need not trouble Comyn scruples."

Hastur said bitterly, "You say you are prohibited from taking sides in local political decisions. Do you realize that this would effectively throw all the force of the Terran Empire against the very existence of the Compact?"

"You leave me no choice, sir."

"You know, don't you, that such a move would mean war? War not of the Comyn's making but, the Compact once abandoned, war would inevitably come. We have had no war here for many years. Small skirmishes, yes. But the enforcement of the Compact has kept such battles within reasonable limits. Do you want the responsibility for letting a different kind of war loose?"

"Of course not," Ramsay said. He was a nontelepath and his emotions were muddy, but I could tell that he was distressed. This distress made me like him just a little more. "Who would?"

"Yet you would hide behind your laws and your orders and your superiors, and let our world be plunged into war again? We had our Ages of Chaos, Ramsay, and the Compact brought them to an end. Does that mean nothing to you?"

The Terran looked straight at Hastur. I had a curious mental picture, a flash picked up from someone in the room, that they were like two massive towers facing one another, as the Comyn Castle and the Terran headquarters faced one another across the valley, gigantic armored figures braced for single combat. The image thinned and vanished and they were just two old men, both powerful, both filled with stubborn integrity, each doing the best for his own side. Ramsay said, "It means a very great deal to me, Lord Hastur. I want to be honest with you. If there was a major war here, it would mean closing and sealing the Trade Cities to be certain of keeping to our law against interference. I don't want to move the spaceport to Caer Donn. It was built there, a good many years ago. When the Comyn offered us this more convenient spot, down here in the plains at Thendara, we were altogether pleased to abandon the operation at Caer Donn, except for trade and certain transport. The Thendara location has been to our mutual advantage. If we are forced to move back to Caer Donn we would be forced to reschedule all our traffic, rebuild our headquarters back in the mountains where the climate is more difficult for Terrans to tolerate and, above all, rely on inadequate roads and inhospitable countryside. I don't want to do that, and we will do anything within reason to avoid it."

Dyan said, "Mr. Ramsay, are you not in command of all the Terrans on Darkover?"

"You have been misinformed, Lord Dyan. I'm a legate, not a dictator. My authority is mostly over spaceport personnel stationed here, and only in matters which for one reason or another supersede that of their individual departments of administration. My major business is to keep order in the Trade City. Furthermore, I have authority from Administration Central to deal with Darkovan citizens through *their* duly constituted and appointed rulers. I have no authority over any individual Darkovan except for a few civilian employees who choose to hire themselves to us, nor over any individual Empire citizen who comes here to do business, beyond determining that his business is a lawful one for a Class D world. Beyond that, if his business disturbs the peace between Darkover and the Empire, I may intervene. But unless someone appeals to me, I have no authority outside the Trade City."

It sounded intolerably complicated. How did the Empire manage to get its business done at all? My father had, as yet, said nothing; now he raised his head and said bluntly, "Well we're appealing to you. These Empire citizens selling blasters in the marketplace of Caer Donn are *not* doing lawful business for a Class D Closed World, and you know it as well as I do. It's up to you to do something about it, and do it now. That *does* come within your responsibility."

The Legate said, "If the offense were here in Thendara, Lord Alton, I would do so with the greatest pleasure. In Caer Donn I can do nothing unless Lord Kermiac of Aldaran should appeal to me."

My father looked and sounded angry. He *was* angry, with

a disrupting anger which could have struck the Legate unconscious if he had not been trying hard to control it. "Always the same old story on Terra, what's your saying, *pass the buck*? You're like children playing that game with hot chestnuts, tossing them from one to another and trying not to get burned! I spent eight years on Terra and I never found even one man who would look me in the eye and say, 'This is my responsibility and I will accept it whatever the consequences.' "

Ramsay sounded harried. "Is it your contention that it is the Empire's business, or mine, to police your ethical systems?"

"I always thought," Callina said in her clear, still voice, "that ethical conduct was the responsibility of every honest man."

Hastur said, "One of our fundamental laws, sir, however law is defined, is that the power to act confers the responsibility to do so. Is it otherwise with you?"

The Legate leaned his chin on his clasped hands. "I can admire that philosophy, my lord, but I must respectfully refuse to debate it with you. I am concerned at this moment with avoiding great inconvenience for both our societies. I will inquire into this matter and see what can legitimately be done without interfering in your political decisions. And if I may make a respectful suggestion, Lord Hastur, I suggest that you take this matter up directly with Kermiac of Aldaran. Perhaps you can persuade him of the rightness of your view, and he will take it upon himself to stop the traffic in weapons, in those areas where the final legal authority is his."

The suggestion shocked me. Deal, negotiate, with that renegade Domain, exiled from Comyn generations ago? But no one seemed inordinately shocked at the idea. Hastur said, "We shall indeed discuss this matter with Lord Aldaran, sir. And it may be that since you refuse to take personal responsibility for enforcing the Empire's agreement with all of Darkover, that I shall myself take the matter directly before the Supreme Tribunal of the Empire. If it is adjudged *there* that the agreement for Darkover does indeed require planet-wide enforcement of the Compact, Mr. Ramsay, have I then your assurance that you would enforce it?"

I wondered if the Legate was even conscious of the absolute contempt in Hastur's voice for a man who required orders from a supreme authority to enforce ethical conduct. I felt almost ashamed of my Terran blood. But if Ramsay heard the contempt, he revealed nothing.

"If I receive orders to that effect, Lord Hastur, you may be assured that I will enforce them absolutely. And permit me to say, Lord Hastur, that it would in no way displease me to receive such orders."

A few more words were exchanged, mostly formal courtesies. But the meeting was over, and I had to gather my scattered thoughts and reassemble the honor guard, conduct the Council members formally out of the headquarters building and the spaceport and through the streets of Thendara. I could sense my father's thoughts, as I always could when we were in each other's presence.

He was thinking that no doubt it would be left to him to go to Aldaran. Kermiac would have to receive him, if only as my mother's kinsman. And I felt the utter weariness, like pain, in the thought. That journey into the Hellers was terrible, even in high summer; and summer was fast waning. Father was thinking that he could not shirk it. Hastur was too old. Dyan was no diplomat, he'd want to settle it by challenging Kermiac to a duel. But who else was there? The Ridenow lads were too young. . . .

It seemed to me, as I followed my father through the streets of Thendara, that in fact almost everyone in Comyn was either too old or too young. What was to become of the Domains?

It would have been easier if I could have been wholly convinced that the Terrans were all evil and must be resisted. Yet against my will I had found much that was wise in what Ramsay said. Firm laws, and never too much power concentrated in one pair of hands, seemed to me a strong barrier to the kind of corruption we now faced. And a certain basic law to fall back on when the men could not be trusted. Men, as I had found out when Dyan was placed at the head of the cadets, were all too often fallible, acting from expediency rather than the honor they talked so much about. Ramsay might hesitate to act without orders, but at least he acted on the responsibility of men and laws he could trust to be wiser than himself. And there was a check on his power too, for he knew that if he acted on his own responsibility against the will of wiser heads, he would be removed before he could do too much damage. But who would be a check on Dyan's power? Or my father's? They had the power to act, and therefore the right to do it.

And who could question their motives, or call a halt to their acts?

Chapter SEVEN

The day remained clear and cloudless. At sunset Regis stood on the high balcony which looked out over the city and the spaceport. The dying sunlight turned the city at his feet to a gleaming pattern of red walls and faceted windows. Danilo said, "It looks like the magical city in the fairy tale."

"There's nothing much magical about it," Regis said. "We learned that this morning on honor guard. Look, there's the ship that takes off every night about this time. It's too small to be an interstellar ship. I wonder where it's going?"

"Port Chicago, perhaps, or Caer Donn. It must be strange to have to send messages to other people by writing them, instead of by using linked minds as we do through the towers," Danilo said. "And it must feel very, very strange never to know what other people are thinking."

Of course, Regis thought. Dani was a telepath. Suddenly he realized that he'd been in contact with him again and again, and it had seemed so normal that neither had recognized it as telepathy. Today at the Council had been different, terribly different. He must have *laran* after all—but how and when, after Lew had failed?

And then the questions and the doubts came back. There had been so many telepaths there, spreading *laran* everywhere, even a nontelepath might have picked it up. It did not necessarily mean anything. He felt wrung, half desperately hoping that he was not cut off anymore and half fearing.

He went on looking at the city spread out below. This was the hour off-duty, when if a cadet had incurred no demerit or punishment detail, he might go where he chose. Morning and early afternoon were spent in training, swordplay and unarmed combat, the various military and command skills they would need later as Guards in the city and in the field. Later in the afternoon, each cadet was assigned to special duties. Danilo, who wrote the clearest hand among the cadets, had been assigned to assist the supply-officer. Regis had the relatively menial task of walking patrol in the city with a seasoned veteran or two, keeping order in the streets, preventing brawls, discouraging sneak-thieves and footpads. He found that he liked it, liked the very idea of keeping order in the city of the Comyn.

Life in the cadet corps was not intolerable, as he had feared. He did not mind the hard beds, the coarse food, the continual demands on his time. He had been even more strictly disciplined at Nevarsin, and life in the barracks was easy by contrast. What troubled him most was always being surrounded by others and yet still being lonely, isolated from the others by a gulf he could not bridge.

From their first day, he and Danilo had drifted together, at first by chance, because their beds were side by side and neither of them had another close friend in the barracks. The officers soon began to pair them off for details needing partners like barrack room cleaning, which the cadets took in turns; and because Regis and Danilo were about the same size and weight, for unarmed-combat training and practice. Within the first-year group they were good-naturedly, if derisively, known as "the cloistered brethren" because, like the Nevarsin brothers, they spoke *casta* by choice, rather than *cahuenga*.

At first they spent much of their free time together too. Presently Regis noticed that Danilo sought his company less, and wondered if he had done something to offend the other boy. Then by chance he heard a second-year cadet jeeringly congratulating Danilo about his cleverness in choosing a friend. Something in Danilo's face told him it was not the first time this taunt had been made. Regis had wanted to reveal himself and do something, defend Danilo, strike the older cadet, anything. On second thought he knew this would embarrass Danilo more and give a completely false impression. No taunt, he realized, could have hurt Danilo more. He was poor, indeed, but the Syrtis were an old and honorable family who had never needed to curry favor or patronage. From that day Regis began to make the overtures himself—not an easy thing to do, as he was diffident and agonizingly afraid of a rebuff. He tried to make it clear, at least to Danilo, that it was he who sought out Dani's company, welcomed it and missed it when it was not offered. Today it was he who had suggested the balcony, high atop Comyn castle, where they could see the city and the spaceport.

The sun was sinking now, and the swift twilight began to race across the sky. Danilo said, "We'd better get back to barracks." Regis was reluctant to leave the silence here, the sense of being at peace, but he knew Danilo was right. On a sudden impulse to confide, he said, "Dani, I want to tell you something. When I've spent my three years in the Guards—I must, I promised—I'm planning to go offworld. Into space. Into the Empire."

Dani stared in surprise and wonder. "Why?"

Regis opened his mouth to pour out his reasons, and found himself suddenly at a loss for words. Why? He hardly knew. Except that it was a strange and different world, with the excitement of the unknown. A world that would not remind him at every turn that he had been born defrauded of his heritage, without *laran*. Yet, after today . . .

The thought was curiously disturbing. If in truth he had *laran*, then he *had* no more reasons. But he still didn't want to give up his dream. He couldn't say it in words, but evidently Danilo did not expect any. He said, "You're Hastur. Will they let you?"

"I have my grandfather's pledge that after three years, if I still want to go, he will not oppose it." He found himself thinking, with a stab of pain that if he had *laran* they certainly would never let him go. The old breathless excitement of the unknown gripped him again; he shivered as he decided not to let them know.

Danilo smiled shyly and said, "I almost envy you. If my father weren't so old, or if he had another son to look after him, I'd want to come with you. I wish we could go together."

Regis smiled at him. He couldn't find words to answer the warmth that gave him. But Danilo said regretfully, "He does need me, though. I can't leave him while he's alive. And anyway"—he laughed just a little,—"from everything I've heard, our world is better than theirs."

"Still, there must be things we can learn from them. Kennard Alton went to Terra and spent years there."

"Yes," Dani said thoughtfully, "but even after that, I notice, he came back." He glanced at the sun and said, "We're going to be late. I don't want to get any demerits; we'd better hurry!"

It was dim in the stairwell that led down between the towers of the castle and neither of them saw a tall man coming down another staircase at an angle to this one, until they all collided, rather sharply, at its foot. The other man recovered first, reached out and took Regis firmly by the elbow, giving his arm a very faint twist. It was too dark to see, but Regis *felt*, through the touch, the feel and presence of Lew Alton. The experience was such a new thing, such a shock, that he blinked and could not move for a moment.

Lew said good-naturedly, "And now, if we were in the Guard hall, I'd dump you on the floor, just to teach you what to do when you're surprised in the dark. Well, Regis, you do know you're supposed to be alert even when you're off duty, don't you?"

Regis was still too shaken and surprised to speak. Lew let go his arm and said in sudden dismay, "Regis, did I really hurt you?"

"No—it's just—" He found himself almost unable to speak because of his agitation. He had not seen Lew. He had not heard his voice. He had simply touched him, in the dark, and it was clearer than seeing and hearing. For some reason it filled him with an almost intolerable anxiety he did not understand.

Lew evidently sensed the distress he was feeling. He let him go and turned to Danilo, saying amiably, "Well, Dani, are you learning to walk with an eye to being surprised and thrown from behind?"

"Am I ever," Danilo said, laughing. "Gabriel—Captain Lanart-Hastur—caught up with me yesterday. *This* time, though, I managed to block him, so he didn't throw me. He just showed me the hold he'd used."

Lew chuckled. "Gabriel is the best wrestler in the Guards," he said. "I had to learn the hard way. I had bruises everywhere. Every one of the officers had me marked down as the easiest to throw. After my arm had been dislocated by—by accident," he said, but Regis felt he had started to say something else, "Gabriel finally took pity on me and taught me a few of his secrets. Mostly, though, I relied on keeping out of the officers' reach. At fourteen I was smaller than you, Dani."

Regis' distress was subsiding a little. He said, "It's not so easy to keep out of the way, though."

Lew said quietly, "I know. I suppose they have their reasons. It *is* good training, to keep your wits about you and be on the alert all the time; I was grateful for it later when I was on patrol and had to handle hefty drunks and brawlers twice my size. But I didn't enjoy the learning, believe me. I remember Father saying to me once that it was better to be hurt a little by a friend than seriously hurt, some day, by an enemy."

"I don't mind being hurt," said Danilo, and with that new and unendurable *awareness*, Regis realized his voice was trembling as if he was about to cry. "I was bruised all over when I was learning to ride. I can stand the bruises. What I do mind is when—when someone thinks it's funny to see me take a fall. I didn't mind it when Lerrys Ridenow caught me and threw me halfway down the stairs yesterday, because he said that was always the most dangerous place to be attacked and I should always be on guard in such a spot. I don't mind when they're trying to teach me something. That's what I'm here for. But now and then someone seems to—to enjoy hurting me, or frightening me."

They had come away from the stairs now and were walking along an open collonade; Regis could see Lew's face, and it was grim. He said, "I know that happens. I don't understand it either. And I've never understood why some people seem to feel that making a boy into a man seems to mean making him into a brute. If we'd all been in the Guard hall, I'd have felt compelled to throw Regis ten feet, and I don't suppose I'd have been any gentler than any other officer. But I don't like hurting people when there's no need either. I suppose your cadet-master would think me shamefully remiss in my duty. Don't tell him, will you?" He grinned suddenly and his hand fell briefly on Danilo's shoulder, giving him a little shake. "Now you two had better hurry along; you'll be late." He turned a corridor at right angles to their own and strode away.

The two cadets hurried down their own way. Regis was thinking that he had never known Lew felt like that. They must have been hard on him, especially Dyan. But how did he know that?

Danilo said, "I wish all the officers were like Lew. I wish he were the cadet-master, don't you?"

Regis nodded. "I don't think Lew would want to be cadet-master, though. And from what I've heard, Dyan is very serious about honor and responsibility. You heard him speak at Council."

Danilo's mouth twisted. "Anyhow, you don't have to worry. Lord Dyan likes you. Everybody knows *that*!"

"Jealous?" Regis retorted good-naturedly.

"You're Comyn," Danilo said, "you get special treatment."

The words were a sudden painful reminder of the distance between them, a distance Regis had almost ceased to feel. It hurt. He said, "Dani, don't be a fool! You mean the fact that he uses me for a partner at sword practice? That's an honor I'd gladly change with you! If you think it's love-pats I'm getting from him, take a look at me naked some day—you're welcome and more than welcome to Dyan's love-pats!"

He was completely unprepared for the dark crimson flush that flooded Danilo's face, the sudden fierce anger as he swung around to face Regis. "What the hell do you mean by *that* remark?"

Regis stared at him in dismay. "Why, only that sword-practice with Lord Dyan is an honor I'd gladly do without. He's much stricter than the arms-master and he hits harder! Look at my ribs, you'll see that I'm black and blue from shoulder to knee! What did you think I meant?"

Danilo turned away and didn't answer directly. He only said, "We're going to be late. We'd better run."

Regis spent the early evening hours on street-patrol in the city with Hjalmar, the giant young Guardsman who had first tested him for swordplay. They broke up two budding brawls, hauled an obstreperous drunk to the brig, directed half a dozen lost country bumpkins to the inn where they had left their horses and gently reminded a few wandering women that harlots were restricted by law to certain districts in the city. A quiet evening in Thendara. When they returned to the Guard hall to go off duty, they fell in with Gabriel Lanart and half a dozen officers who were planning to visit a small tavern near the gates. Regis was about to withdraw when Gabriel stopped him.

"Come along with us, brother. You should see more of the city than you can from the barracks window!"

Thus urged, Regis went with the older men. The tavern was small and smoky, filled with off-duty Guardsmen. Regis sat next to Gabriel, who took the trouble to teach him the card game they were playing. It was the first time he had been in the company of older officers. Most of the time he was quiet, listening much more than he talked, but it was good to be one of the company and accepted.

It reminded him, just a little, of the summers he'd spent at Armida. It would never have occurred to Kennard or Lew or old Andres to treat the solemn and precocious boy as a child. That early acceptance among men had put him out of step, probably forever, he realized with a remote sadness, with lads his own age. Now though, and the knowledge felt as if a weight had fallen from him, he knew that he did feel at home among men. He felt as if he was drawing the first really free breaths he had drawn since his grandfather pushed him, with only a few minutes to prepare for it, into the cadets.

"You're quiet, kinsman," Gabriel said as they walked back together. "Have you had too much to drink? You'd better go and get some sleep. You'll be all right tomorrow." He said a good-natured good night and went off to his own quarters.

The night officer patrolling the court said, "You're a few minutes late, cadet. It's your first offense, so I won't put you on report this time. Just don't do it again. Lights are out in the first-year barracks; you'll have to undress in the dark."

Regis made his way, a little unsteadily, into the barracks. Gabriel was right, he thought, surprised and not altogether displeased, he had had too much to drink. He was not used to drinking at all, and tonight he had drunk several cups of wine. He realized, as he hauled off his clothes by the moonlight, that he felt confused and unfocused. It had, he thought with a strange fuzziness, been a meaningful day, but he didn't know yet what it all meant. The Council. The somehow shocking realization that he had reached his grandfather's mind, recognized Lew by touch without seeing or hearing him. The odd half-quarrel with Danilo. It added to the confusion he felt, which was more than just drunkenness. He wondered if they had put *kirian* in his wine, heard himself giggle aloud at the thought, then fell rapidly into an edgy, nightmare-ridden half-sleep.

. . . He was back in Nevarsin, in the cold student dormitory where, in winter, snow drifted through the wooden shutters and lay in heaps on the novices' beds. In his dream, as had actually happened once or twice, two or three of the students had climbed into bed together, sharing blankets and body warmth against the bitter cold, to be discovered in the morning and severely scolded for breaking this inflexible rule. This dream kept recurring; each time, he would discover some strange naked body in his arms and, deeply disturbed, he would wake up with an admixture of fear and guilt. Each time he woke from this repeated dream he was more deeply upset and troubled by it, until he finally escaped into a deeper, darker realm of sleep. Now it seemed that he was his own father, crouched on a bare hillside in darkness, with strange fires exploding around him. He was shuddering with fright as men dropped dead around him, closer and closer, knowing that within moments he too would be blasted into fragments by one of the erupting fires. Then he felt someone close to him in the dark, holding him, sheltering his body with his own. Regis started awake again, shaking. He rubbed his eyes and looked around him at the quiet barracks room, dimly lit with moonlight, seeing the dim forms of the other cadets, snoring or muttering in their sleep. None of it was real, he thought, and slid down again on his hard mattress.

After a while he began to dream again. This time he was wandering in a featureless gray landscape in which there was nothing to see. Someone was crying somewhere in the gray spaces, crying miserably, in long painful sobs. Regis kept turning in another direction, not at first sure whether he was looking for the source of the weeping or trying to get away from the wretched sound. Small shuddering words came through the sobs, *I won't, I don't want to, I can't.* Every time the crying lessened for a moment there was a cruel voice, an almost familiar voice, saying, *Oh, yes you will, you know you cannot fight me,* and at other times, *Hate me as much as you will, I like it better that way.* Regis squirmed with fear. Then he was alone with the weeping, the inarticulate little sobs of protest and pleading. He went on searching in the lonely grayness until a hand touched him in the dark, a rude indecent searching, half painful and half exciting. He cried out "No!" and fled again into deeper sleep.

This time he dreamed he was in the student's court at Nevarsin, practicing with the wooden foils. Regis could hear the sound of his own panting breaths, doubled and multiplied in the great echoing room as a faceless opponent moved before him and kept quickening his movements insistently. Suddenly Regis realized they were both naked, that the blows struck were landing on his bare body. As his faceless op-

ponent moved faster and faster Regis himself grew almost
paralyzed, sluggishly unable to lift his sword. And then a
great ringing voice forbade them to continue, and Regis
dropped his sword and looked up at the dark cowl of the for-
bidding monk. But it was not the novice-master at Nevarsin
monastery, but Dyan Ardais. While Regis stood, frozen with
dread, Dyan picked up the dropped sword, no longer a
wooden practice sword, but a cruelly sharpened rapier. Dyan,
holding it out straight ahead while Regis looked on in dread
and horror, plunged it right into Regis' breast. Curiously, it
went in without the slightest pain, and Regis looked down in
shaking dread at the sight of the sword passing through his
entire body. "That's because it didn't touch the heart," Dyan
said, and Regis woke with a gasping cry, pulling himself upright in bed. "Zandru," he whispered, wiping sweat from his
forehead, "what a nightmare!" He realized that his heart was
still pounding, and then that his thighs and his sheets were
damp with a clammy stickiness. Now that he was wide awake
and knew what had happened, he could almost laugh at the
absurdity of the dream, but it still gripped him so that he
could not lie down and go to sleep again.

It was quiet in the barrack room, with more than an hour
to go before daybreak. He was no longer drunk or fuzzy-
headed, but there was a pounding pain behind his eyes.

Slowly he became aware that Danilo was crying in the
next bed, crying helplessly, desperately, with a kind of
hopeless pain. He remembered the crying in his dream. Had
he heard the sound, woven it into nightmare?

Then, in a sort of slow amazement and wonder, he realized
that Danilo was not crying.

He could see, by the dimmed moonlight, that Danilo was
in fact motionless and deeply asleep. He could hear his
breath coming softly, evenly, see his turned-away shoulder
moving gently with his breathing. The weeping was not a
sound at all, but a sort of intangible pattern of vibrating misery and despair, like the lost little crying in his dream, but
soundless.

Regis put his hands over his eyes in the darkness and
thought, with rising wonder, that he hadn't heard the crying,
but *knew* it just the same.

It was true, then. *Laran.* Not randomly picked up from another telepath, but his.

The shock of that thought drove everything else from his

mind. How did it happen? When? And formulating the question brought its own answer: that first day in barracks, when Dani had touched him. He had dreamed about that conversation tonight, dreaming he was his father for a moment. Again he felt that surge of closeness, of emotion so intense that there was a lump in his throat. Danilo slept quietly now, even the telepathic impression of noiseless weeping having died away. Regis worried, troubled and torn with even the backwash of his friend's grief, wondering what was wrong.

Quickly he shut off the curiosity. Lew had said that you learned to keep your distance, in order to survive. It was a strange, sad thought. He could not spy on his friend's privacy, yet he was still near to tears at the awareness of Dani's misery. He had sensed it, earlier that day, when Lew talked to them. Had someone hurt him, ill-treated him?

Or was it simply that Danilo was lonely, homesick, wanting his family? Regis knew so little about him.

He recalled his own early days at Nevarsin. Cold and lonely, heartsick, friendless, hating his family for sending him here, only a fierce remnant of Hastur pride had kept him from crying himself to sleep every night for a long time.

For some reason that thought filled him again with an almost unendurable sense of anxiety, fear, restlessness. He looked across at Danilo and wished he could talk to him about this. Dani had been through it; he would know. Regis knew he would have to tell someone soon. But who should he tell? His grandfather? The sudden realization of his own *laran* had left Regis strangely vulnerable, shaken again and again by waves of emotion; again he was at the edge of tears, this time for his grandfather, reliving that fierce, searing moment of anguish of his only son's terrible death.

And, still vulnerable, he swung from grief to rebellion. He was sure his grandfather would force him to walk the path ready-made for a Hastur heir with *laran*. He would never be free! Again he saw the great ship taking off for the stars, and his whole heart, his body, his mind, strained to follow it outward into the unknown. If he cherished that dream, he could never tell his grandfather at all.

But he could share it with Dani. He literally ached to step across the brief space between their beds, slip into bed beside him, share with him this incredible dual experience of grief and tremendous joy. But he held himself back, recalling with an imperative strange sharpness what Lew had said; it was like living with your skin off. How could he impose this burden of his own emotions on Dani, who was himself so burdened with unknown sorrow, so troubled and nightmare-driven that his unshed tears penetrated even into Regis' dreams as a sound of weeping? If he was to have the telepathic gift, Regis thought sadly, he had to learn to live by the rules of the telepath. He realized that he was cold and cramped, and crawled under his blankets again. He huddled them around him, feeling lonely and sad. He felt curiously unfocused again, drifting in anxious search, but in answer to his questioning mind he saw only flimsy pictures in imagination, men and strange nonhumans fighting along a narrow rock-ledge; the faces of two little children fair and delicate and baby-blurred in sleep, then cold in death with a grief almost too terrible to be borne; dancing figures whirling, whirling like wind-blown leaves in a mad ecstasy; a great towering form, blazing with fire . . .

Exhausted with emotion, he slept again.

Chapter EIGHT

(Lew Alton's narrative)

There are two theories about Festival Night, the great midsummer holiday in the Domains. Some say that it is the birthday of the Blessed Cassilda, foremother of the Comyn. Others say that it commemorates the time of year when she found Hastur, Son of Aldones, Lord of Light, sleeping on the shores of Hali after his journey from the realms of Light. Since I don't believe that either of them ever existed, I have no emotional preference about either theory.

My father, who in his youth traveled widely in the Empire, told me once that every planet he has ever visited, and most of those he hasn't, have both a midsummer and midwinter holiday. We're no exception. In the Domains there are two traditional celebrations for summer Festival; one is a private family celebration in which the women are given gifts, usually fruit or flowers, in the name of Cassilda.

Early this morning I had taken my foster-sister Linnell Aillard some flowers, in honor of the day, and she had reminded me of the other celebration, the great Festival ball, held every year in the Comyn Castle.

I've never liked these enormous affairs, even when I was too young for the ball and taken to the children's party in the afternoon; I've disliked them ever since my first one, at the age of seven, when Lerrys Ridenow hit me over the head with a wooden horse.

It would be unthinkable to absent myself, however. My father had made it clear that attending was just one of the unavoidable duties of an heir to Comyn. When I told Linnell that I was thinking of developing some illness just severe enough to keep me away, or changing duty with one of the

105

Guard officers, she pouted. "If you're not there, who'll dance with me?" Linnell is too young to dance at these affairs except with kinsmen so, ever since she's been allowed to attend at all, I've been reminded that unless I'm there to dance with her she will find herself watching from the balcony. My father, of course, has the excellent excuse of his lameness.

I resolved to put in an appearance, dance a few dances with Linnell, be polite to a few old ladies and make an unobtrusive exit as early as politeness allowed.

I came late, having been on duty in the Guard hall where I'd heard the cadets gossiping about the affair. I didn't blame them. All Guardsmen, whatever their rank, and all cadets not actually on duty, have the privilege of attending. To youngsters brought up in the outlands, I suppose it's an exciting spectacle. I was more disinclined to go than ever because Marius had come in while I was dressing. He'd been taken to the children's party, had made himself sick with sweets and had skinned knuckles and a black eye from a fight with some supercilious little boy, distantly kin to the Elhalyns, who had called him a Terran bastard. Well, I'd been called worse in my day and told him so, but I really had no comfort for him. I was ready to kick them all in the shins by the time I went down. It was, I reflected, a hell of a good start to the evening.

As was customary, the beginning dances were exhibitions by professionals or gifted amateurs. A troupe of dancers in the costume of the far mountains was doing a traditional dance, with a good deal of skirt-swirling and boot-stamping. I'd seen it danced better, a while since, on my trip into the foothills. Perhaps no professionals can ever give the mountain dances the true gaiety and excitement of the people who dance them for pure pleasure.

I moved slowly around the edges of the room. My father was being polite to elderly dowagers on the sidelines. Old Hastur was doing the same thing with a group of Terrans who had probably been invited for political or ceremonial reasons. The Guardsmen, especially the young cadets, had already discovered the elegant buffet spread out along one wall and kept replenished by a whole troop of servants. So early in the evening, they were almost the only ones there. I grinned reminiscently. I am no longer required to share the men's mess, but I remembered my cadet years vividly enough to

know how good the plentiful delicacies would look after what
passes for supper in the barracks.

Danilo was there, in dress uniform. A little self-consciously, he wished me a joyous Festival. I returned the greeting. "Where is Regis? I don't see him anywhere."

"He was on duty tonight, sir. I offered to change with
him—all his kinsmen are here—but he said he would have
years of it, and I should go and enjoy myself."

I wondered which officer, in malice or by way of em-
phasizing that a Hastur could expect no favors in the cadets,
had made certain that Regis Hastur would draw a tour of
duty on Festival Night. I only wished I had so good an excuse.

"Well, enjoy yourself by all means, Dani," I told him.

The hidden musicians had struck up a sword dance and
Danilo turned eagerly to watch as two Guardsmen came with
torches to place the swords. The hall lights were lowered to
emphasize the ancient and barbaric quality of this oldest of
traditional mountain dances. It is usually danced by one of
the greatest dancers in Thendara; to my surprise, it was Dyan
Ardais who strode forward, wearing the brilliantly barbaric
costume whose history was lost before the Ages of Chaos.

There are not many amateurs, even in the Hellers, who
still know all the traditional steps and patterns. I'd seen Dyan
dance it when I was a child at Armida, in my father's hall. I
thought that it went better there, to the music of a single
drone-pipe, by the glare of firelight and a torch or two, than
here in the elaborate ballroom, surrounded by ladies in fancy
party costumes and bored noblemen and city folk.

Yet even the elaborately garbed ladies and noblemen fell
silent, impressed by the strange solemnity of the old dance.
And yes—I give him his due—by Dyan's performance. For
once he looked grave, stern, free of the flippant cynicism I
detested so, wholly caught up in the tense, treading-on-eggs
quality of the weaving steps. The dance displays a fierce,
almost tigerish masculinity, and Dyan brought a sort of
leashed violence to it. As he snatched up the swords in the final figure and held them poised over his head, there was not
a sound anywhere in the ballroom. Because I had been impressed against my will, I tried deliberately to break the spell.

I said aloud to Danilo, "I wonder who he's showing off to
this time? It's a pity Dyan's indifferent to women; after this
he'd have to beat them off with a pitchfork!"

I found myself pitying any woman—or any man, for that matter—who allowed himself to be charmed by Dyan. I hoped for his own sake that Danilo was not one of them. It's natural enough for boys that age to be strongly attracted to any strong character, and a cadet-master is a natural object for such romantic identification. If the older man is an honorable and kindly one, it does no harm and wears off in a short time. I long since grew out of any such childish attachments and, although I've been on the receiving end a time or two, I made sure it went no further than a few exchanged smiles.

Well, I wasn't Dani's guardian, and it had been made clear that Dyan was beyond my reach. Besides, I had enough worries of my own.

Dyan was moving toward the buffet; I saw him stop for a glass of wine, speaking to the Guardsmen there with a show of affability. We came briefly face to face. Resolving that if there was any discourtesy among Comyn I would not be the one to show it, I made some brief polite comment on the dance. He replied with equally meaningless courtesy, his eyes straying past me. I wondered who he was looking for and received in return—my barriers must have been lowered for a moment—a surge of violent anger. *Perhaps after tonight this meddlesome bastard will be busy with his own affairs and have less time for interfering in mine!*

I made the briefest possible polite bow and moved away for my promised dance with Linnell. The floor was filling quickly with dancers; I took Linnell's fingertips and led her to the floor.

Linnell is a pretty child, with soft bronze-brown hair and blue eyes framed in lashes so long and dark they looked unreal. She was, I thought, considerably prettier than her kinswoman Callina, who had looked so severe and stern at Council yesterday.

The Aillard Domain is the only one in which *laran* and Council-right pass not in the male line, but in the female; males are not allowed to hold full Domain rights in Council. The last *comynara* in the direct line had been Cleindori, the last of the Keepers trained completely in the old, cloistered virginal tradition. While still quite young, she had left the tower, rebelled against the old superstitions surrounding the matrix circles and especially the Keepers and had, in defiance of tradition and belief, taken a consort and borne him a child while continuing to use the powers she had been taught. She had been horribly murdered by fanatics who thought a Keeper's virginity was more important than her competence or her powers. But she had broken the ancient mold, defied the superstitions and created a new scientific approach to what is now called matrix mechanics. For years her very name had been abhorred as a renegade. Now her memory was revered by every psi technician on Darkover.

But she had left no daughters. The old Aillard line had finally died out and Callina Lindir-Aillard, a distant kinswoman of my father's and of the male head of the Aillard Domain, had been chosen *comynara*, as nearest female successor. Linnell had come to Armida for my father to foster and had been brought up as my sister.

Linnell was an expert dancer, and I enjoyed dancing with her. I have little interest in feminine fripperies, but Linnell had taught me the courtesies of such things, so I took polite notice of her gown and ornaments. When the dance came to an end, I led Linnell to the sidelines and asked her if she thought I should ask Callina to dance; Callina, too, by Comyn custom for unwed women, was restricted to dancing with kinsmen except at masked balls.

"I don't know if Callina cares to dance," Linnell said, "she's very shy. But you should ask her. I'm sure she'll tell you if she'd rather not. Oh, there is Javanne Hastur! Every time I've seen her in the last nine years, it seems, she's been pregnant. But she's actually pretty, isn't she?"

Javanne was dancing with Gabriel. She had a high color in her cheeks and looked as if she were enjoying herself. I suppose that any young matron would be happy, after four closely spaced pregnancies, to be in society again. Javanne was very tall and excessively thin, a dark girl in an elaborate green-and-golden gown. I did not think her pretty, but she was undeniably handsome.

I conducted Linnell to Callina, but before I could speak to her, my father approached me.

"Come along, Lew," he said, in a tone I had learned to regard, however politely phrased, as a command. "You should pay your respects to Javanne."

I stared. Javanne? She had never liked me, even when we were going to children's parties. Once we had both been whipped impartially for getting into a kicking-and-scratching fight, at seven or so, and later, when we were about eleven, she rudely refused to dance with me, saying I stepped on her feet. I probably did, but I had already been telepath enough to know that was not her reason. "Father," I said patiently, "I'm quite sure Lady Javanne can dispense with any compliments from me." Had he quite lost his wits?

"And Lew promised to dance with me again," Linnell said sulkily. Father patted her cheek and assured her there would be time enough for that, with a look at me which admitted no further delay unless I wanted to defy him openly and make a scene.

Javanne was standing in a little cluster of younger women, sipping a glass of wine. My father's voice seemed more deliberate than usual, as he presented me.

"I wish you a joyous Festival, kinsman," she said with a courteous bow. Kinsman! Well, Gabriel and I were friendly enough; perhaps she had learned, from husband and brother, that I was not such a scandal after all. At least for once she seemed to speak to me as if I were a human being. She beckoned to one of the young girls in the crowd surrounding her. "I wish to present to you a young kinswoman of your own, Lew, Linnea Storn-Lanart."

Linnea Storn-Lanart was very young, certainly no older than Linnell, with russet hair falling in soft curls around a heart-shaped face. The Storns were old mountain nobility from the region near Aldaran who had intermarried years ago with Lanarts and Leyniers. What was a maiden so young doing alone in Thendara?

Linnea, although she seemed modest enough, raised her eyes with frank curiosity to my face. Mountain girls—I had heard this from my father—did not follow the exaggerated custom of the lowlands, where a direct glance at a strange man is immodest; hence mountain girls are often considered, here in the Domains, to be over-bold. She looked straight at me for a moment, smiling, then caught Javanne's eyes, flushed crimson and looked quickly at the toes of her slippers. I supposed Javanne had given her a lesson in proper manners for the Domains, and she did not wish to be thought countrified.

I was at a loss what to say to her. She was my kinswoman, or had been so presented to me, although the relationship could not be very close. Perhaps that was it—Javanne wished to spend her time dancing, not looking after a kinswoman too young to dance with strangers. I said, "Will you honor me with a dance, *damisela*?"

She glanced quickly at Javanne for permission, then nodded. I led her to the floor. She was a good dancer and seemed to enjoy it, but I kept wondering why my father should go out of his way to make life easy for Javanne. And why had he looked at me so meaningfully as we moved on to the dance floor? And why had he introduced her as a kinswoman, when the relationship must surely be far too distant to notice officially? When the music ended, it was still perplexing me.

I bluntly said, "What is this all about?"

Forgetting her careful briefing in manners, she blurted out, "Didn't they tell you? They told me!" Then her sudden blush flooded her face again. It made her look very pretty, but I was in no mood to appreciate it.

"Tell me *what*?" I demanded.

Her cheeks were like banners of crimson. She stammered. "I was t-told that—that we should look each other over, get to know one another, and that if we l-liked each other, then a—a marriage would be—" My face must have shown what I was thinking, for she broke off, leaving the sentence unfinished.

Damn them! Trying to run my life again!

The girl's gray eyes were wide, her childish mouth trembling. I quickly fought to control my anger, barrier myself. She was obviously very sensitive, at least an empath, perhaps a telepath. I hoped, helplessly, that she wouldn't cry. None of this was her fault. I could just guess how her parents had been bribed or threatened, how she herself had been coaxed and flattered with the lure of a fine marriage to the heir of the Domain.

"Just what did they tell you about me, Linnea?"

She looked confused. "Only that you're Lord Alton's son, that you've served in the Arilinn Tower, that your mother was Terran—"

"And you think you can bear that disgrace?"

"Disgrace?" She looked puzzled. "Many of us in the Hellers have Terran blood; there are Terrans in my family. Do you think it is a disgrace?"

What could anyone her age know of this kind of court intrigue? I felt revolted, remembering Dyan's gloating look.

Busy with his own affairs . . . Evidently he had known this was in the wind.

"*Damisela*, I have no mind to marry, and if I did I would not let Council choose a wife for me." I tried to smile, but I suspect it was grim enough. "Don't look so downcast, *chiya*, a maiden as pretty as you will soon find a husband you'll like better."

"I have no particular wish to marry," she said with composure. "I had intended to apply for admission at one of the towers; my great-granddame was trained as a Keeper, and it seemed to her I was well fitted for it. But I have always obeyed my family and if they had chosen me a husband, I was not ill-content. I am only sorry that I seem not to please you."

She was so calm that I felt trapped, almost frantic. "It is not that you displease me, Linnea. But I would not marry at their bidding." My wrath flared up again; I felt her flinch from its impact. Her hand still rested lightly on my arm, as when we were dancing; she drew it away as if she had been burned. I felt like storming away and actually made a faint move to leave her, when I realized, just in time, that this would be a disgraceful thing to do. To abandon a young girl in the middle of a dance-floor would be a rudeness no man of breeding would ever commit against a gently reared young girl of unquestionable manners and reputation! I couldn't expose her to such gossip for, inevitably, everyone would be wondering what unspeakable thing she could possibly have done to deserve it. I glanced around. Javanne was dancing at the far end of the ballroom so I led Linnea toward the buffet. I offered her a glass of wine; she refused it with a headshake. I got her *shallan* instead, and stood sipping irritably at the wine myself. I didn't like it.

When I was a little calmer I said, "Nothing is irrevocable yet. You can tell whoever put you up to this—my father, old Hastur, whoever—you can tell them you don't like me and that will be the end of it."

She smiled, a faint amused flicker. "But I do like you, Dom Lewis," she said. "I won't lie about it, even if I thought I could. Lord Kennard would know it at once if I tried to lie to him. You're angry and unhappy, but I think if you weren't so angry, you'd be very nice. I would be well content with such a marriage. If you wish to refuse it, Lew, you must do the refusing."

If she had been less young, less naïve, I might have flung at her that she could hardly be expected to give up a marriage into Comyn with protest. Even so, I am sure she caught the thought, for she looked distressed.

I shut out her thoughts and said flatly, "A woman should have the privilege of refusing. I thought to spare you the offense of hearing me say to my father that I did not—" I discovered that I could not simply say that I did not like her. I amended it and said, "That I did not intend to marry at their bidding."

Her composure was disquieting. "No one marries at his own will. Do you really feel that a marriage between us would be unendurable, Lew? It is obvious that they will arrange some marriage or other for you."

For a moment I wavered. She was evidently sensitive and intelligent; she had been considered for tower training, which meant *laran*. My father had evidently gone to some pains to choose a woman who would be maximally acceptable to me, one with Terran blood, one capable of that emotional and mental fusion a telepath must have in any woman he is to know intimately. She was pretty. She was no empty-minded doll, but had wit and poise. For a second I considered. Sooner or later I must marry, I had always known that. A Comyn heir must father children. And, the Gods knew, I was lonely, lonely . . .

And my father, damn him, had counted on just this reaction! My anger flared anew. *"Damisela*, I have told you why I will not be party to any marriage made as this one was made. If you choose to believe that I have rejected you personally, that is your affair." I drank the last in my wineglass and set it down. "Allow me to conduct you to my kinswomen, since Javanne is much occupied."

Javanne was dancing again. Well, let her enjoy herself. She had been married off at fifteen and had spent the last nine years doing her duty to her family. They wouldn't catch me in that trap!

Gabriel had claimed a dance from Linnell—I was glad to see it—but Callina was standing at the edge of the floor. The crimson draperies she was wearing only accentuated the colorlessness of her bland features. I presented Linnea to her and asked Callina to look after her while I had a word with my father. She looked curious, evidently sensing my anger. I must be broadcasting it right and left.

My rage mounted as I circled the floor, looking for my father. Dyan had known and Hastur had known—how many others had been dragged into this? Had they held a Council meeting to discuss the fate of Lord Alton's bastard heir? How long had it taken them to find a woman who would have me? They'd had to go far afield, I noticed, and get one young enough to obey her father and mother without question! I supposed I ought to feel flattered that they'd picked a nice looking one!

I found myself face to face with the Regent. I gave him a curt greeting and started to pass him by; he laid a hand on my arm to detain me, wishing me the greetings of the season.

"I thank you, my lord. Have you seen my father?"

The old man said mildly, "If you're storming off to complain, Lew, why not come directly to me? It was I who asked my granddaughter to present the girl to you." He turned to the buffet. "Have you had supper? The fruits are exceptional this season. We have ice-melons from Nevarsin; they're not usually obtainable in the market."

"Thank you but I'm not hungry," I said. "Is it permitted to ask why you take such an interest in my marriage, my lord? Or am I to feel flattered that you interest yourself, without asking why?"

"I take it the girl was not to your liking, then."

"What could I possibly have against her? But forgive me, sir, I have a certain distaste for airing my personal affairs before half the city of Thendara." I moved my hand to indicate the dancing crowds. He smiled genially.

"Do you really think anyone here is intent on anything but his own affairs?" He was calmly filling a plate for himself with assorted delicacies. Sullenly, I followed suit. He moved toward a couple of reasonably isolated chairs and said, "We can sit here and talk, if you like. What's the matter, Lew? You're just about the proper age to be married."

"Just like that," I said, "and I'm not to be consulted?"

"I thought we were consulting you," Hastur said, taking a forkful of some kind of shredded seafood mixed with greens. "We did not, after all, summon you to the chapel at a few hours' notice, to be married on the spot, as was done only a few years ago. I was given no chance even to see my dear wife's face until a few minutes before the bracelets were locked on our wrists, yet we lived together in harmony for forty years."

My father, speaking of his first years on Terra and being plunged abruptly into their alien customs, had once used a phrase for the way I felt now: *culture shock.* "With all deference, Lord Hastur, times have changed too much for that to be a suitable way of making marriages. Why is there such a hurry?"

Hastur's face suddenly hardened. "Lew, do you really understand that if your father had broken his neck on those damnable stairs, instead of a few ribs and his collarbone, you would now be Lord Alton of Armida, with all that implies? My own son never lived to see his son. With our world in the shape it's in, none of us can afford to take chances with the heirship of a Domain. What is your specific objection to marriage? Are you a lover of men?" He used the very polite *casta* phrase and I, used to the much coarser one customary in the Guards, was not for a moment quite certain what he meant. Then I grinned without amusement. "*That* arrow went wide of the mark, my lord. Even as a boy I had small taste for such games. I may be young, but that young I am not."

"Then what can it possibly be?" He seemed honestly bewildered. "Is it Linnell you wish to marry? We had other marriage-plans for her, but if both of you really wish—"

I said in honest outrage, "Evanda protect us both! Lord Hastur, Linnell is my *sister!*"

"Not blood-kin," he said, "or not so close as to be a grave risk to your children. It might be a suitable match after all."

I took a spoonful of the food on my plate. It tasted revolting and I swallowed and set the plate down. "Sir, I love Linnell dearly. We were children together. If it were only to share my life, I could think of no happier person to spend it with. But," I fumbled to explain, a little embarrassed, "after you've slapped a girl for breaking your toys, taken her into bed with you when she had a nightmare or was crying with a toothache, pinned up her skirts so she could wade in a brook, or dressed her, or brushed her hair—it's almost impossible to think of her as a—a bedmate, Lord Hastur. Forgive this plain speaking."

He waved that away. "No, no. No formalities. I asked you to be honest with me. I can understand that. We married your father very young to a woman the Council thought suitable, and I have been told they lived together in complete harmony and total indifference for many years. But I don't want to wait until you've fixed your desire on someone wholly unsuitable, either. Your father married at the last to please himself and—forgive me, Lew—you and Marius have been suffering for it all your lives. I am sure you would rather spare your own sons that."

"Can't you wait until I *have* sons? Don't you *ever* get tired of arranging other people's lives for them?"

His eyes blazed at me. "I got tired of it thirty years ago but someone has to do it! I'm old enough to sit and think over my past, instead of carrying the burden of the future, but it seems to be left to me! What are *you* doing to arrange your life in the proper way and save me the trouble?" He took another forkful of salad and chewed it wrathfully.

"How much do you know of the history of Comyn, Lew? In the far-back days, we were given power and privilege because we *served* our people, not because we ruled them. Then we began to believe we had these powers and privileges because of some innate superiority in ourselves, as if having *laran* made us so much better than other people that we could do exactly as we pleased. Our privileges are used now, not to compensate us for all the things we have given up to serve the people, but to perpetuate our own powers. You're complaining that your life isn't your own, Lew. Well, it isn't and it shouldn't be. You have certain privileges—"

"Privileges!" I said bitterly. "Mostly duties I don't want and responsibilities I can't handle."

"Privileges," he repeated, "which you must earn by serving your people." He reached out and lightly touched the mark of Comyn, deeply blazed in my flesh just above the wrist. His own arm bore its twin, whitened with age. He said, "One of the obligations which goes with that, a sacred obligation, is to make certain your gift does not die out, by fathering sons and daughters to inherit it from you, to serve the people of Darkover in their turn."

Against my will, I was moved by his words. I had felt this way during my journey to the outlands, that my position as heir to Comyn was a serious thing, a sacred thing, that I held an important link in an endless chain of Altons, stretching from prehistory to the future. For a moment I felt that the old man followed my thoughts, as he laid his fingertip again on the mark of Comyn on my wrist. He said, "I know what this cost you, Lew. You won that gift at risk of your life. You have begun well by serving at Arilinn. What little remains of our ancient science is preserved there against the day when it may be fully recovered or rediscovered. Do you think I don't know that you young people there are sacrificing your personal lives, giving up many things a young man, a young woman, holds dear? I never had that option, Lew, I was born with a bare minimum of *laran*. So I do what I can with secular powers, to lighten that burden for you others who bear the heavier ones. So far as I know, you have never misused your powers. Nor are you one of those frivolous young people who want to enjoy the privilege of rank and spend your life in amusements and folly. Why, then, do you shrink from doing this duty to your clan?"

I suddenly wished that I could unburden my fears and misgivings to him. I could not doubt the old man's personal integrity. Yet he was so completely entangled in his single-minded plan for political aims on Darkover that I distrusted him, too. I would not let him manipulate me to serve those aims. I felt confused, half convinced, half more defiant than ever. He was waiting for my answer; I shrank from giving it. Telepaths get used to facing things head-on—you have to, in order to stay even reasonably sane—but you don't learn to put things easily into words. You get used, in a place like Arilinn, to knowing that everyone in your circle can share all your feelings and emotions and desires. There is no reticence there, none of the small evasions and courtesies which outsiders use in speaking of intimate things. But Hastur could not read my thoughts, and I fumbled at putting it into words that would not embarrass either of us too much.

"Mostly I have never met a woman I wished to spend my life with . . . and, being a telepath, I am not willing to . . . to gamble on someone else's choice." No. I wasn't being completely honest. I would have gambled on Linnea willingly, if I had not felt I was being manipulated, used as a helpless pawn. My anger flared again. "Hastur, if you wanted me to marry simply for the sake of perpetuating my gift, of fathering a son for the Domain, you should have had me married off before I was full-grown, before I was old enough to have any feelings about any woman, and would have wanted her just because she *was* a woman and available. Now it's different." I fell silent again.

How could I tell Hastur, who was old enough to be my grandfather, and not even a telepath, that when I took a woman, all her thoughts and feelings were open to me and mine to her, that unless rapport was complete and sympathy almost total, it could quickly unman me? Few women could endure it. And how could I tell him about the paralyzing failures which a lack of sympathy could bring? Did he actually think I could manage to live with a woman whose only interest in me was that I might give her a *laran* son? I know some men in the Comyn manage it. I suppose that almost any two people with healthy bodies can give each other *something* in bed. But not tower-trained telepaths, accustomed to that full sharing. . . . I said, and I knew my voice was shaking uncontrollably, "Even a god cannot be constrained to love on command."

Hastur looked at me with sympathy. That hurt, too. It would have been hard enough to strip myself this way before a man my own age. Finally he said gently, "There's never been any question of compulsion, Lew. But promise me to think about it. The Storn-Lanart girl has applied to Neskaya Tower. We need Keepers and psi technicians. But we also need sensitive women, telepaths, to marry into our families. If you could come to like one another, we would welcome her."

I said, drawing a deep breath, "I'll think about it." Linnea was a telepath. It might be enough. But to put it bluntly, I was afraid. Hastur gestured to a servant to take his emptied plate and my nearly untouched one. "More wine?"

"Thank you, sir, but I have already drunk more than I usually do in a week. And I promised my foster-sister another dance."

Kind as he had been, I was glad to get away from him. The conversation had rubbed me raw-edged, rousing thoughts I had learned to keep firmly below the surface of my mind.

Love—to put it more precisely, sex—is never easy for a telepath. Not even when you're very young and still childishly playing around, discovering your own needs and desires, learning to know your own body and its hungers.

I suppose, from the way other lads talk—and there's plenty of talk in the cadets and the Guards—for most people, at least for a time, anyone of the right sex who is accessible and not completely repulsive will do. But even during those early experiments I had always been too conscious of the other party's motives and reactions, and they would rarely stand up to so close an examination. And after I went to Arilinn and submerged myself in the intense sharing and closeness there, it had changed from merely difficult to impossible.

Well, I had promised Linnell a dance. And what I had told Hastur was true. Linnell was not a woman to me and she would not disturb me emotionally at all.

But Callina was alone, watching a group of classic dancers do a rhythmic dance which mimicked the leaves in a spring storm. Their draperies, gray-green, yellow-green, blue-green, flickered and flowed in the lights like sunshine. Callina had thrown back her hood and, preoccupied in watching the dancers, looked rather forlorn, very small and fragile and solemn. I came and stood beside her. After a moment she turned and said, "You promised Linnell to dance again, didn't you? Well, you can save yourself the trouble, cousin, she and the Storn-Lanart child are in the balcony, watching and chattering to one another about gowns and hair-dressing." She smiled, a small whimsical smile which momentarily lightened her pale stern face. "It's foolish to bring little girls that age to a formal ball, they'd be just as happy at a dancing class!"

I said, letting out my pent-up bitterness, "Oh, they're old enough to be up for auction to the highest bidder. It's how we make fine marriages in the Comyn. Are you for sale too, *damisela*?"

She smiled faintly. "I don't imagine you're making an offer? No, I'm not for sale this year at least. I'm Keeper at Neskaya Tower, and you know what that means."

I knew, of course. The Keepers are no longer required to be cloistered virgins to whom no man dares raise even a careless glance. But while they are working at the center of the energon relays, they are required, by harsh necessity, to remain strictly chaste. They learned not to attract desires they dared not satisfy. Probably they learned not to feel them, either, which is a good trick if you can manage it. I wished I could.

I relaxed. Against Callina, tower-trained and a working Keeper, I need not be on my guard. We shared a deeper kinship than blood, the strong tie of the tower-trained telepath.

I've been a matrix technician long enough to know that the work uses up so much physical and nervous energy that there's not much left over for sex. The will may be there, but not the energy. The Keepers are required, for their physical and emotional safety, to remain celibate. The others in the circle—technicians, mechanics, psi monitors—are usually generous and sensitive about satisfying what little remains. In any case you get too close for playing the elaborate games of flirt and retreat that men and women elsewhere are given to playing. And Callina understood all this withoug being told, having been part of it.

She was also sensitive enough to be aware of my mood. She said, with a faint tinge of gentle malice, "I have heard Linnea will be sent to Arilinn next year, if you both choose not to marry. You'll have time for second thoughts. Shall I ask them to be sure she is not made Keeper, in case you should change your mind?"

I felt somewhat abashed. That was an outrageous thing to say! But what would have infuriated me from an outsider did not trouble me from her. Within a tower circle such a statement would not have embarrassed me, although I would not have felt constrained to answer, either. She was simply treating me like one of our own kind. In the rapport of the tower circles, we were all very much aware of each other's needs and hungers, eager to keep them from reaching a point of frustration or pain.

But now my circle was scattered, others serving in my place, and somehow I had to cope with a world full of elaborate games and complex relationships. I said, as I would have said to a sister, "They're pressuring me to marry, Callina. What shall I do? It's too soon. I'm still—" I gestured, unable to put it into words.

She nodded gravely. "Perhaps you should take Linnea after all. It would mean they couldn't put any constraint on you for someone less suitable." She was seriously considering my problem, giving it her full attention. "I suppose, mostly, what they want is for you to father a son for Armida. If you could do *that*, they wouldn't care whether you married the girl or not, would they?"

It wouldn't have been difficult to have fathered a child on one of the women in my circle at Arilinn, even though pregnancy makes it too dangerous for a woman to remain in the tower. But the thought of that was like salt in a raw wound. I said at last, and heard my voice crack, "I am a bastard myself. Do you honestly think I would ever inflict that on any son of mine? And Linnea is very young and she was . . . honest with me." This whole conversation troubled me for obscure reasons. "And how do you come to know so much about this? Has my love life become a subject for Council debate, Callina *comynara?*"

She shook her head pityingly. "No, of course not. But Javanne and I played dolls together, and she still tells me things. Not Council gossip, Lew, just women's talk."

I hardly heard her. Like all Altons, I sometimes have a disturbing tendency to see time out of focus, and Callina's image kept wavering and trembling, as if I saw her through running water or through flowing time. For a moment I would lose sight of her as she was now, pale and plain and crimson-draped, as she shimmered in an ice-blue glittering mist. Then she would seem to float, cold and aloof and beautiful, shimmering with a darkness like the midnight sky. I was tormented, struggling with mingled rage and frustration, my whole body aching with it—

I blinked, trying to get the world back in focus.

"Are you ill, kinsman?"

I realized with sheer horror that I had been, for an instant, on the very edge of taking her into my arms. Since she was not now Keeper within the circle, this was only a rudeness, not an unthinkable atrocity. Still, I must be mad! I was actually trembling. This was insane! I was still looking at Callina, reacting to her as if she were a desirable woman, not bared from me by double taboo and the oath of a tower technician.

She met my eyes, deeply troubled. There was cool sympathy and kindliness in her glance, but no response to my surge of uncontrollable emotion. Of course not!

"*Damisela,* I apologize profoundly," I said, feeling my breath raw in my throat "It's this crowd. Plays hell with my . . . barriers."

She nodded, accepting the excuse. "I hate such affairs. I try never to come to them, except when I must. Let's get into the air for a moment, Lew." She led the way out to one of the small balconies where a thin fine rain was falling. I breathed the cold dampness with relief. She was wearing a long, fine, shimmering black veil that spun out behind her like wings, gleaming in the darkness. I could not resist the impulse to seize her in my arms, crush her against me, press her lips against mine—Again I blinked, staring at the cool rainless night, the clear stars, Callina calm in her brilliant drapery. Suddenly I felt sick and faint and clung to the balcony railing. I felt myself falling into infinite distances, a wild nowhere of empty space. . . .

Callina said quietly, "This isn't just the crowd. Have you some *kirian*, Lew?"

I shook my head, fighting to get the world in perspective. I was too old for this, damn it. Most telepaths outgrow these psychic upheavals at puberty. I hadn't had threshold sickness since before I went to Arilinn. I had no idea why it should overcome me just now.

Callina said gently, "I wish I could help you, Lew. You know what's really wrong with you, don't you?" She brushed past me with a feather-light touch and left me. I stood in the cold damp air of the balcony, feeling the sting of the words. Yes, I knew what was wrong and resented it, bitterly, that she should remind me from behind the barricade of her own invulnerability. She did not share my needs, desires; it was a torment from which she, as Keeper, was free. For the moment, in my flaring anger at the girl, I forgot the cruel discipline behind her hard-won immunity.

Yes, I knew what was really wrong with me. At Arilinn I had grown accustomed to women who were sensitive to my needs, who shared them. Now I had been a long time away, a long time alone. I was even barred, being what I am, from the kind of uncomplicated relief which the least of my fellow Guardsmen might find. The few times—very few times— when, in desperation, I had been driven to seek it, it had only made me sick. Sensitive women don't take up that particular profession. Or if they do I've never met them. Leaning my head on the railing, I gave way to envy . . . a bitter envy of a man who could find even temporary solace with any woman with a willing body.

Momentarily, knowing it would make it worse in the end, I let myself think of the girl Linnea. Terran blood. A sensitive, a telepath. Perhaps I had been too hasty.

Rage gripped me again. So Hastur and my father thought they could manipulate me no other way, now they tried to bribe me with sex. They had bribed Dyan by putting him in charge of a barracks-full of half-grown boys, who at the very least would feed his ego by admiring him and flattering him. And however discreetly, he thrived on it.

And they would bribe me, too. Differently, of course, for my needs were different, but essentially still a bribe. They would keep me in control, pliable, by dangling a young, beautiful, sexually exciting girl before me, a half-spoken agreement.

And my own needs, which my telepathic father knew all too well, would do the rest. I felt sick at the knowledge of how nearly I had fallen into their trap.

The festivities inside the ballroom were breaking up. The cadets had long gone back to barracks. A few lingerers were still drinking at the buffet, but servants were moving around, beginning to clear away. I strode through the halls toward the Alton rooms, still alive with rage.

The central hall was deserted, but I saw a light in my father's room and went in without knocking. He was half-dressed, looking weary and off guard.

"I want to talk to you!"

He said mildly, "You didn't have to charge in here like a *cralmac* in rut for that." He reached out briefly and touched my mind. He hasn't done that much since I was grown up, and it made me angry that he should treat me like a child after so many years. He withdrew quickly and said, "Can't it wait till morning, Lew? You're not well."

Even his solicitude added to my wrath. "If I'm not, you know whose fault it is. What in the hell do you mean, trying to marry me off without a word of warning?"

He met my anger head-on. "Because, Lew, you're too proud and too damned stubborn to admit you *need* anything. You're ready, past ready, for marriage. Don't be like the man in the old tale, who when the devil bade him take the road to paradise, set off on the high-road to hell!" He sounded as raw as I felt. "Damn it, do you think I don't *know* how you feel?"

I thought about that for a moment. I've wondered, now and then, if my father has lived alone all these years since my mother died. He'd certainly had no acknowledged mistress. I had never tried to spy on him, or inquire even in thought about his most private life, therefore I was doubly angered that he left me no rag of privacy to cover my nakedness, had forced me to strip myself naked before Hastur and disgrace myself before my cousin Callina.

"It won't work," I flung at him in a fury. "I wouldn't marry the girl now if she was as beautiful as the Blessed Cassilda, and came dowered with all the jewels of Carthon!"

My father shrugged, with a deep sigh. "Of course not," he said wearily. "When did you ever do anything so sensible? Suit yourself. I married to please myself; I told Hastur I would never compel you."

"Do you think you *could*?" I was still raging.

"Since I'm not trying, what does it matter?" My father sounded as weary as I felt. "I think you're a fool, but if it helps you feel independent and virtuous to go around with an ache in your"—to my surprise and shock he used a vulgar phrase from the Guard hall, one I'd never suspected him of knowing—"then be just as damned stubborn as you want. You're my son all right: you have no more sense than I had at your age!" He shrugged in a way that indicated he was through with the subject. "Threshold sickness? I have some *kirian* somewhere, if you need it."

I shook my head, realizing that something, perhaps just the flooding of my system with violent anger, had dispelled the worst of it.

"I had something to say to you, but it can wait till morning if you're not in shape to listen. Meanwhile, I want another drink." He started to struggle to his feet; I said, "Let me serve you, Father," and brought him a glass of wine, got one for myself and sat beside him to drink it. He sat sipping it slowly. After a time he reached out and laid a hand on my shoulder, a rare gesture of intimacy from childhood. It did not make me angry now.

Finally he said, "You were at the Council. You know what's going on."

"You mean Aldaran." I was glad he had actually changed the subject.

"The worst of it is, I cannot be spared from Thendara, and what's more, I don't think I can make the journey, Lew." His barriers were down, and I could feel his weariness. "I've never admitted, before, that there was anything I could not do. But now," and he gave me his quick, rare smile, "I have a son I can trust to take my place. And since we've both defied Hastur, Thendara might not be too comfortable for you in the next weeks. I'm going to send you to Aldaran as my deputy, Lew."

"Me, Father?"

"Who else? There is no one else I can trust so well. You did as well as I could have done on the fire-beacon business. And you can claim blood-kinship there; old Kermiac of Aldaran is your great-uncle." I had known I was of the Aldaran kin, but I had not known it was so high in the clan, nor so close. "Also, you have Terran blood. You can go and find out, beyond all rumors, what is really happening back there in the mountains."

I felt both elated and uncertain about being sent on this highly sensitive mission, knowing that Father trusted me with it. Hastur had spoken of our duty to serve the Comyn, our world. Now I was ready to take my place among those of our Domain who had done so for more generations than any of us could count. "When do I start?"

"As soon as I can arrange escort and safe-conduct for you. There's no time to be lost," he said. "They know you are heir to Comyn. But you are also kinsman to Aldaran; they will welcome you as they would never welcome me."

I was grateful to my father for giving me this mission, then, a new feeling and a good one, I realized that the gratitude need not be all mine. He genuinely needed me. I had a chance to serve him, too, to do something for him better than he could do it himself. I was eager to begin.

Chapter NINE

At this season the sun was already up when the rising-bell rang in the barracks. Little runnels of snow were melting in the court as they crossed the cobblestones toward the mess hall. Regis was still sleepy in spite of the icy water he had splashed on his face. He felt that he'd almost rather miss breakfast than get up for it at this hour. But he was proud of his good record; he was the only cadet who had never incurred a punishment detail for sleeping through the bell and stumbling in late and half asleep. Nevarsin had done him some good, after all.

He slid into his assigned seat between Danilo and Gareth Lindir. An orderly slapped battered trays in front of them: thick crockery bowls of porridge mixed with nuts, heavy mugs of the sour country beer Regis hated and never touched. He put a spoon distastefully into the porridge.

"Does the food really get worse every morning, or am I imagining it?" Damon MacAnndra asked.

"It gets worse," said Danilo. "Who's capable of imagining anything at this God-forgotten hour? What's *that*?"

There was a small commotion at the door. Regis jerked up his head and stared. After a brief scuffle a cadet was flung off his feet and went reeling across the room, crashed headfirst into a table and lay still. Dyan Ardais was standing in the doorway waiting for the unfortunate cadet to rise. When he did not stir, Dyan motioned to an orderly to go and pick him up.

Damon said, "Zandru's hells, it's Julian!" He got up from his seat and hurried to his friend's side. Dyan was standing over him, looking grim.

"Back to your seat, cadet. Finish your meal."

"He's my friend. I want to see if he's hurt." Ignoring Dyan's angry glare, Damon knelt beside the fallen cadet; the other cadets, craning their necks, could see the bright smear

126

of blood where Julian's head had struck the table. "He's bleeding! You've killed him!" Damon said in a shrill, shaking voice.

"Nonsense!" Dyan rapped out. "Dead men don't bleed like that." He knelt, quickly ran his fingertips over the boy's head and motioned to two third-year cadets. "Take him back to the staff offices and ask Master Raimon to have a look at him."

As Julian was carried out, Gabriel Vyandal muttered across the table, "It's not fair to pick on us at this hour of the morning when we're all half asleep." It was so quiet in the mess room that his voice carried; Dyan strode across the room and said, looking down at him with a curl of his lip, "Times like this are when you should be most on guard, cadet. Do you think that footpads in the city, or catmen or bandits on the border, will pick an hour of your convenience to attack? This part of your training is to teach you to be on your guard literally every moment, cadets." He turned his back on them and walked out of the room.

Gareth muttered, "He's going to kill one of us some day. I wonder what he'll say then?"

Damon came back to his seat, looking very white. "He wouldn't even let me go with them and hold his head."

Gabriel laid a comforting hand on his arm. He said, "Don't worry, Master Raimon will take good care of him."

Regis had been shocked at the sight of blood, but a sense of scrupulous fairness made him say, "Lord Dyan is right, you know. When we're really in the field, a moment of being off guard can get us killed, not just hurt."

Damon glared at Regis. "It's all right for *you* to talk, Hastur. I notice he never picks on *you*."

Regis, whose ribs were chronically black and blue from Dyan's battering at sword practice, said, "I suppose he thinks I get enough lumps working out with him in armed-combat training." It occurred to him that there was an element of cruelty in this too. Kennard Alton had taught him to handle a sword when he was believed to be the best swordsman in the Domains. Yet in daily practice with either Kennard or Lew for two years, he had collected fewer bruises than he had had from Dyan in a few weeks.

A second-year man said audibly, "What do you expect of the Comyn? They all hang together."

Regis bent his head to the cold porridge. What's the use?

he thought. He couldn't show everybody his bruises—he shouldn't have opened his mouth. Danilo was trying to eat with trembling hands. The sight filled Regis with distress but he did not know what he could say that would not be an intrusion.

In the barracks room, Regis quickly made up his bed, helped Damon fix up Julian's cot and arrange his possessions; when Julian returned, at least he would not have to face demerits for leaving his bed and shelf in disorder. After the other cadets had gone off for arms-drill, he and Danilo remained. It was their turn to sweep the room and clean the fireplace. Regis went meticulously about the work of scraping ashes from the fireplace and cleaning the hearth. You never knew which officer would make inspection and some were stricter than others. He did the work with all the more thoroughness because he detested it, but his thoughts were busy. Had Julian really been hurt? Dyan *had* been too rough.

He was aware that Danilo, shoving the heavy push-broom with scowling determination at the far end of the room, was filled with a kind of sullen misery that overlaid everything else. Regis wondered if there was any way to block *out* other people's emotions, for he was far too sensitive to Danilo's moods. If he knew what Dani was thinking, or why he was so angry and miserable all the time, it might not be so bad, but all Regis got were the raw emotions.

He sensed Lew Alton's presence and looked up to see him coming along the room. "Not finished? Take your time, cadet, I'm a little early."

Regis relaxed. Lew could be strict enough, but he did not go out of his way to look for hidden fragments of dust. He continued his work with the hearth-broom, but after a minute felt Lew bend and touch his arm. "I want a word with you."

Regis rose and followed him to the door of the barracks room, turning to say over his shoulder, "I'll be with you in a minute, Dani, don't try to shift that table until I can help you." Just outside, aware of the touch of Lew's thoughts, he looked up to face his smiling eyes.

"Yes, I knew the other day, in Council," Lew said, "but I had no chance to speak to you then. When did this happen, Regis? And how?"

"I'm not sure," Regis said, "but somehow, I—touched—Danilo, or he touched me, I'm not really sure which it was, and some kind of—of barrier seemed to go down. I don't know how to explain it."

Lew nodded. "I know," he said, "there aren't any words for most of these experiences, and the ones there are, aren't very enlightening. But Danilo? I sensed he had *laran* the other day, but if he could do that, then—" He stopped, his brow furrowed, and Regis followed the thought, *that would mean he's a catalyst telepath! They're rare, I thought there were no functioning ones left.*

"I'll speak to my father before I leave for Aldaran."

"You're going instead of Uncle Kennard? When?"

"A few days before Council season is over, not long now. The trip into the mountains is hard at any season, and impossible after the snows really begin in earnest."

Danilo was standing in the doorway of the barracks room and Regis, recalled abruptly to his work, said, "I'd better get back; Dani will think I'm shirking my share."

Lew took a perfunctory glance inside the room. "Go ahead. It looks all right; I'll sign the inspection report. Finish up at your leisure." He came to Danilo and said, "I'm leaving for Aldaran in a day or two, Dani. I shall be passing Syrtis on my road. Have you any message for Dom Felix?"

"Only that I strive to do my duty among my betters, Captain." His voice was sullen.

"I'll tell him you do us credit, Danilo." The boy did not answer, going off toward the fireplace, dragging the broom. Lew looked after him with curiosity. "What do you think is bothering him?"

Regis was worried about Danilo's moods. His silent weeping had wakened Regis twice more, and again he had been torn between the desire to console his friend and the wish to respect his privacy. He wished he could ask Lew what to do, but they were both on duty and there was no time for personal problems. Anyway, Lew might be required by Guard regulations—he didn't really know—to tell him he should ask his cadet-master about any personal problem. Regis said at last, "I don't know. Homesick, maybe," and left it at that. "How is Julian? *Not dead?*"

Lew looked at him, startled. "No, no. He'll be all right. Just a bit of a knock on the head." He smiled again and went out of the barracks.

Danilo leaned the broom against the wall and began to

shift the heavy wooden table to get at the litter under it.
Regis jumped to catch the other end.

"Here, I *told* you I'd give you a hand; you could hurt your
insides trying to lift a heavy thing like that." Danilo looked
up, glowering, and Regis said, "I wasn't shirking, I only
wanted to say goodbye to my kinsman. You were rude to
him, Dani."

"Well, are we going to work or gossip?"

"Work by all means," said Regis, giving his end of the table a heave. "I've nothing to say to you when you're in this
mood." He went to fetch the broom. Danilo muttered something under his breath and Regis swung around, demanding,
"What did you say?"

"Nothing." Danilo turned his back. It had sounded suspi-
ciously like, "Don't get your hands dirty," and Regis stared.

"What's the matter? Do you think I ought to finish up? I
will if you want me to, but I don't think I was away talking
that long, was I?"

"Oh, I'd never think of imposing on you, Lord Regis! Allow me to serve you!" The sneer was openly apparent in
Danilo's voice now and Regis stared in bewilderment.

"Danilo, are you trying to fight with me?"

Danilo looked Regis up and down slowly. "No, I thank
you, my lord. Fight, with an heir to Comyn? I may be a fool,
but not such a fool as all that." He squared his shoulders and
thrust his lip out belligerently. "Run along to your fencing
lesson with Lord Ardais and leave the dirty work to me."

Regis' bewilderment gave way to rage. "When did I ever
leave any dirty work for you or anyone else around here?"
Danilo stared at the floor and did not answer. Regis advanced on him menacingly. "Come on, you started this, answer me! You say I haven't been doing my fair share?" No
other accusation could have made him so furious. "And take
that look off your face or I'll knock it off!"

"Must I watch the very look on my face, *Lord Hastur*?"
The title, as he spoke it, was an open insult, and Regis hit
him. Danilo staggered back, sprang up raging and started for
him, then stopped short.

"Oh no. You can't get me in trouble *that* way. I told you
I'm not going to fight, Lord Hastur."

"Yes you will, damn you. You started this! Now put up
your fists, damn you, or I'll use you for a floor-mop!"

"That would be fun, wouldn't it," Danilo muttered, "force

me to fight and get me in trouble for fighting? Oh, no, Lord Regis, I've had too much of that!"

Regis stepped back. He was now more troubled than angry, wondering what he could possibly have done to upset Dani this way. He reached out to try to touch his friend's mind, met nothing but surging rage that covered everything else. He moved toward Danilo; Dani sprang defensively alert.

"Zandru's hells, what are you two about?" Hjalmar stepped inside the door, took it all in at a glance and collared Regis, not gently. "I heard you, shouting halfway across the court! Cadet Syrtis, your lip is bleeding."

He let Regis go, came and took Danilo by the chin, turning his face gently up to look at the wound. Danily exploded into violence, pushing his hand away, his hand dropping to knife-hilt. Hjalmar grabbed his wrist.

"Zandru's hells! Lad, don't do *that*! Drawing a knife in barracks will break you, and I'd have to report it! What the hell's the matter, boy, I only wanted to see if you were hurt!" He sounded genuinely concerned. Danilo lowered his head and stood trembling.

"What's between you two? You've been close as brothers!"

"It was my fault," said Regis quietly, "I struck him first."

Hjalmar gave Danilo a shove. It looked rude but was, in truth, rather gentle. "Go and put some cold water on your lip, cadet. Hastur can finish doing the barracks alone. It will teach him to keep his big mouth shut." When Danilo had vanished into the washroom he scowled angrily at Regis. "This is a fine example to set for the lads of lower rank!"

Regis did not argue or excuse himself. He stood and accepted the tongue-lashing Hjalmar gave him, and the three days of punishment detail. He felt almost grateful to the young officer for interrupting a nasty situation. Why, *why*, had Danilo exploded that way?

He finished sweeping the barracks, thinking that it was not like Dani to pick a fight.

And he had picked it, Regis thought soberly, throwing the last of the trash, without realizing it, into the newly cleaned fireplace. But why? Had they been tormenting him again about trying to curry favor with a Hastur?

All that day he went about his duties preoccupied and wretched, wondering what had brought his friend to such a point of desperation. He had halfway decided to seek Danilo out in their free time, brave his anger and ask him outright what was wrong. But he was reminded that he was on punishment detail, which turned out to be the distasteful duty of working with the orderlies sweeping the stables. Afterward it took him a long time to get himself clean and free of the stable stink and he had to hurry to be in time for his new assignment, which he found boring beyond words. Mostly it consisted of standing guard at the city gates, checking permits and safe-conducts, questioning travelers who had neither, reminding incoming merchants of the rules covering their trade. After that he and a junior officer were assigned supervision of night guard at the city gates, his first use of authority over any of the Guardsmen. He had known, in theory, that the cadets were in training for officers, but until now he had felt like a menial, a flunky, junior to everyone. Now, after a scant half season, he had a responsible duty of his own. For a time he forgot his preoccupation with his friend's trouble.

He came back to barracks near midnight, wondering what duty Danilo had been assigned at this mid-year rotation. It was strange to walk in and see the night officer simply marking off his name as being on late duty, rather than scolding him for being tardy. He paused to ask the man, "Do you know anything about Julian—cadet MacAran, sir?"

"MacAran? Yes, he has a concussion, they took him to the infirmary, but he'll be all right in a few days. They sent for his friend to come and stay with him there. His wits were wandering, and they were afraid he'd climb out of bed and hurt himself. But he recognized Damon's voice. He didn't seem to hear anyone else but when MacAnndra told him to keep quiet and stay put, they say he went to sleep quiet as a baby. Concussion's like that sometimes."

Regis said he was glad to hear Julian was no worse, and went in to his bed. His end of the dormitory was almost empty, with Damon and Julian in the infirmary. Danilo's bed, too, was empty. He must be on night duty. He felt regretful, having hoped for a word with him, a chance, perhaps, to find out what was troubling him, make friends again.

He was wakened, an hour or two later, by the sounds of heavy rain on the roof and raised voices at the doorway. The night officer was saying, "I'll have to put you on report for this," and Danilo answering roughly, "I don't give a damn, what do you think it matters to me now?" A few minutes later he came into the room with blundering steps.

What is the matter with him? Regis wondered. Was he drunk? He decided not to speak to him. If Danilo was drunk enough, or agitated enough, to be rude to the night officer, he might make another scene and find himself in worse trouble yet.

Danilo bumped into Regis' cot, and Regis could feel that Danilo's clothing was soaked through, as if he had been wandering around in the rain. By the dim light left in the washroom at night Regis could see him blundering around, flinging his clothes off every which way, heard the *bump* as he threw his sword down on his clothing chest instead of hanging it on the wall. He stood under the window for a moment, naked, hesitating, and Regis almost said something. He could have spoken in a low voice without attracting attention; with Damon and Julian both out of the barracks, they were a considerable distance from the other cadets. But the old agonizing fear of a rebuff seized him. He could not face the thought of another quarrel. So he remained silent, and after a time Danilo turned away and got into his own bed.

Regis slept lightly, fitfully, and after a long time woke with a start, hearing again the sound of weeping. This time, although the vibration of misery was there, direct to his senses, Danilo was awake and he was really crying, softly, hopelessly, miserably. Regis listened to the sound for some time, wretchedly torn, unwilling to intrude, unable to endure such grief. Finally his sense of friendship drew him out of bed.

He knelt beside Danilo's cot and whispered, "Dani, what's the matter? Are you sick? Have you had bad news from home? Is there anything I can do?"

Danilo muttered drearily, his head still turned away. "No, no, there's nothing anyone can do, it's too late for that. And for that, for that—Holy Bearer of Burdens, what will my father say?"

Regis said, in a whisper that could not be heard three feet away, "Don't talk like that. Nothing's so bad it can't be helped somehow. Would you feel better to tell me about it? Please, Dani."

Danilo turned over, his face only a white blob in the darkness. He said, "I don't know what to do. I think I must be going mad—" Suddenly he drew a long, gasping sob. He said, "I can't see—who—Damon, is that you?"

Regis whispered, "No. Damon's in the infirmary with Julian. And everyone else is asleep. I don't think anyone heard you coming in. I wasn't going to say anything, but you sounded so unhappy . . ." Forgetting their quarrel, forgetting everything except this was his friend in some desperate trouble, he leaned forward and laid his hand on Danilo's bare shoulder, a shy, tentative touch. "Isn't there anything I can—"

He felt the explosion of rage and something else—fear? shame?—running up his arm through his fingers, like an electric shock. He drew his hand away sharply as if it had been burned. With a violent, tigerish movement, Danilo thrust Regis angrily away with both hands. He spoke in a strained whisper.

"Damnable—filthy—*Comyn,* get the hell away from me, get your stinking *hands* off me, you—" He used a word which made Regis, used as he was to Guard hall coarseness, gasp aloud and draw away, shaking and almost physically sick.

"Dani, you're wrong," he protested, dismayed. "I only thought you were sick or in trouble. Look, whatever's gone wrong with you, I haven't done anything to you, have I? You'll really make yourself ill if you go on like this, Dani. Can't you tell me what's happened?"

"Tell *you?* Sharra's chains, I'd sooner whisper it to a wolf with his teeth in my throat!" He gave Regis a furious push and said, half aloud, "You come near me again, you filthy *ombredin,* and I'll break your stinking neck!"

Regis rose from his side and silently went back to his own bed. His heart was still pounding with the physical shock of that burst of violent rage which he had felt when he touched Danilo, and he was trembling with the assault on his mind. He lay listening to Danilo's strained breathing, quite simply aghast and almost physically sick under that burst of hatred and his own failure to get through to him. Somehow he had thought that between two people, both with *laran,* this kind of misunderstanding could not possibly arise! He lay listening to Danilo's gasping, heard it finally subside into soft sobbing and at last into a restless, tossing sleep. But Regis himself hardly closed his eyes that night.

Chapter TEN

(*Lew Alton's narrative*)

Heavy rain after midnight had turned to wet snow; the day I was to leave for Aldaran dawned gray and grim, the sun hidden behind clouds still pregnant with unfallen snow. I woke early and lay half asleep, hearing angry voices from my father's room. At first I thought Marius was getting a tongue-lashing for some minor naughtiness, but so early? Then I woke a little further and detected a quality in Father's voice never turned on any of us. All my life I have known him for a harsh, hasty and impatient man, but usually his anger was kept on a leash; the fully-aroused anger of an Alton can kill, but he was tower-disciplined, control normally audible in every syllable he spoke. Hastily I put on a few clothes and went into the central hall.

"Dyan, this isn't worthy of you. Is it so much a matter of personal pride?"

Lord of Light, it happened again! Well, at least, if I knew that note in Father's voice, he wouldn't get off unpunished!

Dyan's voice was a heavy bass, muted to a rumble by the thick walls, but no walls could filter out my father's answering shout; "No, damn it, Dyan, I won't be party to any such monstrous—"

Out in the hall I heard Dyan repeat implacably, "Not personal pride, but the honor of the Comyn and the Guards."

"Honor! You don't know the meaning of—"

"Careful, Kennard, there are some things even you cannot say! As for this—in Zandru's name, Ken, I cannot overlook this. Even if it had been your own son. Or mine, poor lad, had he lived so long. Would you be willing to see a cadet draw steel on an officer and go unpunished? If you cannot

135

accept that I am thinking of the honor of the Guards, what of discipline? Would you have condoned such conduct even in your own bastard?"

"Must you draw Lew into every—"

"I'm trying not to, which is why I came directly to you with this. I do not expect *him* to be sensitive to a point of honor."

My father cut him off again, but they had both lowered their voices. Finally Dyan spoke again, in a tone of inflexible finality. "No, don't speak to me of circumstances. If you let the respect due to the Comyn be eroded away in times like this, in full sight of every insolent little cadet and bastard in Thendara, how can *you* speak of honor?"

The violent rage was gone from my father's voice now, replaced by a heavy bitterness. He said, "Dyan, you use the truth as other men use a lie, to serve your own ends. I've known you since we were boys, and this is the first time I've come close to hating you. Very well, Dyan. You leave me no choice. Since you bring me this complaint officially, as cadet-master to commander, it shall be done. But I find it hard to believe you couldn't have kept it from coming to this."

Dyan thrust the door open and came striding out into the hall. He gave me a brief contemptuous glance, said, "Still spying on your betters?" and went out.

I went to the door he had left open. My father looked up at me blankly, as if he could not remember my name, then sighed and said, "Go and tell the men to gather after breakfast in the main Guard hall. All duty-lists suspended for the morning."

"What . . .?"

"Disciplinary assembly." He raised his thick, knotted hands, gnarled and stiff from the joint-disease which has ravaged him since I can remember. "You'll have to stand by. I haven't the strength for a sword-breaking any more and I'm damned if I'll leave it to Dyan."

"Father, what happened?"

"You'll have to know," Kennard said. "One of the cadets drew his sword on Dyan."

I felt my face whiten with dismay. That was indeed something which could not be overlooked. Of course I wondered—who wouldn't?—what provocation Dyan had given. In my own cadet year, he had dislocated my arm, but even then I had known better than that. Even if two cadets in some childish squabble drew their pocketknives, it would have been sufficient to have them both expelled in disgrace.

I was amazed that my father had even tried to interfere. It seemed that for once I had misjudged Dyan.

Even so, I made a quick guess at what had happened. If the MacAran boy had died of his concussion and Damon held Dyan responsible—three different officers had told me of the event and all of them agreed Dyan had been inexcusably rough—then Damon would have held himself honor-bound to avenge his friend. Both boys were mountain-bred and friendship went deep in the Kilghard hills. I did not blame the boy, but I was angry with Dyan. A kinder man would have understood; Dyan, being what he was, might well have shown understanding of the love between them.

Father reminded me that I would need full-dress uniform. I hurried with my tunic-laces, wanting to reach the mess hall while the men were still at breakfast.

The sun had broken through the cloud cover; the melting snow lay in puddles all over the cobblestone court, but it was still gray and threatening to the north. I'd hoped to leave the city shortly after daybreak. If it started snowing again later, I'd have a soggy journey.

Inside the mess room there were sausages for breakfast, their rich spicy smell reminding me that I had not eaten yet. I was tempted to ask the orderly for a plate of them, but remembered I was in full-dress uniform. I came to the center of the crowded tables and called for attention.

As I announced the assembly, I glanced at the table where the cadets were seated. To my surprise, Julian MacAran was there, his head heavily bandaged, but there and looking only a little pale. So much for my theory about what had happened! Regis was there, looking so white and sick that for a moment, in dismay, I wondered if he were the disgraced cadet. But no, he would have been under arrest somewhere.

My way back led me past the first-year barracks room and I heard voices there, so I stopped to see if I should repeat my message to anyone. As I approached I heard the voice of old Domenic. He should have been cadet-master, I thought bitterly.

"No, son, there's no need for that. Your sword is an heirloom in your family. Spare your father that, at least. Take this plain one."

I had often thought during my own cadet years that old

Domenic was the kindest man I had ever known. Any sword would do for breaking. The answer was soft, indistinguishable, blurred by a pain which, even at this distance, clamped around me like an iron band gripping my forehead.

Hjalmar's deep voice rebuked gently, "None of that now, my lad. I'll not hear a word against Comyn. I warned you once, that your temper would get you into trouble."

I glanced in, then wished I hadn't. Danilo was sitting on his cot, hunched over in misery, and the arms-master and Hjalmar were helping him gather his possessions. *Danilo!* What in all of Zandru's nine hells could have happened? No wonder Father had been willing to plead with Dyan! Could any sane man make a point of honor against such a child? Well, if he was old enough to be a cadet, he was old enough to bear the consequences of a rash act.

I hardened my conscience and went on without speaking. I too had had such provocation—for some time, while my arm was still in a sling, I'd put myself to sleep nights thinking up ways to kill him—but I had kept my hands off my sword. If Danilo was not capable of self-restraint, the cadet corps was no place for him.

By the time I came back to the Guard hall the men were gathering. Disciplinary assemblies were not common since minor offenses and punishments were handled by the officers or the cadet-master in private, so there was a good deal of whispered curiosity and muttered questions. I had never seen a cadet formally expelled. Sometimes a cadet dropped out because of illness or family trouble, or was quietly persuaded to resign because he was unable physically or emotionally, to handle the duties or the discipline. Octavien Vallonde's case had been hushed up that way. Damn him, that was Dyan's doing too!

Dyan was already in place, looking stern and self-righteous. My father came in, limping worse than I had ever seen him. Di Asturien brought in Danilo. He was as white as the plastered wall, his face taut and controlled, but his hands were shaking. There was an audible murmur of surprise and dismay. I tried to barrier myself against it. Any way you looked at it, this was tragedy, and worse.

My father came forward. He looked as bad as Danilo. He took out a long and formal document—I wondered if Dyan had brought it already drawn up—and unfolded it.

"Danilo-Felix Kennard Lindir-Syrtis, stand forth," he said

wearily. Danilo looked so pale I thought he would faint and I was glad di Asturien was standing close to him. So he was my father's namesake, as well?

Father began to read the document. It was written in *casta*. Like most hillsmen, I had been brought up speaking *cahuenga* and I followed the legal language only with difficulty, concentrating on every word. The gist of it I knew already. Danilo Syrtis, cadet, in defiance of all order and discipline and against any and all regulations of the cadet corps, had willfully drawn bared steel against a superior officer, his cadetmaster, Dyan-Gabriel, Regent of Ardais. He was therefore dismissed, disgraced, stripped of all honor and privilege and so forth and so on, two or three times over in different phraseology, until I suspected that reading the indictment had taken longer than the offense.

I was trembling myself with the accumulated leakage of emotion I could not entirely barracade in this crowd. Danilo's misery was almost physical pain. Regis looked ready to collapse. Get it over, I thought in anguish, listening to the interminable legal phrases, hearing the words now only through their agonized reverberations in Danilo's mind. Get it over before the poor lad breaks down and has hysterics, or do you want to see that humiliation, too?

". . . and shall therefore be stripped of honorable rank and returned to his home in disgrace . . . in token of which . . . his sword to be broken before his eyes and in the sight of all the Guardsmen together assembled. . . ."

This was my part of the dirty work. Hating it, I went and unfastened his sword. It was a plain Guardsman's sword, and I blessed the kind old man for that much mercy. And besides, I thought sourly, those heirloom swords are of such fine temper you'd need the forge-folk and Sharra's fires to make any impression on one!

I had to touch Danilo's arm. I tried to give him a kindly thought of reassurance, that this wasn't the end of the world, but I knew it wasn't getting through to him. He flinched from my gauntleted hand as if it had been a red-hot branding iron. This would have been a frightful ordeal for any boy who was not a complete clod; for one with *laran*, possibly a catalyst telepath, I knew it was torture. Could he come through it at all without a complete breakdown? He stood motionless, staring straight forward, eyes half closed, but he kept blinking as if to avoid breaking into anguished tears. His hands were clenched into tight fists at his side.

I took Danilo's sword and walked back to the dais. I gripped it between my heavily gauntleted hands and bent it across my knee. It was heavy and harder to bend than I'd realized, and I had time to wonder what I'd do if the damned thing didn't break or if I lost my grip and it went flying across the room. There was a little nervous coughing deep in the room. I strained at the blade, thinking, Break, damn you, break, let's get this filthy business over before we all start screaming!

It broke, shattered with a sound shockingly like breaking glass. If anything, I'd expected a noisy metallic resonance. One half slithered away to the floor; I let it lie.

Straightening my back I saw Regis' eyes full of tears. I looked across at Dyan.

Dyan. . . .

For an instant his barriers were down. He was not looking at me, or at the sword. He was staring at Danilo with a hateful, intense, mocking, *satiated* look. A look of horrid, satisfied lust. There was simply no other word for it.

And all at once I knew—I should have known all along—exactly how and why Danilo had been persecuted, until in a moment of helpless desperation he had been goaded into drawing a knife against his persecutor . . . or possibly against himself.

Either way, the moment the knife was loose from the sheath, Dyan had him exactly where he wanted him. Or the next best thing.

I don't think I'll ever know how I got through the rest of the ceremony. My mind retains only shaken vignettes: Danilo's face as white as his shirt after the full-dress uniform tabard had been cut away. How shabby he looked. And how young! Dyan taking the sword from my hand, smirking. By the time my brain fully cleared again, I was out of the Guard hall and on the stairs to the Alton rooms.

My father was wearily taking off his dress-uniform. He looked drawn and exhausted. He was really ill, I thought, and no wonder. This would make anyone sick. He looked up, saying tiredly, "I have all your safe-conducts arranged. There is an escort ready for you, with pack animals. You can get away before midday, unless you think the snow's likely to be too heavy before nightfall."

He handed me a packet of folded papers. It looked very official, hung with seals and things. For a minute I could hardly remember what he was talking about. The trip to Aldaran had receded very far. I put the papers into my pocket without looking at them.

"Father," I said, "you *cannot* do this. You cannot ruin a boy's life through Dyan's spite, not again."

"I tried to talk him out of it, Lew. He could have condoned it or handled it privately. But since he made it official, I couldn't pass it over. Even if it had been you, or the Hastur boy."

"And what of Dyan? Is it soldierly to provoke a child?"

"Leave Dyan out of it, son. A cadet must learn to control himself under any and all conditions. He will have the life and death of dozens, of hundreds, of men in his hands some day. If he cannot control his personal feelings . . ." My father reached out, laying his hand on my wrist in a rare caress. "My son, do you think I never knew how hard he tried to provoke you to the same thing? But I trusted you, and I was right. I'm disappointed in Dani."

But there was a difference. Though he was perhaps harsher than most people thought an officer should be, Dyan had done nothing to me that was not permitted by the regulations of the cadet corps. I said so, adding, "Do the regulations require that the cadets must endure *that* from an officer too? Cruelty, even sadistic discipline, is bad enough. But persecution of this kind, the threat of sexual attack—"

"What proof have you of that?"

It was like a deluge of ice water. Proof. I had none. Only the satisfied, triumphant look on Dyan's face, the sickness of shame in Danilo, a telepathic awareness I had had no right to read. Moral certainty, yes, but no proof. I just *knew*.

"Lew, you're too sensitive. I'm sorry for Dani, too. But if he had reason to complain of Dyan's treatment of him, there is a formal process of appeal—"

"Against the Comyn? He would have heard what happened to the *last* cadet to try that," I said bitterly. Again, against all reason, Father was standing with the Comyn, with Dyan. I looked at him almost in disbelief. Even now I could not believe he would not right this wrong.

Always. *Always* I had trusted him utterly, implicitly, certain that he would somehow see justice done. Harsh, yes, demanding, but he was always fair. Now Dyan had done—

again!—what I had always known Dyan would do, and my father was prepared to gloss it over, let this monstrous injustice remain, let Dyan's corrupt and vicious revenge or whatever prevail against all honor and reason.

And I had trusted him! Trusted him literally with my life. I had known that if he failed in testing me for the Alton gift, I would die a very quick, very painful death. I felt I would burst into a flood of tears that would unman me. Once again time slid out of focus and again, eleven years old, terrified but wholly trusting, I stood trembling before him, awaiting the touch that would bring me into full Comyn birthright ... or kill me! I felt the solemnity of that moment, horribly afraid, yet eager to justify his faith in me, his faith that I was his true-born son who had inherited his gift and his power. . . .

Power! Something inside me exploded into anguish, an anguish I must have been feeling through all the years since that day, which I had never dared let myself feel.

He had been willing to kill me! Why had I never seen this before? Cold-blooded, he had been willing to risk my death, against the hope that he would have a tool to power. Power! Like Dyan, he didn't care what torture he inflicted to get it! I could still remember the exploding agony of that first contact. I had been so deathly ill for a long time afterward that, in his attentive love and concern, I had forgotten—more accurately, had buried—the knowledge that he had been willing to risk my death.

Why? Because if I had proved *not* to have the gift, why, then . . . why, then, my life was of small concern to him, my death no worse than the death of a pet puppy!

He was looking up at me, appalled. He whispered, "No. No, my son, no. Oh, my boy, my boy, it wasn't like that!" But I slammed my mind shut, for the first time deaf to the loving words.

Loving words merely to force his will on me again! And his pain now was for seeing his plans all go awry, when his puppet, his blind tool, his creature, turned in his hand!

He was no better than Dyan then. Honor, justice, reason—all these could be swept aside in the ruthless hunger for power! Did he even *know* that Danilo was a catalyst telepath, that most sensitive and powerful of talents, that talent thought to be almost extinct?

For a moment it seemed that would be the last argument

to move him. Danilo was no ordinary cadet, expendable to salve Dyan's bruised pride. He must be saved for the Comyn at all costs!

With the very words on my lips, I stopped. No. If I told Father that, he would find some way to use Danilo too, as a tool in his driving quest for more power! Danilo was well freed of the Comyn and lucky to be beyond our reach!

My father drew back his extended hands. He said coldly, "Well, it's a long road to Aldaran; maybe you'll calm down and see sense before you get there."

I felt like saying Aldaran, hell! Go do your own dirty work this time, I'm still sick from the last job! I don't give a fart in a high wind for all your power politics! Go to Aldaran yourself and be damned to you!

But I didn't. I recalled that I, too, was Aldaran, and Terran. I'd had it flung in my face often enough. They all took it for granted that I would feel enough shame at the disgrace of my origins to do anything, *anything*, to be accepted as Comyn and my father's heir. He'd kept me subservient, unquestioning, all my life, that way.

But Terran blood, so Linnea had said, was no disgrace in the mountains. It had amazed her that I thought it so. And the Aldarans, too, were kinsmen.

My father had allowed me to think the Terrans and the Aldarans were evil. It had suited his purposes to let me think so.

And maybe that was another lie, a step on his road to power.

I bowed with ironic submissiveness. "I am entirely at your command, Lord Alton," I said and turned my back, leaving him without a farewell embrace or a word.

And sealed my own doom.

Chapter ELEVEN

Since Danilo's departure the cadet barracks had been silent, hostile, astir with little eddies of gossip from which Regis was coldly excluded. He was not surprised. Danilo had been a favorite and they identified Regis with the Comyn who had brought about his expulsion.

His own suffering, his loneliness—all the worse because for a time it had been breached—was nothing, he knew, to what his friend must have been feeling. Dani had turned on him that night, he realized, because he was no longer just Regis, he was another persecutor. Another Comyn. But what could have made him so desperate?

He went over it again and again in his mind, without reaching any conclusions at all. He wished he could talk it over with Lew, who had been just as shocked and horrified by it. Regis had felt it in him. But Lew had gone to Aldaran, and Regis had no idea when he would be back.

The day before the cadets were dismissed to their homes, to return next summer in Council season, Regis was scheduled for his regular practice session with Dyan Ardais. He went with the usual blend of excitement and apprehension. He enjoyed his reputation among the cadets as a swordsman too expert for ordinary teaching and the sessions with Dyan challenged him to the utmost, but at the same time he knew these sessions alienated him further from the other cadets. Besides he emerged from them battered, bruised and completely exhausted.

Cadets were readying for practice in the little dressing room off the armory, strapping on the padded surcoats which were worn to protect against the worst blows. The heavy wood and leather practice swords could not kill, but they could inflict substantial injury and pain and even break bones. Regis flung off his cloak and tunic, pulling the padded coat over his head and flinching as he twisted his body to fasten the straps. His ribs were always sore these days.

As he fastened the last buckle, Dyan strode in, threw his jerkin on a bench and got quickly into his own practice outfit. Behind the thick fencing-mask he looked like some giant insect. Impatiently he gestured Regis toward the practice room. In his haste to obey Regis forgot to pick up his gauntlets, and the older man said harshly, "After all these months? Look here—" He thrust out his own clenched fist, pointed to the lump on the tendons on the back of the hand. "I got that when I was about your age. I ought to make you try it one day without gloves; forget again and I will do just that. I promise you'd never forget another time!"

Feeling like a slapped child, Regis went back hastily and snatched up the heavily padded gauntlets. He hurried back. At the far end, one of the arms-master's aides was giving young Gareth Lindir a lesson, patiently positioning and repositioning his arms and legs, shoulders and hands, after every separate stroke. Regis could not see their faces behind the masks, but they both moved as if they were bored with the business. Bruises were better than that, Regis thought as he hurried to join Dyan.

The bout was brief today. Dyan moved more slowly than usual, almost awkwardly. Regis found himself recalling, with a faint embarrassment, a dream he had had some time ago, about fencing with Dyan. He couldn't remember the details, but for some unremembered reason it filled him with anxiety. He touched Dyan at last and waited for the older man to regain his stance. Instead Dyan flung the wooden sword aside.

"You will have to excuse me for today," he said. "I am somewhat—" He paused. "Somewhat—disinclined to go on." Regis had the impression that he had intended to plead illness. "If you want to continue, I can find someone to practice with you."

"As you wish, Captain."

"Enough, then." He pulled off his mask and went back into the dressing room. Regis followed slowly. Dyan was breathing hard, his face dripping with sweat. He took up a towel and plunged his head into it. Regis, unbuckling his padding, turned away. Like most young people, he felt embarrassed at witnessing the weakness of an elder. Under the thick surcoat his own shirt was dripping wet; he pulled it off and went to his locker for the spare one he had learned to keep there.

Dyan put aside the towel and came up behind him. He stood looking at Regis' naked upper body, darkened with new and healing bruises, and finally said, "You should have told me. I had no idea I'd been so heavy-handed." But he was smiling. He reached out and ran both his hands, firmly and thoroughly, over Regis' ribs. Regis flinched from the touch and laughed nervously. Dyan shrugged, laughing in return. "No bones broken," he said, running his fingers along the lowest ribs, "so no harm done."

Regis hurriedly drew on his clean shirt and tunic, thinking that Dyan knew precisely to the inch every time he hit an old bruise—or made a fresh one!

Dyan sat on the bench, lacing up his boots. He threw his fencing-slippers into his locker. "I want to talk to you," he said, "and you're not on duty for another hour. Walk down to the tavern with me. You must be thirsty too."

"Thank you." Regis picked up his cloak and they went down the hill to the inn near the military stables, not the big one where the common soldiers went to drink, but the small wineshop where the officers and cadets spent their leisure time. At this hour the place was not crowded. Dyan slid into an empty booth. "We can go into the back room if you'd rather."

"No, this will do very well."

"You're wise," said Dyan impersonally. "The other cadets would resent it if you kept away from their common haunts and amusements. What will you drink?"

"Cider, sir."

"Nothing stronger? Please yourself." Dyan called the waiter and gave his order, commanding wine for himself. He said, "I think that's why so many cadets take to heavy drinking: the beer they serve in the mess is so near undrinkable they take to wine instead! Perhaps we should improve the beer they're given as a way of keeping them sober!"

He sounded so droll that Regis could not help laughing. At that moment half a dozen cadets came in, started to sit at the next table, then, seeing the two Comyn seated there and laughing together, went back and crowded at a smaller table near the door. Dyan had his back turned to them. Several of them were Regis' barracks-mates; he nodded politely to them, but they pretended not to see.

"Well, tomorrow your first cadet season will be over," Dyan said. "Have you decided to come back for a second?"

"I'd expected to, Captain."

Dyan nodded. "If you survive the first year, everything else is easy. It's that first year which separates the soldiers from the spoiled children. I spoke to the arms-master and suggested he try you as one of his aides next year. Do you think you can teach the brats some of the things I've been trying to pound into you?"

"I can try, sir."

"Just don't be too gentle with them. A few bruises at the right time can save their lives later on." He grinned suddenly. "I seem to have done better by you than I thought, kinsman, judging by the look of your ribs!"

The grin was infectious. Regis laughed and said, "Well, you haven't spared the bruises. No doubt I'll be properly grateful for them, some day."

Dyan shrugged. "At least you haven't complained," he said. "I admire that in someone your age." He held Regis' eyes for a split second longer than Regis felt comfortable, then took a long drink from his mug. "I would have been proud of such behavior from my own son."

"I didn't know you had a son, sir."

Dyan poured himself more wine and said, not looking up, "I *had* a son." His tone did not alter even a fraction, but Regis felt the genuine pain behind Dyan's carefully steady voice. "He was killed in a rockslide at Nevarsin a few years ago."

"I am sorry, kinsman. I had never been told."

"He came to Thendara only once, when I had him legitimated. He was in his mother's care so, I saw him very seldom. We never really got to know one another."

The silence stretched. Regis could not barricade the sharp sense of regret, of loss, he could feel in Dyan. He had to say something.

"Lord Dyan, you are not yet an old man. You could have many sons."

Dyan's smile was a mere mechanical stretching of his mouth. "More likely I shall adopt one of my father's bastards," he said. "He strewed them all about the countryside from the Hellers to the Plains of Valeron. It should be easy enough to find one with *laran,* which is all the Council cares about. I have never been a man for women, nor ever made any secret of it. I forced myself to do my duty by my clan. Once. That was enough." To Regis' awakened sensitivity he sounded immeasurably bitter. "I refuse to think of myself as a very special sort of stud animal whose fees are paid to Comyn. I am sure that you"—he raised his eyes and met Regis', again prolonging the glance with intensity—"can understand what I mean."

Dyan's words struck home, yet his intent look, the feeling he was apparently trying to create, that there was a special rapport between them, suddenly embarrassed the boy. He lowered his eyes and said, "I'm not sure just what you mean, kinsman."

Dyan shrugged and the sudden intensity was gone as quickly at it had come. "Why, just that, being heir to Hastur, they've already begun placing you under pressure to marry, just as they did with me when I was your age. Your grandsire has a reputation in Council as a most persistent and tenacious matchmaker. Do you mean he let Festival Night pass without parading a dozen suitable maidens in front of you, in the hope you'd develop an intolerable itch for one of them?"

Regis said stiffly, "Indeed he did not, sir. I was on duty Festival Night."

"Truly?" Dyan raised an expressive eyebrow. "There were a dozen high-born maidens there, all pretty, and I thought they were all intended for you! I'm surprised he allowed you to stay away."

"I've never asked to be excused from duty, sir. I'm sure Grandfather would not have asked it for me."

"A most commendable attitude," Dyan said, "and one I might have expected from your father's son. But how disappointed the old man must have been! I've accused him to his face of being a disgraceful old procurer!" Dyan was grinning again. "But he assured me that he is always careful to have the wedding properly in order before the bedding."

Regis could not help laughing, although he knew he should be ashamed to join in making fun of his grandfather. "No, Lord Dyan, he hasn't spoken of marriage. Not yet. He only said that I should have an heir as young as possible."

"Why, I'm ashamed of him!" Dyan said and laughed again. "He had Rafael married off by the time he was your age!"

Regis had resented the memory of his father, whose death had robbed him of so much; now he felt an almost wistful longing to know what kind of man he had been. "Kinsman, am I so like my father as they say? Did you know him well?"

"Not as well as I could have wished," Dyan said. "He married young, while I was in Nevarsin where my father's ... debaucheries . . . could not contaminate me. Yes, I suppose you are like him." He looked attentively at Regis. "Although you are handsomer than Rafael, handsomer by far."

He was silent, staring down at the swirl in his wineglass. Regis picked up the mug of cider and sipped at it, not looking up. He had grown sensitive to the far-too-frequent comments on his good looks at Nevarsin and in the barracks. From Dyan they seemed somehow more pointed. He gave a mental shrug, recalling what else they said in the barracks, that Lord Dyan had an eye for pretty boys.

Dyan looked up suddenly from his glass. "Where do you intend to spend the winter, kinsman? Will you return to Castle Hastur?"

"I think not. Grandfather is needed here, and I think he would rather have me close at hand. The estate is in good hands, so I'm not needed there."

"True. He lost so much of Rafael's life, I suspect it's a mistake he doesn't want to repeat. I imagine I'll be here too, with crisis on crisis in the city and Kennard ill much of the time. Well, Thendara is an interesting place to spend the winter. There are concerts enough to satisfy any music-lover. And there are fashionable restaurants, balls and dances, all manner of amusements. And, for a young man your age, one should not omit the houses of pleasure. Are you familiar with the House of Lanterns, cousin?"

In contrast to the other flashes of intensity, this was almost too casual. The House of Lanterns was a discreet brothel, one of the very few which were not specifically forbidden to the cadets and officers. Regis knew that some of the older cadets visited the place occasionally but although he shared the curiosity of the other first-year cadets, curiosity had not yet overcome his distaste for the idea. He shook his head. "Only by reputation."

"I find the place tiresome," Dyan said offhandedly. "The Golden Cage is rather more to my liking. It's at the edge of the Terran Zone, and one can find various exotic entertainments there, even aliens and nonhumans, as well as all kinds of women. Or," he added, again in that carefully casual tone, "all kinds of men or boys."

Regis blushed hard and tried to hide it by coughing as if he'd choked on his cider.

Dyan had seen the blush, and grinned. "I had forgotten how conventional young people can be. Perhaps a taste for . . . exotic entertainments . . . needs to be cultivated, like a taste for fine wine instead of cider. And three years in a monastery hardly cultivates the taste for *any* of the finer amusements and luxuries which help a young man to make the most of his life." As Regis only blushed more furiously, he reached out and laid a hand on his arm. "Cousin, the monastery is behind you; have you truly realized that you are no longer bound by all its rules?"

Dyan was watching him carefully. When Regis said nothing, he continued, "Kinsman, one can waste years, precious years of youth, trying to cultivate tastes which turn out to be mistaken. You can miss too much that way. Learn what you want and what you are while you're young enough to enjoy it. I wish someone had given me such advice at your age. My own son never lived to need it. And your father is not here to give it . . . and your grandfather, I have no doubt, is more concerned with teaching you your duty to family and Comyn than with helping you enjoy your youth!"

Dyan's intensity did not embarrass him now. Regis realized that for a long time he had felt starved for just such an opportunity to talk about these things with a man of his own caste, one who understood the world he must live in. He set down his mug and said, "Kinsman, I wonder if that isn't why Grandfather insisted I should serve in the cadets."

Dyan nodded. "Probably so," he said. "It was I who advised him to send you into the cadets, instead of letting you spend your time in idleness and amusements. There's a time for that, of course. But it's true I felt that time spent in the cadets would teach you, more quickly, the things you'd failed to learn before."

Regis looked at him eagerly. "I didn't want to go in the cadets. I hated it at first."

Dyan laid a light hand on his shoulder again and said affectionately, "Everyone does. If you hadn't, I'd be disturbed; it would mean you'd hardened too young."

"But now I think I know why Comyn heirs have to serve in the cadets," Regis said. "Not just the discipline. I got plenty of that in Nevarsin. But learning how to be one of the people, doing the same work they do, sharing their lives and their problems, so we—" He bit his lip, searching carefully for words. "So we'll know what our people are."

Dyan said softly, "That was eloquent, lad. As your cadet-master, I'm content. As your kinsman, too. I wish more boys your age had that kind of understanding. I've been accused of being ruthless. But whatever I've done, I've done it out of allegiance to Comyn. Can you understand that, Regis?"

Regis said, "I think so." He felt warmed, somehow less lonely, by having someone care how he felt or what he thought.

Dyan said, "Do you also understand what I said about how the other cadets would take it ill if you shunned their common amusements."

Regis bit his lip. He said, "I know what you mean. I do, really. Just the same, I feel very strange about—" He was suddenly embarrassed again. "About places like the House of Lanterns. Maybe it will wear off as I get older. But I'm a . . . a telepath—" How strange it felt to say it! How strange that Dyan should be the first one he told! "And it feels . . . wrong," he said, stumbling from phrase to phrase.

Dyan lifted his glass and drank the last in it before he answered. "Maybe you're right. Life can be complicated enough for a telepath, without that, too. Some day you'll know what you want, and then will be the time to trust your instincts and your needs." He fell silent, brooding, and Regis found himself wondering what bitter memories lay behind the pensive look. Finally Dyan said, "You'd probably do well, then, to keep clear of such places and wait until, if the Gods are good to you, someone you can love helps you discover that part of your life." He sighed heavily and said, "If you can. You may discover needs even more imperative than those instincts. It's always a difficult balance for a telepath. There are physical needs. And there are needs which can be even stronger. Emotional needs. And that's a balance which can tear any of us to pieces." Regis had the curious feeling that Dyan was not really talking to him at all, but to himself.

Abruptly, Dyan set down his empty wineglass and rose. He said, "But one pleasure which has no danger attached is to watch young people grow in wisdom, cousin. I hope to see much of that growth in you this winter, and I'll watch with interest. Meanwhile, keep this in mind: I know the city well and it would be a pleasure to show you anything you wish to see." He laughed aloud suddenly and said, "And believe me, cousin, such instruction would at least leave no bruises."

He strode quickly away. Regis, collecting his cloak from

the seat, felt more puzzled than ever, feeling there was something else Dyan had wanted to say.

He had to pass the table crowded with cadets, lounging over cider or beer; he noticed that they were staring at him in no friendly fashion. None of them offered him even the bare civility of a formal greeting. He set his chin and turned his back on them. He heard one say in a low tone, "Catamite!"

Regis felt a flood of intense anger washing over him. He wanted to turn on the boy and beat him to a crimson pulp. Then he set his jaw, disciplining himself to walk away and pretend he had not heard. *If you listen to dogs barking, you'll go deaf and never learn much.*

He remembered various insults he had pretended not to hear, mostly to the intent that the Comyn hung together, that he had had special favors because he was a Comyn heir. But this one was new. He recalled the taunt Danilo had flung at him the night before his expulsion. Dani was a *cristoforo* and to him it was more than an insult.

He knew Dyan would have nothing but scorn for such gossip. He never made any secret of his tastes. Yet Regis felt oddly protective toward his kinsman, having sensed his bitterness. He felt a strange wish to defend him.

It occurred to him again, with frustration too new for him to realize it was a commonplace among telepaths, that there were times when *laran* was absolutely no help at all in personal relationships.

The season ended. The cadets were dismissed to their homes and Regis moved into the Hastur apartments in Comyn Castle. He appreciated the peace and quiet and felt a certain pleasure in being able to sleep as late as he pleased in the morning. And the Hastur cooks were certainly better than those in the Guards mess. The prolonged austerity, though, first in Nevarsin, then in the barracks, had made him almost guilty about this kind of luxury. He couldn't appreciate it as he wanted to.

One morning he was at breakfast with his grandfather when Lord Hastur said abruptly, "You're not looking like yourself. Is something wrong?"

Regis thought that his grandfather had seen so little of him that he would have no idea what he usually looked like. He was too polite to say it, of course, so answered, "Bored, maybe. Not getting enough exercise."

It disturbed him that he could not help picking up his grandfather's thoughts: *It's wrong to keep the boy hanging about here when I've so little time to spend with him.*

Hastur said aloud, "I'm afraid I've been too busy to notice, my boy. I'm very sorry. Would you like to return to Castle Hastur, or go somewhere else?"

"I wasn't complaining, sir. But I feel I'm no use to you. When you asked me to stay for the winter, I thought there was something I could do to help you."

"I wish you could. Unfortunately, you haven't the experience to be a great deal of help yet," Hastur said, but could not conceal a faint flicker of satisfaction. *He's beginning to be interested.* "Some time this winter you might attend a few sessions of the *Cortes* and find out about the problems we're facing. I'll get you a pass. Or you could ride to Edelweiss, spend a few days with Javanne."

Regis shrugged. He found Edelweiss dull. There was no hunting except for rabbits and squirrels, the rain kept them indoors much of the time, and he and Javanne were too far apart in age and too unlike in personality to find much pleasure in each other's company.

"I know it's not very exciting there either," Hastur said, almost apologizing, "but she is your sister, and we do not have so many kinfolk that we can neglect one another. If you want hunting, you know, you are free to go to Armida at any time. Lew is away and Kennard too ill to travel, but you can go there and take a friend."

But the only friend he'd made in the cadets, Regis thought, was sent home in disgrace. "Kennard is ill, sir? What's wrong?"

Danvan sighed. "This climate doesn't agree with him. He grows more crippled every year. He'll be better when the rains—" He broke off as a servant came in with a message. "Already? Yes, I have to go and talk with a trade delegation from the Dry Towns," he said with weary resignation, laying down his napkin. He excused himself to Regis, adding, "Let me know your plans, lad, and I'll arrange for escort."

Left alone, Regis poured himself another cup of Terran coffee, one of the few luxuries the austere old man allowed himself, and thought it over. The duty visit to Javanne could not, of course, be avoided. A visit to Armida could await

Lew's return; he could hardly be intending to spend the winter at Aldaran.

If Kennard was ill, courtesy demanded that Regis pay him a visit in his suite, but for some unknown reason he was unwilling to face the Alton lord. He did not know why. Kennard had always been kind to him. After a time he focused it down to resentment: he stood by and watched Danilo's disgrace and didn't say a word. Lew wanted to interfere, but he couldn't. Kennard didn't care.

And Kennard was one of the most powerful telepaths in the Comyn. Regis, feeling this much resentment, was reluctant to face him. Kennard would know immediately how he felt.

He knew, rationally, that he should go to Kennard at once, if only to tell him about his newly developing *laran*. There were training techniques to help him master and control his new facilities. But in the cadets it had not seemed to matter, and the proper time to speak to Lew about it had never come till too late. Dyan had seemed to take it for granted that he already had what training he needed. Kennard was the obvious one to tell. He admonished himself sternly that he should go at once, now, today.

But he was still reluctant to face him. He decided to go to Javanne for a few days first. By that time perhaps Lew would be back.

A few days later he rode north, the weight of it still on his mind. Syrtis lay half a mile from the northward road and, on an impulse, he told his escort to wait in a nearby village. He rode alone toward Syrtis.

It lay at the far end of a long valley, leading downward to the lake country around Mariposa. It was a clear autumn day, with ripening fruit trees hanging low under their thick harvest and small animals making scurrying noises in the dry brushwood at the side of the road. The sounds and smells made Regis feel well content as he rode along, but as he came down toward the farm his spirits sank. He had been thinking Danilo well off, to be coming home to this pleasant country, but he had not realized how poor the place was. The main house was small, one wing falling into such disrepair that it could hardly have been safe for human habitation. The sparse outbuildings showed how few men must live on the place. The old moat had been drained, ditched and put to kitchen-gardens with neat rows of vegetables and pot-herbs.

An old, bent servant told him, touching his breast in rustic courtesy, that the master was just returning from the hunt. Regis suspected that in a place like this rabbit would be more plentiful on the table than butcher's meat.

A tall, aging man in a once-fine threadbare cloak rode slowly toward him. He was moustached and bearded, and sat his horse with the erect competence of an old soldier. A fine hawk sat, hooded, on his saddle.

"Greetings," he said in a deep voice. "We see few travelers at Syrtis. How may I serve you?"

Regis alighted from his horse, making him a courteous bow. "Dom Felix Syrtis? Regis-Rafael Hastur, *para servirte.*"

"My house and I are at your service, Lord Regis. Let me see to your mount. Old Mauris is half blind; I'd not trust him with such a fine animal. Will you come with me?"

Leading his horse, Regis followed the old man toward a stone barn in better repair than most of the outbuildings, being weathertight and newly roofed. At the far end was a screened-off enclosure; nearer were open box stalls, and Regis tethered his horse in the closest while Dom Felix took a cluster of small birds from the hook at his saddle and unsaddled his mount. Regis saw Danilo's beautiful black gelding in another stall, the old bony hunter Dom Felix had been riding and two good, but aging mares. The other stalls were empty, except for a couple of clumsy plowhorses and a milk animal or two. This was abysmal poverty indeed for a family of noble blood and Regis was ashamed to witness it. He remembered that Danilo had hardly had a whole shirt to his back when he joined the cadets.

Dom Felix was looking at Regis' black mare with the kind of love that men of his type bestowed openly only on their horses and hawks. "A fine mount, *vai dom.* Armida-bred, no doubt? I know that pedigree."

"True. A birthday gift from Lord Kennard, before I went to Nevarsin."

"Might I ask her name, Lord Regis?"

"Melisande," Regis told him, and the old man stroked the velvet muzzle tenderly. Regis nodded to Danilo's fine black. "And there is another of the same breed; they might well be foals of the same dam."

"Aye," said Dom Felix curtly, "Lord Alton does not withdraw a gift, however unworthy given." He shut his mouth with a snap and Regis' heart sank; it promised ill for his mission. Dom Felix turned away to see to the hawk, and Regis asked politely, "Had you good hunting, sir?"

"Indifferent," said Dom Felix shortly, taking the hawk from his saddle and carrying her to the enclosure at the far end. "No, my lord, you will frighten a haggard I have here. Be pleased to remain where you are."

Rebuked, Regis kept his distance. When the old man returned, he complimented him on a well-trained bird.

"It is my life's work, Lord Regis. I was hawk-master to your grandsire, when your father was a lad."

Regis raised a mental eyebrow, but in these disturbed days it was not unusual to find a former courtier out of favor.

"How is it that you honor my house, Dom Regis?"

"I came to see your son Danilo."

The old man's tight-pressed lips almost disappeared between moustache and chin. Finally he said, "My lord, by your uniform you know of my son's disgrace. I beg you, leave him in peace. Whatever his crime, he has paid more than you can know."

Regis said, in shock, "No! I am his friend!"

Now the pent-up hostility exploded.

"The friendship of a Comyn lord is as the sweetness of a beehive: it bears a deadly sting! I have lost one son already to the love of a Hastur lord; must I lose the last child of my old age as well?"

Regis spoke gently. "All my life, Dom Felix, I have heard nothing but good of the man who gave his life in a vain attempt to shield my father. Do you think me evil enough to wish harm on the house of such a man? Whatever your grudge against my forefathers, sir, you have no quarrel with me. If Danilo has, he must tell me himself. I had not known your son was so young he must seek a parent's leave to welcome a guest."

A faint, unlovely flush spread slowly over the bearded face. Regis realized too late that he had been impertinent. It came as no surprise that Danilo should be under his father's displeasure, yet he had spoken the truth: by the law of the Domains, Danilo was a responsible adult.

"My son is in the orchard, Dom Regis. May I send to summon him? We have but few servants to bear messages."

"I'll walk down, if I may."

"Forgive me, then, if I do not accompany you, since you

say your business is with my son. I must take these birds to my kitchen folk. The path will lead you to the orchard."

Regis walked down the narrow lane the old man pointed out. At its end the path opened out to an orchard of apple and pear trees. The fruit, fully ripe, hung glistening among the darkening leaves. Danilo was there at the far end of the grove, his back to Regis, stooping to rake up some mulch around the tree roots. He was stripped to the waist, his feet thrust into wooden clogs. A damp sweat-rag was tied around his forehead, his dark hair in disorder above it.

The smell of apples was sweet and winy. Danilo slowly straightened his back, picked up a windfall and thoughtfully bit into it. Regis stood watching him, unseen, for a moment. He looked tired, preoccupied and, if not content, at least lulled by hard physical work and the warm sun into a momentary peace.

"Dani?" Regis said at last, and the boy, startled, dropped the apple and stumbled over his rake as he turned. Regis wondered what to say.

Danilo took a step toward him. "What do *you* want?"

"I was on the road to my sister's house; I stopped to pay my respects to your father and to see how you did."

He saw Danilo visibly struggling between the impulse to fling the polite gesture back into his face—what more had he to lose?—and the lifelong habit of hospitality. At last he said, "My house and I are at your service, Lord Regis." His politeness was exaggerated almost to a caricature. "What is my lord's will?"

Regis said, "I want to talk to you."

"As you see, my lord, I am very much occupied. But I am entirely at your bidding."

Regis ignored the irony and took him at his word.

"Come here, then, and sit down," he said, taking his seat on a fallen log, felled so long ago that it was covered with gray lichen. Silently Danilo obeyed, keeping as far away as the dimensions of the log allowed.

Regis said after a moment, "I want you to know one thing: I have no idea why you were thrown out of the Guards, or rather, I only know what I heard that day. But from the way everyone acted, you'd think I left you to take the blame for something I myself did. Why? What did I do?"

"You know—" Danilo broke off, kicking a windfall apple

with the point of his clog. It broke with a rotten, slushy *clunk*. "It's over. Whatever I did to offend you, I've paid."

Then for a moment the rapport, the awareness Danilo had wakened in him, flared again between them. He could feel Danilo's despair and grief as if it were his own. He said, harsh with the pain of it, "Danilo Syrtis, speak your grudge and let me avow or deny it! I tried not to think ill of you even in disgrace! But you called me foul names when I meant you nothing but kindness, and if you have spread lies about me or my kinsmen, then you deserve everything they have done to you, and you still have a score to settle with me!" Without realizing it, he had sprung to his feet, his hand going to the hilt of his sword.

Danilo stood defiant. His gray eyes, gleaming like molten metal beneath dark brows, blazed with anger and sorrow. "*Dom* Regis, I beg you, leave me in peace! Isn't it enough that I am here, my hopes gone, my father shamed forever—I might as well be dead!" he cried out desperately, his words tumbling over themselves. "Grudge, Regis? No, no, none against you, you showed me nothing but kindness, but you were one of them, one of those, those—" He stopped again, his voice tight with the effort not to cry. At last he cried out passionately, "Regis Hastur, as the Gods live, my conscience is clear and your Lord of Light and the God of the *cristoforos* may judge between the Sons of Hastur and me!"

Almost without volition, Regis drew his sword. Danilo, startled, took a step backward in fear; then he straightened and stiffened his mouth. "Do you punish blasphemy so quickly, lord? I am unarmed, but if my offense merits death, then kill me now where I stand! My life is no good to me!"

Shocked, Regis lowered the point of the sword. "Kill you, Dani?" he said in horror. "God forbid! It never crossed my mind! I wished ... Dani, lay your hand on the hilt of my sword."

Confused, startled into obedience, Danilo put a tentative hand on the hilt. Regis gripped hand and hilt together in his own fingers.

"Son of Hastur who is the Son of Aldones who is the Lord of Light! May this hand and this sword pierce my heart and my honor, Danilo, if I had part or knowledge in your disgrace, or if anything you say now shall be used to work you harm!" Again, from the hand-touch, he felt that odd little shock running up his arm, blurring his own thoughts, felt Danilo's sobs tight in his own throat.

Danilo said on a drawn breath, "No Hastur would forswear that oath!"

"No Hastur would forswear his naked word," Regis retorted proudly, "but if it took an oath to convince you, an oath you have." He sheathed the sword.

"Now tell me what happened, Dani. Was the charge a lie, then?"

Danilo was still visibly dazed. "The night I came in—it had been raining. You woke, you *knew*—"

"I knew only that you were in pain, Dani. No more. I asked if I could help, but you drove me away." The pain and shock he had felt that night returned to him in full force and he felt his heart pounding again with the agony of it, as he had done when Danilo thrust him away.

Danilo said, "You are a telepath. I thought—"

"A very rudimentary one, Danilo," said Regis, trying to steady his voice. "I sensed only that you were unhappy, in pain. I didn't know why and you would not tell me."

"Why should you care?"

Regis put out his hand, slowly closed it around Danilo's wrist. "I am Hastur and Comyn. It touches the honor of my clan and my caste that anyone should have cause to speak ill of us. With false slanders we can deal, but with truth, we can only try to right the wrong. We Comyn can be mistaken." Dimly, at the back of his mind, he realized he had said "We Comyn" for the first time. "More," he said, and smiled fleetingly, "I like your father, Dani. He was willing to anger a Hastur in order to have you left in peace."

Danilo stood nervously locking and unlocking his hands. He said, "The charge is true. I drew my dagger on Lord Dyan. I only wish I had cut his throat while I was about it; whatever they did to me, the world would be a cleaner place."

Regis stared, disbelieving. *"Zandru!* Dani—"

"I know, in days past, the men who touched Comyn lord in irreverence would have been torn on hooks. In those days, perhaps, Comyn were worth reverence—"

"Leave that," Regis said sharply. "Dani, I am heir to Hastur, but even I could not draw steel on an officer without disgrace. Even if the officer I struck were no Comyn lord but young Hjalmar, whose mother is a harlot of the streets."

Danilo stood fighting for control. "If I struck young Hjalmar, Regis, then I would have deserved my punishment; he is an honorable man. It was not as my officer I drew on Lord Dyan. He had forfeited all claim to obedience or respect."

"Is that for you to judge?"

"In those circumstances . . ." Danilo swallowed. "Could I respect and obey a man who had so far forgotten himself as to try to make me his—" He used a *cahuenga* word Regis did not know, only that it was unspeakably obscene. But he was still in rapport with Danilo, so there was no scrap of doubt about his meaning. Regis went white. He literally could not speak under the shock of it.

"At first I thought he was joking," Danilo said, almost stammering. "I do not like such jests—I am a *cristoforo*—but I gave him some similar joke for an answer and thought that was the end of it, for if he meant the jest in seriousness, then I had given him his answer without offense. Then he made himself clearer and grew angry when I answered him no, and swore he could force me to it. I don't know what he did to me, Regis, he did something with his mind, so that wherever I was, alone or with others, I *felt* him touching me, heard his . . . his foul whispers, that awful, mocking laugh of his. He pursued me, he seemed to be inside my mind all the time. All the time. I thought he meant to drive me out of my mind! I had thought . . . a telepath could not inflict pain. . . . I can't stand it even to be *around* anyone who's really unhappy, but he took some awful, hateful kind of pleasure in it." Danilo sobbed suddenly. "I went to him, then, I begged him to let me be! Regis, I am no gutter-brat, my family has served the Hasturs honorably for years, but if I were a whore's foundling and he the king on his throne, he would have had no right to use me so shamefully!" Danilo broke down again and sobbed. "And then . . . and then he said I knew perfectly well how I could be free of him. He *laughed* at me, that awful, hideous laugh. And then I had my dagger out, I hardly know how I came to draw it, or what I meant to do with it, kill myself maybe. . . ." Danilo put his hands over his face. "You know the rest," he said through them.

Regis could hardly draw breath. "Zandru send him scorpion whips! Dani, why didn't you lay a charge and claim immunity? He is subject to the laws of Comyn too, and a telepath who misuses his *laran* that way . . ."

Danilo gave a weary little shrug. It said more than words.

Regis felt wholly numbed by the revelation. How could he ever face Dyan again, knowing this?

I knew it wasn't true what they said of you, Regis. But you were Comyn too, and Dyan showed you so much favor, and that last night, when you touched me, I was afraid . . .

Regis looked up, outraged, then realized Danilo had not spoken at all. They were deeply in rapport; he felt the other boy's thoughts. He sat back down on the log, feeling that his legs were unable to hold him upright.

"I touched you . . . only to quiet you." he said at last.

"I know that now. What good would it do to say I am sorry for that, Regis? It was a shameful thing to say."

"It is no wonder you cannot believe in honor or decency from my kin. But it is for us to prove it to you. All the more since you are one of us. Danilo, how long have you had *laran*?"

"I? *Laran*? I, Lord Regis?"

"Didn't you know? How long have you been able to read thoughts?"

"That? Why, all my life, it seems. Since I was twelve or so. Is *that* . . ."

"Don't you know what it means, if you have one of the Comyn gifts? You do, you know. Telepaths aren't uncommon, but you opened up my own gift, even after Lew Alton failed." With a flood of emotion, he thought, *you brought me my heritage.* "I think you're what they call a catalyst telepath. That's very rare and a precious gift." He forebore to say it was an Ardais gift. He doubted if Danilo would appreciate that information just now. "Have you told anyone else?"

"How could I, when I didn't know myself? I thought everyone could read thoughts."

"No, it's rarer than that. It means you too are Comyn, Dani."

"Are you saying my parentage is—"

"Zandru's hells, no! But your family is noble, it may well be that your mother had Comyn kinsmen, Comyn blood, even generations ago. With full *laran*, though, it means you yourself are eligible for Comyn Council, that you should be trained to use these gifts, sealed to Comyn." He saw revulsion on Danilo's face and said quickly, "Think. It means you are Lord Dyan's equal. He can be held accountable for having misused you."

Regis blessed the impulse that had brought him here. Alone, his mind burdened with the brooding, hypersensitive nature of the untrained telepath, under his father's grim displeasure . . . Danilo might have killed himself after all.

"I won't, though," Danilo said aloud. Regis realized they had slid into rapport again. He reached out to touch Danilo, remembered and didn't. To conceal the move he bent and picked up a windfall apple. Danilo got to his feet and began putting on his shirt. Regis finished the apple and dropped the core into a pile of mulch.

"Dani, I am expected to sleep tonight at my sister's house. But I give my word: you shall be vindicated. Meanwhile, is there anything else I can do for you?"

"Yes, Regis! Yes! Tell my father the disgrace and dishonor were not mine! He asked no questions and spoke no word of reproach, but no man in our family has ever been dishonored. I can bear anything but his belief that I lied to him!"

"I promise you he shall know the full—no." Regis broke off suddenly. "Isn't that why you dared not tell him yourself? He would kill—" He saw that he had, in truth, reached the heart of Danilo's fear.

"He would challenge Dyan," Danilo said haltingly, "and though he looks strong he is an old man and his heart is far from sound. If he knew the truth—I *wanted* to tell him everything, but I would rather have him . . . despise me . . . than ruin himself."

"Well, I shall try to clear your name with your father without endangering him. But for yourself, Dani? We owe you something for the injury."

"You owe me nothing, Regis. If my name is clean before my kinsmen, I am content."

"Still, the honor of Comyn demands we right this injustice. If there is rot at our heart, well, it must be cleansed." At this moment, filled with righteous anger, he was ready to fling himself against a whole regiment of unjust men who abused their powers. If the older men in Comyn were corrupt or power-mad, and the younger ones idle, then boys would have to set it right!

Danilo dropped to one knee. He held out his hands, his voice breaking. "There is a life between us. My brother died to shield your father. As for me, I ask no more than to give my life in the service of Hastur. Take my sword and my oath, Lord Regis. By the hand I place on your sword, I pledge my life."

Startled, deeply moved, Regis drew his sword again, held out the hilt to Danilo. Their hands met on the hilt again as Regis, stumbling on the ritual words, trying to recall them one by one, said, "Danilo-Felix Syrtis, be from this day paxman and shield-arm to me . . . and this sword strike me if I be not just lord and shield to you. . . ." He bit his lip, fighting to remember what came next. Finally he said, "The Gods witness it, and the holy things at Hali." It seemed there was something else, but at least their intention was clear, he thought. He slid the sword back into its sheath, raised Danilo to his feet and shyly kissed him on either cheek. He saw tears on Danilo's eyelids and knew that his own were not wholly dry.

He said, trying to lighten the moment, "Now you've only had formally what we both knew all along, *bredu*." He heard himself say the word with a little shock of amazement, but knew he meant it as he had never meant anything before.

Danilo said, trying to steady his voice, "I should have . . . offered you my sword. I'm not wearing one, but here—"

That was what had been missing in the ritual. Regis started to say that it did not matter, but without it there was something wanting. He looked at the dagger Danilo held out hilt-first to him. Regis drew his own, laid it hilt-to-blade along the other before giving it to Danilo, saying quietly, "Bear this, then, in my service."

Danilo laid his lips to the blade for a moment, saying, "In your service alone I bear it," and put it into his own sheath.

Regis thrust Danilo's knife into the scabbard at his waist. It did not quite fit, but it would do. He said, "You must remain here until I send for you. It will not be long, I promise, but I have to think what to do."

He did not say goodbye. It was not necessary. He turned and walked back along the lane. As he went into the barn to untie his horse, Dom Felix came slowly toward him.

"Lord Regis, may I offer you some refreshment?"

Regis said pleasantly, "I thank you, but grudged hospitality has a bitter taste. Yet it is my pleasure to assure you, on the word of a Hastur"—he touched his hand briefly to sword-hilt—"you may be proud of your son, Dom Felix. His dishonor should be your pride."

The old man frowned. "You speak riddles, *vai dom*."

"Sir, you were hawk-master to my grandsire, yet I have not seen you at court in my lifetime. To Danilo a choice even more bitter was given: to win favor by dishonorable means, or to keep his own honor at the price of apparent disgrace. In brief, sir, your son offended the pride of a man who has power but none of the honor which gives power its dignity. And this man revenged himself."

The old man's brow furrowed as he slowly puzzled out what Regis was saying. "If the charge was unjust, an act of private revenge, why did my son not tell me?"

"Because, Dom Felix, Dani feared you would ruin yourself to avenge him." He added quickly, seeing a thousand questions forming in the old man's eyes, "I promised Danilo I would tell you no more than this. But will you accept the word of a Hastur that he is blameless?"

Light broke in the troubled face. "I bless you for coming and I beg you to pardon my rough words, Lord Regis. I am no courtier. But I am grateful."

"And loyal to your son," Regis said. "Have no doubt, Dom Felix, he is worthy of it."

"Will you not honor my house, Lord Regis?" This time the offer was heartfelt, and Regis smiled. "I regret that I cannot, sir, I am expected elsewhere. Danilo has shown me your hospitality; you grow the finest apples I have tasted in a long time. And I give you my word that one day it shall be my pleasure to show honor to the father of my friend. Meanwhile, I beg you to be reconciled to your son."

"You may be sure of it, Lord Regis." He stood staring after Regis as the boy mounted and rode away, and Regis could sense his confusion and gratitude. As he rode slowly down the hill to rejoin his bodyguard, he realized what he had, in substance, pledged himself to do: to restore Danilo's good name and make certain that Dyan could not again misuse power this way. What it meant was that he, who had once sworn to renounce the Comyn, now had to reform it from inside out, single-handedly, before he could enjoy his own freedom.

Chapter TWELVE

(Lew Alton's narrative)

The hills rise beyond the Kadarin, leading away into the mountains, into the unknown country where the law of the Comyn does not run. In my present state, as soon as I had forded the Kadarin I felt that a weight had been lifted from my shoulders.

In this part of the world, five days' ride north of Thendara, my safe-conducts meant nothing. We slept at night in tents, with a watch set. It was a barren country, long deserted. Only perhaps three or four times in a day's ride did we see some small village, half a dozen poor houses clustered in a clearing, or some small-holding where a hardy farmer wrested a bare living from the stony and perpendicular forest. There were so few travelers here that the children came out to watch us as we passed.

The roads got worse and worse as we went further into the hills, degenerating at times into mere goat-tracks and trails. There are not many good roads on Darkover. My father, who lived on Terra for many years, has told me about the good roads there, but added that there was no way to bring that system here. For roads you needed slave labor or immense numbers of men willing to work for the barest subsistence, or else heavy machinery. And there have never been slaves on Darkover, not even slaves to machinery.

It was, I thought, small wonder that the Terrans were reluctant to move their spaceport into these hills again.

I was the more surprised when, on the ninth day of traveling, we came on to a wide road, well-surfaced and capable of handling wheeled carts and several men riding abreast. My father had also told me that when he last visited the hills

near Aldaran, Caer Donn had been little more than a substantial village. Reports had reached him that it was now a
good-sized city. But this did not diminish my astonishment
when, coming to the top of one of the higher hills, we saw it
spread out below us in the valley and along the lower slopes
of the next mountain.

It was a clear day, and we could see a long distance. Deep
in the lowest part of the valley, where the ground was most
even, there was a great fenced-in area, abnormally smooth-
surfaced, and even from here I could see the runways and
the landing strips. This, I thought, must be the old Terran
spaceport, now converted to a landing field for their aircraft
and the small rockets which brought messages from Thendara and Port Chicago. There was a similar small landing
field near Arilinn. Beyond the airfield lay the city, and as my
escort drew to a halt behind me, I heard the men murmuring
about it.

"There was no city here when I was a lad! How could it
grow so fast?"

"It's like the city which grew up overnight in the old fairy
tale!"

I told them a little of what Father had said, about prefab-
ricated construction. Such cities were not built to stand for
ages, but could be quickly constructed. They scowled skeptically and one of them said, "I'd hate to be rude about the
Commander, sir, but he must have been telling you fairy
tales. Even on Terra human hands can't build so quick."

I laughed. "He also told me of a hot planet where the na-
tives did not believe there was such a thing as snow, and accused him of tale-telling when he spoke of mountains which
bore ice all year."

Another pointed. "Castle Aldaran?"

There was nothing else it could have been, unless we were
unimaginably astray: an ancient keep, a fortress of craggy
weathered stone. This was the stronghold of the renegade
Domain, exiled centuries ago from Comyn—no man alive
now knew why. Yet they were the ancient Seventh Domain,
of the ancient kin of Hastur and Cassilda.

I felt curiously mingled eagerness and reluctance, as if taking some irrevocable step. Once again the curiously unfocused time-sense of the Altons thrust fingers of dread at me.
What was waiting for me in that old stone fortress lying at
the far end of the valley of Caer Donn?

With a scowl I brought myself back to the present. It needed no great precognition to sense that in a completely strange part of the world I might meet strangers and that some of them would have a lasting effect on my life. I told myself that crossing that valley, stepping through the gates of Castle Aldaran, was *not* some great and irrevocable division in my life which would cut me off from my past and all my kindred. I was here at my father's bidding, an obedient son, disloyal only in thought and will.

I struggled to get myself back in focus. "Well, we might as well try to reach it while we still have some daylight," I said, and started down the excellent road.

The ride across Caer Donn was in a strange way dream-like. I had chosen to travel simply, without the complicated escort of an ambassador, treating this as the family visit it purported to be, and I attracted no particular attention. In a way the city was like myself, I thought, outwardly all Darkovan, but with a subliminal difference somewhere, something that did not quite belong. For all these years I had been content to accept myself as Darkovan; now, looking at the old Terran port as I had never looked at the familiar one at Thendara, I thought that this too was my heritage ... if I had courage to take it.

I was in a curious mood, feeling a trifle fey, as if, without knowing what shape or form it would take, I could smell a wind that bore my fate.

There were guards at the gates of Aldaran, mountain men, and for the first time I gave my full name, not the one I bore as my father's *nedestro* heir, but the name given before either father or mother had cause to suspect anyone could doubt my legitimacy. "I am Lewis-Kennard Lanart-Montray Alton y Aldaran, son of Kennard, Lord Alton, and Elaine Montray-Aldaran. I have come as envoy of my father, and I ask a kinsman's welcome of Kermiac, Lord Aldaran."

The guards bowed and one of them, some kind of major-domo or steward, said, "Enter, *dom*, you are welcome and you honor the house of Aldaran. In his name I extend you welcome, until you hear it from his own lips." My escort was taken away to be housed elsewhere while I was led to a spacious room high in one of the far wings of the castle; my saddle bags were brought and servants sent to me when they found I traveled with no valet. In general they established me in luxury. After a while the steward returned.

"My lord, Kermiac of Aldaran is at dinner and asks, if you are not too weary from travel, that you join him in the hall. If you are trail-wearied, he bids you dine here and rest well, but he bade me say he was eager to welcome his sister's grandson."

I said I would join him with pleasure. At that moment I was not capable of feeling fatigue; the fey mood of excitement was still on me. I washed off the dust of travel and dressed in my best, a fine tunic of crimson-dyed leather with breeches to match, low velvet boots, a dress cape lined with fur—not vanity, this, but to show honor to my unknown kinsman.

Dusk was falling when the servant returned to conduct me to the great dining hall. Expecting dim torchlight, I was struck amazed by the daylight flood of brilliance. Arc-light, I thought, blinking, arc-light such as the Terrans use in their Trade City. It seemed strange to go at night into a room flooded by such noonday brilliance, strange and disorienting, yet I was glad, for it allowed me to see clearly the faces in the great hall. Evidently, despite his use of the newfangled lights, Kermiac kept to the old ways, for the lower part of his hall was crammed with a motley conglomeration of faces, Guardsmen, servants, mountain people, rich and poor, even some Terrans and a *cristoforo* monk or two in their drab robes.

The servant led me toward the high table at the far end where the nobles sat. At first they were only a blur of faces: a tall man, lean and wolfish, with a great shock of fair hair; a pretty, red-haired girl in a blue dress; a small boy about Marius' age; and at their center, an aging man with a dark reddish beard, old to decrepitude but still straight-backed and keen-eyed. He bent his eyes on me, studying my face intently. This, I knew, must be Kermiac, Lord Aldaran, my kinsman. He wore plain clothes, of a simple cut like those the Terrans wore, and I felt briefly ashamed of my barbarian finery.

He rose and came down from the dais to greet me. His voice, thinned with age, was still strong.

"Welcome, kinsman." He held out his arms and gave me a kinsman's embrace, his thin dry lips pressing each of my cheeks in turn. He held my shoulders between his hands for a moment. "It warms my heart to see your face at last, Elaine's son. We hear tidings in the Hellers here, even of the *Hali'imyn*." He used the ancient mountain word, but without offense. "Come, you must be weary and hungry after this long journey. I am glad you felt able to join us. Come and sit beside me, nephew."

He led me to a place of honor at his side. Servants brought us food. In the Domains the choicest food is served a guest without asking his preference, so that he need not in courtesy choose the simplest; here they made much of asking whether I would have meat, game-bird or fish, whether I would drink the white mountain wine or the red wine of the valleys. It was all cooked well and served to perfection, and I did it justice after days of trail food.

"So, nephew," he said at last, when I had appeased my hunger and was sipping a glass of white wine and nibbling at some strange and delicious sweets, "I have heard you are tower-trained, a telepath. Here in the mountains it's believed that men tower-trained are half eunuch, but I can see you are a man; you have the look of a soldier. Are you one of their Guardsmen?"

"I have been a captain for three years."

He nodded. "There is peace in the mountains now, although the Dry-Towners get ideas now and then. Yet I can respect a soldier; in my youth I had to keep Caer Donn by force of arms."

I said, "In the Domains it is not known that Caer Donn is so great a city."

He shrugged. "Largely of Terran building. They are good neighbors, or we find them so. Is it otherwise in Thendara?"

I was not yet ready to discuss my feelings about the Terrans, but to my relief he did not pursue that topic. He was studying my face in profile.

"You are not much like your father, nephew. Yet I see nothing of Elaine in you, either."

"It is my brother Marius who is said to have my mother's face and her eyes."

"I have never seen him. I last saw your father twelve years ago, when he brought Elaine's body here to rest among her kin. I asked then for the privilege of fostering her sons, but Kennard chose to rear you in his own house."

I had never known that. I had been told nothing of my mother's people. I was not even sure what degree of kin I was to the old man. I said something of this to him, and he nodded.

"Kennard has had no easy life," Kermiac said. "I cannot

blame him that he never wanted to look back. But if he
chose to tell you nothing of your mother's kin, he cannot
take offense that I tell you now in my own fashion. Years
ago, when the Terrans were mostly stationed at Caer Donn
and the ground had just been broken for the fine building at
Thendara—I hear it has been finished in this winter past—
years ago, then, when I was not much more than a boy, my
sister Mariel chose to marry a Terran, Wade Montray. She
dwelt with him many years on Terra. I have heard the marriage was not a happy one and they separated, after she had
borne him two children. Mariel chose to remain with her
daughter Elaine on Terra; Wade Montray came with his son
Larry, whom we called Lerrys, back to Darkover. And now
you may see how the hand of fate works, for Larry Montray
and your father, Kennard, met as boys and swore friendship.
I am no great believer in predestination or a fate foretold,
but so it came about that Larry Montray remained on
Darkover to be fostered at Armida and your father was sent
back to Terra, to be fostered as Wade Montray's son, in the
hope that these two lads would build again the old bridge between Terra and Darkover. And there, of course, your father
met Montray's daughter, who was also the daughter of my
sister Mariel. Well, to make a long tale short, Kennard returned to Darkover, was given in marriage to a woman of
the Domains, who bore him no child, served in Arilinn
Tower—some of this you must have been told. But he bore
the memory of Elaine, it seems, ever in his heart, and at last
sought her in marriage. As her nearest kinsman, it was I who
gave consent. I have always felt such marriages are fortu-
nate, and children of mixed blood the closest road to friendship between people of different world. I had no idea, then,
that your Comyn kinsmen would not bless the marriage as I
had done, and rejoice in it."

All the more wrong of the Comyn, I thought, since it was
by their doing that my father had first gone to Terra. Well, it
was all of a piece with their doings since. And another score
I bore against them.

Yet my father stood with them!

Kermiac concluded, "When it was clear they would not accept you, I offered to Kennard that you should be fostered
here, honored at least as Elaine's son if not as his. He was
certain he could force them, at last, to accept you. He must
have succeeded, then?"

"After a fashion," I said slowly. "I am his heir." I did not want to discuss the costs of that with him. Not yet.

The steward had been trying to attract Lord Kermiac's attention; he saw it and gave a signal for the tables to be cleared. As the great crowd who dined at his table began to disperse, he led me into a small sitting room, dimly lighted, a pleasant room with an open fireplace. He said, "I am old, and old men tire quickly, nephew. But before I go to rest, I want you to know your kinsmen. Nephew, your cousin, my son Beltran."

To this day, even after all that came later, I still remember how I felt when I first looked on my cousin. I knew at last what blood had shaped me such a changeling among the Comyn. In face and feature we might have been brothers; I have known twins who were less like. Beltran held out his hand; drew it back and said, "Sorry, I have heard that telepaths don't like touching strangers."

"I won't refuse a kinsman my hand," I said, and returned the clasp lightly. In the strange mood I was in the touch gave me a swift pattern of impressions: curiosity, enthusiasm, a disarming friendliness. Kermiac smiled at us as we stood close together and said, "I leave your cousin to you, Beltran. Lew, believe me, you are at home." He said good night and left us, and Beltran drew me toward the others. He said, "My father's foster-children and wards, cousin, and my friends. Come and meet them. So you're tower-trained? Are you a natural telepath as well?"

I nodded and he said, "Marjorie is our telepath." He drew forward the pretty, red-haired girl in blue whom I had noticed at the table. She smiled, looking directly into my eyes in the way mountain girls have. She said, "I am a telepath, yes, but untrained; so many of the old things have been forgotten here in the mountains. Perhaps you can tell us what you were taught at Arilinn, kinsman."

Her eyes were a strange color, a tint I had never seen before: gold-flecked amber, like some unknown animal. Her hair was almost red enough for the valley Comyn. I gave her my hand, as I had done with Beltran. It reminded me a little of the way the women at Arilinn had accepted me, simply as a human being, without fuss or flirtatiousness. I felt strangely reluctant to let her fingers go. I asked, "Are you a kinswoman?"

Beltran said, "Marjorie Scott, and her sister and brother,

too, are my father's wards. It's a long story, he may tell you some day if he will. Their mother was my own mother's foster-sister, so I call them, all three, sister and brother." He drew the others forward and presented them. Rafe Scott was a boy of eleven or twelve, not unlike my own brother Marius, with the same gold-flecked eyes. He looked at me shyly and did not speak. Thyra was a few years older than Marjorie, a slight, restless, sharp-featured woman, with the family eyes but a look of old Kermiac, too. She met my eyes but did not offer her hand. "This is a long and weary journey for a lowlander, kinsman."

"I had good weather and skilled escort for the mountains," I said, bowing to her as I would have done to a lady of the Domains. Her dark features looked amused, but she was friendly enough, and for a little we talked of weather and the mountain roads. After a time Beltran drew the conversation back.

"My father was greatly skilled in his youth and has taught all of us some of the skills of a matrix technician. Yet I am said to have but little natural talent for it. You have had the training, Lew, so tell me, which is the most important, talent or skill?"

I told him what I had been told myself. "Talent and skill are the right hand and the left; it is the will that rules both, and the will must be disciplined. Without talent, little skill can be learned; but talent alone is worth little without training."

"I am said to have the talent," said the girl Marjorie. "Uncle told me so, yet I have no skill, for by the time I was old enough to learn, he was old past teaching. And I am half-Terran. Could a Terran learn those skills, do you think?"

I smiled and said, "I too am part-Terran, yet I served at Arilinn—Marjorie?" I tried to speak her Terran name and she smiled at my stumbling formation of the syllables.

"*Marguerida*, if you like that better," she said softly in *cahuenga*. I shook my head. "As you speak it, it is rare and strange . . . and precious," I said, wanting to add, "like you."

Beltran curled his lip disdainfully and said, "So the Comyn actually let you, with your Terran blood, into their sacred towers? How very condescending of them! I'd have laughed in their faces and told them what they could do with their tower!"

"No, cousin, it wasn't like that," I said. "It was only in the towers that no one took thought of my Terran blood. Among the Comyn I was *nedestro*, bastard. In Arilinn, no one cared what I was, only what I could do."

"You're wasting your time, Beltran," said a quiet voice from near the fire. "I am sure he knows no more of history than any of the *Hali'imyn*, and his Terran blood has done him little good." I looked across to the bench at the other side of the fire and saw a tall thin man, silver-gilt hair standing awry all around his forehead. His face was shadowed, but it seemed to me for a moment that his eyes came glinting out of the darkness like a cat's eyes by torchlight. "No doubt he believes, like most of the valley-bred, that the Comyn fell straight from the arms of the Lord of Light, and has come to believe all their pretty romances and fairy tales. Lew, shall I teach you your own history?"

"Bob," said Marjorie, "no one questions your knowledge. But your manners are terrible!"

The man gave a short laugh. I could see his features now by firelight, narrow and hawklike, and as he gestured I could see that he had six fingers on either hand, like the Ardais and Aillard men. There was something terribly strange about his eyes, too. He unfolded his long legs, stood up and made me an ironic bow.

"Must I respect the chastity of your mind, *via dom*, as you respect that of your deluded sorceresses? Or have I leave to ravish you with some truths, in hope that they may bring forth the fruits of wisdom?"

I scowled at the mockery. "Who in hell are you?"

"In hell, I am no one at all," he said lightly. "On Darkover, I call myself Robert Raymon Kadarin, *s'dei par servu.*" On his lips the elegant *casta* words became a mockery. "I regret I cannot follow your custom and add a long string of names detailing my parentage for generations. I know no more of my parentage than you Comyn know of yours but, unlike you, I have not yet learned to make up the deficiency with a long string of make-believe gods and legendary figures!"

"Are you Terran?" I asked. His clothing looked it.

He shrugged. "I was never told. However, it's a true saying: only a race-horse or a Comyn lord is judged by his pedigree. I spent ten years in Terran Empire intelligence, though they wouldn't admit it now; they've put a price on my head because, like all governments who buy brains, they like to limit what the brains are used for. I found out, for instance," he added deliberately, "just what kind of game the Empire's been playing on Darkover and how the Comyn have been playing along with them. No, Beltran," he said, swinging around to face my cousin, "I'm going to tell him. He's the one we've been waiting for."

The harsh, disconnected way he spoke made me wonder if he was raving or drunk. "Just what do you mean, a game the Terrans are playing, with the Comyn to help?"

I had come here to find out if Aldaran was dangerously allied with Terra, to the danger of Comyn. Now this man Kadarin accused the Comyn of playing Terra's games. I said, "I don't know what in the hell you're talking about. It sounds like rubbish."

"Well, start with this," Kadarin said. "Do you know who the Darkovans are, where we came from? Did anyone ever tell you that we're the first and oldest of the Terran colonies? No, I thought you didn't know that. By rights we should be equal to any of the planetary governments that sit in the Empire Council, doing our part to make the laws of the Empire, as other colonies do. We should be part of the galactic civilization we live in. Instead, we're treated like a backward, uncivilized world, poor relations to be content with what crumbs of knowledge they're willing to dole out to us drop by drop, kept carefully apart from the mainstream of the Empire, allowed to go on living as barbarians!"

"Why? If this is true, why?"

"Because the Comyn want it that way," Kadarin said. "It suits their purposes. Don't you even *know* Darkover is a Terran colony? You said they mocked your Terran blood. Damn them, what do they think *they* are? Terrans, all of them."

"You're stark raving mad!"

"You'd like to think so. So would they. More flattering, isn't it, to think of your father's precious caste as being descended from gods and divinely appointed to rule all Darkover. Too bad! They're just Terrans, like all the rest of the Empire colonies!" He stopped pacing and stood, staring down at us from his great height, he was a full head taller than I am, and I am not small. "I tell you, I've seen the records on Terra, and in the Administrative Archives on the Coronis colony. The facts are buried there, or supposed to be buried, but anybody with a security clearance can get them quickly enough."

I demanded, "Where did you get all this *stuff?*" I could have used a much ruder word; out of deference to the women I used one meaning, literally, stable-sweepings.

He said, "Remarkable fertile stuff, stable-sweepings. Grows good crops. The facts are there. I have a gift for languages, like all telepaths—oh, yes, I am one, Dom Lewis. By the way, do you know you have a Terran name?"

"Surely not," I said. Lewis had been a given name among the Altons for centuries.

"I have stood on the island of Lewis on Terra itself," said the man Kadarin.

"Coincidence," I said. "Human tongues evolve the same syllables, having the same vocal mechanism."

"Your ignorance, Dom Lewis, is appalling," said Kadarin coldly. "Some day, if you want a lesson in linguistics, you should travel in the Empire and hear for yourself what strange syllables the human tongue evolves for itself when there is no common language transmitted in culture." I felt a sudden twinge of dread, like a cold wind. He went on. "Meanwhile, don't make ignorant statements which only show what an untraveled boy you are. Virtually every given name ever recorded on Darkover is a name known on Terra, and in a very small part of Terra at that. The drone-pipe, oldest of Darkovan instruments, was known once on Terra, but they survive only in museums, the art of playing them lost; musicians came here to relearn the art and found music that survived from a very small geographical area, the British or Brictish Islands. Linguists studying your language found traces of three Terran languages. Spanish in your *casta*; English and Gaelic in your *cahuenga*, and the Dry-Town languages. The language spoken in the Hellers is a form of pure Gaelic which is no longer spoken on Terra but survives in old manuscripts. Well, to make a long tale short, as the old wife said when she cropped her cow's brush, they soon found the record of a single ship, sent out before the Terran colonies had bound themselves together into the Empire, which vanished without trace and was believed crashed or lost. And they found the crewlist of that ship."

"I don't believe a word of it."

"Your belief wouldn't make it true; your doubt won't make it false," Kadarin said. "The very name of this world, Darkover, is a Terran word meaning," he considered a minute, translated, " 'color of night overhead.' On that crewlist there were di Asturiens and MacArans and these are, you would say, good old Darkovan names. There was a ship's officer named Camilla Del Rey. Camilla is a rare name among Terrans now, but it is the most common name for girl-children in the Kilghard Hills; you have even given it to one of your Comyn demi-goddesses. There was a priest of Saint Christopher of Centaurus, a Father Valentine Neville, and how many of the Comyn's sons have been taught in the *cristoforo* monastery of Saint-Valentine-of-the-Snows? I brought Marjorie, who is a *cristoforo*, a little religious medal from Terra itself; its twin is enshrined in Nevarsin. Must I go on with such examples, which I assure you I could quote all night without tiring? Have your Comyn forefathers ever told you so much?"

My head was reeling. It sounded infernally convincing.

"The Comyn cannot know this. If the knowledge was lost—"

"They know, all right," Beltran said with contempt. "Kennard knows certainly. He has lived on Terra."

My father knew this and had never told me?

Kadarin and Beltran were still telling me their tale of a "lost ship" but I had ceased to listen. I could sense Marjorie's soft eyes on me in the dying firelight, though I could no longer see them. I felt that she was following my thoughts not intruding on them but rather responding to me so completely that there were no longer any barriers between us. This had never happened before. Even at Arilinn, I had never felt so wholly attuned to any human being. I felt she knew how distressed and weary all this had made me.

On the cushioned bench she stretched out her hand to me and I could feel her indignation running up from her small fingers into my hand and arm and all along my body. She said, "Bob, what are you trying to *do* to him? He comes here weary from long travel, a kinsman and a guest; is this our mountain hospitality?"

Kadarin laughed. "Set a mouse to guard a lion!" he said. I felt those unfathomably strange eyes piercing the darkness to see our hands clasped. "I have my reasons, child. I don't know what fate sent him here, but when I see a man who has lived by a lie, I try to tell him the truth if I feel he's worth hearing it. A man who must make a choice must make it on facts, not fuzzy loyalties and half-truths and old lies. The tides of fate are moving—"

I said rudely, "Is fate one of your facts? You called *me* superstitious."

He nodded. He looked very serious. "You're a telepath, an Alton; you know what precognition is."

Beltran said, "You're going too fast. We don't even know why he's come here, and he *is* heir to a Domain. He may even have been sent to carry tales back to the old graybeard in Thendara and all his deluded yes-men."

Beltran swung around to face me. "Why *did* you come here?" he demanded. "After all these years, Kennard cannot be all that eager for you to know your mother's kin, otherwise you would have been my foster-brother, as Father wished."

I thought of that with a certain regret. I would willingly have had this kinsman for foster-brother. Instead I had never known of his existence till now, and it had been our mutual loss. He demanded again, "Why have you come, cousin, after so long?"

"It's true I came at my father's will," I said at last, slowly. "Hastur heard reports that the Compact was being violated in Caer Donn; my father was too ill to travel and sent me in his place." I felt strangely pulled this way and that. Had Father sent me to spy on kinsfolk? The idea filled me with revulsion. Or had he, in truth, wished me to know my mother's kin? I did not know, and not knowing made me uncertain, wretched.

"You see," said the woman Thyra, from her place in Kadarin's shadow, "it's useless to talk to him. He's one of the Comyn puppets."

Anger flared through me. "I am no man's puppet. Not Hastur's. Not my father's. Nor will I be yours, cousin or no. I came at my free will, because if Compact is broken it touches all our lives. And more than that, whatever my father said, I wished to know for myself whether what they had told me of Aldaran and Terra was true."

"Spoken honestly," Beltran said. "But let me ask you this, cousin. Is your loyalty to Comyn . . . or to Darkover?"

Asked that question at almost any other time, I would have said, without hesitation, that to be loyal to Comyn *was* to be loyal to Darkover. Since leaving Thendara I was no longer so sure. Even those I wholly trusted, like Hastur, had no power, or perhaps no wish, to check the corruption of the others. I said, "To Darkover. No question, to Darkover."

He said vehemently, "Then you should be one of us! You were sent to us at this moment, I think, because we needed you, because we couldn't go on without someone like you!"

"To do what?" I wanted no part in any Aldaran plots.

"Only this, kinsman, to give Darkover her rightful place, as a world belonging to our own time, not a barbarian backwater! We deserve the place on the Empire Council which we should have had, centuries ago, if the Empire had been honest with us. And we are going to have it!"

"A noble dream," I said, "if you can manage it. Just how are you going to bring this about?"

"It won't be easy," Beltran said. "It's suited the Empire, and the Comyn, to perpetuate their idea of our world: backward, feudal, ignorant. And we have become many of these things."

"Yet," Thyra said from the shadows, "we have one thing which is wholly Darkovan and unique. Our psi powers." She leaned forward to put a log on the fire and I saw her features briefly, lit by flame, dark, vital, glowing. I said, "If they are unique to Darkover, what of your theory that we are all Terrans?"

"Oh, yes," she said, "these powers are all recorded and remembered on Terra. But Terra neglected the powers of the mind, concentrating on material things, metal and machinery and computers. So their psi powers were forgotten and bred out. Instead we developed them, deliberately bred for them—that much of the Comyn legend is true. And we had the matrix jewels which convert energy. Isolation, genetic drift and selective breeding did the rest. Darkover is a reservoir of psi power and, as far as I know, is the only planet in the galaxy which turned to psi instead of technology."

"Even with matrix amplification, these powers are dangerous," I said. "Darkovan technology has to be used with caution, and sparsely. The price, in human terms, is usually too high."

The woman shrugged. "You cannot take hawks without climbing cliffs," she said.

"Just what is it you intend to do?"

"Make the Terrans take us seriously!"

"You don't mean war?" That sounded like suicidal nonsense and I said so. "Fight the Terrans, weapons against weapons?"

"No. Or only if they need to be shown that we are neither

ignorant nor helpless," Kadarin said. "A high-level matrix, I understand, is a weapon to make even the Terrans tremble. But I hope and trust it will never come to that. The Terran Empire prides itself on the fact that they don't conquer, that planets *ask* to be admitted to the Empire. Instead, the Comyn committed Darkover to withdrawal, barbarianism, a search for yesterday, not tomorrow. We have something to give the Empire in return for what they give us, our matrix technology. We can join as equals, not suppliants. I have heard that in the old days there were matrix-powered aircraft in Arilinn—"

"True," I said, "as recently as in my father's time."

"And why not now?" He did not wait for me to answer. "Also, we could have a really effective communications technique—"

"We have that now."

"But the towers work only under Comyn domination, not for the entire population of the world."

"The risks—"

"Only the Comyn seem to know anything about those risks," Beltran said. "I'm tired of letting the Comyn decide for everyone else what risks we may take. I want us to be accepted as equals by the Terrans. I want us to be part of Terran trade, not just the trickle which comes in and out by the spaceports under elaborate permits signed and countersigned by their alien culture specialists to make certain it won't disturb our primitive culture! I want good roads and manufacturing and transportation and some control over the God-forgotten weather on this world! I want our students in the Empire universities, and theirs coming here! Other planets have these things! And above all I want star-travel. Not as a rich man's toy, as with the Ridenow lads spending a season now and then on some faraway pleasure world and bringing back new toys and new debaucheries, but free trade, with Darkovan ships coming and going at our will, not the Empire's!"

"Daydreams," I said flatly. "There's not enough metal on Darkover for a spaceship's hulk, let alone fuel to power it!"

"We can trade for metal," Beltran said. "Do you think matrices, manned by psi power, won't power a spaceship? And wouldn't that make most of the other power sources in the Galaxy obsolete overnight?"

I stood motionless for a moment, gripped by the force of

his dream. Starships for Darkover . . . matrix-powered! By all the Gods, what a dream! And Darkovans comrades, competitors, not forgotten stepchildren of the Empire. . . .

"It can't be possible," I said, "or the matrix circles would have done it in the old days."

"It *was* done," Kadarin said. "The Comyn stopped it. It would have diluted their power on this world. We turned our back on a Galactic civilization because that crew of old women in Thendara decided they liked our world the way it was, with the Comyn up there with the Gods and everyone else running around bowing and scraping to them! They even disarmed us all. Their precious Compact sounds very civilized, but what it's done, in effect, is to make it impossible to organize any kind of armed rebellion that could endanger the Comyn's power!"

This went along, all too uncomfortably, with some of my own thoughts. Even Hastur spoke noble words about the Comyn devoting themselves to the service of Darkover, but what it came to was that he knew what was best for Darkover, and wanted no independent ideas challenging his power to enforce that "best."

"It's a noble dream. I said that before. But what have I to do with it?"

It was Marjorie who answered, squeezing my hand eagerly. "Cousin, you're tower-trained. You know the skills and techniques, and how they can be used even by latent telepaths. So much of the old knowledge has been lost, outside the towers. We can only experiment, work in the dark. We don't have the skills, the disciplines with which we could experiment further. Those of us who are telepaths have no chance to develop our natural gifts; those who are not have no way to learn the mechanics of matrix work. We need someone— someone like you, cousin!"

"I don't know . . . I have only worked within the towers. I have been taught it is not safe . . ."

"Of course," Kadarin said contemptuously. "Would they risk any trained man experimenting on his own and perhaps learning more than the little they allow? Kermiac was training matrix technicians here in the Hellers when you people in the Domains were still working in guarded circles, looked on as sorceresses and warlocks! But he is very old and he cannot guide us now." He smiled, a brief, bleak smile. "We need someone who is young and skilled and above all fearless. I think you have the strength for it. Have you the will?"

I found myself recalling the fey sense of destiny which had gripped me as I rode here. Was this the destiny I had foreseen, to break the hold of a corrupt clan on Darkover, to overthrow their grip at our throats, set Darkover in its rightful place among the equals of the Empire?

It was almost too much to grasp. I was suddenly very tired. Marjorie, still stroking my hand gently in her small fingers, said without looking up, "Enough, Beltran, give him time. He's weary from traveling and you've been jumping at him till he's confused. If it's right for him, he'll decide."

She was thinking of me. Everyone else was thinking of how well I could fit into their plans.

Beltran said with a rueful, friendly smile, "Cousin, my apologies! Marjorie is right, enough for now! After that long journey, you're more in need of a quiet drink and a soft bed than a lecture on Darkovan history and politics! Well, the drink for now and the bed soon, I promise!" He called for wine and a sweet fruit-flavored cordial not unlike the *shallan* we drank in the valley. He raised his glass to me. "To our better acquaintance, cousin, and to a pleasant stay among us."

I was glad to drink to that. Marjorie's eyes met mine over the rim of her glass. I wanted to take her hand again. Why did she appeal to me so? She looked young and shy, with an endearing awkwardness, but in the classic sense, she was not beautiful. I saw Thyra sitting within the curve of Kadarin's arm, drinking from his cup. Among valley folk that would have proclaimed them admitted lovers. I didn't know what, if anything, it meant here. I wished I were free to hold Marjorie like that.

I turned my attention to what Beltran was saying, about Terran methods used in the rapid building of Caer Donn, of the way in which trained telepaths could be used for weather forecasting and control. "Every planet in the Empire would send people here to be trained by us, and pay well for the privilege."

It was all true, but I was tired, and Beltran's plans were so exciting I feared I would not sleep. Besides, my nerves were raw-edged with trying to keep my awareness of Marjorie under control. I felt I would rather be beaten into bleeding pulp than intrude, even marginally, on her sensitivities. But I kept wanting to reach out to her, test her awareness of me, see if she shared my feelings or if her kindness was the courtesy of a kinswoman to a wearied guest. . . .

"Beltran," I said at last, cutting off the flow of enthusiastic ideas, "there's one serious flaw in your plans. There just aren't enough telepaths. We haven't enough trained men and women even to keep all nine of the towers operating. For such a galactic plan as you're contemplating, we'd need dozens, hundreds."

"But even a latent telepath can learn matrix mechanics," he said. "And many who have inherited the gifts never develop them. I believed the tower-trained could awaken latent *laran*."

I frowned. "The Alton gift is to force rapport. I learned to use it in the towers to awaken latents if they weren't too barricaded. I can't always do it. That demands a catalyst telepath. Which I'm not."

Thyra said sharply, "I told you so, Bob. *That* gene's extinct."

Something in her tone made me want to contradict her. "No, Thyra," I said, "I know of one. He's only a boy, and untrained, but definitely a catalyst telepath. He awakened *laran* in a latent, even after I failed."

"Much good that does us," Beltran said in disgust. "Comyn Council has probably bound him so tight, with favors and patronage, that he'll never see beyond their will! They usually do, with telepaths. I'm surprised they haven't already bribed and bound *you* that way."

I thought, but did not say, that they had tried.

"No," I said, "they have not. Dani has no reason at all to love the Comyn . . . and reason enough to hate."

I smiled at Marjorie and began to tell them about Danilo and the cadets.

Chapter THIRTEEN

Regis lay in the guest chamber at Edelweiss, tired to exhaustion, but unable to sleep. He had come to Edelweiss through a late-afternoon fall of snow, still too stunned and sickened to talk, or to eat the supper Javanne had had prepared for him. His head throbbed and his eyes flickered with little dots of light which remained even when his eyes were shut, crawling, forming odd visual traceries behind the eyelids.

Dyan, he kept thinking. In charge of cadets, misusing power like that, and no one knew, or cared, or interfered.

Oh, they knew, he realized. They must have known. He would never believe Dyan could have deceived Kennard!

He remembered that curious unsatisfactory talk in the tavern with Dyan and his head throbbed harder, as if the very violence of his emotions would burst it asunder. He felt all the worse because he had, in truth, liked Dyan, had admired him and been flattered by his attention. He had welcomed the chance to talk to a kinsman as an equal ... like a stupid, silly child! Now he knew what Dyan was trying to find out, so subtle it was never even an invitation.

It was not the nature of Dyan's desires that troubled him so greatly. It was not considered anything so shameful to be an *ombredin*, a lover of men. Among boys too young for marriage, rigidly kept apart by custom from any women except their own sisters or cousins, it was considered rather more suitable to seek companionship and even love from their friends than to consort with such women as were common to all. It was eccentric, perhaps, in a man of Dyan's years, but certainly not shameful.

What sickened Regis was the *kind* and *type* of pressure used against Danilo, the deliberate, sadistic cruelty of it the particularly subtle revenge Dyan had taken for the wound to his pride.

183

Petty harrassment would have been cruel but understandable. But to use *laran* against him! To force himself on Danilo's mind, to torment him that way! Regis felt physically ill with disgust.

Besides, he thought, still tossing restlessly, there were enough men or young lads who would have welcomed Dyan's interest. Some, perhaps, only because Dyan was a Comyn lord, rich and able to give presents and privileges to his friends, but others, certainly, would find Dyan a charming, pleasing and sophisticated companion. He could have had a dozen minions or lovers and no one would have thought of criticizing him. But some perverse cruelty made him seek the one boy in the cadets who would have none of him. A *cristoforo*.

He turned on his side, thrust a pillow over his face to shut out the light of the single candle he was too weary to get up and extinguish, and tried to sleep. But his mind kept going back to the frightening, disturbingly sexual nightmares which had preceded the wakening of his own *laran*. He knew now how Dyan had pursued Danilo even in sleep, enjoying the boy's fright and shame. And he knew now the ultimate corruption of power: to make another person a toy to do your will.

Was Dyan mad, then? Regis considered. No, he was very sane, to choose a poor boy, one without powerful friends or patrons. He played with Dani as a cat plays with a captive bird, torturing where he could not kill. Regis felt sick again. Pleasure in pain. Did it give Dyan that kind of pleasure to batter him black and blue at swordplay? With the vivid tactile memory of a telepath he relived that moment when Dyan had run his hands over his bruised body, the deliberate sensual quality of the touch. He felt physically used, contaminated, shamed. If Dyan had been physically present then, Regis would have struck him and dared the consequences himself.

And Dani was a catalyst telepath. That terrible force, that loathsome compulsion, against the rarest and most sensitive of telepaths!

Again and again, compulsively, he returned to that night in the barracks when he had tried—and failed—to reach out to Danilo and comfort him. He felt again and again the pain, the physical and mental shock of that wild rejection, the flood of guilt, terror, shame which had flooded him from that brief and innocent touch on Danilo's bare shoulder. Cassilda, blessed Mother of the Comyn! Regis thought in scalding shame, I touched him! Is it any wonder he thought me no better than Dyan!

He turned over on his back and lay staring at the vaulted ceiling, feeling his body ice over with dread. Dyan was a member of Council. They could not be so corrupt that they would know what Dyan had done, and say nothing. But who could tell them?

The single candle near his bed wavered, flickered in and out of focus; colors looped and spun across his visual field and the room swelled up, receded and shrank until it seemed to lie far away, then loom enormously around him in great echoing space.

He recognized the feeling from when Lew gave him *kirian,* but he was not drugged now!

He clutched at the bedclothes, squeezing his eyes shut. He could still see the candleflame, a dark fire printed inside his eyelids, the room around him lit with blazing brilliance, reversed afterimages, dark to bright and bright to dark, and a roaring in his ears like the distant roaring of a forest fire . . .

. . . The fire-lines at Armida! For an instant it seemed that he saw Lew's face again, crimson, gazing into a great fire, drawn with terror and wonder, then the face of a woman, shining, ecstatic, crowned with fire, burning, burning alive in the flames . . . Sharra, golden-chained Forge-Goddess. The room was alive with the fire and he burrowed beneath the blankets, sunk, battered, swirled. The room was dissolving around him, tilting . . . every thread in the smooth fine linen of the blankets seemed to cut into him, hard and rough, the twisted fibers of blanket trying to curl and frizzle and dig painfully into his skin, like cutting edges. He heard someone moan aloud and wondered who was there moaning and crying like that. The very air seemed to separate itself and come apart against his skin as if he had to sort it out into little droplets before he could breathe. His own breath hissed and whistled and moaned as it went in and out, like searing fire, to be quenched by the separate droplets of water in his lungs. . . .

Pain crashed through his head. He felt his skull smashing, shattering into little splinters; Another blow sent him flying high, falling into darkness.

"Regis!" Again the crashing, reeling sickness of the blow

and the long spin into space. The sound was only meaningless vibration but he tried to focus on it, make it mean something. *"Regis!"* Who was Regis? The roaring candleflame died to a glimmer and Regis heard himself gasp aloud. Someone was standing over him, calling his name, slapping him hard and repeatedly. Suddenly, noiselessly, the room fell into focus.

"Regis, wake up! Get up and walk around, don't drift with it!"

"Javanne . . ." he said, struggling fuzzily upright to catch her hand as it was descending for another blow. "Don't, sister . . ."

He was surprised at how weak and faraway his voice sounded. She gave a faint cry of relief. She was standing beside his bed, a white shawl slipping from her shoulders above her long nightgown. "I thought one of the children cried out, then heard you. Why didn't you tell me you were likely to have threshold sickness?"

Regis blinked and dropped her hand. Even without the touch he could feel her fear. The room was still not quite solid around him. "Threshold sickness?" He thought about it a moment. He'd heard of it, of course, born into a Comyn family: a physical and psychic upheaval of awakening telepaths in adolescence, the inability of the brain to cope with sudden overloads of sensory and extrasensory data, resulting in perceptual distortions of sight, sound, touch. . . . "I never had it before. I didn't know what it was. Things seemed to thin out and disappear, I couldn't see properly, or feel . . ."

"I know. Get up now and walk around a little."

The room was still tilting around him; he clung to the bed-frame. "If I do, I'll fall. . . ."

"And if you don't, your balance centers will start drifting out of focus again. Here," she said with a faint laugh, tossing the white shawl to him, looking courteously away as he wrapped it around his body and struggled to his feet. "Regis, did no one warn you of this when your *laran* wakened?"

"Didn't *who* warn me? I don't think anyone knew," he said, taking a hesitant step and then another. She was right; under the concentrated effort of getting up and moving, the room settled into solidity again. He shuddered and went toward the candle. The little lights still danced and jiggled behind his eyes, but it was candle-sized again. How had it grown to a raging forest fire out of childhood? He picked it up, was amazed to see how his hand shook. Javanne said sharply, "Don't touch the candle when your hand's not steady, you'll set something afire! Regis, you frightened me!"

"With the candle?" He set it down.

"No, the way you were moaning. I spent half a year at Neskaya when I was thirteen, I saw one of the girls go into convulsions in crisis once."

Regis looked at his sister as if for the first time. He could sense, now, the emotion behind her cross, brisk manner, real fear, a tenderness he had never guessed. He put his arm around her shoulders and said, wonderingly, "Were you really afraid?" The barriers were wholly down between them and what she heard was, *Would you really care if something happened to me?* She reacted to the wondering amazement of that unspoken question with real dismay.

"How can you doubt it? You are my only kinsman!"

"You have Gabriel, and five children."

"But you are my father's son and my mother's," she said, giving him a short, hard hug. "You seem to be all right now. Get back into that bed before you take a chill and I must nurse you like one of the babies!"

But he knew now what the sharpness of her voice concealed and it did not trouble him. Obediently he got under the covers. She sat on the bed.

"You should spend some time in one of the towers, Regis, just to learn control. Grandfather can send you to Neskaya or Arilinn. An untrained telepath is a menace to himself and everyone around him, they told me so when I was your age."

Regis thought of Danilo. Had anyone thought to warn him?

Javanne drew the covers up under his chin. He recalled now that she had done this when he was very small, before he knew the difference between elder sister and a never-known mother. She was only a child herself, but she had tried to mother him. Why had he forgotten that?

She kissed him gently on the forehead and Regis, feeling safe and protected for the moment, toppled over the edge of a vast gulf of sleep.

The next day he felt ill and dazed, but although Javanne told him to keep to his bed, he was too restless to stay there.

"I must return at once, at once to Thendara," he insisted. "I've learned something which makes it necessary to talk to

Grandfather. You said, yourself, I should arrange to go to one of the towers. What can happen to me with three Guardsmen for escort?"

"You know perfectly well you're not able to travel! I should spank you and put you to bed as I'd do with Rafael if he were so unreasonable," she said crossly.

His new insight into her made him speak with gentleness. "I'd like to be young enough for your cosseting, sister, even if it meant a spanking. But I know what I must do, Javanne, and I've outgrown a woman's rule. Please don't treat me like a child."

His seriousness sobered her, too. Still unwilling, she sent for his escort and horses.

All that long day's ride, he seemed to move through torturing memories, repeating themselves over and over, and a growing unease and uncertainty: would they believe him, would they even listen? Danilo was out of Dyan's reach, now; there was time enough to speak if he endangered another. Yet Regis knew that if he was silent, he connived at what Dyan had done.

In midafternoon, still miles from Thendara, wet snow and sleet began to fall again, but Regis ignored the suggestions of his escort that he should seek shelter and hospitality somewhere. Every moment between him and Thendara now was a torture; he yearned to be there, to have this frightening confrontation over. As the long miles dragged by, and he grew more and more soggy and wretched, he drew his soaked cape around him, huddling inside it like a protective cocoon. He knew his guards were talking about him, but he shut them firmly away from his consciousness, withdrawing further and further into his own misery.

As they came over the top of the pass he heard the distant vibration from the spaceport, carried thick and reverberating in the heavy, moist air. He thought with wild longing of the ships taking off, invisible behind the wall of rain and sleet, symbols of the freedom he wished he had now.

He let the thickening storm batter him, uncaring. He welcomed the icy wind, the sleet freezing in layers on his heavy riding-cloak, on his eyelashes and hair. It kept him from sliding back into that strange, hypersensitive, hallucinatory awareness.

What shall I say to Grandfather?

How did you face the Regent of Comyn and tell him his

most trusted counselor was corrupt, a sadistic pervert using his telepathic powers to meddle with a mind placed in his charge?

How do you tell the Commander of the Guard, your own commanding officer, that his most trusted friend, holding the most trusted and responsible of posts, has ill-treated and shamefully misused a boy in his care. How do you accuse your own uncle, the strongest telepath in Comyn, of standing by, indifferent, watching the rarest and most sensitive of telepaths being falsely accused, his mind battered and bruised and dishonored, while he, a tower-trained psi technician, did nothing?

The stone walls of the Castle closed about them, cutting off the biting wind Regis heard his escort swearing as they led their horses away. He knew he should apologize to them for subjecting them to this cold, wearying ride in such weather. It was a totally irresponsible thing to do to loyal men and the fact that they would never question his motives made it worse. He gave them brief formal thanks and admonished them to go quickly for supper and rest, knowing that if he offered them any reward they would be offended beyond measuring.

The long steps to the Hastur apartments seemed to loom over him, shrinking and expanding. His grandfather's aged valet rushed at him, blurred and out of focus, clucking and shaking his head with the privilege of long service. "Lord Regis, you're soaked through, you'll be ill, let me fetch you some wine, dry clothes—"

"Nothing, thank you." Regis blinked away the drops of ice melting on his eyelashes. "Ask the Lord Regent if he"—he tensed to keep his teeth from chattering—"if he can receive me."

"He's at supper, Lord Regis. Go in and join him."

A small table had been laid before the fire in his grandfather's private sitting room, and Danvan Hastur looked up, dismayed, almost comically echoing the elderly servant's dismay.

"My boy! At this hour, so wet and dripping? Marton, take his cloak, dry it at the fire! Child, you were to be with Javanne some days, what has happened?"

"Necessary—" Regis discovered his teeth were chattering so hard he could not speak; he clenched them to get control. "To return at once—"

The Regent shook his head skeptically. "Through a blizzard? Sit down there by the fire." He picked up the jug on his table, tilted a thick stream of steaming soup into a stoneware mug and held it out to Regis. "Here. Drink this and warm yourself before you say anything."

Regis started to say he did not want it, but he had to take it to keep it from falling from the old man's hand. The hot fragrant steam was so enticing that he began to sip it, slowly. He felt enraged at his own weakness and angrier at his grandfather for seeing it. His barriers were down and he had a flash of Hastur as a young man, a commander in the field, knowing his men, judging each one's strengths and weaknesses, knowing what each one needed and precisely how and when to get it to him. As the hot soup began to spread warmth through his shivering body he relaxed and began to breathe freely. The heat of the stoneware mug comforted his fingers, which were blue with cold, and even when he had finished the soup he held it between his hands, enjoying the warmth.

"Grandfather, I must talk to you."

"Well, I'm listening, child. Not even Council would call me out in such weather."

Regis glanced at the servants moving around the room. "Alone, sir. This concerns the honor of the Hasturs."

A startled look crossed the old man's face and he waved them from the room. "You're not going to tell me Javanne has managed to disgrace herself!"

Even the thought of his staid and fastidious sister playing the wanton would have made Regis laugh, if he could have laughed. "Indeed not, sir, all at Edelweiss is well and the babies thriving." He was not cold now, but felt an inner trembling he did not even recognize as fear. He put down the empty mug which had grown chill in his hands, shook his head at the offer of a refill.

"Grandfather. Do you remember Danilo Syrtis?"

"Syrtis. The Syrtis people are old Hastur folk, your father's paxman and bodyguard bore that name, old Dom Felix was my hawk-master. Wait, was there not some shameful thing in the Guards this year, a disgraced cadet, a sword-breaking? What has this to do with the honor of Hastur, Regis?"

Regis knew he must be very calm now, must keep his voice steady. He said, "The Syrtis men are our wards and paxmen, sir. From their years of duty to us, is it not our duty to safeguard them from being attacked and abused, even by Comyn? I have learned ... Danilo Syrtis was wrongfully attacked and disgraced, sir, and it's worse than that. Danilo is a ... a catalyst telepath, and Lord Dyan ill-used him, contrived his disgrace for revenge—"

Regis' voice broke. That searing moment of contact with Danilo flooded him again. Hastur looked at him in deep distress.

"Regis, this cannot possibly be true!"

He doesn't believe me! Regis heard his voice crack and break again. "Grandfather, I swear—"

"Child, child, I know you are not lying, I know you better than that!"

"You don't know me at all!" Regis flung at him, almost hysterical.

Hastur rose and came to him, laying a concerned hand on his forehead. "You are ill, Regis, feverish, perhaps delirious."

Regis shook the hand off. "I know perfectly well what I am saying. I had an attack of threshold sickness at Edelweiss, it's better now."

The old man looked at him with startled skepticism. "Regis, threshold sickness is nothing to take lightly. One of the symptoms is delusion, hallucination. I cannot accuse Lord Dyan of the wild ravings of a sick child. Let me send for Kennard Alton; he is tower-trained and can deal with this kind of illness."

"Send to Kennard indeed," Regis demanded, his voice wavering, "he is the one man in Thendara who will know for a fact that I am neither lying nor raving! This was by his contrivance, too; he stood by and watched Danilo disgraced and the cadet corps shamed!"

Hastur looked deeply troubled. He said, "Can it not wait—" He looked at Regis sharply and said, "No. If you rode through a blizzard at this hour to bring me such news, it certainly cannot wait. But Kennard is very ill, too. Can you possibly manage to go to him, child?"

Regis cut off another angry outburst and only said, with tight control, "I am not ill. I can go to him."

His grandfather looked at him steadily. "If you are not ill you will soon be so, if you stand there shivering and dripping. Go to your room and change your clothes while I send word to Kennard."

He was angry at being sent like a child to change his

clothes but he obeyed. It seemed the best way to convince his grandfather of his rationality. When he returned, dry-clad and feeling better, his grandfather said shortly, "Kennard is willing to talk to you. Come with me."

As they went through the long corridors, Regis was aware of his grandfather's bristling disapproval. In the Alton rooms, Kennard was seated in the main hall, before the fire. He rose and took one step toward them and Regis saw with deep compunction that the older man looked terribly ill, his gaunt face flushed, his hands looking hugely swollen and shapeless. But he smiled at Regis with heartfelt welcome and held out the misshapen hand. "My lad, I'm glad to see you."

Regis touched the swollen fingers with awkward carefulness, unable to blur out Kennard's pain and exhaustion. He felt raw-edged, hypersensitive. Kennard could hardly stand!

"Lord Hastur, you honor me. How may I serve you?"

"My grandson has come to me with a strange and disturbing story. It's his tale, I'll leave him to tell it."

Regis felt consuming relief. He had feared to be treated like a sick child dragged unwilling to a doctor. For once he was being treated like a man. He felt grateful, a little disarmed.

Kennard said, "I cannot stand like this long. You there—" He gestured to a servant. "An armchair for the Regent. Sit beside me, Regis, tell me what's troubling you."

"My lord Alton—"

Kennard said kindly, "Am I no longer Uncle, my boy?"

Regis knew if he did not resist that fatherly warmth with all his strength, he would sob out his story like a beaten child. He said stiffly, "My lord, this is a serious matter concerning the honor of the Guardsmen. I have visited Danilo Syrtis at his home—"

"That was a kindly thought, nephew. Between ourselves, that was a bad business. I tried to talk Dyan out of it, but he chose to make an example of Dani and the law is the law. I couldn't have done anything if Dani had been my own son."

"Commander," Regis said, using the most formal of Kennard's military titles, "on my most solemn word as a cadet and a Hastur, there has been a terrible injustice done. Danilo was, I swear, wrongly accused, and Lord Dyan guilty of something so shameful I hardly dare name it. Is a cadet forced to submit—"

"Now you wait a minute," Kennard said, turning blazing

eyes on him. "I had this already from Lew. I don't know what those three years among the *cristoforos* did to you, but if you're going to come whining to me about the fact that Dyan likes young lads for lovers, and accuse—"

"*Uncle!*" Regis protested in shock. "What kind of ninny do you think me? No, Commander. If that had been all—" He stopped, hunting for words, in confusion.

He said, "Commander, he would not accept refusal. He persecuted him day and night, invaded his mind, used *laran* against him. . . ."

Kennard's eyes sharpened. "Lord Hastur, what do you know of this wild tale? The boy looks ill. Is he raving?"

Regis stood up with a surge of violent anger that matched Kennard's own. "Kennard Alton, I am a Hastur *and I do not lie*! Send for Lord Dyan if you will, and question me in his presence!"

Kennard met his eyes, not angry now, but very serious. He said, "Dyan is not in the city tonight. Regis, tell me, how do you know this?"

"From Danilo's own lips, and from rapport with his mind, Regis said quietly. "You of all men know there is no way to lie to the mind."

Kennard did not release his eyes. "I did not know you had *laran*."

Regis held out his hand to Kennard, palm upward, a gesture he had never seen before, yet instinct guided him to it. He said, "*You* have. You will know. See for yourself, sir."

He saw dawning respect in the older man's gaunt, feverish face in the instant before he felt, with a thrill of fear, the touch on his mind. He heard Lew saying in Kennard's memory, *I've known grown men who dared not face that test.* Then he felt Kennard's touch, the shock of rapport . . . the moment he had stood before Danilo in the orchard, reeling with the shock of Danilo's anger and shame . . . his own liking for Dyan, the moment of half-shamed response to him . . . Kennard's own memories of Dyan blurring his own, a younger Dyan, a slender, eager boy, to be loved and protected and cherished . . . Danilo's sick, stunned terror, the flood of nightmarish dreams and cruelties he had shared with Danilo, the weeping in the dark, the harsh hawklike laughter. . . .

The blur of memories and impressions was gone. Kennard had covered his eyes with his hands. His eyes were dry and blazing, but just the same Regis got the impression that the older man was weeping in dismay. He said in a whisper, "Zandru's hells, *Dyan!*" Regis could feel the knifing anguish in the words. Kennard sank down on the bench again and Regis knew that he would have fallen if he had not, but for the first time Regis felt the iron strength and control with which a tower-trained telepath can control himself when he must. He had a frightening flash of agony, as if Kennard were holding his hand steadily in a fire, but Kennard only drew a deep breath and said, "So Danilo has *laran.* Lew did not tell me, nor did he tell me Dani had awakened you." A long silence. "That is a crime, and a terrible one—to use *laran* to force the will. I trusted Dyan; I never thought to question him. We were *bredin.* It is my responsibility and I will bear the guilt."

He looked shattered, dazed. "Aldones, Son of Light! I trusted him with *my* cadets! And Lew tried to warn me and I would not hear. I sent my own son from me in wrath because he tried to make me hear. . . . Hastur, what shall we do?"

Hastur looked grieved. "All the Ardais are unstable," he said. "Dom Kyril has been mad these twenty years. But you know the law as well as I do. You forced us to name Lew your heir with that same law. There must be one in the direct line, male and healthy, to represent every Domain, and Dyan has appointed no heir. We cannot even dismiss him from Comyn Council, as we did with Kyril when he began to rave. I do not know how we can send him from Council even long enough to heal his mind, if he is truly mad. Is he sane enough even to choose an heir?"

Regis felt angry and bruised. They seemed to care only about Dyan. Dani was nothing to them, no more than he was to Dyan. He said aggressively, "What of Danilo? What of his disgrace and his suffering? He has the rarest of the Comyn gifts, and the way he has been treated dishonors us all!"

Both men turned to look at him as if they had forgotten him. He felt like a noisy rude child intruding on the counsels of his elders, but he stood his ground, watching the torchlight make flickering patterns on the antique swords over the fire, saw Dyan, the sharp foil in hand, plunging it into his breast. . . .

"Amends shall be made," Hastur said quietly, "but you must leave it to us."

"I'll leave Dyan to you. But Dani is *my* responsibility! I pledged him my sworn word. I am a Hastur, and the heir to a Domain, and I demand—"

"You demand, do you?" said his grandfather, swinging around to face him. "I deny your right to demand anything! You have told me you wish to renounce that right, to go off-world. It took all I had even to extract your promise to give the minimum duty to the cadets! You have refused, even as Dyan refused, to give an heir to your Domain. By what right do you dare criticize him? You have renounced your heirship to Hastur; by what right do you stand here in front of us and make demands? Sit down and behave yourself or go back to your room and leave these things to your betters!"

"Don't you treat me like a child!"

"You are a child," said Hastur, his lips pressed tightly together, "a sick, silly child."

The room was flickering in and out of focus with the firelight. Regis clenched his fists, fighting for words. "An injury to anyone with *laran* . . . dishonors us all." He turned to Kennard, pleading. "For the honor of the Guards . . . for your own honor . . ."

Kennard's crippled hands touched him gently; Regis could feel pain ripping through those swollen hands as he wrenched them away. He felt himself sliding in and out of his body, unable to bear the jangle and confusion of all their thoughts. He thought with wild longing of being aboard a starship outward bound, *free*, leaving this little world behind with all its intrigue. He stood for a moment in Kennard's memory on the faraway surface of Terra, struggling with the pull of honor and duty against all he longed for, back to the heritage laid out for him before he was born, a path he must walk whether he would or not . . . felt his grandfather's anguish, *Rafael, Rafael, you would not have deserted me like this* . . . heard Dyan's slow cynical voice, *a very special stud animal whose fees are paid to Comyn* . . .

It forced him physically to his knees with the weight of it. Past, present, future spun together, whirling, he saw Dani's hand meet his on the hilt of a gleaming sword, felt it rip his mind open, overshadowing him. *Son of Hastur who is the Son of Light!* He was crying like a child. He whispered, "To the House of Hastur . . . I swear . . ."

Kennard's hands, hot and swollen, touched his temples; he felt for an instant that Kennard was holding him upright.

Gradually the seething flood of emotion, foreknowledge, memory, receded. He heard Kennard say, "Threshold sickness. Not crisis, but he's pretty sick. Speak to him, sir."

"Regis . . ."

Regis struggled, whispered, "Grandfather, Lord Hastur . . . I swear, I will swear . . ."

His grandfather's arms enfolded him gently. "Regis, Regis, I know. But I cannot accept any pledge from you now. Not in your present state. The Gods know I want to, but I cannot. You must leave this to us. You *must*, child. We will deal with Dyan. You have done all you need to do. Just now your task is to go, as Kennard says, to Neskaya, to teach yourself to control your gift."

He tried again to fight his way upright . . . kneeling on cold stones, crystal lights around him. Words came slowly, painfully, yet he could not escape them: *I pledge my life and honor . . . to Hastur, forever* . . . and terrible pain, knowing he spoke into a closing door, he gave away his life and his freedom. He could not get a word out, not a syllable, and he felt his body and brain would explode with the words bursting in him. He whispered and knew no one could hear him, as his senses slipped away, " . . . swear . . . honor . . ."

His grandfather's eyes met his briefly, a momentary anchor over a swaying darkness where he hung. He heard his grandfather's voice, deep and compassionate, saying firmly, "The honor of the Comyn has been safe in my hands for ninety years, Regis. You can leave it to me now."

Regis let them lay him, nearly senseless, on the stone bench.

He let himself slip away into unconsciousness like a little death.

Chapter FOURTEEN

(Lew Alton's narrative)

For three days a blizzard had raged in the Hellers. On the fourth day I woke to sunshine and the peaks behind Castle Aldaran gleaming under their burden of snow. I dressed and went down into the gardens behind the castle, standing atop the terraces and looking down on the spaceport below where great machines were already moving about, as tiny at this distance as creeping bugs, to shift the heavy layers of snow. No wonder the Terrans didn't want to move their main port here!

Yet, unlike Thendara, here spaceport and castle seemed part of a single conjoined whole, not warring giants, striding toward battle.

"You're out early, cousin," said a light voice behind me. I turned to see Marjorie Scott, warmly wrapped in a hooded cloak with fur framing her face. I made her a formal bow.

"Damisela."

She smiled and stretched her hand to me. "I like to be out early when the sun's shining. It was so dark during the storm!"

As we walked down the terraces she grasped my cold hand and drew it under her cloak. I had to tell myself that this freedom did not imply what it would mean in the lowlands, but was innocent and unaware. It was hard to remember that with my hand lying between her warm breasts. But damn it, the girl was a telepath, she had to know.

As we went along the path, she pointed out the hardy winter flowers, already thrusting their stalks up through the snow, seeking the sun, and the sheltered fruits casting their snow-pods. We came to a marble-railed space where a water-fall tumbled, storm-swollen, away into the valley.

"This stream carries water from the highest peaks down into Caer Donn, for their drinking water. The dam above here, which makes the waterfall, serves to generate power for the lights, here and down in the spaceport, too."

"Indeed, *damisela*? We have nothing like this in Thendara." I found it hard to keep my attention on the stream. Suddenly she turned to face me, swift as a cat, her eyes flashing gold. Her cheeks were flushed and she snatched her hand away from mine. She said, with a stiffness that con-cealed anger, "Forgive me, Dom Lewis. I presumed on our kinship," and turned to go. My hand, in the cold again, felt as chilled and icy as my heart at her sudden wrath.

Without thinking, I reached out and clasped her wrist.

"Lady, how have I offended you? Please don't go!"

She stood quite still with my hand clasping her wrist. She said in a small voice, "Are all you valley men so queer and formal? I am not used to being called *damisela*, except by servants. Do you . . . dislike me . . . Lew?"

Our hands were still clasped. Suddenly she colored and tried to withdraw her wrist from my fingers. I tightened them, saying, "I feared to be burned . . . too near the fire. I am very ignorant of your mountain ways. How should I ad-dress you, cousin?"

"Would a woman of your valley lands be thought too bold if she called you by name, Lew?"

"Marjorie," I said, caressing the name with my voice. "Marjorie." Her small fingers felt fragile and live, like some small quivering animal that had taken refuge with me. Never, not even at Arilinn, had I known such warmth, such accept-ance. She said my hands were cold and drew them under her cloak again. All she was telling me seemed wonderful. I knew something of electric power generators—in the Kilghard Hills great windmills harnessed the steady winds—but her voice made it all new to me, and I pretended less knowledge so she would go on speaking.

She said, "At one time matrix-powered generators provid-ed lights for the castle. That technique is lost."

"It is known at Arilinn," I said, "but we rarely use it; the cost is high in human terms and there is some danger." Just the same, I thought, in the mountains they must need more energy against the crueler climate. Easy enough to give up a luxury, but here it might make the difference between civilized life and a brutal struggle for existence.

"Have you been taught to use a matrix, Marjorie?"

"Only a little. Kermiac is too old to show us the techniques. Thyra is stronger than I because she and Kadarin can link together a little, but not for long. The techniques of making the links are what we do not know."

"That is simple enough," I said, hesitating because I did not like to think of working in linked circles outside the safety of the tower force-fields. "Marjorie, who is Kadarin, where does he come from?"

"I know no more than he told you," she said. "He has traveled on many worlds. There are times when he speaks as if he were older than my guardian, yet he seems no older than Thyra. Even she knows not much more than I, yet they have been together for a long time. He is a strange man, Lew, but I love him and I want you to love him too."

I had warmed to Kadarin, sensing the sincerity behind his angry intensity. Here was a man who met life without self-deception, without the lies and compromises I had lived with so long. I had not seen him for days; he had gone away before the blizzard on unexplained business.

I glanced at the strengthening sun. "The morning's well on. Will anyone be expecting us?"

"I'm usually expected at breakfast, but Thyra likes to sleep late and no one else will care." She looked shyly up into my face and said, "I'd rather stay with you."

I said, with a leaping joy, "Who needs breakfast?"

"We could walk into Caer Donn and find something at a food-stall. The food will not be as good as at my guardian's table. . . ."

She led the way down a side path, going by a flight of steep steps that were roofed against the spray from the waterfall. There was frost underfoot, but the roofing had kept the stairway free of ice. The roaring of the waterfall made so much noise that we left off trying to talk and let our clasped hands speak for us. At last the steps came out on a lower terrace leading gently downslope to the city. I looked up and said, "I don't relish the thought of climbing back!"

"Well, we can go around by the horse-path," she said. "You came up that way with your escort. Or there's a lift on the far side of the waterfall; the Terrans built it for us, with chains and pulleys, in return for the use of our water power."

A little way inside the city gates Marjorie led the way to a food-stall. We ate freshly baked bread and drank hot spiced cider, while I pondered what she had said about matrices for generating power. Yes, they had been used in the past, and misused, too, so that now it was illegal to construct them. Most of them had been destroyed, not all. If Kadarin wanted to try reviving one there was, in theory at least, no limit to what he could do with it.

If, that was, he wasn't afraid of the risks. Fear seemed to have no part in that curious enigmatic personality. But ordinary prudence?

"You're lost somewhere again Lew. What is it?"

"If Kadarin wants to do these things he must know of a matrix capable of handling that kind of power. What and where?"

"I can only tell you that not on any of the monitor screens in the towers. It was used in the old days by the forge-folk to bring their metals from the ground. Then it was kept at Aldaran for centuries, until one of Kermiac's wards, trained by him, used it to break the siege of Storn Castle."

I whistled. The matrix had been outlawed as a weapon centuries ago. The Compact had not been made to keep us away from such simple toys as the guns and blasters of the Terrans, but against the terrifying weapons devised in our Ages of Chaos. I wasn't happy about trying to key a group of inexperienced telepaths into a really large matrix, either. Some could be harnessed and used safely and easily. Others had darker histories, and the name of Sharra, Goddess of the forge-folk, was linked in old tales with more than one matrix. This one might, or might not, be possible to bring under control.

She said, looking incredulous, "Are you afraid?"

"Damn right," I said. "I thought most of the talismans of Sharra-worship had been destroyed before the time of Regis Fourth. I *know* some of them were destroyed."

"This one was hidden by the forge-folk and given back for their worship after the siege of Storn." Her lip curled. "I have no patience with that kind of superstition."

"Just the same, a matrix is no toy for the ignorant." I stretched my hand out, palm upward over the table, to show her the coin-sized white scar, the puckered seam running up my wrist. "In my first year of training at Arilinn I lost control for a split second. Three of us had burns like this. I'm not joking when I speak of risks."

For a moment her face contracted as she touched the puckered scar tissue with a delicate fingertip. Then she lifted her firm little chin and said, "All the same, what one human mind can build, another human mind can master. And a matrix is no use to anyone lying on an altar for ignorant folk to worship." She pushed aside the cold remnants of the bread and said, "Let me show you the city."

Our hands came irresistibly together again as we walked, side by side, through the streets. Caer Donn was a beautiful city. Even now, when it lies beneath tons of rubble and I can never go back, it stands in my memory as a city in a dream, a city that for a little while *was* a dream. A dream we shared.

The houses were laid out along wide, spacious streets and squares, each with plots of fruit trees and its own small glass-roofed greenhouse for vegetables and herbs seldom seen in the hills because of the short growing season and weakened sunlight. There were solar collectors on the roofs to collect and focus the dim winter sun on the indoor gardens.

"Do these work even in winter?"

"Yes, by a Terran trick, prisms to concentrate and reflect more sunlight from the snow."

I thought of the darkness at Armida during the snow-season. There was so much we could learn from the Terrans!

Marjorie said, "Every time I see what the Terrans have made of Caer Donn I am proud to be Terran. I suppose Thendara is even more advanced."

I shook my head. "You'd be disappointed. Part of it is all Terran, part of it all Darkovan. Caer Donn . . . Caer Donn is like you, Marjorie, the best of each world, blended into a single harmonious whole . . ."

This was what our world could be. Should be. This was Beltran's dream. And I felt, with my hands locked tight in Marjorie's, in a closeness deeper than a kiss, that I would risk anything to bring that dream alive and spread it over the face of Darkover.

I said something about how I felt as we climbed together upward again. We had elected to take the longer way, reluctant to end this magical interlude. We must have known even then that nothing to match this morning would ever come

again, when we shared a dream and saw it all bright and
new-edged and too beautiful to be real.

"I feel as if I were drugged with *kirian!*"

She laughed, a silvery peal. "But the *kireseth* no longer
blooms in these hills, Lew. It's all real. Or it can be."

I began as I had promised later that day. Kadarin had not
returned, but the rest of us gathered in the small sitting
room.

I felt nervous, somehow reluctant. It was always nerve-
racking to work with a strange group of telepaths. Even at
Arilinn, when the circle was changed every year, there was
the same anxious tension. I felt naked, raw-edged. How much
did they know. What skills, potentials, lay hidden in these
strangers? Two women, a man and a boy. Not a large circle.
But large enough to make me quiver inside.

Each of them had a matrix. That didn't really surprise me
since tradition has it that the matrix jewels were first found
in these mountains. None of them had his or her matrix what
I would call properly safeguarded. That didn't surprise me either. At Arilinn we're very strict in the old traditional ways.
Like most trained technicians, I kept mine on a leather thong
around my neck, silk-wrapped and inside a small leather bag,
lest some accidental stimulus cause it to resonate.

Beltran's was wrapped in a scrap of soft leather and thrust
into a pocket. Marjorie's was wrapped in a scrap of silk and
thrust into her gown between her breasts, where my hand
had lain! Rafe's was small and still dim; he had it in a small
cloth bag on a woven cord around his neck. Thyra kept hers
in a copper locket, which I considered criminally dangerous.
Maybe my first act should be to teach them proper shielding.

I looked at the blue stones lying in their hands. Marjorie's
was the brightest, gleaming with a fiery inner luminescence,
giving the lie to her modest statement that Thyra was the
stronger telepath. Thyra's was bright enough, though. My
nerves were jangling. A "wild telepath," one who has taught
himself by trial and error, extremely difficult to work with.
In a tower the contact would first be made by a Keeper,
not the old carefully-shielded *leronis* of my father's day, but
a woman highly trained, her strength safeguarded and disciplined. Here we had none. It was up to me.

It was harder than taking my clothes off before such an assembly, yet somehow I had to manage it. I sighed and looked from one to the other.

"I take it you all know there's nothing magical about a matrix," I said. "It's simply a crystal which can resonate with, and amplify, the energy-currents of your brain."

"Yes, I know that," said Thyra with amused contempt. "I didn't expect anyone trained by Comyn to know it, though."

I tried to discipline my spontaneous flare of anger. Was she going to make this as hard for me as she could?

"It was the first thing they taught me at Arilinn, kinswoman, I am glad you know it already." I concentrated on Rafe. He was the youngest and would have least to unlearn.

"How old are you, little brother?"

"Thirteen this winter, kinsman," he said, and I frowned slightly. I had no experience with children—fifteen is the lowest age limit for the Towers—but I would try. There was light in his matrix, which meant that he had keyed it after a fashion.

"Can you control it?" We had none of the regular test materials; I would have to improvise. I made brief contact. *The fireplace. Make the fire flame up twice and die down.*

The stone reflected blue glimmer on his childish features as he bent, his forehead wrinkling up with the effort of concentration. The light grew; the fire flamed high, sank, flared again, sank down, down . . .

"Careful," I said, "don't put it out. It's cold in here." At least he could receive my thoughts; though the test was elementary, it qualified him as part of the circle. He looked up, delighted with himself, and smiled.

Marjorie's eyes met mine. I looked quickly away. Damn it, it's never easy to make contact with a woman you're attracted to. I'd learned at Arilinn to take it for granted, for psi worked used up all the physical and nervous energy available. But Marjorie hadn't learned that, and I felt shy. The thought of trying to explain it to her made me squirm. In the safe quiet of Arilinn, chaperoned by nine or ten centuries of tradition, it was easy to keep a cool and clinical detachment. Here we must devise other ways of protecting ourselves.

Thyra's eyes were cool and amused. Well, *she* knew. If she and Kadarin had been working together, no doubt she'd found it out already. I didn't like her and I sensed she didn't like me either, but thus far, at least, we could touch one another with easy detachment; her physical presence did not embarrass me. Where, working alone, had she picked up that cool, knife-like precision? Was I glad or sorry that Marjorie showed no sign of it?

"Beltran," I said, "what can you do?"

"Children's tricks," he said, "little talent, less skill. Rafe's trick with the fire." He repeated it, more slowly, with somewhat better control. He reached an unlighted taper from a side table and bent over it with intense concentration. A narrow flame leaped from the fireplace to the tip of the taper, where it burst into flame.

A child's trick, of course, one of the simplest tests we used at Arilinn. "Can you call the fire without the matrix?" I asked.

"I don't try," he said. "In this area it's too great a danger to set something on fire. I'd rather learn to put fires *out*. Do your tower telepaths do that, perhaps, in forest-fire country?"

"No, though we do call clouds and make rain sometimes. Fire is too dangerous an element, except for baby tricks like these. Can you call the overlight?"

He shook his head, not understanding. I held out my hand and focused the matrix. A small green flame flickered, grew in the palm of my hand. Marjorie gasped. Thyra held out her own hand; cold white light grew, pale around her fingers, lighting up the room, flaring up like jagged lightning. "Very good," I said, "but you must control it. The strongest or brightest light is not always the best. Marjorie?"

She bent over the blue shimmer of her matrix. Before her face, floating in the air, a small blue-white ball of fire appeared, grew gradually larger, then floated to each of us in turn. Rafe could make only flickers of light; when he tried to shape them or move them, they flared up and vanished. Beltran could make no light at all. I hadn't expected it. Fire, the easiest of the elements to call forth, was still the hardest to control.

"Try this." The room was very damp; I condensed the moist air into a small splashing fountain of water-drops, each sizzling a moment in the fire as it vanished. Both of the women proved able to do this easily; Rafe mastered it with little trouble. He needed practice, but had excellent potential.

Beltran grimaced. "I told you I had small talent and less skill."

"Well, some things I can teach you without talent, kinsman," I said. "Not all mechanics are natural telepaths. Do you read thoughts at all?"

"Only a little. Mostly I sense emotions," he said.

Not good. If he could not link minds with us, he would be no use in the matrix circle. There were other things he could do, but we were too few for a circle, except for the very smallest matrices.

I reached out to touch his mind. Sometimes a telepath who has never learned the touching technique can be *shown*, when all else fails. I met slammed, locked resistance. Like many who grow up with minimal *laran*, untrained, he had built defenses against the use of his gift. He was cooperative, letting me try again and again to force down the barrier, and we were both white and sweating with pain by the time I finally gave up. I had used a force on him far harder than I had used on Regis, to no avail.

"No use," I said at last. "Much more of this will kill both of us. I'm sorry, Beltran. I'll teach you what I can outside the circle, but without a catalyst telepath this is as far as you can go." He looked miserably downcast, but he took it better than I had hoped.

"So the women and children can succeed where I fail. Well, if you've done the best you can, what can I say?"

It was, on the contrary, easy to make contact with Rafe. He had built no serious defense against contact, and I gathered, from the ease and confidence with which he dropped into rapport with me, that he must have had a singularly happy and trusting childhood, with no haunting fears. Thyra sensed what we had done; I felt her reach out, and made the telepathic overture which is the equivalent of an extended hand across a gulf. She met it quickly, dropping into contact without fumbling, and . . .

A savage animal, dark, sinuous, prowling an unexplored jungle. A smell of musk . . . claws at my throat . . .

Was this her idea of a joke? I broke the budding rapport, saying tersely, "This is no game, Thyra. I hope you never find that out the hard way."

She looked bewildered. Unconscious, then. It was just the inner image she projected. Somehow I'd have to learn to live with it. I had no idea how she perceived *me*. That's one thing you can never know. You try, of course, at first. One girl in my Arilinn circle had simply said I felt "steady." Another tried, confusedly, to explain how I "felt" to her mind and wound up saying I felt like the smell of saddle-leather. You're trying, after all, to put into words an experience that has nothing to do with verbal ideas.

I reached out for Marjorie and sensed her in the fragmentary circle . . . a falling swirl of golden snowflakes, silk rustling, like her hand on my cheek. I didn't need to look at her. I broke the tentative four-way contact and said, "Basically, that's it. Once we learn to match resonances."

"If it's so simple, why could we never do it before?" Thyra demanded.

I tried to explain that the art of making a link with more than one other mind, more than one other matrix, is the most difficult of the basic skills taught at Arilinn. I felt her fumbling to reach out, to make contact, and I dropped my barriers and allowed her to touch me. *Again the dark beast, the sense of claws* . . . Rafe gasped and cried out in pain and I reached out to knock Thyra loose. "Not until you know how," I said. "I'll try to teach you, but you have to learn the precise knack of matching resonance *before* you reach out. Promise me not to try it on your own, Thyra, and I'll promise me to teach you. Agreed?"

She promised, badly shaken by the failure. I felt depressed. Four of us, then, and Rafe only a child. Beltran unable to make rapport at all, and Kadarin an unknown quantity. Not enough for Beltran's plans. Not nearly enough.

We needed a catalyst telepath. Otherwise, that was as far as I could go.

Rafe's attempts to lower the fire and our experiments with water-drops had made the hearth smolder; Marjorie began to cough. Any of us could have brought it back to brightness, but I welcomed the chance to get out of the room. I said, "Let's go into the garden."

The afternoon sunshine was brilliant, melting the snow. The plants which had just this morning been thrusting up spikes through snow were already budding. I asked, "Will Kermiac be angry if we destroy a few of his flowers?"

"Flowers? No, take what you need, but what will you do with them?"

"Flowers are ideal test and practice material," I said. "It would be dangerous to experiment with most living tissue; with flowers you can learn a very delicate control, and they live such a short time that you are not interfering with the balance of nature very much. For instance." Cupping matrix in hand, I focused my attention on a bud full-formed but not yet opened, exerting the faintest of mental pressures. Slowly, while I held my breath, the bud uncurled, thrusting forth slender stamens. The petals unfolded, one by one, until it stood full-blown before us. Marjorie drew a soft breath of excitement and surprise.

"But you didn't destroy it!"

"In a way I did; the bud isn't fully mature and may never mature enough to be pollinated. I didn't try; maturing a plant like that takes deep intercellular control. I simply manipulated the petals." I made contact with Marjorie. *Try it with me. Try first to see deep into the cell structure of the flower, to see exactly how each layer of petals is folded. . . .*

The first time she lost control and the petals crushed into an amorphous, colorless mass. The second time she did it almost as perfectly as I had done. Thyra, too, quickly mastered the trick, and Rafe, after a few tries. Beltran had to struggle to achieve the delicate control it demanded, but he did it. Perhaps he would make a psi monitor. Nontelepaths sometimes made good ones.

I saw Thyra by the waterfall, gazing into her matrix. I did not speak to her, curious to see what she could do unaided. It was growing late—we had spent considerable time with the flowers—and dusk was falling, lights appearing here and there in the city below us. Thyra stood so still she hardly appeared to breathe. Suddenly the raging, foaming torrent next to her appeared to freeze motionless, arrested in midair, only one or two of the furthest droplets floating downward. The rest hung completely stopped, poised, frozen as if time itself and motion had stopped. Then, deliberately, the water began to flow uphill.

Beneath us, one after another, the lights of Caer Donn blinked and went out.

Rafe gasped aloud; in the eerie stillness the small sound brought me back to reality. I said sharply, "Thyra!" she started, her concentration broken, and the whole raging torrent plunged downward with a crash.

Thyra turned angry eyes on me. I took her by the shoulder and drew her back from the edge, to where we could hear ourselves speak above the torrent.

"Who gave you leave to meddle——!"

I deliberately smothered my flare of anger. I had assumed responsibility for all of them now, and Thyra's ability to make me angry was something I must learn to control. I said, "I am sorry, Thyra, had you never been told that this is dangerous?"

"Danger, always danger! Are you such a coward, Lew?"

I shook my head. "I'm past the point where I have to prove my courage, child." Thyra was older than I, but I spoke as to a rash, foolhardy little girl. "It was an astonishing display. but there are wiser ways to prove your skill." I gestured. "Look, you have put their lights out; it will take repair crews some time to restore their power relays. That was thoughtless and silly. Second, it is unwise to disturb the forces of nature without great need, and for some good reason. Remember, rain in one place, even to drown a forest fire, may mean drought elsewhere, and balance disturbed. Until you can judge on planet-wide terms, Thyra, don't presume to meddle with a natural force, and never, *never*, for your pride! Remember, I asked Beltran's leave even to destroy a few flowers!"

She lowered her long lashes. Her cheeks were flaming, like a small girl lectured for some naughtiness. I regretted the need to lay down the law so harshly, but the incident had disturbed me deeply, rousing all my own misgivings. Wild telepaths were dangerous! How far could I trust any of them?

Marjorie came up to us; I could tell that she shared Thyra's humiliation, but she made no protest. I turned and slipped my arm around her waist, which would have proclaimed us acknowledged lovers in the valley. Thyra sent me a sardonic smile of amusement beneath her meekly dropped lashes, but all she said was, "We are all at your orders, Dom Lewis."

"I've no wish to give orders, cousin," I said, "but your guardian would have small cause to love me if I disregarded the simplest rules of safety in your training!"

"Leave him alone, Thyra," Marjorie flared. "He knows what he's doing! Lew, show her your hand!" She seized the palm, turned it over, showing the white ridged scars. "He has learned to follow rules, and learned it with pain! Do you want to learn like that?"

Thyra flinched visibly, averting her eyes from the scar as if it sickened her. I would not have thought her squeamish. She said, visibly shaken, "I had never thought ... I did not know. I'll do what you say, Lew. Forgive me."

"Nothing to forgive, kinswoman," I said, laying my free

hand on her wrist. "Learn caution to match your skill and you will be a strong *leronis* some day." She smiled at the word which, taken literally, meant *sorceress*.

"Matrix technician, if you like. Some day, perhaps, there will be new words for new skills. In the towers we are too busy mastering skills to worry about words for them, Thyra. Call it what you like."

Thin fog was beginning to move down from the peaks behind the castle. Marjorie shivered in her light dress and Thyra said, "We'd better go in, it will be dark soon." With one bleak look at the darkened city below, she walked quickly toward the castle. Marjorie and I walked with our arms laced, Rafe tagging close to us.

"Why do we need the kind of control we practiced with the flowers, Lew?"

"Well, if someone in the circle gets so involved in what he's doing that he forgets to breathe, the monitor outside has to start him breathing again without hurting him. A well-trained empath can stop bleeding even from an artery, or heal wounds." I touched the scar. "This would have been worse, except that the Keeper of the circle worked with it, to heal the worst damage." Janna Lindir had been Keeper at Arilinn for two of my three years. At seventeen, I had been in love with her. I had never touched her, never so much as kissed her fingertips. Of course.

I looked at Marjorie. *No. No, I have never loved before, never. . . . The other women I have known have been nothing. . . .*

She looked at me and whispered, half laughing, "Have you loved so many?"

"Never like this. I swear it—"

Unexpectedly she threw her arms around me, pressed herself close. "I love you," she whispered quickly, pulled away and ran ahead of me along the path into the hall.

Thyra smiled knowingly at me as we came in, but I didn't care. You had to learn to take that kind of thing for granted. She swung around toward the window, looking into the gathering darkness and mist. We were still close enough that I followed her thoughts. *Kadarin, where was he, how did he fare on his mission?* I began to draw them together again, Marjorie's delicate touch, Rafe alert and quick like some small frisking animal, Thyra with the strange sense of a dark beast prowling.

Kadarin. The interlinked circle formed itself and I discovered to my surprise, and momentary dismay, that Thyra was at the center, weaving us about her mind. But she seemed to work with a sure, deft touch, so I let her keep that place. Suddenly I *saw* Kadarin, and heard his voice speaking in the middle of a phrase;

" . . . refuse me then, Lady Storn?"

We could even see the room where he was standing, a high-arched old hall with the blue glass windows of almost unbelievable antiquity. Directly before his eyes was a tall old woman, proudly erect, with gray eyes and dazzling white hair. She sounded deeply troubled.

"Refuse you, *dom*? I have no authority too give or refuse. The Sharra matrix was given into the keeping of the forge-folk after the siege of Storn. It had been taken from them without authority, generations ago, and now it is safe in their keeping, not mine. It is theirs to give."

Kadarin's deep exasperation could be felt by all of us—*stubborn, superstitious old beldame!*—as he said, "It is Kermiac of Aldaran who bids me remind you that you took Sharra's matrix from Aldaran without leave—"

"I do not recognize his right."

"Desideria," he said, "let's not quarrel or quibble. Kermiac sent me to bring the Sharra matrix back to Aldaran; Aldaran is liege-lord to Storn and there's an end to it."

"Kermiac does not know what I know, sir. The Sharra matrix is well where it is; let it lie there. There are no Keepers today powerful enough to handle it. I myself called it up only with the aid of a hundred of the forge-folk, and it would be ill done of me to deprive them of their goddess. I beg you say to Kermiac that by my best judgment, which he trusted always, it should stay where it is."

"I am sick of this superstitious talk of goddesses and talismans, lady. A matrix is a machine, no more."

"Is it? So I thought when I was a maiden," the old woman said. "I knew more of the art of a matrix at fifteen, sir, than you know now, and I know how old you really are." I felt the man flinch from her sharp, steady gaze. "I know *this* matrix, you do not. Be advised by me. You could not handle it. Nor could Kermiac. Nor could I, at my age. Let it lie, man! Don't wake it! If you do not like the talk of goddesses, call it a force basically beyond human control in these days, and evil."

Kadarin paced the floor and I paced with him, sharing a restlessness so strong it was pain. "Lady, a matrix can be no more good or evil in itself than the mind of the man who wields it. Do you think me evil, then?"

She waved that away with an impatient gesture. "I think you honest, but you will not believe there are some powers so strong, so far from ordinary human purpose, that they warp all things to evil. Or to evil in ordinary human terms, at least. And what would you know of that? Let it be, Kadarin."

"I cannot. There is no other force strong enough for my purposes, and these are honest. I have safeguarded all, and I have a circle ready to my hand."

"You do not mean to use it alone, then, or with the Darriell woman?"

"*That* foolhardy I am not. I tell you, I have safeguarded all. I have won a Comyn telepath to aid me. He is cautious and skilled," Kadarin said persuasively, "and trained at Arilinn."

"Arilinn," said Desideria at last. "I know how they were trained at Arilinn. I did not believe that knowledge still survived. That should be safe, then. Promise me, Kadarin, to place it in his hands and leave all things to his judgment, and I will give you the matrix."

"I promise you," Kadarin said. We were so deeply in rapport that it seemed it was I myself, Lew Alton, who bowed before the old Keeper, feeling her gray eyes search *my* very soul rather than his.

It is in the memory of that moment that I will swear, even after all the nightmare that came later, that Kadarin was honest, that he meant no evil. . . .

Desideria said, "Be it so, then, I will entrust it to you." Again the sharp gray eyes met his. "But I tell you, Robert Kadarin, or whatever you call yourself now, *beware!* If you have any flaw, it will expose it brutally; if you seek only power, it will turn your purposes to such ruin as you cannot even guess; and if you kindle its fires recklessly, they will turn on you, and consume you and all you love! I *know*, Kadarin! I have stood in Sharra's flame and though I emerged unburnt, I was not unscarred. I have long put aside my power, I am old, but this much I can still say—*beware!*"

And suddenly the identity swirled and dissolved. Thyra sighed, the circle dropped like strands of cobweb and we stood, staring at one another dazed, in the darkening hallway.

Thyra was white with exhaustion and I felt Marjorie's hands trembling on mine.

"Enough," I said firmly, knowing that until it was certain who was to take the centerpolar place, until we knew which of us was Keeper, it was my responsibility to safeguard them all. I motioned to the others to separate, draw apart physically, to break the last clinging strands of rapport. I let Marjorie's hands go with regret. "Enough. We all need rest and food. You must learn never to overtax your physical strength." I spoke deliberately, in a firm, didactic manner, to minimize any emotional contact or concern. "Self-discipline is just as important as talent, and far more important than skill."

But I was not nearly as detached as I sounded, and I suspected they knew it.

Three days later, at dinner in the great lighted hall, I spoke of my original mission to Kermiac. Beltran, I knew, felt that I had wholly turned my back on Comyn. It was true that I no longer felt bound to my father's will. He had lied to me, used me ruthlessly. Kadarin had spoken of Compact as just another Comyn plot to disarm Darkover, to keep the Council's rule intact. Now I wondered how my elderly kinsman felt about it. He had ruled many years in the mountains, with the Terrans ever at hand. It was reasonable he should see everything differently from the Comyn lords. I had heard their side; I had never been given opportunity to know the other view.

When I spoke to him of Hastur's disquiet about the violations of Compact and told him I had been sent to find out the truth, he nodded and frowned, thinking deeply. At last he said, "Danvan Hastur and I have crossed words over this before. I doubt we will ever really agree. I have a good bit of respect for that man: down there between the Dry Towns and the Terrans he has no bed of roses, and all things considered he's managed well. But his choices aren't mine, and fortunately I'm not oath-bound to abide by them. Myself, I believe the Compact has outlived its usefulness, if it ever had any, which I'm no longer sure of."

I had known he felt this way, yet I felt shocked. From childhood I had been taught to think of Compact as the first ethical code of civilized men.

"Stop and think," he said. "Do you realize that we are a

part of a great galactic civilization? The days when any single planet could live in isolation is over forever. Swords and shields belong to that day and must be abandoned with it. Do you realize what an anachronism we are?"

"No, I don't realize that, sir. I don't know that much about any world but this one."

"And not too much even about this one, it seems. Let me ask you this, Lew, when did you learn the use of weapons?"

"At seven or eight, more or less." I had always been proud that I need fear no swordsman in the Domains—or out of them.

"I, too," said the old man. "And when I came to rule in my father's high seat, I took it for granted that I would have bodyguards following me everywhere but my marriage-bed! Halfway through my life I realized I was living inside a dead past, gone for centuries. I sent my bodyguards home to their farms, except for a few old men who had no other skills and no livelihood. I let *them* walk around looking important more for their own usefulness than mine, and yet I sit here, untroubled and free in my own house, my rule unquestioned."

I felt horrified. "At the mercy of any malcontent—"

He shrugged. "I am here, alive and well. By and large, those who give allegiance to Aldaran *want* me here. If they did not, I would persuade them peacefully or step aside and let them try to rule better. Do you honestly believe Hastur keeps authority over the Domains only because he has a bigger and better bodyguard than his rivals?"

"Of course not. I never heard him seriously challenged."

"So. My people too are content with my rule, I need no private army to enforce it."

"But still . . . some malcontent, some madman—"

"Some slip on a broken stair, some lightning-bolt, some misstep by a frightened or half-broken horse, some blunder by my cook with a deadly mushroom for a wholesome one . . . Lew, every man alive is divided from death by that narrow a line. That's as true at your age as mine. If I put down rebellion with armed men, does it prove me the better man, or only the man who can pay the better swordsmen or build the bigger weapons? The long reign of Compact has meant only that every man is expected to settle his affairs with his sword instead of his brains or the rightness of his cause."

"Just the same, it has kept peace in the Domains for generations."

"Flummery!" the old man said rudely. "You have peace in the Domains because, by and large, most of you down there are content to obey Comyn law and no longer put every little matter to the sword. Your celebrated Castle Guard is a police force keeping drunks off the streets! I'm not insulting it, I think that's what it should be. When did *you* last draw your sword in earnest, son?"

I had to stop and think. "Four years ago bandits in the Kilghard hills broke into Armida, stealing horses. We chased them back across the hills and hanged a few of them."

"When did you last fight a duel?"

"Why, never."

"And you last drew your sword against common horse-thieves. No rebellions, wars, invasions from nonhumans?"

"Not in my time." I began to see what he was driving at.

"Then," he said, "why risk law-abiding men, good men and loyal, against horse-thieves, bandits, rabble who have no right to the protection given men of honor? Why not develop really effective protection against the lawless and let your sons learn something more useful than the arts of the sword? I am a peaceful man and Beltran will, I think, have no reason to force himself on my people by armed force. The law in the Hellers states that no man given to breach of the peace may own any weapon, even a sword, and there are laws about how long a pocketknife he may carry. As for the men who keep my laws, they are welcome to any weapon they can get. An honest man is less threat to our world with a Terran's nerve-blaster than a lawless one with my cook's paring knife or a stonemason's hammer. I don't believe in matching good honest men against rogues, both armed with the same weapons. When I left off fairy tales I left off believing that an honest man must always be a better swordsman than a horse-thief or a bandit. The Compact, which allows unlimited handweapons and training in their use to good men and criminals alike, has simply meant that honest men must struggle day and night to make themselves stronger than brutes."

There was certainly some truth in what he said. Now that my father was so lame, Dyan was certainly the best swordsman in the Domains. Did that mean if Dyan fought a duel, and won, that his cause was therefore just? If the horse-thieves had been better swordsmen than ours at Armida, would they have had a right to our horses? Yet there was a flaw in his logic too. Perhaps there was no flawless logic anywhere.

"What you say is true, Uncle, as far as it goes. Yet ever since the Ages of Chaos, it's been known that if an unjust man gets a weapon he can do great damage. With the Compact, and such a weapon as he can get under the Compact, he can do only one man's worth of damage."

Kermiac nodded, acknowledging the truth of what I said. "True. Yet if weapons are outlawed, soon only outlaws can get them—and they always do. Old Hastur's heir so died. The Compact is only workable as long as everybody is willing to keep it. In today's world, with Darkover on the very edge of becoming part of the Empire, it's unenforceable. Completely unenforceable. And if you try to make an unworkable law work and fail, it encourages other men to break laws. I have no love for futile gestures, so I enforce only such laws as I can. I suspect the only answer is the one that Hastur, even though he pays lip service to Compact, is trying to spread in the Domains: make the land so safe that no man seriously needs to defend himself, and let weapons become toys of honor and tokens of manhood."

Uneasily I touched the hilt of the sword I had worn every day of my adult life.

Kermiac patted my wrist affectionately. "Don't trouble yourself, nephew. The world will go as it will, not as you or I would have it. Leave tomorrow's troubles for tomorrow's men to solve. I'll leave Beltran the best world I can, but if he wants a better one he can always build it himself. I'd like to think that some day Beltran and the heir to Hastur could sit down together and build a better world, instead of spitting venom at one another between Thendara and Caer Donn. And I'd like to think that when that day comes you'll be there to help, whether you're standing behind Beltran or young Hastur. Just that you'll be *there*."

He picked up a nut and cracked it with his strong old teeth. I wondered what he knew of Beltran's plans, wondered too how much of what he said was straightforward, how much meant to reach Hastur's ears. I was beginning to love the old man, yet unease nagged at my mind. Most of the crowd at dinner had dispersed; Thyra and Marjorie were gathered with Beltran and Rafe near one of the windows. Kermiac saw the direction of my eyes and laughed.

"Don't sit here among the old men, nephew, take yourself along to the young folk."

"A moment," I said. "Beltran calls them foster-sisters; are they your kinswomen too?"

"Thyra and Marguerida? That's an odd story," Kermiac said. "Some years ago I had a bodyguard in my house, a Terran named Zeb Scott, while I still indulged in such foolishness, and I gave him Felicia Darriell to wife—Does this long tale weary you, Lew?"

"By no means." I was eager to know all I could about Marjorie's parentage.

"Well, then. The Darriell's are an old, old family in these hills, and the last of them, old Rakhal—Rafe's true name is Rakhal, you know, but my Terrans find that hard to say—old Rakhal Darriell dwelt as a hermit, half mad and all drunk, in his family mansion, which was falling to ruins even then. And now and then, when he was maddened with wine or when the Ghost Wind blew—the *kireseth* still grows in some of the far valleys—he would wander crazed in the forests. He'd tell strange tales, afterward, of women astray in the forests, dancing naked in the winds and taking him to their arms—such a tale as any madman might tell. But a long time ago, a very long time now, old Rakhal, they say, came to Storn Castle bearing a girl-child in his arms, saying he had found her like this, naked in the snow at his doorway. He told them the babe was his child by one of the forest-folk, cast out to die by her kin. So the lady of Storn took her in for, whatever the babe was, human or of the forest-folk, old Rakhal could not rear her. She fostered her with her own daughters. And many years after, when I was married to Lauretta Storn-Lanart, Felicia Darriell, as she was called, came with Lauretta among her ladies and companions. Felicia's oldest child—Thyra there—may well be my daughter. When Lauretta was heavy with child it was Felicia, by her wish, that I took to my bed. Lauretta's first child was stillborn and she took Thyra as a fosterling. I have always treated her as Beltran's sister, although nothing is certain. Later, Felicia married Zeb Scott, and these two, Rafe and Marguerida, are half-Terran and none of your kin. But Thyra may well be your cousin."

He added, musing, "Old Rakhal's tale may well have been true. Felicia was a strange woman; her eyes were very strange. I always thought such tales mere drunken babble. Yet, having known Felicia ..." He was silent, lost in memories of time long past. I looked at Marjorie, wondering. I had never believed such tales, either. Yet those eyes . . .

Kermiac laughed and dismissed me. "Nephew, since your eyes and heart are over there with Marguerida, take the rest of yourself along over there too!"

Thyra was gazing intently out into the storm; I could feel the questing tendrils of her thought and knew she was searching, through the gathering darkness, for her lover. Now Thyra, I could well believe, was not all human.

But Marjorie? She reached her hands to me and I caught them in one of mine, circled her waist with my free arm. Beltran said, joining us, "He'll be here soon. What then, Lew?"

"It's your plan," I said, "and Kadarin is certainly enough of a telepath to fit into a circle. You know what we want to do, though there are limits to what can be done with a group this size. There are certainly technologies we can demonstrate. Road-building and surfacing, for instance. It should convince the Terrans we are worth watching. Powered aircraft may be more difficult. There may be records of that at Arilinn. But it won't be fast or easy."

"You still feel I'm not fit to take a place in the matrix circle."

"There's no question of fitness, you're not *able*. I'm sorry, Beltran. Some powers may develop. But without a catalyst . . ."

He set his mouth and for a moment he looked ugly. Then he laughed. "Maybe some day we can persuade the young one at Syrtis to join us, since you say he does not love the Comyn."

There had been no sound I could hear, but Thyra turned from the window and went out of the hall. A few moments later she came back with Kadarin. He held in his arms a long, heavily wrapped bundle, waving away the servants who would have taken it.

Kermiac had risen to leave the table; he waited for Kadarin at the edge of the dais while the other people in the hall were leaving. Kadarin said, "I have it, kinsman, and a fine struggle I had with the old lady, too. Desideria sends you her compliments." He made a wry face. Kermiac said, with a bleak smile, "Aye, Desideria ever had a mind of her own. You didn't have to use strong persuasion?"

There was sarcasm in Kadarin's grin. "You know Lady

Storn better than I. Do you really think it would have availed much? Fortunately, it was not needed. I have small talent for bullying womenfolk."

Kermiac held out his hand to take it, but Kadarin shook his head. "No, I made her a pledge and I must keep it, kinsman, to place it only in the hands of the Arilinn telepath and be guided by his judgment."

Kermiac nodded and said, "Her judgment is good; honor your pledge, then, Bob."

Kadarin laid the long bundle on the bench while he began removing his snow-crusted outer wear. I said, "You look as if you'd been out in the worst weather in the Hellers, Bob. Was it as bad as that?"

He nodded. "I didn't want to linger or be stormbound on the way, carrying *this*." He nodded at the bundle, accepted the hot drink Marjorie brought him and gulped it thirstily. "Season's coming in early; another bad storm on the way. What have you done while I was away?"

Thyra met his eyes and I felt, like a small palpable shock, the quick touch and link as he came into the circle. It was easier than long explanations. He set down the empty cup and said, "Well done, children."

"Nothing's done," I said, "only begun."

Thyra knelt and began to unfasten the knots in the long bundle. Kadarin caught her wrist. "No," he said, "I made a pledge. Take it, Lew."

"We know," said Thyra, "we heard you." She sounded impatient.

"Then will you set my word at nothing, wild-bird?" His hand holding hers motionless was large, brown, heavy-knuckled. Like the Ardais and the Aillards, he had six fingers on his hand. I could easily believe nonhuman blood there, too. Thyra smiled at him and he drew her against him, saying, "Lew, it's for you to take this."

I knelt beside the bundle and began to unfasten the heavy wrappings. It was longer than my arm and narrow, and had been bundled into layer on layer of heavy canvas cloth, the layers bound and knotted with embroidered straps. Marjorie and Beltran came to look over my shoulder as I struggled with the knots. Inside the last layer of heavy canvas was a layer of raw colorless silk, like the insulation of a matrix. When I finally got it unrolled, I saw that it was a ceremonial or ornamental sword, forged of pure silver. An atavistic little prickle went down to the ends of my spine. I had never set eyes on this before. But I knew what it was.

My hands almost refused to take it, despite the thing of beauty the forge-folk had made to cover and guard it. Then I forced myself back to sanity. Was I as superstitious as Thyra thought me? I took the hilt in my hand, sensing the pulsing life within. I seized the sword in both hands and gave the hilt a hard twist.

It came off in my hand. Inside lay the matrix itself, a great blue stone, with an inner glimmer curling fires which, trained as I was, made my head reel and my vision blur.

I heard Thyra gasp aloud. Beltran had quickly turned away. If it made me, after three seasons in Arilinn, fight for control, I could imagine what it had done to him. I quickly wadded it up in the silk, then took it gingerly between my fingers. I was immensely reluctant to look, even for a moment, into those endlessly *live* depths. Finally I bent my eyes to it. Space wrenched, tore at me. For a moment I felt myself falling, saw the face of a young girl shrouded in flame, crimson and orange and scarlet. It was a face I *knew* somehow—*Desideria!* The old woman I had seen in Karadin's mind! Then the face shifted, shrouded, was no more a woman but a looming, towering form of fire, a woman's form, chained in gold, rising, flaming, striking, walls crumbling like dust. . . .

I wrapped it in the silk again and said, "Do you know what this is?"

Kadarin said, "It was used of old by the forge-folk to bring metals from the deeps of the ground, to their fires."

"I'm not so sure," I said. "Some of the Sharra matrices were used that way. Others were . . . less innocent. I'm not sure this is a monitored matrix."

"All the better. We want no Comyn eyes spying on what we do."

"But that means it's essentially uncontrollable," I said. "A monitored matrix has a safety factor: if it gets out of hand the monitor takes over and breaks the circle. Which is why I still have a right hand." I held out the ugly scar. He flinched slightly and said, "Are you afraid?"

"Of this happening again? No, I know what precautions to take. But of this matrix? Yes, I am."

"You Comyn are superstitious cowards! All my life I've heard about the powers of the Arilinn-trained telepaths and mechanics. Now you are afraid—"

Anger surged through me. Comyn, was I? And cowardly? It seemed that the anger pulsed, beat within me, surging up my arm from the matrix in my fist. I thrust it back into the sword, sealing it there. Thyra said, "Nothing's gained by calling names. Lew, *can* this be used for what Beltran has in mind?"

I found I had an incomprehensible desire to take the sword in my hand again. The matrix seemed to call me, demanding that I take it out, master it. . . . It was almost a sensual hunger. Could it really be dangerous, then? I put the canvas wrappings around it and gave Thyra's question some thought.

Finally I said, "Given a fully trained circle, one I can trust, yes, probably. A tower circle is usually seven or eight mechanics and a Keeper, and we seldom handle more than fourth- or fifth-level matrices. I know this one is stronger than that. And we have no trained Keeper."

"Thyra can do that work," Kadarin said.

I considered it for a moment. She had, after all, drawn us all around her, taking the central position with swift precision. But finally I shook my head.

"I won't risk it. She's worked wild too long. She's self-taught and her training could come apart under stress." I thought of the prowling beast I had sensed when the circle formed. I felt Thyra's eyes on me and was painfully embarrassed, but I had been disciplined to rigid honesty within a circle. You can't hide from one another, it's disaster to try.

"I can control her," Kadarin said.

"I'm sorry, Bob. That's no answer. She herself must be in control or she'll be killed, and it's not a nice way to die. I could control her myself, but the essence of a Keeper is that she does the controlling. I trust her powers, Bob, but not her judgment under stress. If I'm to work with her, I must trust her implicitly. And I can't. Not as Keeper. I think Marjorie can do it—if she will."

Kadarin was regarding Marjorie with a curious wry smile. He said, "You're rationalizing. Do you think I don't know you're in love with her, and want her to have this post of honor?"

"You're mad," I said. "Damn it, yes, I'm in love with her! But it's clear you know nothing about matrix circles. Do you think I *want* her to be Keeper in this circle? Don't you know that will make it impossible for me to touch her? As long as she's a functioning Keeper, none of us may touch her, and I least of all, because I love her and want her. Didn't you know that?" I drew my fingers slowly away from Marjorie's. My hand felt cold and alone.

"Comyn superstition," Beltran said scornfully, "driveling nonsense about virgins and purity! Do you really believe all that rubbish?"

"Belief has nothing to do with it," I said, "and no, Keepers don't have to be sheltered virgins in this day and age. But while they're working in the circles they stay strictly chaste. That's a physical fact. It has to do with nerve currents. It's no more superstition than what every midwife knows, that a pregnant woman must not ride too fast or hard, nor wear tight lacing in her dresses. And even so, it's dangerous. Terribly dangerous. If you think I *want* Marjorie to be our Keeper, you are more ignorant than I thought!"

Kadarin looked at me steadily, and I saw that he was weighing what he said. "I believe you," he said at last. "But you believe Marjorie can do it?"

I nodded, wishing I could lie and be done with it. A telepath's love life is always infernally complicated. And Marjorie and I had just found each other. We had had so very little, so very little. . . .

"She can, if she will," I said at last, "but she must consent. No woman can be made Keeper unwilling. It is too strong a weight to carry, except by free will."

Kadarin looked at us both then and said, "So it all hangs on Marjorie, then. What about it, Margie? Will you be Keeper for us?"

She looked at me and, biting her lip, she stretched out her hands to mine. She said, "Lew, I don't know . . ."

She was afraid, and small wonder. And then, like a compelling, magical dream, I remembered the morning when we had walked together through Caer Donn and shared our dreams for this world. Wasn't this worth a little danger, a little waiting for our happiness? A world where we need not feel shame but pride for our dual heritage, Darkovan and Terran? I felt Marjorie catch the dream, too, as without a word, she slowly loosed her hand from mine and we drew apart. From this moment until our work was ended and the circle dissolved, Marjorie would stand inviolate, set apart, alone. The Keeper.

No words were necessary, but Marjorie spoke the simple words as if they were an oath sealed in fire.

"I agree. If you will help me, I will do what I can."

Chapter FIFTEEN

For ten days the storm had raged, sweeping down from the Hellers through the Kilghard Hills and falling on Thendara with fury almost unabated. Now the weather was clear and fine, but Regis rode with his head down, ignoring the bright day.

He'd failed, he felt, having made a pledge and then doing nothing. Now he was being packed off to Neskaya in Gabriel's care, like a sick child with a nanny! But he raised his head in surprise as they made the sharp turn that led down the valley toward Syrtis.

"Why are we taking this road?"

"I have a message for Dom Felix," Gabriel said. "Will the few extra miles weary you? I can send you on to Edelweiss with the Guards. . . ."

Gabriel's careful solicitude set him on edge. As if a few extra miles could matter! He said so, irritably.

His black mare, sure-footed, picked her way down the path. Despite his disclaimer to Gabriel, he felt sick and faint, as he had felt most of the time since his collapse in Kennard's rooms. For a day or two, delirious and kept drugged, he had had no awareness of what was going on, and even now much of what he remembered from the last few days was illusion. Danilo was there, crying out in wild protest, being roughly handled, afraid, in pain. It seemed that Lew was there sometimes too, looking cold and stern and angry with him, demanding again and again, *What is it that you're afraid to know?* He knew, because they told him afterward, that for a day or two he had been so dangerously ill that his grandfather never left his side, and when, waking once between sick intervals of fragmented hallucinations, he had seen his grandfather's face and asked, "Why are you not at Council?" the old man had said violently, "Damn the Council!" Or was that another dream? He knew that once Dyan had come

222

into the room, but Regis had hidden his face in the bedclothes and refused to speak to him, gently though Dyan
spoke. Or was *that* a dream, too? And then, for what seemed
like years, he had been on the fire-lines at Armida, when they
had lived day and night with terror; during the day the hard
manual work kept it at bay, but at night he would wake, sobbing and crying out with fear. . . . *That* night, his grandfather
told him, his half-conscious cries had grown so terrified, so
insistent, that Kennard Alton, himself seriously ill, had come
and stayed with him till morning, trying to quiet him with
touch and rapport. But he kept crying out for Lew and Kennard couldn't reach him.

Regis, ashamed of this childish behavior, had finally agreed
to go to Neskaya. The blur of memory and thought-images
embarrassed him, and he didn't try to sort out the truth from
the drugged fantasies. Just the same, he knew that at least
once Lew *had* been there, holding him in his arms like the
frightened child he had been. When he told Kennard so, Kennard nodded soberly and said, "It's very likely. Perhaps you
were astray in time; or perhaps from where he is, Lew sensed
that you had need for him, and reached you as a telepath
can. I had never known you were so close to him." Regis felt
helpless, vulnerable, so when he was well enough to ride, he
had meekly agreed to go to Neskaya Tower. It was intolerable to live like this. . . .

Gabriel's voice roused him now, saying in dismay, "Look!
What's this? Dom Felix—"

The old man was riding up the valley toward them, astride
Danilo's black horse, the Armida-bred gelding which was the
only really good horse at Syrtis. He was coming at what was,
for a man his age, a breakneck pace. For a few minutes it
seemed he would ride full tilt into the party on the path, but
just a few paces away he pulled up the black and the animal
stood stiff-legged, breathing hard, its sides heaving.

Dom Felix glared straight at Regis. "Where is my son?
What have you thieving murderers done with him?"

The old man's fury and grief were like a blow. Regis said
in confusion, "Your son? Danilo, sir? Why do you ask *me*?"

"What have you vicious, detestable tyrants done with him?
How dare you show your faces on my land, after stealing
from me my youngest—"

Regis tried to interrupt and quell the torrent of words.
"Dom Felix, I do not understand. I parted from Danilo some

days ago, in your own orchard. I have not laid eyes on him since; I have been ill—" The memory of his drugged dream tormented him, of Danilo being roughly handled, afraid, in pain. . . .

"Liar!" Dom Felix shouted, his face red and ugly with rage and pain. "Who but you—"

"That's enough, sir," said Gabriel, breaking in with firm authority. "No one speaks like that to the heir to Hastur. I give you my word—"

"The word of a Hastur lickspittle and toady! *I* dare speak against these filthy tyrants! Did you take my son for your—" He flung a word at Regis next to which "catamite" was a courtly compliment. Regis paled against the old man's rage.

"Dom Felix—if you will hear me—"

"Hear you! My son heard you, sir, all your fine words!"

Two Guardsmen rode close to the enraged old man, grasping the reins of his horse, holding him motionless.

"Let him go," Gabriel said quietly. "Dom Felix, we know nothing of your son. I came to you with a message from Kennard Alton concerning him. May I deliver it?"

Dom Felix quieted himself with an effort that made his eyes bulge. "Speak, then, Captain Lanart, and the Gods deal with you as you Comyn dealt with my son."

"The Gods do so to me and more also, if I or mine harmed him," Gabriel said. "Hear the message of Kennard, Lord Alton, Commander of the Guard: 'Say to Dom Felix of Syrtis that it is known to me what a grave miscarriage of justice was done in the Guards this year, of which his son Danilo-Felix, cadet, may have been an innocent victim; and ask that he send his son Danilo-Felix to Thendara under any escort of his own choosing, to stand witness in a full investigation against men in high places, even within Comyn, who may have misused their powers.' " Gabriel paused, then added, "I was also authorized to say to you, Dom Felix, that ten days from now, when I have escorted my brother-in-law, who is in poor health at this moment, to Neskaya Tower, that I shall myself return and escort your son to Thendara, and that you are yourself welcome to accompany him as his protector, or to name any guardian or relative of your own choosing, and that Kennard Alton will stand personally responsible for his safety and honor."

Dom Felix said unsteadily, "I have never had reason to

doubt Lord Alton's honor or goodwill. Then Danilo is not in Thendara?"

One of the Guards, a grizzled veteran, said, "You know me, sir, I served with Rafael in the war, sixteen years gone. I kept an eye on young Dani for his sake. I give you my word, sir, Dani isn't there, with Comyn conniving or without it."

The old man's face gradually paled to its normal hue. He said, "Then Danilo did not run away to join you, Lord Regis?"

"On my honor, sir, he did not. I saw him last when we parted in your own orchard. Tell me, how did he go, did he leave no word?"

The old man's face was clay-colored. "I saw nothing. Dani had been hunting; I was not well and had kept my bed. I said to him I had a fancy for some birds for supper, the Gods forgive me, and he took a hawk and went for them, such a good obedient son—" His voice broke. "It grew late and he did not return. I had begun to wonder if his horse had gone lame, or he'd gone on some boy's prank, and then old Mauris and the kitchen-folk came running into my chamber and told me, they saw him meet with riders on the path and saw him struck down and carried away. . . ."

Gabriel looked puzzled and dismayed. "On my word, Dom Felix, none of us had art, part or knowledge of it. What hour was this? Yesterday? The day before?"

"The day before, Captain. I swooned away at the news. But as soon as my old bones would bear me I took horse to come and hold . . . someone to account. . . ." His voice faded again. Regis drew his own horse close to Dom Felix and took his arm. He said impulsively, "Uncle," using the same word he used to Kennard Alton, "you are father to my friend; I owe you a son's duty as well. Gabriel, take the Guards, go and look, question the house-folk." He turned back to Dom Felix, saying gently, "I swear I will do all I can to bring Danilo safely back. But you are not well enough to ride. Come with me." Taking the other's reins in his own hands, he turned the old man's mount and led him down the path into the cobbled courtyard. Dismounting quickly, he helped Dom Felix down and guided his tottering steps. He led him into the hall, saying to the old half-blind servant there, "Your master is ill, fetch him some wine."

When it had been brought and Dom Felix had drunk a little, Regis sat beside him, near the cold hearth.

"Lord Regis, your pardon . . ."

"None needed. You have been sorely tried, sir."

"Rafael . . ."

"Sir, as my father held your elder son dear, I tell you Danilo's safety and honor are as dear to me as my own." He looked up as the Guardsmen came into the hall. "What news, Gabriel?"

"We looked over the ground where he was taken. The ground was trampled and he had laid about him with his dagger."

"Hawking, he had no other weapon."

"They cut off sheath and all." Gabriel handed Dom Felix the weapon. He drew it forth a little way, saw the Hastur crest on it. He said, "Dom Regis—"

"We swore an oath," said Regis, drawing Danilo's dagger from his own sheath where he wore it, "and exchanged blades, in token of it." He took the dagger with the Hastur crest, saying, "I will bear this to restore to him. Did you see anything else, Gabriel?"

One of the Guardsmen said, "I found this on the ground, torn off in the fight. He must have fought valiantly for a young lad outnumbered." He held out a long, heavy cloak of thick colorless wool, bound with leather buckles and straps. It was much cut and slashed. Dom Felix sat up a little and said, "That fashion of cloak has not been worn in the Domains in my lifetime; I believe they wear them still in the Hellers. And it is lined with marl-fur; it came from somewhere beyond the river. Mountain bandits wore such cloaks. But why Dani? We are not rich enough to ransom him, nor important enough to make him valuable as a hostage."

Regis thought grimly that Dyan's men came from the Hellers. Aloud he said only, "Mountain men act for whoever pays them well. Have you enemies, Dom Felix?"

"No. I have dwelt in peace, farming my acres, for fifteen years." The old man sounded stunned. He looked at Regis and said, "My lord, if you are sick—"

"No matter," Regis said. "Dom Felix, I pledge you by the oath no Hastur may break that I shall find out who has done this to you, and restore Dani to you, or my own life stand for it." He laid his hand over the old man's for a moment. Then he straightened and said, "One of the Guardsmen shall remain here, to look after your lands in your son's absence. Gabriel, you ride back with the escort to Thendara and carry this news to Kennard Alton. And show him this cloak; he may know where in the Hellers it was woven."

"Regis, I have orders to take you to Neskaya."

"In good time. This must come first," Regis said. "You are a Hastur, Gabriel, if only by marriage-right, and your sons are Hastur heirs. The honor of Hastur is your honor, too, and Danilo is my sworn man."

His brother-in-law looked at him, visibly wavering. There were good things about being heir to a Domain, Regis decided like having your orders obeyed without question. He said impatiently, "I shall remain here to bear my friend's father company, or wait at Edelweiss."

"You cannot stay here unguarded," Gabriel said at last. "Unlike Dani, you *are* rich enough for ransom, and important enough for a hostage." He stood near enough to Comyn to be undecided. "I should send a Guardsman with you to Edelweiss," he said. Regis protested angrily. "I am not a child! Must I have a nanny trotting at my heels to ride three miles?"

Gabriel's own older sons were beginning to chafe at the necessity of being guarded night and day. Finally Gabriel said, "Regis, look at me. You were placed in my care. Pledge me your word of honor to ride directly to Edelweiss, without turning aside from your road unless you meet armed men, and you may ride alone."

Regis promised and, taking his leave of Dom Felix, rode away. As he rode toward Edelweiss, he thought, a little triumphantly, that he had actually outwitted Gabriel. A more experienced officer would have allowed him, perhaps, to ride to Edelweiss on his promise to go directly . . . but he would also have made Regis give his pledge not to depart from there without leave!

His triumph was short-lived. The knowledge of what he must do was tormenting him. He had to find out where—and how—Danilo was taken. And there was only one way to do that: his matrix. He had never touched the jewel since the ill-fated experiment with *kirian*. It was still in the insulated bag around his neck. The memory of that twisting sickness when he looked into Lew's matrix was still alive in him, and he was horribly afraid.

Surprisingly for these peaceful times, the gates of Edelweiss were shut and barred, and he wondered what alarm had sealed them. Fortunately most of Javanne's servants knew his voice, and after a moment Javanne came running down from the house, a servant-woman puffing at her heels. "Regis! We had word that armed men had been seen in the hills! Where is Gabriel?"

He took her hands. "Gabriel is well, and on his way to Thendara. Yes, armed men were seen at Syrtis, but I think it was a private feud, not war, little sister."

She said shakily, "I remember so well the day Father rode to war! I was a child then, and you not born. And then word came that he was dead, with so many men, and the shock killed Mother. . . ."

Javanne's two older sons came racing toward them, Rafael and Gabriel, nine years old and seven, dark-haired, well-grown boys. They stopped short at the sight of Regis and Rafael said, "I thought you were sick and going to Neskaya. What are you doing here, kinsman?"

Gabriel said, "Mother said there would be war. Is there going to be war, Regis?"

"No, as far as I know, there is no war here or anywhere, and you be thankful for it," Regis said. "Go away now, I must talk with your mother."

"May I ride Melisande down to the stables?" Gabriel begged, and Regis lifted the child into the saddle and went up to the house with Javanne.

"You have been ill; you are thinner," Javanne said. "I had word from Grandfather you were on your way to Neskaya. Why are you here instead?"

He glanced at the darkening sky. "Later, sister, when the boys are abed and we can talk privately. I've been riding all the day; let me rest a little and think. I'll tell you everything then."

Left alone, he paced his room for a long time, trying to steel himself to what he knew he must do.

He touched the small bag around his neck, started to draw it out, then thrust it back, unopened. Not yet.

He found Javanne before the fire in her small sitting room; she had just finished nursing the smaller of the twins and was ready for dinner. "Take the baby to the nursery, Shani," she told the nurse, and tell the women I'm not to be disturbed for any reason. My brother and I will dine privately."

"*Su serva, domna,*" the woman said, took the baby and went away. Javanne came and served Regis herself. "Now tell me, brother. What happened?"

"Armed men have taken Danilo Syrtis from his home."

She looked puzzled. "Why? And why should you disturb yourself about it?"

"He is my paxman; we have sworn the oath of *bredin,*" Regis said, "and it may well be private revenge. This is what I must find out." He gave her such an edited version of the affair in the cadet corps as he thought fit for a woman's ears. She looked sick and shocked. "I have heard of Dyan's ... preferences, who has not? At one time there was talk he should marry me. I was glad when he refused, although I, of course, was offered no choice in the matter. He seems to me a sinister man, even cruel, but I had not thought him criminal as well. He is Comyn, and oath-bound never to meddle with the integrity of a mind. You think *he* took Dani, to silence him?"

"I cannot accuse him without proof," Regis said. "Javanne, you spent time in a tower. How much training have you?"

"I spent one season there," she said. "I can use a matrix, but they said I had no great talent for it, and Grandfather said I must marry young."

He drew out his own matrix and said, "Can you show me how to use it?"

"Yes, no great skill is needed for that. But not as safely as they can at Neskaya, and you are not yet wholly well. I would rather not."

"I must know now, at once, what has come to Danilo. The honor of our house is engaged, sister." He explained why. She sat with her plate pushed aside, twirling a fork. At last she said "Wait" and turned away from him, fumbling at the throat of her gown. When she turned back there was something silk-wrapped in her hands. She spoke slowly, the troubled frown still on her features. "I have never seen Danilo. But when I was a little maiden, and old Dom Felix was the hawk-master, I knew Dom Rafael well; he was Father's bodyguard and they went everywhere together. He used to call me pet names and take me up on his saddle and give me rides. ... I was in love with him, as a little girl can be with any handsome man who is kind and gentle to her. Oh, I was not yet ten years old, but when word came that he had been killed, I think I wept more for him than I did for Father. I remember once I asked him why he had no wife and he kissed my cheek and said he was waiting for me to grow up to be a woman." Her cheeks were flushed, her eyes far away. At last she sighed and said, "Have you any token of Danilo, Regis?"

Regis took the dagger with the Hastur crest. He said, "We both swore on this, and it was cut from his belt when he was taken."

"Then it should resonate to him," she said, taking it in her hands and laying it lightly against her cheekbone. Then, the dagger resting in her palm, she uncovered the matrix. Regis averted his eyes, but not before he got a glimpse of a blinding blue flash that wrenched at his gut. Javanne was silent for a moment, then said in a faraway voice, "Yes, on the hillside path, four men—strange cloaks—an emblem, two eagles—cut away his dagger, sheath and all—*Regis*! He was taken away in a Terran helicopter!" She raised her eyes from the matrix and looked at him in amazement.

Regis' heart felt as if a fist were squeezing it. He said, "Not to Thendara; the Terrans there would have no use for him. Aldaran?"

Her voice was shaking. "Yes. The ensign of Aldaran is an eagle, doubled . . . and they would find it easy to beg or borrow Terran aircraft—Grandfather has done it here in urgency. But why?"

The answer was clear enough. Danilo was a catalyst telepath. There had been a time when Kermiac of Aldaran trained Keepers in his mountains, and no doubt there were ways he could still use a catalyst.

Regis said in a low voice, "He has already borne more than any untrained telepath was meant to bear. If further strain or coercion is put on him his mind may snap. I should have brought him back with me to Thendara instead of leaving him there unguarded. This is my fault."

Bleakly, struggling against a horrible fear, he raised his head. "I must rescue him. I am sworn. Javanne, you must help me key into the matrix. I have no time to go to Neskaya."

"Regis, is there no other way?"

"None. Grandfather, Kennard, the council—Dani is nothing to them. If it had been Dyan they might have exerted themselves. If Aldaran's men had kidnapped *me*, they'd have an army on the road! But Danilo? What do *you* think?"

Javanne said, "That *nedestro* heir of Kennard's. He was sent to Aldaran and he's kin to them. I wonder if he had a hand in this."

"Lew? He wouldn't."

Javanne looked skeptical. "In your eyes he can do no wrong. As a little boy you were in love with him as I with Dom Rafael; I have no child's passion for him, to blind me to what he is. Kennard forced him on Council with ugly tricks."

"You have no right to say so, Javanne. He is sealed to Comyn and tower-trained!"

She refused to argue. "In any case, I can see why you feel you must go, but you have no training, and it is dangerous. Is there such need for haste?" She looked into his eyes and said after a moment, "As you will. Show me your matrix."

His teeth clenched, Regis unwrapped the stone. He drew breath, astonished: faint light glimmered in the depths of the matrix. She nodded. "I can help you key it, then. Without that light, you would not be ready. I'll stay in touch with you. It won't do much good, but if you . . . go out and can't get back to your body, it could help me reach you." She drew a deep breath. For an instant then he felt her touch. She had not moved, her head was lowered over the blue jewel so that he saw only the parting in her smooth dark hair, but it seemed to Regis that she bent over him, a slim childish girl still much taller than he. She swung him up, as if he were a tiny child, astride her hip, holding him loosely on her arm. He had not thought of this in years, how she had done this when he was very little. She walked back and forth, back and forth, along the high-arched hall with the blue windows, singing to him in her husky low voice. . . . He shook his head to clear it of the illusion. She still sat with her head bent over the matrix, an adult again, but her touch was still on him, close, protective, sheltering. For a moment he felt that he would cry and cling to her as he had done then.

Javanne said gently, "Look into the matrix. Don't be afraid, this one isn't keyed to anyone else; mine hurt you because you're out of phase with it. Look into it, bend your thoughts on it, don't move until you see the lights waken inside it. . . ."

He tried deliberately to relax; he realized that he was tensing every muscle against remembered pain. He finally looked into the pale jewel, feeling only a tiny shock of awareness, but something inside the jewel glimmered faintly. He bent his thoughts on it, reached out, reached out . . . deep, deep inside. Something stirred, trembled, flared into a living spark.

Then it was as if he had blown his breath on a coal from the fireplace: the spark was brilliant blue fire, moving, pulsing with the very rhythm of his blood. Excitement crawled in him, an almost sexual thrill.

"Enough!" Javanne said. "Look away quickly or you'll be trapped!"

No, not yet. . . . Reluctantly, he wrenched his eyes from the stone. She said, "Start slowly. Look into it only a few minutes at a time until you can master it or it will master you. The most important lesson is that you must always control *it*, never let it control *you*."

He gave it a last glance, wrapped it again with a sense of curious regret, feeling Javanne's protective touch/embrace withdraw. She said, "You can do with it what you will, but that is not much, untrained. Be careful. You are not yet immune to threshold sickness and it may return. Can a few days matter so much? Neskaya is only a little more than a day's ride away."

"I don't know how to explain, but I feel that every moment matters. I'm afraid Javanne, afraid for Danilo, afraid for all of us. I must go now, tonight. Can you find me some old riding-clothes of Gabriel's, Javanne? These will attract too much attention in the mountains. And will you have your women make me some food for a few days? I want to avoid towns nearby where I might be recognized."

"I'll do it myself; no need for the women to see and gossip." She left him to his neglected supper while she went to find the clothing. He did not feel hungry, but dutifully stowed away a slice of roast fowl and some bread. When she came back, she had his saddlebags, and an old suit of Gabriel's. She left him by the fire to put them on, then he followed her down the hall to a deserted kitchen. The servants were long gone to bed. She moved around, making up a package of dried meat, hard bread and crackers, dried fruit. She put a small cooking-kit into the saddlebags, saying it was one which Gabriel carried on hunting trips. He watched her silently, feeling closer to this little-known sister than he had felt since he was six years old and she left their home to marry. He wished he were still young enough to cling to her skirts as he had then. An ice-cold fear gripped at him, and then the thought: before going into danger, a Comyn heir must himself leave an heir. He had refused even to think of it, as Dyan had refused, not wanting to be merely a link in a chain, the son of his father, the father of his sons. Something inside him rebelled, deeply and strongly, at what he must do. Why bother? If he did not return, it would all be the same, one of Javanne's sons named his heir. . . . He could do nothing, say nothing. . . .

He sighed. It was too late for that, he had gone too far. He said, "One thing more, sister. I go where I may never return. You know what that means. You must give me one of your sons, Javanne, for my heir."

Her face blanched and she gave a low, stricken cry. He felt the pain in it but he did not look away, and finally she ·said, her voice wavering, "Is there no other way?"

He tried to make it a feeble joke. "I have no time to get one in the usual way, sister, even if I could find some woman to help me at such short notice."

Her laughter was almost hysterical; it cut off in the middle, leaving stark silence. He saw slow acceptance dawning in her eyes. He had known she would agree. She was Hastur, of a family older than royalty. She had of necessity married beneath her, since there was no equal, and she had come to love her husband deeply, but her duty to the Hasturs came first. She only said, her voice no more than a thread, "What shall I say to Gabriel?"

"He has known since the day he took you to wife that this day might come," Regis said. "I might well have died before coming to manhood."

"Come, then, and choose for yourself." She led the way to the room where her three sons slept in cots side by side. By the candlelight Regis studied their faces, one by one. Rafael, slight and dark, close-cropped curls tousled around his face; Gabriel, sturdy and swarthy and already taller than his brother. Mikhail, who was four, was still pixie-small, fairer than the others, his rosy cheeks framed in light waving locks, almost silvery white. Grandfather must have looked like that as a child, Regis thought. He felt curiously cold and bereft. Javanne had given their clan three sons and two daughters. He might never father a son of his own. He shivered at the implications of what he was doing, bent his head, groping through an unaccustomed prayer. "Cassilda, blessed Mother of the Domains, help me choose wisely. . . ."

He moved quietly from cot to cot. Rafael was most like him, he thought. Then, on some irresistible impulse, he bent over Mikhail, lifted the small sleeping form in his arms.

"This is my son, Javanne."

She nodded, but her eyes were fierce. "And if you do not return he will be Hastur of Hastur; but if you *do* return, what then? A poor relation at the footstool of Hastur?"

Regis said quietly, "If I do not return, he will be *nedestro,* sister. I will not pledge you never to take a wife, even in return for this great gift. But this I swear to you: he shall come second only to my first legitimately born son. My second son shall be third to him, and I will take oath no other *nedestro* heir shall ever displace him. Will this content you, *breda?*"

Mikhail opened his eyes and stared about him sleepily, but he saw his mother and did not cry. Javanne touched the blond head gently. "It will content me, brother."

Holding the child awkwardly in unpracticed arms, Regis carried him out of the room where his brothers slept. "Bring witnesses," he said, "I must be gone soon. You know this is irrevocable, Javanne, that once I take this oath, he is not yours but mine, and must be sealed my heir. You must send him to Grandfather at Thendara."

She nodded. Her throat moved as she swallowed hard, but she did not protest. "Go down to the chapel," she said. "I will bring witnesses."

It was an old room in the depths of the house, the four old god-forms painted crudely on the walls, lights burning before them. Regis held Mikhail on his lap, letting the child sleepily twist a button on his tunic, until the witnesses came, four old men and two old women of the household. One of the women had been Javanne's nurse in childhood, and his own.

He took his place solemnly at the altar, Mikhail in his arms.

"I swear before Aldones, Lord of Light and my divine forefather, that Hastur of Hasturs is this child by unbroken blood line, known to me in true descent. And in default of any heir of my body, therefore do I, Regis-Rafael Felix Alar Hastur y Elhalyn, choose and name him my *nedestro* heir and swear that none save my first-born son in true marriage shall ever displace him as my heir; and that so long as I live, none shall challenge his right to my hearth, my home or my heritage. Thus I take oath in the presence of witnesses known to us both. I declare that my son shall be no more called Mikhail Regis Lanart-Hastur, but—" He paused, hesitating among old Comyn names for suitable new names which would confirm the ritual. There was no time to search the rolls for names of honor. He would commemorate, then, the desperate need which had driven him to this. "I name him Danilo," he said at last. "He shall be called Danilo Lanart Hastur, and I will so maintain to all challenge, facing my father before me and my sons to follow me, my ancestry and my posterity. And this claim may never be renounced by me while I live, nor in my name by any of the heirs of my body." He bent and kissed his son on the soft baby lips. It was done. They had a strange beginning. He wondered what the end would be. He turned his eyes on his old nurse.

"Foster-mother, I place you in charge of my son. When the roads are safe, you must take him to the Lord Hastur at Thendara, and see to it that he is given the Sign of Comyn."

Javanne was dropping slow tears, but she said nothing except, "Let me kiss him once more," and allowed the old woman to carry the child away. Regis followed them with his eyes. His son. It was a strange feeling. He wondered if he had *laran* or the unknown Hastur gift; he wondered if he would ever know, would ever see the child again.

"I must go," he said to his sister. "Send for my horse and someone to open the gates without noise." As they waited together in the gateway, he said, "If I do not return—"

"Speak no ill-omen!" she said quickly.

"Javanne, do you have the Hastur gift?"

"I do not know," she said. "None knows till it is wakened by one who holds it. We had always thought that you had no *laran*. . . ."

He nodded grimly. He had grown up with that, and even now it was too sore a wound to touch.

She said, "A day will came when you must go to Grandfather, who holds it to waken in his heir, and ask for the gift. Then, and only then, you will know what it is. I do not know myself," she said. "Only if you had died before you were declared a man, or before you had fathered a son, it would have been wakened in me so that, before my own death, I might pass it to one of my sons."

And so it might pass, still. He heard the soft clop-clop-clop of hooves in the dark. He prepared to mount, turned back a moment and took Javanne briefly in his arms. She was crying. He blinked tears from his own eyes. He whispered, "Be good to my son, darling." What more could he say?

She kissed him quickly in the dark and said, "Say you'll

come back, brother. Don't say anything else." Without waiting for another word, she wrenched herself free of him and ran back into the dark house.

The gates of Edelweiss swung shut behind him. Regis was alone. The night was dark, fog-shrouded. He fastened his cloak about his throat, touching the small pouch where the matrix lay. Even through the insulation he could feel it, though no other could have, a small live thing, throbbing. . . . He was alone with it, under the small horn of moon lowering behind the distant hills. Soon even that small light would be gone.

He braced himself, murmured to his horse, straightened his back and rode away northward, on the first step of his unknown journey.

Chapter SIXTEEN

(Lew Alton's narrative)

Until the day I die, I am sure I shall return in dreams to that first joyous time at Aldaran.

In my dreams, everything that came after has been wiped out, all the pain and terror, and I remember only that time when we were all together and I was happy, wholly happy for the first and last time in my life. In those dreams Thyra moves with all her strange wild beauty, but gentle and subdued, as she was during those days, tender and pliant and loving. Beltran is there, too, with his fire and the enthusiasm of the dream from which we had all taken the spark, my friend, almost my brother. Kadarin is always there, and in my dreams he is always smiling, kind, a rock of strength bearing us all up when we faltered. And Rafe, the son I shall never have, always beside me, his eyes lifted to mine.

And Marjorie.

Marjorie is always with me in those dreams. But there is nothing I can say about Marjorie. Only that we were together and in love, and as yet the fear was only a little, little shadow, like a breath of chill from a glacier not yet in sight. I wanted her, of course, and I resented the fact that I could not touch her even in the most casual way. But it wasn't as bad as I had feared. Psi work uses up so much energy and strength that there's nothing much left. I was with her every waking moment and it was enough. *Almost* enough. And we could wait for the rest.

I wanted a well-trained team, so I worked with them day by day, trying to shape us all together into a functioning circle which could work together, precisely tuned. As yet we were working with our small matrices; before we joined to-

237

gether to open and call forth the power of the big one, we must be absolutely attuned to one another, with no hidden weaknesses. I would have felt safer with a circle of six or eight, as at Arilinn. Five is a small circle, even with Beltran working outside as a psi monitor. But Thyra and Kadarin were stronger than most of us at Arilinn—I knew they were both stronger than I, though I had more skill and training—and Marjorie was fantastically talented. Even at Arilinn, they would have chosen her the first day as a potential Keeper.

Deep warmth and affection, even love, had sprung up among all of us with the gradual blending of our minds. It was always like this, in the building of a circle. It was closer than family intimacy, closer than sexual love. It was a sort of *blending*, as if we all melted into one another, each of us contributing something special, individual and unique, and somehow all of us together becoming more than the sum of us.

But the others were growing impatient. It was Thyra who finally voiced what they were all wanting to know.

"When do we begin to work with the Sharra matrix? We're as ready as we'll ever be."

I demurred. "I'd hoped to find others to work with us; I'm not sure we can operate a ninth-level matrix alone."

Rafe asked, "What's a ninth-level matrix?"

"In general," I said dryly, "it's a matrix not safe to handle with less than nine workers. And that's with a good, fully trained Keeper."

Kadarin said, "I told you we should have chosen Thyra."

"I won't argue with you about it. Thyra is a very strong telepath; she is an excellent technician and mechanic. But no Keeper."

Thyra asked, "Exactly how does a Keeper differ from any other telepath?"

I struggled to put it into language she could understand. "A Keeper is the central control in the circle; you've all seen that. She holds together the forces. Do you know what *energons* are?"

Only Rafe ventured to ask, "Are they the little wavy things that I can't quite see when I look into the matrix?"

Actually that was a very good answer. I said, "They're a purely theoretical name for something nobody's sure really exists. It's been postulated that the part of the brain which controls psi forces gives off a certain type of vibration which we call energons. We can describe what they do, though we can't really describe them. These, when directed and focused through a matrix—I showed you—become immensely amplified, with the matrix acting as a transformer. It is the *amplified* energons which transform energy. Well, in a matrix circle, it is the Keeper who receives the flow of energons from all members of the circle and weaves them all into a single focused beam, and this, the focused beam, is what goes through the large matrix."

"Why are Keepers always women?"

"They aren't. There have been male Keepers, powerful ones, and other men who have taken a Keeper's place. I can do it myself. But women have more positive energon flows, and they begin to generate them younger and keep them longer."

"You explained why a Keeper has to be chaste," Marjorie said, "but I still don't understand it."

Kadarin said, "That's because it's superstitious drivel. There's nothing to understand; it's gibberish."

"In the old days," I said, "when the really enormous matrix screens were made, the big synthetic ones, the Keepers *were* virgins, trained from early childhood and conditioned in ways you wouldn't believe. You know how close a matrix circle is." I looked around at them, savoring the closeness. "In those days a Keeper had to learn to be part of the circle and yet completely, *completely* apart from it."

Marjorie said, "I should think they'd have gone mad."

"A good many of them did. Even now, most of the women who work as Keepers give it up after a year or two. It's too difficult and frustrating. The Keepers at the towers aren't required to be virgins any more. But while they are working as Keepers, they stay strictly chaste."

"It sounds like nonsense," Thyra said.

"Not a bit of it," I said. "The Keeper takes and channels all that energy from all of you. No one who has ever handled these very high energy-flows wants to take the slightest chance of short-circuiting them through her own body. It would be like getting in the way of a lightning-bolt." I held out the scar again. "A three-second backflow did that to me. Well, then. In the body there are clusters of nerve fibers which control the energy flows. The trouble is that the same nerve clusters carry two kinds of energy: they carry the psi flows, the energons which carry power to the brain; they also carry the sexual messages and energies. This is why some telepaths get threshold sickness when they're in their teens: the two kinds of energy, sexual energies and *laran*, are both wakening at once. If they aren't properly handled, you can get an overload, sometimes a killer overload, because each stimulates the other and you get a circular feedback."

Beltran asked, "Is that why—"

I nodded, knowing what he was going to ask. "Whenever there's an energon drain, as in concentrated matrix work, there's some nerve overloading. Your energies are depleted—have you noticed how we've all been eating?—and your sexual energies are at a low ebb, too. The major side effect for men is temporary impotence." I repeated, smiling reassuringly at Beltran, "*Temporary* impotence. Nothing to worry about, but it does take some getting used to. By the way, if you ever find you can't eat, come to one of us right away for monitoring; that can be an early-warning signal that your energy flows are out of order."

"Monitoring. That's what you're teaching me to do, then?" Beltran asked, and I nodded. "That's right. Even if you can't link into the circle, we can use you as a psi monitor." I knew he was still resentful about this. He knew enough by now to know it was the work usually done by the youngest and least skilled in the circle. The worst of it was that unless he could stop projecting this resentment, we couldn't even use him near the circle. Not even as a psi monitor. There are few things that can disrupt a circle faster than uncontrolled resentments.

I said, "In a sense, the Keeper and the psi monitor are at the two ends of a circle—and almost equally important." This was true. "Often enough, the life of the Keeper is in the hands of the monitor, because she has no energy to waste in watching over her own body."

Beltran grinned ruefully, but he grinned. "So Marjorie is the head and I'm the old cow's tail!"

"By no means. Rather she's at the top of the ladder and you're on the ground holding it steady. You're the lifeline." I remembered suddenly that we had come far astray from the subject, and said, "With a Keeper, if the nerve channels are not *completely* clear they can overload, and the Keeper will burn up like a torch. So while the nerve channels are being used to carry these tremendous energy overloads, they cannot

be used to carry any other form of energy. And only complete chastity can keep the channels clear enough."

Marjorie said, "I can feel the channels all the time now.
Even when I'm not working in the matrices. Even when I'm
asleep."

"Good." That meant she was functioning as a Keeper now.
Beltran looked at her with half shut eyes and said, "I can *see*
them, almost."

"That's good, too," I said. "A time will come when you'll
be able to sense the energy flows from across the room—or a
mile away—and pinpoint any backflows or energy disruptions
in any of us."

I deliberately changed the subject. I asked, "Precisely what
do we want to do with the Sharra matrix, Beltran?"

"You know my plans."

"Plans, yes, precisely what do you want to do *first*? I know
that in the end you want to prove that a matrix this size can
power a starship—"

"Can it?" Marjorie asked.

"A matrix this size, love, could bring one of the smaller
moons right down out of its orbit, if we were insane enough
to try. It would, of course, destroy Darkover along with it.
Powering a starship with one might be possible, but we can't
start there. Among other reasons, we haven't got a starship
yet. We need a smaller project to experiment with, to learn
to direct and focus the force. This force is fire-powered, so
we also need a place to work where, if we lose control for a
few seconds, we won't burn up a thousand leagues of forest."

I saw Beltran shudder. He was mountain-bred too, and
shared with all Darkovans the fear of forest fire. "Father has
four Terran aircraft, two light planes and two helicopters.
One helicopter is away in the lowlands, but would the other
be suitable for experiment?"

I considered. "The explosive fuel should be removed first,"
I said, "so if anything *does* go wrong it won't burn. Otherwise a helicopter might be ideal, experimenting with the rotors to lift and power and control it. It's a question of developing control and precision. You wouldn't put Rafe, here,
to riding your fastest racehorse."

Rafe said shyly, "Lew, you said we need other telepaths.
Lord Kermiac . . . didn't he train matrix mechanics before
any of us were born? Why isn't he one of us?"

True. He had trained Desideria and trained her so well
that she could use the Sharra matrix—

"And she used it alone," said Kadarin, picking up my thoughts. "So why does it worry you that we are so few?"

"She didn't use it alone," I said. "She had fifty to a hundred believers focusing their raw emotion on the stone. More, she did not try to control it or focus it. She used it as a weapon, rather, she let it use *her*." I felt a sudden cold shudder of fear, as if every hair on my body were prickling and standing erect. I cut off the thought. I was tower-trained. I had no will to wield it for power. I was sworn.

"As for Kermiac," I said, "he is old, past controlling a matrix. I wouldn't risk it, Rafe."

Beltran grew angry. "Damn it, you might have the courtesy to ask him!"

That seemed fair enough, when I weighed the experience he must have had against his age and weakness. "Ask him, if you will. But don't press him. Let him make his own choice freely."

"He will not," Marjorie said. She colored as we all turned on her. "I thought it was my place, as Keeper, to ask him. He called it to my mind that he would not even teach me. He said a circle was only as strong as the weakest person in it, and he would endanger all our lives."

I felt both disappointed and relieved. Disappointed because I would have welcomed a chance to join him in that special bond that comes only among the members of a circle, to feel myself truly one of his kin. Relieved, because what he had told Marjorie was true, and we all knew it.

Thyra said rebelliously, "Does he understand how much we need him? Isn't it worth some risk?"

I would have risked the hazards to us, not those to him. At Arilinn they recommended gradual relinquishing of the work after early middle age, as vitality lessened.

"Always Arilinn," Thyra said impatiently, as if I had spoken aloud. "Do they train them there to be cowards?"

I turned on her, tensing myself against that sudden inner anger which Thyra could rouse in me so easily. Then, sternly controlling myself before Marjorie or the others could be caught up in the whirlpool emotion which swirled and raced between Thyra and me, I said, "One thing they *do* teach us, Thyra, is to be honest with ourselves and each other." I held out my hands to her. If she had been taught at Arilinn she would have known already that anger was all too often a concealment for less permissible emotions. "Are you ready to be so honest with me?"

Reluctantly, she took my extended hand between her own. I fought to keep my barriers down, not to barricade myself against her. She was trembling, and I knew this was a new and distressing experience to her, that no man except Kadarin, who had been her lover for so long, had ever stirred her senses. I thought, for a moment, she would cry. It would have been better if she had, but she bit her lip and stared at me, defiant. She whispered, half-aloud, "Don't—"

I broke the trembling rapport, knowing I could not force Thyra, as I would have had to do at Arilinn, to go into this all the way and confront what she refused to see. I couldn't. Not before Marjorie.

It was not cowardice, I told myself fiercely. We were all kinsmen and kinswomen. There was simply no need.

I said, changing the subject quickly, "We can try keying the Sharra matrix tomorrow, if you want. Have you explained to your father, Beltran, that we will need an isolated place to work, and asked leave to use the helicopter?"

"I will ask him tonight, when we are at dinner," Beltran promised.

After dinner, when we were all seated in the little private study we had made our center, he came to us and told us permission had been given, that we could use the old airstrip. We talked little that night, each thinking his or her own thoughts. I was thinking that it had certainly cost Kadarin a lot to turn the matrix over to me. All along, he had expected that he and Beltran would be wholly in charge of this work, that I would be only a helper, lending skill but with no force to decisions. Beltran probably still resented my taking charge, and his inability to be part of the circle was most likely the bitterest dose he had ever had to swallow.

Marjorie was a little apart from us all, the heartbreaking isolation of a Keeper having already begun to slip down over her, forcing her away from the rest. I hated myself for having condemned her to this. With one part of myself I wanted to smash it all and take her into my arms. Maybe Kadarin was right, maybe the chastity of a Keeper was the stupidest of Comyn superstitions, and Marjorie and I were going through all this hell unnecessarily.

I let myself drift out of focus, trying to see ahead to a day when we would be free to love one another. And strangely, though my life was here and I felt I had wholly renounced my allegiance to Comyn, I still tried to see myself breaking the news to my father.

I came up to ordinary awareness and saw that Rafe was asleep on the hearth. Someone should wake him and send him to bed. Was this work too strenuous for a boy his age? He should be playing with button-sized matrices, not working seriously in a circle like this!

My eyes dwelt longest, with a cruel envy, on Kadarin and Thyra, side by side on the hearthrug, gazing into the fire. No prohibition lay between them; even separated, they had each other. I saw Marjorie's eyes come to rest on them, with the same remote sadness. That, at least, we could share ... and for now it was all we could share.

I turned my hand over and looked with detached sorrow at the mark tattooed on my right wrist, the seal of Comyn. The sign that I was *laran* heir to a Domain. My father had sworn for me, before that mark was set there, for service to Comyn, loyalty to my people.

I looked at the scar from my first year at Arilinn. It ached whenever I was doing matrix work like this; it ached now. That, not the tattoo mark of my Domain, was the real sign of my loyalty to Darkover. And now I was working for a great rebirth of knowledge and wisdom to benefit all our world. I was breaking the law of Arilinn by working with untrained telepaths, unmonitored matrices. Breaking their letter, perhaps, to restore their spirit all over Darkover!

When, yawning wearily, Rafe and the women went their way to bed, I detained Kadarin for a moment. "One thing I have to know. Are you and Thyra married?"

He shook his head. "Freemates, perhaps, we never sought formal ceremonies. If she had wished I would have been willing, but I have seen too many marriage customs on too many worlds to care about any of them. Why?"

"In a tower circle this would not arise; here it must be taken into account," I said. "Is there any possibility that she could be carrying a child?"

He raised his eyebrow. I knew the question was an inexcusable intrusion, but it was necessary to know. He said at last, "I doubt it. I have traveled on so many worlds and been exposed to so many things ... I am older than I look, but I have fathered no children. Probably I cannot. So I fear if Thyra really wants a child she will have to have it fathered elsewhere. Are you volunteering?" he asked, laughing.

I found the question too outrageous even to think about. "I only felt I should warn you that matrix circle work could be dangerous if there was the slightest chance of pregnancy.

Not so much for her, but for the unborn child. There have been gruesome tragedies. I felt I should warn you."

"I should think you'd have done better to warn *her*," he said, "but I appreciate your delicacy." He gave me an odd, unreadable look and went away. Well, I had done no more than my duty in asking, and if the question distressed him, he would have to absorb and accept it, as I absorbed my frustration over Marjorie and accpeted the way Thyra's physical presence disturbed me. My dreams that night were disturbing, Thyra and Marjorie tangling into a single woman, so that again and again I would see one in dreams and suddenly discover it was the other. I should have recognized this as a sign of danger, but I only knew that when it was too late.

The next day was gray and lowering. I wondered if we would have to wait till spring for any really effective work. It might be better, giving us time to settle into our work together, perhaps find others to fit into the circle. Beltran and Kadarin would be impatient. Well, they would just have to master their impatience.

Marjorie looked cold and apprehensive; I felt the same way. A few lonesome snowflakes were drifting down, but I could not make the snow an excuse for putting off the experiment. Even Thyra's high spirits were subdued.

I unwrapped the sword in which the matrix was hidden. The forge-folk must have done this; I wondered if they had known, even halfway, what they were doing. There were old traditions about matrices like this, installed in weapons. They came out of the Ages of Chaos, when, it is said, everything it's possible to know about matrices was known, and our world nearly destroyed in consequence.

I said to Beltran, "It's very dangerous to key into a matrix this size without a very definite end in mind. It must always be controlled or it will take control of us."

Kadarin said, "You speak as if the matrix was a live thing."

"I'm not so sure it's not. I gestured at the helicopter, standing about eighty feet away at the near edge of the deserted airfield, the snow faintly beginning to edge its tail and rotors. "What I mean is this. We cannot simply key into the matrix, say 'fly' and stand here watching that thing take off. We must know precisely *how* the mechanism works, in order to know precisely what forces we must exert, and in what directions. I suggest we begin by concentrating on turning the rotor blade mechanism and getting enough speed to lift it. We don't really need a matrix this size for that, nor five workers. I could do it with this." I touched the insulated bag which held my own. "But we must have some precise way of learning to direct forces. We will discover, then, how to lift the helicopter and, since we don't want it to crash, we'll limit ourselves to turning the rotors until it lifts a few inches, then gradually diminish the speed again until we set it down. Later we can try for direction and control in flight." I turned to Beltran. "Will this demonstrate to the Terrans that psi power has material uses, so they'll give us help in developing a way to use this for a stardrive?"

It was Kadarin who answered, "Hell yes! If I know the Terrans!"

Marjorie checked Rafe's mittened hands. "Warm enough?" He pulled away indignantly, and she admonished, "Don't be silly! Shivering uses up too much energy; you have to be able to concentrate!" I was pleased at her grasp of this. My own chill was mental, not physical. I placed Beltran at a little distance from the circle. I knew it was a bitter pill to swallow, that the twelve-year-old Rafe could be part of this and he could not, and I was intensely sorry for him, but the first necessity of matrix work was to know and accept for all time your own limitations. If he couldn't, he had no business within a mile of the circle.

There was really no need for a physical circle, but I drew us close enough that the magnetic energy of our bodies would overlap and reinforce the growing bond.

I knew this was folly, a partly trained Keeper, a partly trained psi monitor ... an illegal, unmonitored matrix ... and yet I thought of the pioneers in the early days of our world, first taming the matrices. Terran colonists? Kadarin thought so. Before the towers rose, before their use was guarded by ritual and superstition. And it was given to us to retrace their steps!

I separated hilt and blade, taking out the matrix. It was not yet activated, but at its touch the old scar on my palm contracted with a stab of pain. Marjorie moved with quiet sureness into the center of the circle. She stood facing me, laying one hand on the blue stone ... *a vortex seeking to draw me into its depths, a maelstrom. . . .* I shut my eyes, reaching out for contact with Marjorie, steadying myself as I made contact with her cool silken strength. I felt Thyra drop into place, then Kadarin; the sense of an almost-unendurable burden lessened with his strength, as if he shifted a great weight onto his shoulders. Rafe dropped in like some small furry thing nestling against us.

I had the curious sense that power was flowing *up* from the stone and into the circle. It felt like being hooked up to a powerful battery, vibrating in us all, body and brain. That was wrong, that was very wrong. It was curiously invigorating, but I knew we must not succumb to it even for a moment. With relief I felt Marjorie seize control and with a determined effort direct the stream of force, focusing it through her, outward.

For a moment she stood bathed in flickering, transparent flames, then for an instant she took on the semblance of a woman . . . *golden, chained, kneeling, as the forge-folk depicted their goddess.* . . . I knew this was an illusion, but it seemed that Marjorie, or the great flickering fire-form which seemed to loom around and over and through her, reached out, seized the helicopter's rotors and spun them as a child spins a pinwheel. With my physical ears I heard the humming sound as they began to turn, slowly at first under the controlling force, then winding to a swift spinning snarl, a drone, a shriek that caught the air currents. Slowly, slowly, the great machine lifted, hovering lightly a foot or so above the ground.

Straining to be gone . . .

Hold it there! I was directing the power outward as Marjorie formed and shaped it; I could feel all the others pressed tightly against me, though physically none of us were touching. As I trembled, feeling the vast outflow of that linked conjoined power, I saw in a series of wild flashes the great form of fire I had seen before, Marjorie and not Marjorie, a raw stream of force, a naked woman, sky-tall with tossing hair, each separate lock a streamer of fire . . . I felt a curious rage surging up and through me. *Take the helicopter, hanging there useless a few inches high, hurl it into the sky, high, high, fling it down like a missile against the towers of Castle Aldaran, burning, smashing, exploding the walls like sand, hurling a rain of fire into the valley, showering fires on Caer Donn, laying the Terran base waste.* . . . I struggled with these images of fire and destruction, as a rider struggles with the bit of a hard-mouthed horse. *Too strong, too strong.* I smelled musk, a wild beast prowled the jungle of my impulses, rage, lust, a constellation of wild emotions . . . a small

skittering animal bolting up a tree in terror ... the shriek of
the rotor blades, a scream, a deafening roar. . . .

Slowly the noise lessened to a whine, a drone, a faint whir,
silence. The copter stood vibrating faintly, motionless. Marjorie, still flickering with faint glimmers of invisible fire, stood
calm, smiling absently. I felt her reach out and break the
rapport, the others slipping away one by one until we stood
alone, locked together. She withdrew her hand from the matrix and I stood cold and alone, struggling against spasms of
lust, raging violence spinning in my brain, out of control, my
heart racing, the blood pounding in my head, vision
blurred. . . .

Beltran touched me lightly on the shoulder; I felt the tu-
mult subside and with a shudder of pain managed to withdraw my consciousness. I covered the matrix quickly and
drew my aching hand over my forehead. It came away dripping.

"Zandru's hells!" I whispered. Never, not in three years at
Arilinn, had I even guessed such power. Kadarin, looking at
the helicopter thoughtfully, said, "We could have done anything with it."

"Except maybe controlled it."

"But the power is *there*, when we do learn to control it,"
Beltran said. "A spaceship. Anything."

Rafe touched Marjorie's wrist, very lightly. "For a minute
I thought you were on fire. Was that real, Lew?"

I wasn't sure if this was simply an illusion, the way generations upon generations of the forge-folk had envisioned their
goddess, the power which brought metal from the deeps of
the earth to their fires and forges. Or was this some objective
force from that strange otherworld to which the telepath
goes when he steps out of his physical body? I said, "I don't
know, Rafe. How did it seem, Marjorie?"

She said, "I saw the fire. I even felt it, a little, but it didn't
burn me. But I *did* feel that if I lost control, even for an instant, it would burn up inside and ... and take over, so that
I *was* the fire and could leap down and ... and destroy. I'm
not saying this very well. . . ."

Then it was not only me. She too had felt the weapon-
rage, the lust for destruction. I was still struggling with their
physical aftereffects, the weak trembling of adrenalin expended. If these emotions had actually arisen from within *me*, I
was not fit for this work. Yet, searching within myself, with

the discipline of the tower-trained, I found no trace of such emotion within me now.

This disquieted me. If my own hidden emotions—anger I did not acknowledge, repressed desire for one of the women, hidden hostility toward one of the others—had been wrested out of my mind to consume me, then it was a sign I had lost, under stress, my tower-imposed discipline. But those emotions, being mine, I could control. If they were not mine, but had come from elsewhere to fasten upon us, we were all in danger.

I said, "I'm more disturbed than ever about this matrix. The power's there, yes. But it's been used as a weapon. . . ."

"And it wants to destroy," Rafe said unexpectedly, "like the sword in the fairy tale; when you drew it, it would never go back into the scabbard until it had had its drink of blood."

I said soberly, "A lot of those old fairy tales were based on garbled memories of the Ages of Chaos. Maybe Rafe's right and it *does* want blood and destruction."

Thyra, her eyes brooding, asked, "Don't all men, just a little? History tells us they do. Darkovans and Terrans too."

Kadarin laughed. "You were brought up in the Comyn, Lew, so I'll forgive you for being superstitious." He put his arm around my shoulders in a warm hug. "I have more faith in the human mind than in forge-folk superstitions." We were still linked; again I felt the strength that lifted a great weight from my shoulders. I let myself lean against him. He was probably right. My mind had been filled from childhood with these old gods and powers. The science of matrix mechanics had been formulated to get rid of that. I was a skilled technician; why was I letting imagination run away with me?

Kadarin said, "Try again. Now that we know we *can* control it, it's all a matter of learning how."

"It's always up to the Keeper to decide that," I said. It troubled me that Marjorie still deferred to me. It was natural enough, for I had trained her, but she must learn that the initiative was hers, to lead, not follow.

She stretched her hand to me, setting up the primary line of force. One by one she brought us into the circle, each of us dropping into his appointed place as if we were scouts on a battlefield. This time I felt her touch Beltran, too, and *place* him so that he could maintain rapport just outside the circle. This time the force was easier to carry . . . *chained fire, electricity firmly stored in a battery, a firmly bridled racehorse.* . . . I saw the fire leap up around Marjorie, but this time I could see through it. It wasn't real, just a way of visualizing a force with no physical reality.

We stood linked, holding the pulsing power suspended. *If the Terrans will not give us what we need and deserve, we can force them to it, we need not fear their bombs nor their blasters. Do they think we are barbarians armed with swords and pitchforks?*

Clearly now, as the form of fire built up, I saw a woman, a sky-tall goddess clothed in flame, restlessly reaching to strike.

... fire raining on Caer Donn, smashing the city into rubble, starships falling like comets out of the sky ...

Firmly Marjorie reached for control, like at one of those riding-exhibitions where a single rider controls four horses with one rein, bringing us back to the physical airfield. It shimmered around us, but it was there. The helicopter blades began to hum again, to turn with a clattering roar.

We need more power, more strength. For a moment I clearly saw my father's face, felt the strong line of rapport. He had awakened my gift; we were never wholly out of touch. I felt the amazement, the *fear* with which he felt the matrix touch him, momentarily draw him in.... He was gone. Had never been there. Then I felt Thyra reach out with a sure touch and draw Kermiac within the circle as if he had been physically present. For an instant the circle expanded with his strength, burning brilliantly, and the helicopter rose easily from the ground, hung there quivering, rotors spinning with emphasis and force. I saw, I *felt* Kermiac crumple, withdraw. The lines of force went ragged . . . Kadarin and I locked hard together, supporting Marjorie as she controlled the wavering forces, lowering, lowering. . . . The helicopter bumped, hard, and the sound shattered the link. Pain crashed through me. Marjorie collapsed, sobbing. Beltran had seized Thyra by the shoulders, was shaking her like a dog shaking a rodent. He swung back his hand and slapped her full in the face. I felt—we all felt—the stinging pain of that blow.

"Vicious bitch! Damned she-devil," Beltran shouted. "How dare you, damn you, how dare you—"

Kadarin grabbed him, pulled him from Thyra by main force. Beltran was still fighting, struggling. Cold terror clutching at me, I reached out for Kermiac. *Uncle, have they killed you?* After a moment, sick with relief, I felt his presence, a thread of life, weak, collapsed, but alive. Alive, thank God!

Kadarin was still holding Beltran off Thyra; he let him go, flinging him violently to the ground. He said, raging, "Lay a hand on her again, Beltran, and I'll kill you with my own hands!" He hardly looked human at all now.

Marjorie was crying, trembling so violently I feared she would fall senseless. I caught and supported her. Thyra put a hand to her bruised face. She said, trying to be defiant, "What a fuss about nothing! He's stronger than any of us!"

My fear for Kermiac had turned to anger almost as great at Beltran's own. How dared Thyra do this against his will and Marjorie's judgment? I knew I couldn't trust her, damned sneaking bitch! I turned on her, still holding Marjorie with one arm; she shrank away as if from a blow. That shocked me back to my senses. Strike a woman? Slowly, lowering my head, I thrust the wadding around the matrix. This rage was ours. It was as dangerous as what Thyra did.

Marjorie could stand alone now. I put the matrix in her hand and went toward Thyra. I said, "I'm not going to hurt you, child. But what possessed you to do such a thing?" One of the strongest laws of every telepath was never to force another's will or judgment. . . .

The defiance was gone from her face. She fingered the cheek Beltran had struck. "Truly, Lew," she said, almost in a whisper, "I don't know. I felt we *needed* someone, and in days past this matrix had known the Aldarans, wanted Kermiac—no, that doesn't make sense, does it? And I felt that I could and I must because Marjorie wouldn't ... I couldn't stop myself, I watched myself do it and I was afraid. . . ." She began to cry helplessly.

I stepped forward and took her into my arms, holding her against me, her face wet on my shoulder. I felt a shaking tenderness. We had all been helpless before that force. My own emotion should have warned me, but I was too distressed to feel alarm. The feel of her warm body in my arms should have warned me, too, at that stage, but I let her cling to me, sobbing, for a minute or two before I patted her shoulders tenderly, wiped her tears away and turned to help Beltran rise. He stood up stiffly, rubbing his hip. I sighed and said, "I know how you feel, Beltran. It was a dangerous thing to do. But you were in the wrong, too, losing your temper. A matrix technician must have control, must at all times."

Defiance and contrition warred in his face. He fumbled for

words. I should have waited for them—I was responsible for this whole circle—but I felt too sick and drained to try. I said curtly, "Better see if any harm was done to the helicopter when it crashed."

"From three inches off the ground?" He sounded contemptuous now. That also troubled me but I was too tired to care. I said, "Suit yourself. It's your craft. If this is what comes of having you in the circle, I'll make damned sure you're a good long way away from it." I turned my back on him.

Marjorie was leaning on Rafe. She had stopped crying but her eyes and nose were red. Absurdly I loved her more than ever like that. She said in a small shaking voice, "I'm all right now, Lew. Honestly."

I looked at the ground at our feet. It was covered with more than an inch of snow. You always lost track of time inside a matrix. It was snowing harder than ever, and the sky was darkening. The shaking of my own hands warned me. I said, "We all need food and rest. Run ahead, Rafe, and ask the servants to have a meal ready for us."

I heard a familiar clattering roar and looked up. The other helicopter was circling overhead, descending. Beltran was walking away toward it. I started to call after him, summon him—he too would be drained, needing the replenishment of food and sleep. At that moment, though, my only thought was to let him collapse. It would do him good to learn this wasn't a game! We left him behind.

I'd have an apology to make to Kermiac, too. It didn't matter that it had been done against my orders. I was operating the matrix. I had trained this circle. I was responsible for everything that happened to it.

Everything.

Everything. Aldones, Lord of Light . . . everything: Ruin and death, a city in flames and chaos, Marjorie . . .

I shook myself out of the maelstrom of misery and pain, staring at the quiet path, the dark sky, the gently falling snow. None of it was real. I was hallucinating. Merciful Avarra, if, after three years at Arilinn, any matrix ever built could make *me* hallucinate, I was in trouble!

Kermiac's servants had laid a splendid meal for us, though I was so hungry I could as readily have eaten bread and milk. As I ate the drained weakness receded, but the vague, formless guilt remained. Marjorie. Had she been burned by the flare of fire? I kept wanting to touch her and make sure she was there, alive, unhurt. Thyra ate with tears running down her face, the bruise gradually swelling and darkening until her eye was swollen shut. Beltran did not come. I supposed he was with Kermiac. I didn't give a damn where he was. Marjorie self-consciously thrust aside her third plateful, saying, "I'm ashamed to be so greedy!"

I began to reassure her. Kadarin did it instead. "Eat, child, eat, your nerves are exhausted, you need the energy. Rafe, what's the matter, child?" The boy was restlessly pushing his food around on his plate. "You haven't touched a bite."

"I can't, Bob. My head aches. I can't swallow. If I try to swallow anything I'm afraid I'll be sick."

Kadarin met my eyes. "I'll take care of him," he said. "I know what to do, I went through it when I was his age." He lifted Rafe in his arms and carried him, like a small child, out of the room. Thyra rose and went after them.

Left alone with Marjorie, I said, "You should rest, too, after all that."

She said in a very small voice, "I'm afraid to be alone. Don't leave me alone, Lew."

I didn't intend to, not until I was sure she was safe. A Keeper in training has stresses no other matrix mechanic suffers, and I was still responsible for her. Although emotional upheavals were common enough when first keying into one of the really big matrices, such frightful blowups as this between Beltran and Thyra were not common. Fortunately. No wonder we were all literally sick from it.

I had never seen Marjorie's room before. It was at the top of a small tower, isolated, reached by a winding stair, a wedge-shaped room with wide windows. In clear weather it would have looked out on tremendous mountain ranges. Now it was all a dismal gray, gloomy, with hard beating snow rattling and whining against the glass. Marjorie slipped off her outdoor boots and knelt by the window, looking into the storm. "It's lucky we came in when we did. I've known the snow to come up so quickly you can lose your way a hundred paces from your own doorway. Lew, will Rafe be all right?"

"Of course. Just stress, maybe a touch of threshold sickness. Beltran's tantrum didn't help any, but it won't last long." Once a telepath gained full control of his matrix, and to do this he must have mastered the nerve channels, recurrences of threshold sickness were not serious. Rafe was probably feeling rotten, but it wouldn't last.

Marjorie leaned against the window, pressing her temples to the cold glass. "My head aches."

"Damn Beltran anyway!" I said, with violence that surprised me.

"It was Thyra's fault, Lew. Not his."

"What Thyra did is Thyra's responsibility, but Beltran must bear the responsibility for losing control, too."

My mind slid back to that strange interval within the matrix—whether it had been a few seconds or an hour I had no way of knowing—when I had sensed my father's presence. It occurred to me to wonder if at any of the towers, Hali or Arilinn or Neskaya, they had sensed the wakening of this enormous matrix, stirring to life. My father was an extraordinary telepath; he had served in Arilinn under the last of the old-style Keepers. He must have felt Sharra's wakening.

Did he know what we were doing?

As if following my thoughts Marjorie said, "Lew, what is your father like? My guardian has always spoken well of him."

"I don't want to talk about my father, Marjorie." But my barriers had been breached and that furious parting came back to me, with all the old bitterness. *He had been willing to kill me, to have his own way. He cared no more for me than a . . .*

Marjorie said in a low voice, "You're wrong, Lew. Your father loved you. Loves you. No, I'm not reading your mind. You were . . . broadcasting. But you are a loving person, a gentle person. To be so loving, you must have been loved. Greatly loved."

I bent my head. Indeed, indeed, all those years I had been so secure in his love, he could never have lived a lie. Not to me. We had been open to one another. Yet somehow that made it worse *Loving me, to risk me so ruthlessly . . .*

She whispered, "I know you, Lew. You could not have lived—would you have wanted to be without *laran*? Without the full potential of your gift? He knew your life wouldn't have been worth living without it. Blind, deaf, crippled . . . so he let you risk it. To become what he knew you *were*."

I laid my head on her knees, blind with pain. She had given me back something I never knew I had lost; she had returned to me the security of my father's love. I couldn't look up, couldn't let her see my face was contorted, that I was crying like a child. She knew anyway. I supposed this was my form of throwing a tantrum. Thyra disobeyed orders. Rafe got threshold sickness, Kadarin and Beltran started slamming each other . . . I started crying like a child. . . .

After a time I lifted her hand and kissed the slender finger-tips. She looked worn and exhausted. I said, "You must rest too, darling." I was deeply proud of the skill with which she had seized control. She lay back against her pillows. I bent and, as I would have done at Arilinn, ran my fingertips lightly along her body. Not touching her, of course, simply feeling out the energy flows, monitoring the nerve centers. She lay quietly, smiling at the touch that was not a touch. I felt that she was still depleted, drained of energy, but that would not last. The channels were clear. I was glad she had come through this strenous beginning so well, so undamaged.

I was not, at the moment, actively suffering because she was forbidden to me, that even a kiss would have been un-thinkable. I was remotely aware of her but there was no sexual element in it. I simply felt an intense and overwhelm-ing love such as I had never known for anyone alive. I didn't have to speak of it. I knew she shared it.

If I couldn't have reached Marjorie's mind I'd have gone mad with wanting her, needing her with every nerve in me. But we had this, and it was enough. Almost enough, and we had the promise of the rest.

I knew the answer, but I wanted to say the words aloud.

"When this is over, you will marry me, Marjorie?"

She said, with a simplicity that made my heart turn over, "I want to. But will the Comyn let you?"

"I won't ask them. By then the Comyn may have learned it's not for them to arrange everyone's life!"

"I wouldn't want to make trouble, Lew. Marriage doesn't mean that much to me."

"It does to *me*," I said fiercely. "Do you think I want our children to be bastards? I want them at Armida after me, without the struggle my father had to get it for me. . . ."

Her laugh was adorable. Quickly, she sobered. "Lew, Lew, I'm not laughing at *you*, darling. Only it makes me so happy, to think that it means all this to you—not just wanting me, but thinking of all that will come afterward, our children, our children's children, a household to stand into the future. Yes, Lew. I want to have your children, I'm sorry we have to wait so long for them. Yes, I'll marry you if you want me to, in the Comyn if they'll have it, if not, then any way we can, any way you choose." For a moment, a feather-touch, she laid her lips against the back of my hand.

My heart was so full I could bear no more. I had desired women before, but never with this wholeness, going far beyond any moment of desire, stretching into the future, all our lives. For a moment time went out of focus again . . .

. . . I was kneeling beside the cot of a little girl. five or six perhaps, a tiny child with a heart-shaped face and wide eyes fenced in long lashes, golden eyes just the color of Marjorie's . . . I felt a strange wonder, pain in my right hand, *dismayed, torn with anguish* . . .

Marjorie whispered, "What is it, Lew?"

"A flash of precognition," I said, coming back to myself, strangely shaken. "I saw—I saw a little girl. With your eyes." But why had I felt so bewildered, so agonized? I tried to see it again, but as these flashes come unbidden, so they can never be recalled. I felt Marjorie's thoughts, and hers were wholly joyful: *It will be all right then. We will be together as we wish, we will see that child.* Her lashes were dropping shut with weariness and, kneeling beside her, I looked into her face again. She thought drowsily, *We should have a son first*, and I knew she had seen the child's face in my mind. She smiled with pure happiness and her lids slipped shut. Her hand tightened on my own.

"Don't leave me," she whispered, half asleep.

"Never. Sleep, beloved." I stretched out beside her, holding her fingers in mine, my love encircling her sleep. After a moment. I slept too. in the deepest happiness I had ever known.

Or was ever to know again.

It was dark when I woke, the snow still rattling the windows. Kadarin was standing above us, holding a light. Marjorie was still deeply asleep. His glance at her was filled with a deep tenderness that warmed me to him as nothing else could have done.

And then, for a moment, I felt his face wrenched, contorted with rage . . . It was gone. He said softly, "Beltran sent to ask if you would come down. Let Margie sleep if you like, she's very tired."

I slid from the bed. She stirred, made a faint protesting noise—I thought she had murmured my name. I covered her gently with a shawl, picked up my boots in my hand and noiselessly went out, feeling her sink back into deep sleep.

"Rafe?"

"He's fine. I gave him a few drops of *kirian*, got him to drink some hot milk and honey, left him asleep." Kadarin wore his sad, tender smile on his face. "I've been looking for you everywhere. After all your warnings, I never expected—

it was Thyra who suggested you might be with Marjorie." He laughed. "But I hadn't expected to find you in her bed!"

I said stiffly, "I assure you—"

"Lew, in the name of all the damned obscene gods of the Dry-Towners, do you think it matters a damn to me?" He was laughing again. "Oh, I believe you, you're just scrupulous enough, and bound hand and foot with your own idiot super-stitions! I think you're putting a considerable strain on human nature, myself—I wouldn't trust myself to lie down with a woman I loved and never touch her—but if you happen to enjoy self-torture, that's your own choice. As the Dry-Towner said to the *cralmac* . . ." And he launched into a long, good-humored and incredibly obscene tale which took my mind off my embarrassment as nothing else could have. Not a word of it was suitable for repeating in polite company, but it was exactly what the situation demanded.

When we reached the fireside room, he said, "You heard the helicopter land this afternoon?"

I was still chuckling at the adventures of the Dry-Towner, the spaceman and the three nonhumans; the sudden gravity of his voice shocked me back to normal.

"I saw it, yes. Has it to do with me?"

"A special guest," Kadarin said. "Beltran feels you should speak with him. You told us he is a catalyst telepath with no reason to love the Comyn, and Beltran sent to persuade him—"

Seated on one of the stone benches near the fire, his dark hair awry, looking cold and ruffled and angry, was Danilo Syrtis. Beltran said, "Perhaps you can explain that we mean no harm, that he is not a prisoner, but an honored guest."

Danilo tried to sound defiant, but despite his best efforts I could hear that his voice was shaking. "You carried me off with armed men and my father will be ill with fright! Is this how you mountain men welcome guests, taking them away in infernal Terran machines?" He looked no older than Rafe.

I called "Danilo—" and his mouth dropped open. He sprang up. "They told me you were here, but I thought it was just another of their lies." The childish face hardened. "Was it by your orders they had me kidnapped? How long will the Comyn persecute me?"

I shook my head. "Not my orders, nor Comyn. Until this moment I had no idea you were here."

He turned on Beltran in childish triumph. His voice, still

unbroken, sounded shrill. "I knew you were lying, when you told me Lew Alton ordered me brought here—"

I swung toward Beltran and said in real anger, "I told you Danilo might be *persuaded* to join us! Did you take that as license to kidnap him?" I held out both hands to the boy and said, "Dani, forgive me. It is true I told them of you and your *laran*; I suggested that one day they might seek you out and persuade you to join us in what we are doing." His hands felt cold. He had been badly frightened. "Don't be afraid. I swear on my honor, no one will hurt you."

"I am not *afraid* of such rabble," he said scornfully, and I saw Beltran wince. Well, if he was going to behave like some Brynat Scarface or Cyrillon des Trailles, he must expect to be called uncomplimentary names! Danilo added, his voice shaking, "My father is old and feeble. He has already suffered my disgrace. Now to lose me again . . . he will surely grieve himself to death."

I said to Beltran, "You fool, you utter fool! Send a message at once, send it through the Terran relays if you must, that Danilo is alive and well, and that someone must inform his family that he is here, an honored guest! Do you want a friend and ally, or a mortal enemy?"

He had the grace to look ashamed. He said, "I gave no orders to hurt or frighten him or his father. Did anyone lay rough hands on either of you, lad?"

"I was certainly issued no polite invitation, Lord Aldaran. Do you disarm all your honored guests?"

I said, "Go and send that message, Beltran. Let me talk to him alone." Beltran went and I mended the fire, leaving Danilo to recover his composure. At last I asked, "Tell me the truth, Danilo, have you been ill-treated?"

"No, though they were not gentle. We were some days riding, then the sky-machine. I do not know its name. . . ."

The helicopter. I had seen it land. I knew I should have gone after Beltran. If I had been there when Danilo was brought from it—well, it was done. I said, "A helicopter is safer, in the peaks and crossdrafts of the Hellers, than any ordinary plane. Were you very frightened?"

"Only for a little, when we were forced down by weather. Mostly I feared for my father."

"Well, a message will be sent. Have you had anything to eat?"

"They offered me something when we first landed," he said. He did not say he had been too shaken and frightened to eat, but I surmised that. I called a servant and said, "Ask my uncle to excuse me from his table, and say that Lord Beltran will explain. Then send some food here for my guest and myself." I turned back to the boy. "Dani, am I your enemy?"

"Captain, I—"

"I've left the Guards," I said. "Not captain, now."

To my amazement he said, "Too bad. You were the only officer everybody liked. No, you're not my enemy, Lew, and I always thought your father was my friend. It was Lord Dyan—you *do* know what happened?"

"More or less," I said. "Whatever it may have been this time, I know damn well that by the time you drew your dagger he'd given you enough provocation for a dozen duels anywhere else. You don't have to tell me all the nasty little details. I know Dyan."

"Why did the Commander—"

"They were children together," I said. "In his eyes Dyan can do no wrong. I'm not defending him, but didn't you ever do anything you thought was wrong, for a friend's sake?"

"Did you?" he asked. I was still trying to think how to answer when our supper was brought. I served Dani, but found I was not hungry and sat nibbling at some fruit while the boy satisfied his appetite. I wondered if they had fed him at all since his capture. No, boys that age were always hungry, that was all.

While he ate I worried what Marjorie would think when she woke and found herself alone. Was Rafe really all right, or should I go and make certain? Had Kermiac suffered any lasting ill-effects from Thyra's rashness? I didn't approve of what Beltran had done, but I knew why he had been tempted to do it. We needed someone like Danilo so badly that it terrified me.

I poured Dani a glass of wine when he had finished. He merely tasted it for courtesy's sake, but at least now he was willing to go through the motions of courtesy again. I took a sip of mine and set it aside.

"Danilo, you know you have *laran*. You also have one of the rarest and most precious Comyn gifts, one we've thought extinct. If Comyn Council finds out, they'll be ready and willing to make all kinds of amends for the stupid and cruel thing Dyan did to you. They'll offer you anything you want, up to and including a seat in Comyn Council if you want that, marriage with someone like Linnell Aillard—you name it, you can probably have it. You attended that Council meeting among the Terrans. Are you interested in power of that sort? If so, they'll be lining up two and three deep to offer it to you. Is that what you want?"

"I don't know," he said, "I never thought about it. I expected, after I finished in the cadets, to stay quietly at home and look after my father while he lived."

"And then?"

"I hadn't thought about that either. I suppose I thought when that time came, I'd be grown up, and then I'd know what I wanted."

I smiled wryly. Yes, at fifteen I too had been sure that by the time I was twenty or so my life would have arranged itself in simple patterns.

"That's not the way it happens when you have *laran*," I said. "Among other things, you must be trained. An untrained telepath is a menace to himself and everyone around him."

He made a grimace of revulsion. "I've never wanted to be a matrix technician."

"Probably not," I said. "It takes a certain temperament." I couldn't see Danilo in a tower; I, on the other hand, had never wanted anything else. I still didn't. "Even so, you must learn to control what you are and what gifts you have. All too many untrained telepaths end up as madmen."

"Then whether I'm interested in Comyn Council or not, what choice do I have? Isn't this training only in the hands of the Comyn and the towers? And they can train me to do whatever they want me to do."

"That's true in the Domains," I said. "They do draw all telepaths to their service there. But you still have a choice." I began to tell him about Beltran's plan, and a little about the work we had begun.

He listened without comment until I had finished. "Then," he said, "it seems I have a choice between taking bribes for the use of my *laran* from the Comyn—or from Aldaran."

"I wouldn't put it that way. We're asking you to come into this of your own free will. If we do achieve what we want, then the Comyn will no longer have the power to demand that all telepaths serve them or be left prey to madness. And there would be an end to the kind of power-hunger that left you at the mercy of a man like Dyan."

He thought that over, sipping the wine again and making a childish wry face. Then he said, "It seems as if something like that's always going to be happening to people like me, like us. Someone's always going to be bribing us to use our gifts, for their good, not our own." He sounded terribly young, terribly bitter.

"No, some of us may have a choice now. Once we are a legitimate part of the Terran Empire—"

"Then I suppose the Empire will find some way to use us," Danilo said. "The Comyn makes mistakes, but don't they know more about us and our world than the Terrans ever could?"

"I'm not sure," I said. "Are you willing to see them stay in power, controlling all our lives, putting corrupt men like Dyan in charge—"

"No, I'm not," he said, "nobody would want that. But if people like you and me—you said I could have a seat on the Council if I wanted it—if people like you and me were on the Council, the bad ones like Dyan wouldn't have everything their own way, would they? Your father's a good man but, like you said, Dyan can do no wrong in his eyes. But when *you* take a seat on the Council, you won't feel that way, will you?"

"What I want," I said with concealed violence, "is *not* to be forced to take a seat on the Council, or do all the other damned things the Comyn wants me to do!"

"If good men like you can't be bothered," said Danilo, "then who's left, except the bad ones who *shouldn't?*"

There was some truth in that, too. But I said vehemently, "I have other skills and I feel I can serve my people better in other ways. That's what I'm trying to do now, to benefit everyone on Darkover. I'm not trying to smash the Comyn, Dani, only to give everyone more of a choice. Don't you think it's an ambition worth achieving?"

He looked helpless. "I can't judge," he said. "I'm not even used to thinking of myself as a telepath yet. I don't know what I ought to do."

He looked up at me with that odd, trustful look which made me think somehow, of my brother Marius. If it were Marius standing here before me, gifted with *laran,* would I try to persuade him to face Sharra? A cold chill iced my spine and I shivered, even though the room was warm. I said, "Can you trust me, then?"

"I'd like to," he said. "You never lied to me or hurt me. But I don't think I'd trust any of the Aldarans."

"Is your mind still full of schoolroom bogeymen?" I asked. "Do you believe they are all wicked renegades because they

have an old political quarrel with Comyn? You have reason
to distrust the Comyn too, Danilo."

"True," he said. "But can I trust a man who begins by kid-
napping me and frightening my father to death? If he had
come to me, explained what he wanted to do, and that you
and he together thought my gift could be useful, then asked
my father to give me leave to visit him . . ."

The hell of it was, Dani was entirely right. What had possessed Beltran to do such a thing? "If he had consulted me,
that is exactly how I would have suggested he should do it."

"Yes, I know," Dani said. "You're *you*. But if Beltran isn't
the kind of man to do it that way, how can you trust him?"

"He's my kinsman," I said helplessly. "What do you expect
me to say? I expect his eagerness got the better of him. He
didn't hurt you, did he?"

Dani raged. "You're talking just the way you said your father did about Lord Dyan!"

It wasn't the same, I knew that, but I couldn't expect
Danilo to see it. Finally I said, "Can't you look beyond per-
sonalities in this, Dani? Beltran was wrong, but what we're
trying to do is so enormous that maybe it blinds people to
smaller aims and ends. Keep your eyes on what he's doing,
and forgive him. Or are you waiting," and I spoke deliberately, with malice, to make him see how cynical it sounded,
"for the Comyn to make a better offer?"

He flushed, stung to the depths. I hadn't overestimated either his intelligence or his sensitivity. He was a boy still, but
the man would be well worth knowing, with strong integrity
and honor. I hoped with all my heart he would be our ally.

"Danilo," I said, "we need you. The Comyn cast you out in
disgrace, undeserved. What loyalty do you owe them?"

"The Comyn, nothing," he said quietly. "Yet I am pledged
and my service given. Even if I wanted to do what you ask,
Lew, and I'm not sure, I am not free."

"What do you mean?"

Danilo's face was impassive, but I could sense the emotion
behind his words. "Regis Hastur sought me out at Syrtis," he
said. "He did not know how or why, but he knew I had been
wronged. He pledged himself to set it right."

"We're trying to set many wrongs right, Dani. Not just
yours."

"Maybe," he said. "But we swore an oath together and I
pledged him my sword and my service. I am his paxman,
Lew, so if you want me to help you, you must ask *his* con-

sent. If my lord gives me leave, then I am at your service. Otherwise I am his man: I have sworn."

I looked at the solemn young face and knew there was nothing I could say to that. I felt a quite irrational anger at Regis because he had forestalled me here. For a moment I wrestled with strong temptation. I could make him see it my way . . .

I recoiled in horror and shame at my own thoughts. The first pledge I had sworn at Arilinn was this: never, never force the will or conscience of another, even for his own good. I could persuade. I could plead. I could use reason, emotion, logic, rhetoric. I could even seek out Regis and beg him for his consent; he too had reason to be disaffected, to rebel against the corruption in the Comyn. But further than this I could not go. I could *not*. That I had even thought of it made me feel a little sick.

"I may indeed ask Regis for your aid, Dani," I said quietly. "He too is my friend. But I will never force you. I am not Dyan Ardais!"

That made him smile a little. "I never thought you were, Lew. And if my lord gives me leave, then I will trust him, and you. But until that time shall come, Dom Lewis"—he gave me my title very formally, though we had been using the familiar mode before this—"have I your permission to depart and return to my father?"

I gestured at the snow, a white torrent whipping the windows, sending little spits of sleet down the chimney. "In *this*, lad? Let me at least offer you the hospitality of my kinsman's roof until the weather suits! Then you shall be given proper escort and company out of these mountains. You cannot expect me to set you adrift in these mountains, at night and in winter, with a storm blowing up?" I summoned a servant again, and requested that he provide proper lodging for a guest, near my own quarters. Before Danilo went away to his bed, I gave him a kinsman's embrace, which he returned with a childlike friendliness that made me feel better.

But I was still deeply troubled. Damn it, I'd have a word with Beltran before I slept!

Chapter SEVENTEEN

Regis rode slowly, head down against the biting wind. He told himself that if he ever got out of these mountains, no place on Darkover would ever seem cold to him again.

A few days ago he had stopped in a mountain village and traded his horse for one of the sturdy little mountain ponies. He felt a sort of despairing grief at the necessity—the black mare was Kennard's gift and he loved her—but this one attracted less attention and was surer-footed along the terrible trails. Poor Melisande would surely have died of the cold or broken a leg on these steep paths.

The trip had been a long nightmare: steep unfamiliar trails, intense cold, sheltering at night in abandoned barns or shepherd's huts or wrapped in cloak and blanket against a rock wall, close curled against the horse's body. He tried in general to avoid being seen, but every few days he had gone into a village to bargain for food and fodder for his pony. He aroused little curiosity; he thought life must be so hard in these mountains that the people had no time for curiosity about travelers.

Now and again, when he feared losing his way, he had drawn out the matrix, trying by furious concentration to fix his attention on Danilo. The matrix acted like one of those Terran instruments Kennard had once told him about, guiding him, with an insistent subliminal pull, toward Aldaran and Danilo.

By now he was numbed to fear, and only determination kept him going, that, and the memory of his pledge to Dani's father. But there were times when he rode in a dark dream, losing awareness of Danilo and the roads where he was. Images would spin in his mind, which seemed to drink up pictures and thoughts from the villages he passed. The thought of looking again into the matrix filled him with such a crawling sickness that he could not force himself to draw it out. Threshold sickness again. Javanne had warned him. At

the last few villages he had simply inquired the road to Aldaran.

All the morning he had been riding up a long slope where
forest fires had raged a few seasons ago. He could see miles
of scorched and blackened hillside, ragged stumps sticking up
gaunt and leafless through the gullied wasteland. In his hyper-
suggestible state the stink of burned woods, ashes and soot
swirling up every time his pony put a hoof down, brought
him back to that last summer at Armida and his first turn on
the fire-lines, the night the fire came so close to Armida that
the outbuildings burned.

That evening he and Lew had eaten out of the same bowl
because supplies were running short. When they had laid
down the stink of ashes and burned wood was all around
them. Regis had smelled it even in his sleep, the way he was
smelling it now. Toward midnight something woke him, and
he had seen Lew sitting bolt upright, staring at the red glow
where the fire was.

And Regis had known Lew was afraid. He'd touched Lew's
mind, and *felt* it: *his fear,* the pain of his burns, everything.
He could feel it as if it had been in his own mind. And Lew's
fear hurt so much that Regis couldn't stand it. He would
have done anything to comfort Lew, to take his mind off the
pain and the fear. It had been too much. Regis couldn't shut
it out, couldn't stand it.

But he had forgotten. Had made himself forget, till now.
He had blocked away the memory until, later that year,
when he was tested for *laran* at Nevarsin, he had not even
remembered anything but the fire.

And that, he realized, was why Lew was surprised when
Regis told him he did not have *laran.* . . .

The mountain pony stumbled and went down. Regis
scrambled to his feet, shaken but unhurt, taking the beast by
the bridle and gently urging him to his feet. He ran his hand
up and down the animal's legs. No bones were broken, but
the pony flinched when Regis touched his rear right hock. He
was limping, and Regis knew the pony could not bear his
weight for a while. He led him along the trail as they crested
the pass. The downward trail was even steeper, black and
mucky underfoot where recent rains had soaked the remnants
of the fire. The stench in his nostrils was worse than ever,
restimulating again the memories of the earlier fire and the
shared fear. He kept asking himself why he forgot, why he
made himself forget.

The sun was hidden behind thick clouds. A few drifting snowflakes, not many but relentless, began to fall as he went down toward the valley. He guessed it was about midday. He felt a little hungry, but not enough to stop and dig into his pack and get out something to eat.

He hadn't been eating much lately. The villagers had been kind to him, often refusing to take payment for food, which was tasty, though unfamiliar. He was usually on the edge of nausea, though, unwilling to start up that reflex again by actually chewing and swallowing something. Hunger was less painful.

After a time he did dig some grain out of his pack for the horse. The trail was well-traveled now; there must be another village not far away. But the silence was disturbing. Not a dog barked, no wild bird or beast cried. There was no sound but his own footsteps and the halting rhythm of the lame pony's steps. And, far above, the unending wind moaning in the gaunt snags of the dead forest.

It was too much solitude. Even the presence of a bodyguard would have been welcome now, or two, chatting about the small chances of the trail. He remembered riding in the hills around Armida with Lew, hunting or checking the herdsmen who cared for the horses out in the open uplands. Suddenly, as if the thought of Lew had brought him to mind again, Lew's face was before him, lighted with a glow—not forest fire now! It was aglow, blazing in a great blue glare, space-twisting, gut-wrenching, the glare of the matrix! The ground was reeling and dipping under his feet, but for a moment, even as Regis dropped the pony's reins and clapped his hands over his tormented eyes, he saw a great form sketch itself on the inside of his eyelids, inside his very brain.

. . . *a woman, a golden goddess, flame-clothes, flame-crowned, golden-chained, burning, glowing, blazing, consuming . . .*

Then he lost consciousness. Over his head the mountain pony edged carefully around, uneasily nuzzling at the unconscious lad.

It was the pony's nuzzling that woke him, some time later. The sky was darkening, and it was snowing so hard that when he got stiffly to his feet, a little cascade of snow showered off him. A faint sickening smell told him that he had vomited as he lay senseless. What in Zandru's hells happened to me?

He dug his water bottle from his saddlebag, rinsed his mouth and drank a little, but was still too queasy to swallow much.

It was snowing so hard that he knew he must find shelter at once. He had been trained at Nevarsin to find shelter in unlikely places, even a heap of underbrush would do, but on a road as well-traveled as this there were sure to be huts, barns, shelters. He was not mistaken. A few hundred feet further on, the outline of a great stone barn made a dark square against the swirling whiteness. The stones were blackened with the fire that had swept over it and a few of the roof slates had fallen in, but someone had replaced the door with rough-hewn planking. Drifted ice and snow from the last storm was banked against the door, but he knew that in mountain country doors were usually left unfastened against just such emergencies. After much struggling and heaving Regis managed to shove the rough door partway open and wedge himself and the pony through into a gloomy and musty darkness. It had once been a fodder-storage barn; there were still a few rodent-nibbled bales lying forgotten against the walls. It was bitterly cold, but at least it was out of the wind. Regis unsaddled his pony, fed him and hobbled him loosely at one end of the barn. Then he raked some more of the moldy fodder together, laid his blankets out on it, crawled into them and let sleep, or unconsciousness, take him again.

This long sleep was more like shock, or suspended animation, than any normal sleep. Regis could not know it was the mental and physical reaction of a telepath in crisis. Now it only seemed that he wandered for eternities—certainly for days—in restless nightmares. At times he seemed to leave his aching body behind and wander in gray formless space, shouting helplessly and knowing he had no voice. Once or twice, coming up to dim semiconsciousness, he found his face wet and knew he had been crying in his sleep. Time disappeared. He wandered in what he only dimly knew was the past or the future: now in the dormitories of Nevarsin where the memory of cold, loneliness and an aching frustration held him aloof, frightened, friendless; now by the fireside at Armida, then bending with Lew and an unknown fair-haired girl over the bedside of an apparently dying child, again wandering through thick forests while strange aliens, red-eyed, peered at them through the trees.

Again he was fighting with knives along a narrow ledge,

the ragged red-eyed aliens thrusting at him, trying to kick
him off. He sat in the Council chamber and heard Terrans
arguing; in the Guard hall of Comyn Castle he saw Danilo's
sword breaking with that terrible sound of shattering glass.
He was looking down with a sense of aching tragedy at two
small children, pale and lifeless, lying side by side in their
coffins, dead by treachery, so young, so young, and knew
they were his own. Again he stood in the armory, numb and
shamed into immobility while Dyan's hands ran along his
bare bruised body, and then he and Danilo were standing by
a fountain in the plaza at Thendara, only Danilo was taller
and bearded, drinking from wooden tankards and laughing
while girls threw festival garlands down from windows above
them.

After a time he began to filter these random awarenesses
more critically. He saw Lew and Danilo standing by a fireplace in a room with a mosaic pattern of white birds on the
floor, talking earnestly, and he felt insanely jealous. Then it
seemed as if Kennard was calling his name in the gray dim
spaces, and he could see Kennard drifting far off in the dimness. Only Kennard was not lame now, but young and
straight-backed and smiling as Regis could hardly remember
him. He was calling, with a mounting sense of urgency,
*Regis, Regis, where are you? Don't hide from me! We have
to find you!* All Regis could make of this was that he had left
the Guards without leave and the Commander wanted to
have him brought back and punished. He knew he could
make himself invisible here in these gray spaces, so he did,
running from the voice full speed over a gray and featureless
plain, though by this time he was perfectly well aware that
he was lying half-conscious in the abandoned fodder-barn.
And then he saw Dyan in the gray spaces, only Dyan as a
boy his own age. Somehow he dimly realized that, in this gray
world where bodies did not come but only minds, every man
appeared as he saw himself in his own mind, so of course
Kennard looked well and young. Dyan was saying, *I can't
find him, Kennard, he is nowhere in the overworld,* and Regis
felt himself laughing inside and saying, *I'm here but I don't
have to let you see me here.* Then Kennard and Dyan were
standing close together, their hands joined, and he knew that
together they were seeking him out. Their faces and figures
disappeared, they were only eyes in the grayness, seeking,
seeking. He knew he must leave the gray world or they
would find him now. Where could he go? He didn't want to

go back! He could see Danilo in the distance, then they were both back in the dark barracks room—that night!—and he was bending over his friend, touching him with aching solicitude. And then that terrible, strained whisper, the shock more mental than physical as he thrust him away: *Come near me again, you filthy ombredin, and I'll break your neck . . .*

But I was only trying to reach him, help him. Wasn't I? Wasn't I? And with a shuddering gasp Regis sat up, fully awake at last, staring into the dim light that filtered through a broken roof-slate above him. He was shaking from head to foot and his body ached as if he had been battered and beaten. He was completely conscious, though, and his mind was clear. At the far end of the barn the pony was stamping restlessly. Slowly, Regis got to his feet, wondering how long he had been there.

Far too long. The pony had eaten every scrap of the ample fodder and nosed the floor clear of chaff as far as he could reach.

Regis went to the door and swung it open. It had stopped snowing long since. The sun was out, and melted snow dripped in runnels from the roof. Regis was aware of a raging thirst, but like all lifelong horsemen he thought first of his pony. He led the horse to the door and released him; after a moment the pony made off, deliberately, around the corner to the rear of the building. Regis followed, finding an old well there, covered against the snow, with a workable though creaky and leaking bucket assembly. He watered the pony and drank deeply, then, shivering, stripped off his clothes. He was grateful for the austere discipline of Nevarsin, which made it possible for him to wash in the icy water of the well. His clothes smelled of sweat and sickness; he got fresh ones from his pack. Shivering, but feeling immensely better, he sat down on the well-side and chewed dried fruit. Cold as he was, the interior of the building seemed to reek of his nightmares and echo with the voices he had heard in his delirium, if it had all been delirium. What else could it have been?

Moving slowly until he knew he could rely on his body to do what he told it, he saddled the pony again and collected his belongings. He must be nearing the Aldaran lands now and there was no time to lose.

The snow had drenched the smell of forest fire and he was glad. He had not ridden more than an hour or two when he heard the sound of approaching horses and drew aside to let them pass. Instead they confronted him, blocking the road, demanding his name and business.

He said, "I am Regis-Rafael Hastur, and I am on my way to Castle Aldaran."

"And I," the leader, a big swarthy mountain man, said in a mincing voice that mocked Regis' careful *casta* accent, "am the Terran Legate from Port Chicago. Well, whoever you are, you'll go to Aldaran, and damn quick, too."

It had evidently been nearer than Regis believed; as they reached the top of the next hill he saw the castle, and beyond it the city of Cear Donn and the white Terran buildings.

Now that he was actually within sight of Aldaran his old fears returned. No man knew—or if they did it was the best kept secret on Darkover—why Aldaran had been exiled from the Seven Domains.

They couldn't be that bad, Regis thought. Kennard had married into their kin. And if they were once of the Seven Domains, they too must be of the sacred lineage of Hastur and Cassilda. And why should a Hastur fear his kindred? He asked himself this as he rode through the great gates. Yet he was afraid.

Mountain men dressed in curiously cut leather cloaks took their horses. One of the guards led Regis into a hall, where he talked at length with another guard, then finally said, "We'll take you to Lord Aldaran, but if you're not who you claim you are, you'd better plan on spending the rest of the day in the brig. The old lord is ill, and none of us takes kindly to the notion of bothering him with an impostor!"

They conducted him through long stone corridors and along flights of stairs, pausing at last outside a great door. From inside they could hear voices, one low and undistinguishable, the other a harsh old man's voice, protesting angrily:

"Zandru's hells! *Kirian*, at my age! As if I were a schoolboy—oh, very well, very well! But what you are doing is dangerous if it can have side effects like this, and I want to know more—a great deal more—before I let it go on!"

The guards exchanged glances over Regis' head; one of them knocked lightly and someone told them to come in.

It was a large, high-arched stone chamber, gray with the outdoor light. At the far end, a thin old man lay in a raised bed, propped on many pillows. He glared at them in angry question. "What's this now? What's this?"

"An intruder on the borders, Lord Aldaran, maybe a spy from the Domains."

"Why, he's just a boy," the old man said. "Come here, child." The guards thrust Regis forward, and the old eyes focused, hawk-keen, on him. Then he smiled, an odd amused smile.

"Humph! No need to ask *your* name! If ever a man wore his lineage on his face! You might be Rafael's son. I thought his heir was still in the schoolroom, though. Which one are you, then, some *nedestro* or old Danvan's bastard, maybe?"

Regis lifted his chin. "I am Regis-Rafael Hastur of Hastur!"

"Then in hell's name," said the old man testily, "what were you doing sneaking around the borders alone? Where is your escort? The heir of Hastur should have ridden up to the front gates, properly escorted, and asked to see me. I've never refused a welcome to anyone who comes here in peace! Do you think this is still a bandit fortress?"

Regis felt stung, all the more because he knew the old man was right. "My Lord, I felt there might be warfare of which I had been told nothing. If there is peace between us, what have you done with my sworn man?"

"*I*, young Hastur? I know of no man of yours. Who?"

"My paxman and my friend, Danilo Syrtis. He was taken by armed men, in the hills near his home, men bearing your ensign, my lord."

Aldaran's face narrowed in a frown. He glanced at the tall thin man in Terran clothing who stood near the head of the bed. He said, "Bob, do you know anything at all about this matter? You usually know what Beltran's up to. What's he been doing while I've been lying here sick?"

The man raised his head and looked at Regis. He said, "Danilo Syrtis is here and unharmed, young Hastur. Beltran's men only exceeded their orders; they were told to invite him here with all courtesy. And we were told he had no reason to love the Comyn; how should we know he was your sworn man?" Regis felt unspoken contempt, *And why should we give a damn?* But Kadarin's words were rigidly polite. "He is unharmed, an honored guest."

"I'll have a word with Beltran," Kermiac of Aldaran said. "This isn't the first time his enthusiasm has carried him away. I'm sorry, young Hastur, I didn't know we had anyone of yours here. Kadarin, take him to his friend."

So it was as simple as that? Regis felt vague disquiet. Kadarin said, "There's no need for such haste. Lew Alton talked to the Syrtis boy for hours last night, I'm sure he knows now that he's not a prisoner. Lord Regis, would you like to speak with your kinsman?"

"Is Lew still here? Yes, I would like to see him."

Kermiac looked at Regis' travel-stained garments. He said, "But this is a long journey alone for a boy. You are exhausted. Let us take you to a guest chamber, offer you some refreshment—a meal, a bath—"

Both of them sounded almost unendurably attractive, but Regis shook his head. "Truly, I need nothing now. I am deeply concerned about my friend."

"As you wish, then, lad." He held out a withered old hand, seeming to have trouble moving as he wished. "Damned if I'm going to call a boy your age lord anything! That's half what's wrong with our world!"

Regis bent over it as he would have done over his grandfather's. "If I have misjudged you, Lord Aldaran, I implore your pardon. Let anxiety for my paxman be my excuse."

"Humph," Aldaran said again, "it seems to me that we of Aldaran owe you some apology as well, my boy. Bob, send Beltran to me—at once!"

"Uncle, he is very much occupied with—"

"I don't give a damn what he's occupied with, bring him! And fast!" He released Regis' hand, saying, "I'll see you again soon, lad. You are my guest, remain here in peace, be welcome."

Dismissed and ushered out of Aldaran's presence, Kadarin striding through the halls at his side, Regis felt more confused than ever. What was going on here? What had Lew Alton to do with this? It was warm in the hallway and he wished he had taken off his riding-cloak; he felt suddenly very tired and hungry. He had not had a hot meal, or slept in a bed, for more days than he could reckon, and during his sickness he had completely lost count.

Kadarin turned into a small room, saying, "I think Lew is here with Beltran." Regis blinked in astonishment, seeing, in the first moment, only the blazing fire, the floor inlaid with the mosaic of white birds! Fantasies spun in his mind. Danilo was not here, as in his dream, but Lew was standing near the fire, his back to Regis. He was looking down at a woman who had a small harp across her knees. She was playing and singing. Regis had heard the song at Nevarsin; it was immeasurably old, and had a dozen names and a dozen tunes:

> How came this blood, on your right hand,
>   Brother, tell me, tell me.
> It is the blood of an old gray wolf
> Who lurked behind a tree.

The song broke off in mid-chord; Lew turned, and looked at Regis in amazement.

"Regis!" he said, coming quickly toward the door. "What are you doing here?" He held out his arms to embrace him, then, seeing him clearly, took him by the shoulders, almost holding his upright. He said savagely, "If this is any more of Beltran's—"

Regis drew himself upright. He wanted to let himself collapse into Lew's arms, lean on him, break down with fatigue and long drawn out fear—but not before these strangers. "I came here in search of Danilo; Javanne saw in her crystal that he had been taken by men of Aldaran. Had you any hand in this?"

"God forbid," said Lew. "What do you think I am? It was a mistake, I assure you, only a mistake. Come and sit down, Regis. You look tired and ill. Bob, if he's been mishandled, I'll have someone's head for it!"

"No, no," said Kadarin. "Lord Kermiac welcomed him as his own guest, and sent him to you right away."

Regis let Lew lead him to the bench by the fire. The woman touched the harp again, in soft chords. Another woman, this one very young, with long straight red hair and a pretty, remote face, came and took his cloak, looking at him with bold eyes, straight at him. No girl in the Domains would look at him like that! He had an uncomfortable feeling that she knew what he was thinking and was greatly amused by it. Lew said the women's names but Regis was in no condition to pay attention. He was introduced to Beltran of Aldaran, too, who almost immediately left the room. Regis wished they would all go away. Lew sat beside him, saying, "How came you to ride this long road alone, Regis? Only for Danilo's sake?"

"I am sworn to him, we are *bredin*," Regis said faintly. "He is truly unharmed, not a prisoner?"

"He is housed in luxury, an honored guest. You shall see him as soon as you like."

"But I do not understand all this, Lew. You came on a mission from Comyn, yet I find you here entangled in their affairs. What is this all about?" As soon as their hands

touched they had fallen into rapport, and Regis found himself
wondering, *Has Lew turned traitor to Comyn?* In answer
Lew said quietly, "I am no traitor. But I have come to believe that perhaps service to Comyn and service to Darkover
are not quite the same thing."

The woman had begun the song again, softly.

> No wolf would prowl at this hour of the day,
> Brother, tell me, tell me!
> It is the blood of my own brothers twain
> Who sat at the drink with me.
>
> How came ye fight with your own blood kin,
> Brother, tell me, tell me,
> Your father's sons and your mother's sons
> Who dwelled in peace with thee.

Lew was still talking, through the sound. "The Comyn has
been too often unjust. They threw Danilo aside like a piece
of rubbish, for no better reason than that he had offended a
wicked and corrupt man who should never have been in
power. Danilo is a catalyst telepath. I suggested they bring
him here—I had no idea they would take him by force—and
his services were enlisted to a larger loyalty. I had it in mind he
could serve all our world, not a sick, power-mad clique of
aristocrats bent on keeping themselves in power at whatever
cost. . . ."

The mournful harp-chords were very soft, the woman's
voice very sweet.

> We sat at feast, we fought in jest,
> Sister, I vow to thee;
> A berserker's rage came in my hand,
> And I slew them shamefully.

Lew said, "Enough of this, you are tired and anxious about
Dani, and you must have some rest. When you are well
recovered, I want you to know all about what we are doing.
Then you will know why those who are really loyal to
Darkover may serve us all best by putting some check on the
Comyn powers."

Regis could feel Lew's sincerity through the touch on his
hand, yet there was some hesitation too. He slid his hand up
Lew's arm to touch the tattooed mark there. He said, "You're

not completely sure of this either, Lew. You are sworn, sealed to Comyn."

Lew took his hand away, saying bitterly, "Sworn? No. Vows in which I had no part were sworn for me when I was five years old. But come, we'll talk of this another time. If you've been imagining Danilo a prisoner it will reassure you to find him in the best guest suite, the only one, I suppose, fit to entertain a Hastur. If he's your sworn man he should be lodged with you."

He turned, briefly making his excuses to the women. In his sensitized state Regis could feel their emotions, too: sharp resentment from the older, the singer. The younger one seemed aware of nothing but Lew. Regis didn't want to be part of these complexities! He was glad when they were alone in the corridor.

"Regis, what's really wrong with you? You're ill!"

Regis tried—he knew he didn't succeed too well—to cut off the rapport entirely. He knew that if he told Lew he had threshold sickness on the road, Lew would be immensely concerned. Even Javanne had treated it as a serious matter. For some reason he was anxious to avoid this. He said, "Nothing much; I'm very tired. I'm not used to mountain riding and I may have a chill." Actively he resisted Lew's solicitude. He could feel his kinsman's anxiety about him, and it made him irritible for some unknown reason. He wasn't a child now! And he could sense the bafflement with which Lew gently but definitely withdrew.

Lew paused at an ornate double door, scowling at the guard stationed there. "You guard a guest, sir?"

"Safeguard, Dom Lewis. Lord Beltran ordered me to see that no one disturbed him. Everybody's not friendly to the valley folk here. See?" the guard said, thrusting the door open. "He's not locked in."

Lew went in and called, "Danilo?" Regis, following him, took in at a glance the luxurious old-fashioned surroundings. Danilo came from an inner room, stopped short.

Regis felt overwhelming relief. He couldn't speak. Lew smiled. "You see," he said, "alive and well and unharmed."

Danilo flung back his head in an aggressive gesture. He said, "Did you send to have him captured, too?"

"How suspicious you are, Dani," Lew said. "Ask him yourself. I'll send servants to look after you."

He touched Regis lightly on the arm. "My own honor

pledged on it, no harm shall come to either of you, and you shall depart unharmed when you are able to travel." He added, "Take good care of him, Dani," and withdrew, closing the door.

Chapter EIGHTEEN

When I came back to the fireside room, Thyra was still playing her harp, and I realized how short a time I had been away; she was still singing the ballad of the outlaw berserker.

And when will you come back again,
  Brother, tell me, tell me?
When the sun and the moon rise together in the West,
And that shall never be.

It must be immeasurably old, I thought, and alien, to speak of one moon instead of four! Beltran had returned and was gazing into the fire, looking angry and remote. He must have gotten the scolding he deserved from Kermiac. Before this, the old man's illness had kept any of us from telling Kermiac what Beltran had done. I was distressed because Beltran was distressed—I couldn't help it, I liked him, I understood what had prompted his rash orders. But what he had done to Danilo was unforgivable, and I was angry with him, too.

And he knew it. His voice, when he turned to me, was truculent.

"Now that you've put the child to bed—"

"Don't mock the lad, cousin," I said. "He's young, but he was man enough to cross the Hellers alone. I wouldn't."

Beltran said, "I've had that already from Father; he had nothing but praise for the boy's courage and good manner! I don't need it from you, too!" And he turned his back on me again. Well, I had little sympathy for him. He might well have lost us any chance of Danilo's friendship or help; and Danilo's help, as I saw it now, was all that could save this circle. If Beltran's *laran* could be fully opened, if with Danilo's aid we could discover and open up a few more latent telepaths, there was a chance, a bare chance but one I

277

was willing to take, that we might somehow control the Sharra matrix. Without that it seemed helpless.

Marjorie smiled and said, "Your friend wouldn't speak to me or look at me. But I would like to know him."

"He's a valley man, love, he'd think it rude and boorish to stare at a maiden. But he is my good friend."

Kadarin's lip curled in amusement. "Yet it wasn't for *your* sake he crossed the mountains, but for the Syrtis boy."

"I came here of my free will, and Regis knew it," I retorted, then laughed heartily. "By my probably nonexistent forefathers, Bob, do you think I am jealous? I am no lover of boys, but Regis was put in my charge when he was a little lad. He's dearer to me than my own brother born."

Marjorie smiled her heart-stopping smile and said, "Then I shall love him, too."

Thyra looked up and taunted, through the chords of her harp, "Come, Marjorie, you're a Keeper! If a man touches you you'll go up in smoke or something!"

Icy shudders suddenly racked me. *Marjorie, burning in Sharra's flame. . . .* I took one stride toward the fire, wrenched the harp from Thyra's hands, then caught myself, still rigid. What had I been about to do? Fling the harp across the room, bring it down crashing across that mocking face? Slowly, deliberately, forcing my shaking muscles to relax, I brought the harp down and laid it on the bench.

"*Breda,*" I said, using the word for sister, not the ordinary one but the intimate word which could also mean darling, "such mockery is unworthy of you. If I had thought it possible, or if I had had the training of you from the first, don't you think I would have chosen you rather than Marjorie? Don't you think I would rather have had Marjorie free?" I put my arm around her. For a moment she was defiant, gazing angrily up at me.

"Would you really have trusted me to keep your rule of chastity?" she flung at me. I was too shocked to answer. At last I said, "*Breda,* it isn't you I don't trust, it's your training."

She had been rigid in my arms; suddenly she went limp against me, her arms clinging around my neck. I thought she would cry. I said, still trembling with that mixture of fury and tenderness, "And don't make jests about the fires! Evanda have mercy, Thyra! You were never at Arilinn, you have never seen the memorial, but have you, who are a singer of ballads, never heard the tale of Marelie Hastur? I have no voice for singing, but I shall tell it you, if you need reminding that there is no jesting about such matters!" I had to break off. My voice was trembling.

Kadarin said quietly, "We all saw Marjorie in the fire, but it was an illusion. You weren't hurt, were you, Margie?"

"No. No, I wasn't. No, Lew. Don't, please don't. Thyra didn't mean anything," Marjorie said, shaking. I ached to reach out for her, take her in my arms, keep her safe. Yet that would place her in more danger than anything else I could possibly do.

I had been a fool to touch Thyra.

She was still clinging to me, warm and close and vital. I wanted to thrust her violently away, but at the same time I wanted—and she knew it, damn it, she knew it!—I wanted what I would have had as a matter of course from any woman of my own circle who was not a Keeper. What would have dispelled this hostility and tension. Any woman tower-trained would have sensed the state I was in and felt responsible. . . .

I forced myself to be calm, to release myself from Thyra's arms. It wasn't Thyra's fault, any more than it was Marjorie's. It wasn't Thyra's fault that Marjorie, and not herself, had been forced by lack of any other to be Keeper. It wasn't Thyra who had roused me this way. It wasn't Thyra's fault, either, that she had not been trained to the customs of a tower circle, where the intimacy and awareness is closer than any blood tie, closer than love, where the need of one evokes a real responsibility in the others.

I could impose the laws of a tower circle on this group only so far as was needed for their own safety. I could not ask more than this. Their own bonds and ties went far back, beyond my coming. Thyra had nothing but contempt for Arilinn. And to come between Thyra and Kadarin was not possible.

Gently, so she would not feel wounded by an abrupt withdrawal, I moved away from her. Beltran, staring into the fire as if hypnotized by the darting flames, said in a low voice, "Marelie Hastur. I know the tale. She was a Keeper at Arilinn who was taken by mountain raiders in the Kilghard Hills, ravaged and thrown out to die by the city wall. Yet from pride, or fear of pity, she concealed what had been done to her and went into the matrix screens in spite of the law of the Keepers. . . . And she died, a blackened corpse like one lightning-struck."

Marjorie shrank, and I damned Beltran. Why did he have to tell that story in Marjorie's hearing? It seemed a piece of gratuitous cruelty, very unlike Beltran.

Yes. And I had been about to tell it to Thyra, and I had come near to breaking her own harp across her head. That was very unlike me, too.

What in all the Gods had come to us!

Kadarin said harshly, "A lying tale. A pious fraud to scare Keepers into keeping their virginity, a bogeyman to frighten babies and girl-children!"

I thrust out my scarred hand. "Bob, *this* is no pious fraud!"

"Nor can I believe it had anything to do with your virginity," he retorted, laughing, and laid a kind hand on my shoulder. "You're giving yourself nightmares, Lew. For your Marelie Hastur I give you Cleindori Aillard, who was kinswoman to your own father, and who married and bore a son, losing no iota of her powers as Keeper. Have you forgotten they butchered her to keep *that* secret? That alone should give the lie to all this superstitious drivel about chastity."

I saw Marjorie's face lose a little of its tension and was grateful to him, even if not wholly convinced. We were working here without elementary safeguards, and I was not yet willing to disregard this oldest and simplest of precautions.

Kadarin said, "If you and Marjorie feel safer to lie apart until this work is well underway, it's your own choice. But don't give yourselves nightmares either. She's well in control. I feel safe with her." He bent down, kissing her lightly on the forehead, a kiss completely without passion but altogether loving. He put a free arm around me, drew me against him, smiling. I thought for a moment he would kiss me too, but he laughed. "We're both too old for that," he said, but without mockery. For a moment we were all close together again, with no hint of the terrible violence and disharmony that had thrust us apart. I began to feel hope again.

Thyra asked softly, "How is it with our father, Beltran?" I had forgotten that Thyra was his daughter too.

"He is very weak," Beltran said, "but don't fret, little sister, he'll outlive all of us."

I said, "Shall I go to him, Beltran? I've had long experience treating shock from matrix overload—"

"And so have I, Lew," Kadarin said kindly, releasing me.

"All the knowledge of matrix technology is not locked up at Arilinn, *bredu.* I can do better without sleep than you young people."

I knew I should insist, but I did not have the heart to face down another of Thyra's taunts about Arilinn. And it was true that Kermiac had been training technicians in these hills before any of us were born. And my own weariness betrayed me. I swayed a little where I stood, and Kadarin caught and steadied me.

"Go and rest, Lew. Look, Rafe's asleep on the rug. Thyra, call someone to carry him to bed. Off with you now, all of you!"

"Yes," said Beltran, "tomorrow we have work to do, we've delayed long enough. Now that we have a catalyst telepath—"

I said somberly, "It may take a long time now to persuade him to trust you, Beltran. And you cannot use force on him. You know that, don't you?"

Beltran looked angry. "I won't hurt a hair of his precious little head, kinsman. But you'd better be damned good at persuading. Without his help, I don't know what we'll do."

I didn't either. We needed Danilo so terribly. We separated quietly, all of us sobered. I had a terrible feeling of weight on my heart. Thyra walked beside the burly servant who was carrying Rafe to bed. Kadarin and Beltran, I knew, were going to watch beside Kermiac. I should have shared that vigil. I loved the old man and I was responsible for the moment's lack of control which had struck him down.

I was about to leave Marjorie at the foot of her tower stairway, but she clung hard to my hand.

"Please, Lew. Stay with me. As you did the other day."

I started to agree, then realized something else.

I didn't trust myself.

Whether it was the brief disturbing physical contact with Thyra, whether it was the upsetting force of the quarrel, or the old songs and ballads . . . I didn't trust myself!

Even now, it took all my painfully acquired discipline, all of it, to keep from taking her into my arms, kissing her senseless, carrying her up those stairs and into her room, to the bed we had shared so chastely . . .

I stopped myself right there. But we were deeply in contact; she had seen, felt, *shared* that awareness with me. She was blushing, but she did not turn her eyes from mine. She said at last, quietly, "You told me that when we were working like this, nothing could happen that would harm or . . . or endanger me."

I shook my head in bewilderment. "I don't understand it either, Marjorie. Normally, at this stage," and here I laughed, a short unmirthful sound, "you and I could lie down naked together and sleep like brothers or unweaned babies. I don't know what's happened, Marjorie, but I don't dare. Gods above!" I almost shouted at her. "Don't you think I *want* to?"

Now she did avert her eyes for a moment. She said in a whisper, "Kadarin says it's only a superstition. I'll . . . I'll risk it if you want to, Lew. If you need to."

Now I really felt ashamed. I was better disciplined than this. I made myself take a long breath, unclench my hands from the railings of the stair. "No, beloved. Perhaps I can find out what's gone wrong. But I have to be alone."

I heard her plea, not aloud but straight to my mind, straight to my heart: *Don't leave me! Don't go, Lew, don't . . .* I broke the contact harshly, cutting her off, shutting her out. It hurt horribly, but I knew that if this went on I would never be able to leave her, and I knew where it would end. And her discipline held. She closed her eyes, drawing a deep breath. I saw that curious look of distance, withdrawnness, isolation, slip down over her features. The look Callina had had, that Festival Night. The look I had seen so often on Janna's face, my last season at Arilinn. She had known I loved her, wanted her. It hurt, but I felt relieved, too. Marjorie said quietly, "I understand, Lew. Go and sleep, my darling." She turned and went away from me, up the long stairs, and I went away, blind with pain.

I passed the closed door of the suite where Regis and Danilo had been lodged. I knew I should speak to Regis. He was ill, exhausted. But my own misery made me shrink from the task. He had made it clear he did not want my solicitude. He was reunited with his friend, why should I disturb them now? He would be asleep, I hoped, resting after that terrible journey alone through the Hellers.

I went to my own room and threw myself down without bothering to undress.

Something was wrong. Something was terribly wrong.

I had felt a disruption like this once before, like a vortex of fury, lust, rage, destruction, surging up through us all. It should not be like this. It *could* not be like this!

Normally, matrix work left the workers drained, spent,

without anything left over for any violent emotion. Above all, I had grown accustomed to the fact that there was nothing left over for sexuality. It wasn't that way now.

I had been angry with Thyra at first, not aroused by her. I had been angry when it seemed she mocked Marjorie, and then suddenly I'd been so overcome by my own need that it would have been easy for me to tear off her clothes and take her there before the fire!

And Marjorie. A Keeper. I shouldn't have been capable even of *thinking* about her this way. Yet I *had* thought about it. Damn it, I still ached with wanting her. And she had wanted me to stay with her! Was she weeping now, alone in her room, the tears she had been too proud to shed before me? Should I have risked it? Sanity, prudence, long habit, told me no; no, I had done the only thing it was safe to do.

I glanced briefly at the wrapped bundle of the matrix and felt the faintest thrill of awareness along my nerves. Insulated like that, it should have been wholly dormant. Damn it, I trained at Arilinn and any first-year telepath learns to insulate a matrix! What I insulate stays insulated! I must be dreaming, imagining. I was living on my nerves and by now they were raw, hypersensitive.

That damned thing was responsible for all our troubles. I'd have liked to heave it out the window, or better, send it out on a Terran rocket and let it work its mischief on cosmic dust or something! I heartily wished that Beltran and the Sharra matrix and Kadarin and old Desideria, with all her forge-folk about her, were all frying together on one of their own forges.

I was still in accord with Beltran's dream, but standing between us and the accomplishment of the dream was this ravening nightmare of Sharra. I knew, I knew with the deepest roots of my self, that I could not control it, that Marjorie could not control it, that nothing human could ever control it. We had only stirred the surface of the matrix. If it was roused all the way it might never be controlled again, and tomorrow I would tell Beltran so.

Clutching this resolve, I fell into an uneasy sleep.

For a long time I wandered in confused nightmares through the corridors of Comyn Castle; whenever I met someone, his or her face was veiled or turned away in aversion or contempt. Javanne Hastur refusing to dance with me at a children's ball. Old Domenic di Asturien with his lifted eyebrows. My father, reaching out to me across a great

chasm. Callina Aillard, turning away and leaving me alone
on the rain-swept balcony. It seemed I wandered through
those halls for hours, with no single human face turned to me
in concern or compassion.

And then the dream changed. I was standing on the balcony of the Arilinn Tower, watching the sunrise, and Janna
Lindir was standing beside me. I was dreamily surprised to
see her. I was back again where I had been happy, where I
had been accepted and loved, where there was no cloud on
my mind and heart. But I had thought my circle had been
broken and scattered, the others to their homes, I to the
Guards where I was despised, Janna married . . . no, surely
that had been only a bad dream! She turned and laid her
hand in mine, and I felt a deep happiness.

Then I realized it was not Janna but Callina Aillard, saying
softly, mockingly, "You do know what's really wrong with
you," taunting me from the safe barrier of what she was, a
Keeper, forbidden, untouchable. . . . Maddened by the surge
of need and hunger in me, I reached for her, I tore the veils
from her body while she screamed and struggled. I threw her
down whimpering on the stones and flung myself atop her,
naked, and through her wild cries of terror she *changed*, she
began to flame and glow and burn, the fires of Sharra engulf-
ing us, consuming us in a wild spasm of lust and ecstasy and
terror and agony. . . .

I woke up shuddering, crying out with the mingled terror
and enchantment of the dream. The Sharra matrix lay
shrouded and dormant.

But I dared not close my eyes again that night.

Chapter NINETEEN

After Lew had gone away, closing the door behind him, it was Regis who moved first, stumbling across the floor as if wading through a snowdrift, to clasp Dani's shoulders in a kinsman's embrace. He heard his own voice, hoarse in his ears.

"You're safe. You really are here and safe." He had doubted Lew's word, though never in all his life had he reason to doubt. What kind of evil was here?

"Yes, yes, well and safe," Danilo said, then drew a harsh breath of dismay. "My lord Regis, you're soaked through!"

For the first time Regis became aware of the heat from the fireplace, the hangings sealing off drafts, the warmth after the icy blasts of the corridors. The very warmth touched off a spasm of shivering, but he forced himself to say, "The guards. You are really a prisoner, then?"

"They're here to protect me, so they say. They've been friendly enough. Come, sit here, let me get these boots off, you're chilled to the bone!"

Regis let himself be led to an armchair, so ancient in design that until he was in the seat he was not sure what it was. His feet came out of the boots numb and icy-cold. He was almost too weary to sit up and unlace his tunic; he sat with his hands hanging, his legs stretched out, finally with an effort put his stiff fingers to the tunic-laces. He knew his voice sounded more irritible than he meant.

"I can manage for myself, Dani. You're my paxman, not my body-servant!"

Danilo, kneeling before the fire to dry Regis' boots, jerked upright as if stung. He said into the fire, "Lord Regis, I am honored to serve you in any way I may." Through the stiff formality of the words, Regis, wide open again, *felt* something else, a wordless resonance of despair: *He didn't mean it, then, about accepting my service. It was . . . it was only a way of atoning for what his kinsman had done. . . .*

Without stopping to think, Regis was out of the chair, kneeling beside Dani on the hearth. His voice was shaking, partly with the cold which threatened to rip him apart with shudders, partly with that intense awareness of Dani's hurt.

"The Gods witness I meant it! It's only . . . only . . ." Suddenly he knew the right thing to say. "You remember what a fuss it caused, when I expected anyone to wait on me, in the barracks!"

Their eyes caught and held. Regis had no idea whether it was his own thought or Danilo's: *We were boys then. And now . . . how long ago that seems! Yet it was only last season!* It seemed to Regis that they were looking back, as men, across a great chasm of elapsed time, at a shared boyhood. Where had it gone?

With a sense of fighting off unutterable weariness—it seemed he had been fighting off this weariness as long as he could remember—he reached for Danilo's hands. They felt hard, calloused, real, the only firm anchor-point in a shifting, dissolving universe. Momentarily he felt his hands going *through* Danilo's as if neither of them were quite solid. He blinked hard to focus his eyes, and saw a blue-haloed form in front of him. He could see through Danilo now, to the wall beyond. Trying to focus against the swarming fireflies that spun before his eyes, he remembered Javanne's warning, fight it, move around, speak. He tried to get his voice back into his throat.

"Forgive me, Dani. Who should serve me if not my sworn man . . .?"

And as he spoke the words he *felt*, amazed, the texture of Danilo's relief: *My people have served the Hasturs for generations. Now I too am where I belong.*

No! I do not want to be a master of men . . . !

But the swift denial was understood by both, not as a personal rejection, but the very embodiment of what they both were, so that the giving of Danilo's service was the pleasure and the relief it was, so that Regis knew he must not only accept that service, but accept it fully, graciously.

Danilo's face suddenly looked strange, frightened. His mouth was moving but Regis could no longer hear him, floating bodiless in the sparkling darkness. The base of his skull throbbed with ballooning pain. He heard himself whisper, "I am . . . in your hands . . ." Then the world slid sidewise and he felt himself collapse into Danilo's arms.

He never knew how he got there, but seconds later, it

seemed, he felt searing pain all over his naked body, and found himself floating up to the chin in a great tub of boiling water. Danilo, kneeling at his side, was anxiously chafing his wrists. His head was splitting, but he could see solid objects again, and his own body was reassuringly firm. A servant was hovering around with clean garments, trying to attract Danilo's attention long enough to get his approval of them.

Regis lay watching, too languid to do anything but accept their ministrations. He noticed that Danilo unobtrusively kept his own body between Regis and the Aldaran servant. Danilo chased the man out quickly, muttering under his breath, "I'm not going to trust any of them alone with you!"

At first the water had seemed scalding to his chilled body; now he realized it was barely warm, in fact it must have been drawn for some time, was probably a bath prepared for Danilo before he came in. Danilo was still bending over him, his face tight with worry. Suddenly Regis was filled with such intolerable anxiety that he cut off the intense, sensuous pleasure of the hot water soothing his chilled and stiffened body—eleven nights on the trail and not warm once!—and drew himself upright, hauling himself out of the hot tub, reaching for a towel to wrap himself in. Danilo knelt to dry him, saying, "I sent the servant for a healer-woman, there must be someone of that sort here. Regis, I never saw anyone faint like that before; your eyes were open but you couldn't hear me or see me . . ."

"Threshold sickness." Briefly he sketched in an explanation. "I've had a few attacks before. I'm over the worse." I hope, he added to himself. "I doubt if the healer could do anything with this. Here, give me that, I can dress myself." Firmly he took the towel away from Danilo. "Go and tell her not to bother, and find out if there's anything hot to drink."

Skeptically Danilo retreated. Regis finished drying himself and clambered into the unfamiliar clothing. His hands were shaking almost too hard to tie the knots of his tunic. What's the matter with me, he asked himself why didn't I want Dani to help me dress? He looked at his hands in cold shock, as if they belonged to someone else. I didn't want him to touch me!

Even to him that sounded incongruous. They had lived together in the rough intimacy of the barracks room for months. They had been close-linked, even thinking one another's thoughts.

This was different.

Irresistibly his mind was drawn back to that night in the

barracks, when he had reached out to Danilo, torn by an almost frenzied desire to share his misery, the spasm of loathing and horror with which Danilo had flung him away. . . .

And then, shaken and shamed and terrified, Regis knew what had prompted that touch, and why he was suddenly shy of Danilo now. The knowledge struck him motionless, his bare feet cold through the wolfskin rug on the tile floor.

To touch him. Not to comfort Dani, but to comfort his own need, his own loneliness, his own hunger. . . .

He moved deliberately, afraid if he remained motionless another instant the threshold sickness would surge up over him again. He knelt on the wolfskin, drawing fur-lined stockings up over his knees and deliberately tying the thongs into intricate knots. On the surface of his mind he thought that fur clothing was life-saving here in the mountains. It felt wonderful.

But, relentless, the memory he had barricaded since his twelfth year burst open like a bleeding wound; the memory he had let himself lose consciousness before recovering on the northward trail: Lew's face, alight with fire, his barriers down in the last extremity of exhaustion and pain and fear.

And Regis had shared it all with him, there were no barriers between them. None. Regis had known what Lew wanted and would not ask, was too proud and too shy to ask. Something Regis had never felt before, that Lew thought he was too young to feel or to understand. But Regis had known and had shared it.

And afterward, perhaps because Lew had never spoken of it, Regis was too ashamed to remember. And he had never dared open his mind again. Why? Why? Out of fear, out of shame? Out of . . . longing?

Until Danilo, without even trying, broke that barricade.

And now Regis knew why it was Dani who could break it . . .

He doesn't know, Regis thought, and then with a bleak and spartan pride, He must never know.

He stood up, felt the splitting pain at his forehead again. He knew a frightened moment of disquiet. How could he keep this from him? Dani was a telepath too!

Lew had said it was like living with your skin off. Well, his skin was off and he was doubly naked. Taking a grip on himself, he walked out into the other room, decided his boots weren't dry. Inside he felt cold and trembly, but physically he was quite warm and calm.

How could he face Lew again, knowing this? Coldly, Regis told himself not to be a fool. Lew had always known. He wasn't a coward, he didn't lie to himself! Lew remembered, so no wonder he was astonished when Regis had said he did not have *laran*!

Lew had asked him why he could not bear to remember. . . .

"You should have gone straight to bed and let me bring you supper there," Danilo said behind him, and Regis, firmly taking mastery of his face, looked around. Danilo was looking at him with friendly concern, and Regis remembered, with a shock, that Danilo knew nothing, nothing of the memory and awareness that had flooded him in the scant few minutes they had been parted. He said aloud, trying for a casual neutral tone, "I collapsed before I saw anything of the suite but this room. I have no idea where I'm going to be sleeping."

"And I've had days with nothing to do but explore. Come, I'll show you the way. I told the servant to bring your supper in here. How does it feel to be quartered in a royal suite, after the student dormitory at Nevarsin?"

There was room enough for a regent and all his entourage in this guest suite: enormous bedrooms, servants quarters in plenty, a great hall, even a small octagonal presence chamber with a throne and footstools for petitioners. It was more elaborate than his grandfather's suite in Thendara. Danilo had chosed the smallest and least elaborate bedroom, but it looked like a royal favorite's chamber. There was a huge bed on a dais which would, Regis thought irreverently, have held a Dry-Towner, three of his wives and six of his concubines. The servant he had seen before was warming the sheets with a long-handled warming pan, and there was a fire in the fireplace. He let Danilo help him into the big bed, put a tray of hot food beside him. Danilo sent the man away, saying gravely, "It is my privilege to wait on my lord with my own hands." Regis would have laughed at the solemn, formal words, but knew even a smile would hurt Danilo unspeakably. He kept his composure, until the man was out of earshot, then said, "I hope you're not going to take that formal my-lord tone all the time now, *bredu*."

There was relief in Danilo's eyes too. "Only in front of strangers, Regis." He came and lifted covers off steaming bowls of food, clambered up on the bed and poured hot soup from a jug. He said, "The food's good. I had to ask for cider instead of wine the first day, that's all. I see they brought both tonight, and the cider's hot."

Regis drank the soup and the hot cider thirstily; but although it was his first hot meal in days, he found it almost too hard to chew and swallow.

"Now tell me how you found me here, Regis."

Regis' hand went to the matrix on the thong around his neck. Danilo shrank a little. "I thought such things were to be used only by technicians, with proper safeguards. Isn't it dangerous?"

"I knew no other way."

Danilo looked at him, visibly moved. "And you took that risk for me, *bredu?*"

Regis deliberately withdrew from the moment of emotion. "Take that last cutlet, won't you? I'm not hungry. . . . I'm here and alive, aren't I? I expect I'll have trouble with my kinfolk; I got away from Gabriel and my escort by a trick. I was supposed to be on my way to Neskaya Tower."

The diversion worked. Danilo asked with a faint revulsion, "Are you to be a matrix mechanic, now they know you have *laran?*"

"God forbid! But I have to learn to safeguard myself."

Danilo had made a long mental leap. "Is this—using a matrix, untrained—why you have been having threshold sickness?"

"I don't know. Perhaps. It couldn't help."

Danilo said, "I should have sent for Lew Alton, instead of the healer-woman. He's tower-trained, he'd know what to do for it."

Regis flinched. He didn't want to face Lew just yet. Not till he had his own thoughts in order. "Don't disturb him. I'm all right now."

"Well, if you're sure," Danilo said uncertainly. "No doubt, by now, he's in bed with his girl and wouldn't thank anyone for disturbing him, but just the same—"

"His girl?"

"Aldaran's foster-daughter. The guards are lonely and have nothing to do but gossip, and I thought it just as well to learn as much as I could about what's going on here. They say Lew's madly in love with her, and old Kermiac's arranging a marriage."

Well, Regis thought, that made good sense. Lew had never been happy in the lowlands and he was lonely. If he took a wife from his mountain kinsmen, that was a good thing.

Danilo said, "There's wine, if you want it," but Regis firmly shook his head. He might sleep better for it, but he dared not risk anything that might break down his defenses. He took a handful of sugared nuts and began nibbling them.

"Now, Dani, tell me all about it. Old Kermiac did not know why they had brought you here, and I had no chance to ask Lew alone." He wondered suddenly which of the women in the fireside room was Lew's sweetheart. The hard-faced girl with the harp? Or the delicate remote, younger one in blue?

"But you must have known all about it," said Danilo, "or how could you have come after me? I tried . . . I tried to reach out for you with my mind, but I was afraid. I could *feel* them. I was afraid they'd use that somehow . . ." Regis sensed he was almost crying. "It's terrible! *Laran* is terrible! I don't want it, Regis! I don't want it!"

Impulsively Regis reached out to lay a steadying hand on his wrist, stopped himself. Oh no. Not that. Not so easy an excuse to . . . to touch him. He said, keeping his voice detached, "It seems we have no choice, Dani. It has come to us both."

"It's like—like lightning! It hits people who don't want it, hits them at random—" Danilo's voice shook.

Regis wondered how anyone lived with it. He said, "I don't much want it either, now that I've got it. No more than I want to be heir to Comyn." He sighed. "But we have no choice. Or the only choice we have is to misuse it—like Dyan—or to meet it like men, and honorably." He knew he was not talking only of *laran* now. "Laran cannot be all evil. It helped me find you."

"And if I've brought you into danger of death . . ."

"That's enough of that!" The words were a sharp rebuke; Danilo shrank as if Regis had slapped him, but Regis felt he dared not face another emotional outburst. "Lord Kermiac has called me *guest*. Among mountain people that is a sacred obligation. Neither of us is in danger."

"Not from old Kermiac perhaps. But Beltran wants to use my *laran* to awaken other telepaths, and what's he going to do with them when he's got them awakened? Whatever they're doing . . ." He stared right through Regis and whispered, "It's *wrong*. I can feel it, reaching for me even in my sleep!"

"Surely Lew wouldn't be a party to anything dishonorable?"

"Not knowingly, maybe. But he's very angry with the Comyn, and wholly committed to Beltran now," Danilo said. "This is what he told me."

He began to explain Beltran's plan for revival of the old matrix technology, bringing Darkover from a non-industrial, non-technological culture into a position of strength in a galactic empire. As he spoke of star-travel Regis' eyes brightened, recalling his own dreams. Suppose he need *not* desert his world and his heritage to go out among the stars, but could serve his people and still be part of a great star-spanning culture . . . it seemed too good to be true.

"Surely if it could have been done at all, it would have been done at the height of the strength of the towers. They must have tried this."

"I don't know," said Danilo humbly, "I'm not as well-educated as you, Regis."

And Regis knew so little!

"Let's not sit and make guesses about what they're doing," Regis said. "Let's wait till tomorrow and ask them." He yawned deliberately. "I haven't slept in a bed for a dozen nights. I think I'll try this one out." Danilo was taking away the mugs and bowls; Regis beckoned him back.

"I hope you have no foolish notion of standing guard while I sleep, or sleeping on the floor across my doorway?"

"Only if you want me to," said Dani, but he sounded hurt, and with that unwelcome sensitivity Regis knew he'd have liked to. The picture that had haunted him for days now returned, Dani's brother shielding his father with his body. Did Dani really want to die for him? The thought shocked him speechless.

He said curtly, "Sleep where you damn please, but get some sleep. And if you really like having me give you orders, Dani, that's an order." He didn't wait to see where Dani chose. He slid down into the great bed and dropped into a bottomless pit of sleep.

At first, exhaustion taking its toll of his aching body and overstrained emotions, he was too weary even to dream. Then he began to drift in and out of dreams: the sound of horses' hooves on a road, galloping . . . the armory in Comyn Castle, struggling weakly against Dyan, armed and fresh against an aching lassitude that would not let Regis lift his sword . . . a great form swooping down, touching Castle Aldaran with a finger of fire, flames rising skyward. By the firelight he saw Lew's face alight with terror, and reached out to him, feeling the strange and unfamiliar emotions and sensations, but this time he knew what he was doing. This time he was not a child, his child's body responding half-aware to the most innocent of caresses; this time he knew and accepted it all, and suddenly it was Danilo in his arms, and Danilo was struggling, trying to push him away in pain and terror. Regis, gripped by need and blind cruelty, gripped him more and more tightly, fighting to hold him, subdue him, and then, with a gasp, cried aloud, "No! Oh, *no*!" and flung him away, pulling himself upright in the great bed.

He was alone, the firelight burned down to coals. Across the foot of the enormous bed, like a dark shadow, Danilo slept, wrapped in a blanket, his back turned away. Regis stared at the sleeping boy, unable to shake off the horror of the dream, the shock of knowing what he had tried to do.

No. Not tried to do. Wanted to do. Dreamed of doing. There was a difference.

Or was there, for a telepath?

Once, one of the few times Kennard had spoken of his own years in the tower, Kennard had said, very seriously: "I am an Alton; my anger can kill. A murderous thought is, for me, almost a murder. A lustful thought is the psychological equivalent of a rape."

Regis wondered if he was responsible even for his dreams. Would he ever dare sleep again?

Danilo stirred with a moan. Abruptly he began to gasp and cry out and struggle in his sleep. He muttered aloud, "No— no, please!" and began to cry. Regis stared in horror. Did his own dream disturb Dani! Dyan had reached him, even in sleep. . . . He could not leave him crying. He leaned forward, saying gently, "Dani, it's all right, you were asleep."

Half asleep, Danilo made the safeguarding sign of *cristoforo* prayers. It must be comforting to have their faith, Regis thought. Danilo's smothered sobbing tore at Regis like claws. He had no way of knowing that far away in the castle Lew Alton had also started out of nightmare, shaking with the guilt of the most dreadful crime *he* could imagine, but Regis did find himself wondering what form Danilo's nightmare had taken. He dared not ask, dared not risk the intimacy of midnight confidences.

Danilo had his crying under control now. He asked, "It's not . . . not threshold sickness again?"

"No. No, only a nightmare. I'm sorry I woke you."

"This damned place is full of nightmares . . ." Danilo mut-

tered. Regis felt him reach out for reassurance, for contact.
He held himself aloof from the touch. After a long time he
knew Danilo slept again. He lay awake, watching the dying
remnants of the fire on the hearth. The fire that had been a
raging forest fire from his troubled childhood, that had become the great form of fire. Sharra, of the legends. What, in
the name of all the Gods, were they *doing* here at Aldaran?
Something here was out of control, dangerous.

Fire was the key, he knew, not only because the memory
of a forest fire had brought back the memory he'd buried,
but it was worse than that. Lew looked as if he'd been doing
something dangerous. And all this ... this dislocation of
memory, these nightmares of cruelty and lust ... something
terrible was going on here.

And Regis had Danilo to protect. He came here for that,
and he vowed again to fulfill it.

Weighed down under the unendurable burden of *laran*,
knowing guilt even for his dreams, shouldering the heavy
knowledge of what he had forgotten, Regis dared not sleep
again. He thought instead. The mistake was in sending him to
Nevarsin, he knew. Anywhere else he could have come to
terms with it. He knew, rationally, that what had happened
to him, what was happening to him now, was nothing to
bring such catastrophic guilt and self-hatred. He had even
minded when the cadets thought him Dyan's minion.

But that was before he knew what Dyan had done....

Dyan's shadow lay heavy on Regis. And heavier on Danilo.
Regis knew he could not bear it if Dani were to think of him
as he thought of Dyan ... even if Regis thought of him that
way....

His mind reeling under it, Regis knew suddenly that he *had*
a choice. Faced by this unendurable self-knowledge, he could
do again what he had done when he was twelve years old,
and this time there would be no lifting of the barrier. He
could forget again. He could cut off the unwelcome, un-
wanted self-knowledge, cut off, with it, the undesired, unendurable *laran*.

He could be free of it all, and this time no one would ever
be able to break through it again. Be free of it all: heritage,
and responsibility. If he had no *laran*, it would not matter if
he left the Comyn, went out into the Empire never to return.
He even left an heir to take his place. He had done it once.
He could do it again. He could meet Danilo in the morning
with no guilty knowledge and no fear, meet him innocently,

as a friend. He need never again fear that Danilo could reach his mind and learn what Regis now felt he would rather die than reveal.

He had done it once. Even Lew could not break that barrier.

The temptation was almost unendurable. Dry-mouthed, Regis looked at the sleeping boy lying heavily across his feet. To be free again, he thought, free of it all.

He had accepted Dani's oath, though, as a Hastur. Had accepted his service, and his love.

He was no longer free. He'd said it to Danilo, and it was true for him, too. They had no choice, it had come to them, and they had only the choice to misuse it or meet it with honor.

Regis did not know if he could meet it with honor, but he knew he'd have to try. Chickens couldn't go back into eggs.

Either way, there was nothing but hell ahead.

Chapter TWENTY

(Lew Alton's narrative)

Shortly after sunrise I let myself fall into a fitful drowse. Some time later I was awakened by a strange outcry, women screaming—no, wailing, a sound I had heard only once before ... on my trip into the backwoods, in a house where there was a death.

I threw on some clothes and ran out into the corridor. It was crowded, servants rushing to and fro, no one ready to stop and answer my questions. I met Marjorie at the foot of the little stair from her tower. She was as white as her chamber robe.

"Darling, what is it?"

"I'm not sure. It's the death-wail!" She put out a hand and forcibly stopped one of the women rushing by. "What is it, what's that wailing, what's happened?"

The woman gasped. "It's the old lord, *domna Marguerida*, your guardian, he died in the night—"

As soon as I heard the words I knew I had been expecting it. I felt stricken, grieved. Even in such a short time I had come to love my uncle, and beyond my personal grief I was dismayed at what this must mean. Not only for the Domain of Aldaran, but for all Darkover. His reign had been a long one, and a wise one.

"Thyra," Marjorie whispered, "Evanda pity us, what will she do, how will she live with this?" She clutched my arm. "He's her *father*, Lew! Did you know? My father owned to her, but she was none of his, and it was her doing, her mistake, that has killed him!"

"Not hers," I said gently. "Sharra." I had begun to believe, now, that we were all helpless before it. Tomorrow—no, today, the sooner the better—it should go back to the forge-folk. Desideria had been right: it had lain safe in their keeping, should never have left them. I quailed, thinking of what Beltran would say. Yet Kadarin had pledged Desideria to abide my judgment.

First I must visit the death chamber, pay a kinsman's respects. The high wailing of the death-cries went on from inside, fraying my already ragged nerves to shreds. Marjorie clutched desperately at my fingers. As we entered the great chamber I heard Thyra's voice, bursting out, almost screaming:

"Cease that pagan caterwauling! I'll have none of it here!"

One or two of the women stopped in mid-wail; others, half-hearted, stopped and started again. Beltran's voice was a harsh shout:

"You who killed him, Thyra, would you deny him proper respect?"

She was standing at the foot of the bed, her head thrown back, defiant. She sounded at the ragged end of endurance. "You superstitious idiot, do you really believe his spirit has stayed here to listen to the yowling over his corpse? Is this your idea of a seemly sound of mourning?"

Beltran said, more gently, "More seemly, perhaps, than this kind of brawling, foster-sister." He looked as you would expect after a long night of watching, and a death. He gestured to the women. "Go, go, finish your wailing elsewhere. The days are long gone when anyone must stand and wail to scare away demons from the dead."

Kermiac had been decently laid out, his hands laid crosswise on his breast, his eyes closed. Marjorie made the *cristoforo* sign across the old man's brow, then across her own. She bent and pressed her lips for a moment to the cold brow, whispering, "Rest in peace, my lord. Holy Bearer of Burdens, give us strength to bear our loss . . ." Then she turned quietly away and bent over the weeping Thyra.

"He is past all forgiveness or blame, darling. Don't torment yourself this way. It is for us to bear now, for the living. Come away, love, come away."

Thyra collapsed into terrible sobbing and let Marjorie lead her out of the room. I stood looking down at the calm, composed old face. For a moment it seemed my own father was lying here before me. I bent and kissed the cold brow, as Marjorie had done.

I said to Beltran, "I knew him such a little while. It is my great loss that I did not come here before." I embraced my kinsman, cheek to cheek, feeling the pain of his grief added to my own. Beltran turned away, pale and composed, as

Regis came into the room, Danilo in his wake. Regis spoke a
brief formal phrase of condolence, held out his hand. Beltran
bowed over it but he did not speak. Had his grief dimmed his
awareness of courtesy? He should have bidden Regis welcome as his guest; somehow it made me uneasy that he did
not. Danilo made the *cristoforo* sign over the old man's
brow, as Marjorie had done, whispering, I suppose, one of
their prayers, then made a formal bow to Beltran.

I followed them outside. Regis looked as if he'd had the
same nightmare-ridden sleep I had, and he was fully barriered against me—a new thing, and a disquieting one. He
said, "He was your kinsman, Lew. I'm sorry for your grief.
And I know my grandfather respected him. It's fitting there
should be someone here from the Hasturs, to extend our condolences. Things will be different, now, in the mountains."

I had been thinking that myself. The sight of Regis almost
automatically taking his place as the formal representative of
Comyn was disquieting. I knew his grandfather would approve, but I was surprised.

"He told me, Regis, shortly before his death, that he hoped
for a day when you and Beltran could sit down together and
plan a better future for our world."

Regis smiled bleakly. "That will be for Prince Derik. The
Hasturs are not kings now."

I gave him a skeptical smile. "Yet they stand nearest the
throne. I have no doubt Derik will choose you for his nearest
counselor, as his kinsmen chose your grandsire."

"If you love me, Lew, don't wish a crown on me," Regis
said with a shudder of revulsion. "But enough of politics for
now. I will remain for the funeral, of course; I owe Beltran
no courtesies, but I'll not insult his father's death bed, either."

If Kermiac's untimely death had delayed Regis' immediate
departure, it must also, in all decency, delay my ultimatum to
Beltran. I anticipated less trouble now that he had had a bitter taste of the dangers inherent in Sharra. Kadarin might be
less tractable. Yet I had faith in his good sense and his affection for all of us.

And so, all those days of mourning for the old lord of Aldaran, none of us spoke of Sharra or Beltran's plans. During
the days I could guard myself against the memory and the
fear; only in terrifying dreams did it return, claw at me with
talons of torment. . . .

The funeral services were over; the mountain lords who
had come to pay their respects to the dead, and to give alle-

giance to Beltran, departed one by one. Beltran made an appearance of grave dignity, solemnly accepting their pledges of amity and support, yet I sensed in all of the mountain men an awareness that an era had irrevocably come to an end. Beltran was aware of it, too, and I knew it hardened his resolve not to run peaceably along the track his father had made—resting on his father's accomplishments and accepting their homage because of their goodwill to Kermiac—but to carve his own place.

We were so much alike, he and I, I have known twins less like. And yet we were so different. I had not known he was personally ambitious, too. I had lost the last traces of personal ambition at Arilinn, had resented Father's attempts to rouse it in me, in the Guards. Now I was deeply disturbed. Would he let his plans slip through his fingers without protest? It would take all my persuasion, all my tact, to convince him to a course less dangerous for all our world. Somehow I must make it clear to him that I still shared his dreams, that I would work for his aims and help him to the utmost, even though I had irrevocably renounced the means he and Kadarin had chosen.

When the mountain lords had departed, Beltran courteously asked Regis and Danilo to remain for a few more days. I had not expected either of them to agree and was ready to try to persuade them, but to my surprise, Regis had accepted the invitation. Maybe it was not so surprising. He looked dreadfully ill. I should have talked to him, tried to find out what ailed him. Yet whenever I tried to speak to him alone he rebuffed me, always turning the conversation to indifferent things. I wondered why. As a child he had loved me; did he think me a traitor, or was it something more personal?

Such was my state when we gathered that morning in the small fireside hall where we had met and worked together so often. Beltran bore the marks of stress and grief and he looked older, too, sobered by the new weight of responsibility. Thyra was pale and composed, but I knew how hard-won that composure had been. Kadarin, too, was haggard, grieved. Rafe, though subdued, had suffered the least; his grief was only that of a child who had lost a kindly guardian. He was too young to see the deeper implications of this.

Marjorie had that heartbreaking remoteness I had begun to see in her lately, the isolation of every Keeper. Through it I sensed a deeper disquiet. Beltran was her guardian now. If he and I were to quarrel, the future for us was not bright.

These were my kinsmen. Together we had built a beautiful dream. My heart ached that I must be the one to shatter it.

But when Danilo and Regis were ceremoniously escorted in, I felt again a glimmer of hope. Perhaps, perhaps, if I could persuade them to help us, there was still a way to salvage that dream!

Beltran began with the utmost courtesy, making formal apologies to Danilo for the way his men had exceeded their orders. If the words had more of diplomacy than real regret, I supposed only the strongest of telepaths could feel the difference. He ended by saying, "Let the end I am striving for outweigh personal considerations. A day is coming for Darkover when mountain men and the Domains must forget their ages-old differences and work together for the good of our world. Can we not agree on that at least, Regis Hastur, that you and I speak together for a world, and that our fathers and grandfathers should have wrought together and not separately for its well-being?"

Regis made a formal bow. I noticed he was wearing his own clothes again. "For your sake, Lord Beltran, I wish I were more skilled in the arts of diplomacy, so that I might more fittingly represent the Hasturs here. As it is, I can speak only for myself as a private individual. I hope the long peace between Comyn and Aldaran may endure for our lifetimes and beyond."

"And that it may not be a peace under the thumbs of the Terrans," Beltran added. Regis merely bowed again and said nothing.

Kadarin said with a grim smile, "I see that already you are skilled, Lord Regis, in the greatest of the Comyn arts, that of saying nothing in pleasant words. Enough of this fencing-match! Beltran, tell them what it is you hope to do."

Beltran began to outline, again, his plans to make Darkover independent, self-sufficient and capable of star-travel. I listened again, falling for the last time under the sway of that dream. I wished—all the gods there ever were *know* how I wished—that his plans might work. And they might. If Danilo could help us uncover enough telepaths, if Beltran's own latent powers could be wakened. *If, if, if!* And, above all, if we had some source of power other than the impossible Sharra. . . .

Beltran concluded, and I knew our thoughts ran for the moment at least along the same track: "We have reached a point where we are dependent on your help, Danilo. You are a catalyst telepath; that is the rarest of all psi powers, and if it is in our service, our chances of success are enormously raised. It goes without saying that you will be rewarded beyond your dreams. You will help us, will you not?"

Danilo met the ingratiating smile with a slight frown of puzzlement. "If what you are doing is so just and righteous, Lord Aldaran, why did you resort to violence? Why not seek me out, explain this to me, ask my aid?"

"Come, come," said Beltran good-naturedly, "can't you forgive me for that?"

"I forgive you readily, sir. Indeed, I am a little grateful. Otherwise I might have been charmed into doing what you wish without really thinking about it. Now I am not nearly so sure. I've had too much experience with people who speak fine words, but will do whatever they think justified to get what they want. If your cause is as good as you say, I should think any telepath would be glad to help you. If I am made sure of that by someone I can trust, and if my lord gives me leave"—he turned and made Regis a formal bow—"then I am at your service. But I must first be wholly assured that your motives and your methods are as good as you say"—he looked Beltran straight in the eyes, and I gasped aloud at his audacity—"and not just fine words to cover a will to power and personal ambition."

Beltran turned as red as a turkey-cock. He was not used to being crossed, and for this shabby nobody to read him a lesson in ethics was more than he could face. I thought for a moment that he would strike the boy. Probably he remembered that Danilo was the only catalyst telepath known to be adult and fully functioning, for he controlled himself, although I could see the signs of his inward wrath. He said, "Will you trust Lew Alton's judgment?"

"I have no reason not to trust it, but . . ." And he turned to Regis. I knew he had reached the end of his own defiance.

I knew Regis was as frightened as Danilo, but just as resolute. He said, "I will trust no man's judgment until I have heard what he has to say."

Kadarin said shortly, "Will you two boys, who know nothing of matrix mechanics, presume to sit in judgment upon a trained Arilinn telepath about matters of his own competence?"

Regis gave me a pleading look. After a long pause, during which I could almost feel him searching for the right words, he said, "To judge his competence—no. To judge whether I

can conscientiously support his ... his means and motives—
for that I can trust no man's judgment but my own. I will listen to what he has to say."

Beltran said, "Tell them, then, Lew, that we must do this if
Darkover is to survive as an independent world, not a slave
colony of the Empire!"

All their eyes were suddenly on me. This was the moment
of truth, and a moment of great temptation. I opened my
mouth to speak. Darkover's future was a cause justifying all
things, and we needed Dani.

But did I serve Darkover or my own private ends? Before
the boy whose career was ruined by a misuse of power, I discovered I could not lie. I could not give Danilo the reassurance it would take to enlist his aid, then frantically try to find
some way to make the lie true.

I said, "Beltran, your aims are good and I trust them. But
we cannot do it with the matrix we have to work with. Not
with Sharra, Beltran. It is impossible, completely impossible."

Kadarin swung around. I had seen his rage only once before, turned on Beltran. Now it was turned on me, and it
struck me like a blow. "What folly is this, Lew? You told me
Sharra has all the power we could possibly need!"

I tried to barrier that assault and hold my own wrath
firmly under control. The unleashed anger of an Alton can
kill, and this man was my dear friend. I said, "Power, yes, all
the power we could ever need, for this work or any. But it's
essentially uncontrollable. It's been used as a weapon and
now it's unfit for anything but a weapon. It is—" I hesitated,
trying to formulate my vague impressions. "It's hungry for
power and destruction."

"Comyn superstition again!" Thyra flung at me. "A matrix
is a machine. No more and no less."

"Most matrices, perhaps," I said, "though I am beginning
to think that even at Arilinn we know far too little of them
to use them as recklessly as we do. But this one is more." I
hesitated again, struggling for words for a knowledge, an *experience* which was basically beyond words. "It brings something into our world which is not of this world at all. It be-
longs to other dimensions, other places or spaces. It's a gateway, and once it's opened, it's impossible to shut completely."
I looked from face to face. "Can't you see what it's *doing* to
us?" I pleaded. "It's rousing recklessness, a failure of caution,
a lust for power—" I had felt it myself, the temptation to lie
ruthlessly to Regis and Danilo, just to enlist their aid. "Thyra,

you know what you did under its impulse, and your foster-father lies dead. I'll never believe you would have done that, knowingly, on your own! It's so much stronger than we are, it's playing with us like toys!"

Kadarin said, "Desideria used it with none of this fuss."

"But she used it as a weapon," I said, "and in a righteous cause. She had no wish for personal power, so that it could not take her and corrupt her, as it has done with us; she gave it over to the forge-folk, to lie unused and harmless on their altars."

Beltran said harshly, "Are you saying it has corrupted *me*?"

I looked squarely at him and said, "Yes. Even your father's death has not made you see reason."

Kadarin said, "You talk like a fool, Lew. I hadn't expected this sort of whining cant from you. If we had the power to give Darkover its place in the Empire, how can we shrink from anything we must do?"

"My friend," I pleaded, "listen to me. We cannot use Sharra's matrix for the kind of controlled power you wish to show the Terrans. It cannot be used to power a spaceship; I would not trust it even to control the helicopter now. It is a weapon, only a weapon, and it is not weapons we need. It is technology."

Kadarin's smile was fierce. "But if a weapon is all we have, then we will use that weapon to get what we must from the Terrans! Once we show them what we can do with it—"

My spine iced over with a deadly cold. I saw again the vision: *flames rising from Caer Donn, the great form of fire bending down with a finger of destruction. . . .*

"No!" I almost shouted. "I'll have nothing to do with it!"

I rose and looked around the circle, saying desperately, "Can't you see how this has corrupted us? Was it for war, for murder, for violence, blackmail, ruin, that we forged our link in such love and harmony? Was this your dream, Beltran, when we spoke together of a better world?"

He said savagely, "If we must fight, it will be the fault of the Terrans for denying us our rights! I would rather do it peacefully, but if they force us to fight them—"

Kadarin, coming and laying his hands on my shoulders with real affection said, "Lew, you're foolishly squeamish. Once they know what we can do, there will certainly be no need to do it. But it places us in a position of equal power with the Terrans for once. Can't you see? Even if we never use it, we must have the power, simply in order to control the situation and not be forced to submit!"

I knew what he was trying to say, but I could see the fatal flaw. I said, "Bob, we cannot bluff with Sharra. It *wants* ruin and destruction . . . can't you feel that?"

"It *is* like the sword in the fairy tale," Rafe said. "Remember what it said on the scabbard? 'Draw me never unless I may drink blood.'"

We swung to look at the child and he smiled nervously under all our eyes.

"Rafe's right," I said harshly. "We can't loose Sharra unless we really mean to use it, and no sane human beings would do that."

Kadarin said, "Marjorie. You're the Keeper. Do you believe this superstitious drivel?"

Her voice was not steady, but she stretched her hand to me. "I believe Lew knows more about matrices than any of us, or all of us together. You pledged, Bob, you swore to Desideria to be guided by Lew's judgment. I won't work against it."

Beltran said, "You're both part-Terran! Are you two on their side then, against Darkover?"

I gasped at the old slur. I would never have believed it of Beltran. Marjorie flared. "It was you, yourself, who pointed out not a moment ago that we are *all* Terran! There is no 'side,' only a common good for all! Does the left hand chop off the right?"

I felt Marjorie struggle for control, felt Kadarin, too, fighting to overcome his flaming anger. I had confidence still in his integrity, when he took the time to control that vicious rage which was the one chink in the strong armor of his will.

Kadarin spoke gently at last: "Lew, I know there is some truth in what you say. I trust you, *bredu*." The word moved me more that I could express. "But what alternative have we, my friend? Are you trying to say that we should simply give up our plans, our hopes, our dream? It was your dream, too. Must we forget what we all believed in?"

"The Gods forbid," I said, shaken. "It is not the dream I would see put aside, only Sharra's part in it." Then I appealed directly to Beltran. He was the one I must convince.

"Let Sharra go back to the forge-folk's keeping. They have held it harmless all these years. No, kinsman, hear me out," I pleaded. "Do this, and I will go to Arilinn; I will speak with telepaths at Hali, at Neskaya and Corandolis and Dalereuth.

I will explain to all of them what you are doing for Darkover, plead for you, if need be, before the Comyn Council itself. Do you honestly believe that you are the only man on Darkover who chafes under Terran rule and control? I am as certain as that I stand here, that they will come to your support and work with you freely and wholeheartedly, far better than I alone can do. And they have access to every known, monitored matrix on Darkover, and to the records of what was done with them in old times. We can find one safe for our purpose. Then I will work with you myself, and as long as you like, for your *real* aims. Not bluff with a terrible weapon, but a total, concerted effort by all of us, every one of us together, to recover the *real* strengths of Darkover, something positive to give the Terrans and the Empire, in return for what they can give us."

I met Regis' eyes, and suddenly time was out of focus again. I saw him in a great hall, crowded with men and women, hundreds and hundreds of them, *every telepath on Darkover*! It slid away and the eight of us were alone in the little fireside room again. I said to Regis and Danilo, "You would cooperate in such an endeavor, wouldn't you?"

Regis, his eyes gleaming with excitement, said, "With all my heart, Lord Beltran. I am certain that even Comyn Council would put all the telepaths and towers of Darkover at your service!"

This was a greater dream than the one which had drawn us together! It must be! I had seen it! Beltran must catch fire from it too!

Beltran stared at us all, and before he spoke my heart sank. There was icy contempt in his voice and words.

"You damnable forsworn *traitor*!" he flung at me. "Get me under the heel of Comyn, would you? That I should get on my knees before the *Hali'imyn* and take from them as a gift the power which is my right? Better even to do as my doddering old father did, and grovel to the Terrans! But I am lord of Aldaran now, and I will plunge all Darkover into red chaos first! Never! Never, damn you! Never!" His voice rose to a hoarse shriek of rage.

"Beltran, I beg of you—"

"Beg! Beg, you stinking half-caste! As you would make *me* beg, grovel—"

I clenched my fists, aching with the need to fall on him, beat that sneer off his face . . . no. That was not his true self, either, but Sharra.

"I am sorry, kinsman. You leave me no choice." Whatever happened after, the closeness of this circle was broken; nothing could ever be the same. "Kadarin, you placed Sharra in my hands and pledged to abide my judgment. Before it is too late, the circle must be broken, the link destroyed, the matrix insulated before it controls us all."

"No!" Thyra cried. "If you dare not handle it, I do!"

"*Breda*—"

"No," Marjorie said, her voice shaking, "no, Thyra. It is the only way. Lew's right, it can destroy us all. Bob." She faced Kadarin, her golden eyes swimming in tears. "You made me Keeper. By that authority, I have to say it." Her voice broke in a sob. "The link must be broken."

"No!" Kadarin said harshly, repulsing her outstretched hands. "I did not want you to be Keeper; I feared just this—that you would be swayed by Lew! Sharra's circle must be preserved! You know you cannot break it without my consent!" He stared fiercely at her, and I thought of a hawk I had once seen, hovering over its prey.

Beltran stood in front of Danilo, facing him down. "I ask you for the last time. Will you do what I ask?"

Danilo was trembling. I recalled that he had been the youngest and most timid of the cadets. His voice shook as he said, "N-no, my lord Aldaran. I will not."

Beltran turned his eyes on Regis. His voice was level and grim. "Regis Hastur. You are not now in the Domains, but in Aldaran's stronghold. You came here of your own free will, and you will not depart from here until you command your minion to use his powers as I shall direct."

"My *paxman* is free to follow his own will and conscience. He has refused you; I support his decision. Now, Lord Aldaran, I respectfully request your leave to depart."

Beltran shouted in the mountain tongue. The doors suddenly burst open and a dozen of his guards burst into the fireside room. I realized, in sudden consternation, that he must have meant this all along. One of them approached Regis, who was unarmed; Danilo quickly drew his dagger and stepped between them, but was swiftly disarmed. Beltran's men dragged them back out of the way.

Marjorie faced Beltran in angry reproach.

"Beltran, you cannot! This is treachery! He was our father's guest!"

But not *my* guest," Beltran said, and the words were a snarl, "and I have no patience with barbarian codes under a pretense of honor! Now for you, Lew Alton. Will you honor your pledge to us?"

"*You* speak of honor?" The words seemed to rise from some hidden spring within me, and I spat on the floor at his feet. "I honor my pledge to you as you honor your father's memory!" I turned my back on him. Within the hour I would be in touch with Arilinn by matrix, and the Comyn would know what Beltran planned . . .

I had forgotten the link still strong between us all. Kadarin said, "Oh, no, you won't," and gestured to the guards. "Take him!"

My hand fell to sword-hilt—and found, of course, nothing. *Wear no sword, at kinsman's board.* I had trusted in my safety in my cousin's own house! Two guards seized me, held me motionless between them. Kadarin came to where I was held and raised his hand to my throat, jerking the laces of my tunic undone. He raised his hand to the leather bag containing my personal matrix.

I began to struggle now in deadly fear. It had never been more than a few inches from my body since I had been keyed into it when I was twelve years old. I had been warned what it meant to have anyone else touch it. Kadarin hauled at the leather bag; I brought my knee up into his groin. He yelled with pain, and I felt the shock of the agony through my own body, doubling me up, but it only strengthened his fury. He beckoned to the rest of the guards. It took four of them to do it, but before long I was spread-eagled on the floor, arms and legs pinioned down, while Kadarin knelt atop me, straddling my helpless body, his fists flailing blows on my face. I felt blood breaking from my nose, my eyes; I gagged on my own blood, streaming down my throat from a broken tooth. I could no longer see Marjorie for the blood in my eyes, but I heard her shrieking, sobbing, begging. Were they hurting her too?

Kadarin drew his dagger. He stared straight down into my eyes, his face flickering with that unholy flame. He said between his teeth, "I should cut your throat now and save us all some trouble."

With a swift, downward slash, he cut the thong that held the leather bag; seized it between his hands and wrenched it away.

Until the day I die, I shall never forget that agony. I heard Marjorie scream, a long, death-like shriek of pain and terror, felt my whole body arch backward in a convulsive spasm, then fall limp. I heard my own voice screaming hoarsely, felt steel fingers clutch at my heart, felt my breathing falter. Every nerve in my body was in spasm. I had never known I could live through such anguish. Red haze blurring what was left of my sight, I felt myself dying and instinctively I heard my own tortured shriek:

"Father! *Father!*"

Then it all went dark and blind and I thought, This is death.

I don't know what happened in the next three days. For all I know, I was dead. I know it was three days because I was told so later; it might have been thirty seconds or thirty years later that I came up to foggy awareness that I was alive, and that I would much rather *not* be.

I was lying on the bed in my quarters in Castle Aldaran. I felt bruised, sick, every separate bone and muscle in my body with a separate ache. I staggered into the bathroom and stared at my reflection in the mirror. From the way my face looked, I can only imagine that my body kept on fighting long after I wasn't in it any more.

There were a couple of broken teeth ragged in my mouth, and they hurt like hell. My eyes were so bruised and swollen I could hardly get them open to see. My face had been cut by something hard, the big rings Kadarin wore, maybe. There were going to be scars.

Worse than the physical pain, which was bad enough, was the terrible sense of *emptiness*. Drearily, I wondered why I had not died. Some telepaths do die of shock, if they are forcibly severed from their own personal keyed matrices. I was just one of the unlucky ones.

Marjorie. My last memory was hearing her scream. Had they tortured her too?

If Kadarin had harmed her I would kill him . . .

The thought was wrenching pain. He had been my friend—he could not have pretended—not to a telepath. Sharra had corrupted him. . . .

I wished he *had* cut my throat instead.

Sharra. I went to look for the matrix, but it was gone. I was glad to be rid of the damnable thing, but I was afraid, too. Would it let us go?

I drank cold water, trying to lessen the dry sickness in me. My hand kept fumbling for the place around my neck where the matrix should have been. I couldn't think straight or see properly, and there was a constant dull ringing in my ears. I was really surprised I had survived this shock.

Slowly I realized something else. Sore and aching as I was, there was no blood anywhere on my face or garments. Nor had I fouled my clothes. Someone had therefore been here, tended my wounds after a fashion, put clean clothes on me. Kadarin, when he came to take away the Sharra matrix?

I found I very much disliked the thought of Kadarin coming here, handling my unconscious body. I clenched my teeth, found out it hurt too much and made myself relax. Another score to settle with him.

Well, he'd done him worse, and I was still alive.

I tried the door cautiously. As I had suspected, it was bolted on the outside.

I ached so much that the thought of a long hot bath was tempting. The thought of being surprised naked and defenseless in the bathtub, however, removed all temptation from the idea. I soaked a cloth in the hot water and bathed my bruised face.

I ransacked the apartment, but of course my sword was gone, and the dagger, too. When I rummaged in my saddlebags for my heavy traveling boots, even the small *skean-dhu* in the boot was gone from its sheath.

A grim smile touched my face. Did they think me helpless? I had my Guardsman training still, and Kadarin might—he just might—despise me enough to come back alone.

I dragged up a chair—I still wasn't steady enough on my feet to stand for what might be hours waiting for him—and sat down facing the bolted door.

Sooner or later someone would come. And I would be ready.

It was a long time before I heard a tiny metallic rasp from the door. Someone was stealthily fumbling to draw the bolt back. Finally the door began, very slowly, to open inward.

I leaped, grabbed the hand that had just begun to steal inward and jerked hard—and felt the delicate wrist too late to arrest the force of the swing. Marjorie skidded inside, gasping, slammed against the door-frame. I dropped her wrist as if it was burned. She staggered and I held her quickly upright.

"Quick," she whispered, "shut the door!"

"Gods defend us," I whispered, staring in horror at her. "I could have killed you!"

"I'm glad you're able—" She drew a quick gasp. "Lew, your face! Oh God . . ."

"The loving attention of my kinsmen." I shut the door, shoved the heavy chair up against it.

"I begged them—I begged them—"

I laid my arms around her. "Poor love, I know, I heard you. Did they hurt you?"

"No, even Beltran didn't hurt me, though I scratched and bit him." She said, her voice coming in gasps, "I have your matrix for you. Here, quick." She held the small leather bag out to me. I thrust it inside my tunic, next to my skin. It seemed that my vision cleared at once, the dull ringing inside my head quieted. Even my heart beat more solidly. I was still battered and aching from the terrible beating I had taken, but I felt alive again. "How did you get it?"

"Bob made me take it," she said. "He said I was Keeper, only I could handle it without hurting you. He said you'd die otherwise. So I took it. Lew, only to save you. I swear it—"

"I know. If anyone but a Keeper had kept it long, I would certainly have died." Not that I credited Kadarin with that much kindness for my well-being. He probably knew what too much handling of someone else's keyed matrix would do to *him*.

"Where is the Sharra matrix?"

"Thyra has it, I think," she said doubtfully. "I'm not sure."

"How did you get in here, Marjorie? Are there guards watching me?"

She nodded slowly. "All the guards know me," she said at last. "Most of them were my father's friends and have known me since they held me on their knees. They trust me . . . and I brought them drugged wine. I'm ashamed of that, Lew, but what else could I do? But we must get away at once, as quickly as we can. When they wake up they will know, and tell Beltran . . ." Her voice failed.

"He should thank you for saving the small remnant of his honor," I said grimly. Then I realized she had said "we."

"You will come with me?"

"I must, I dare not stay after what I have done. Lew, don't you *want* me? Do you think I had any part in . . . *oh!*"

I held her tight. "Can you doubt it? But in these mountains, at this season—"

"I was born in these mountains; I've traveled in worse weather than this."

"We must be gone, then, before the guards wake. What did you give them?"

She told me and I shook my head. "No good. They'll wake within the hour. But maybe I can do better now." I touched the matrix. "Let's go." Hastily I gathered my things together. She had dressed warmly, I saw, heavy boots, a long riding-skirt. I looked out the windows. It was nightfall, but by some god's mercy it was not snowing.

In the dim hallway two figures sprawled in sodden, snoring sleep. I bent and listened to their breathing. Marjorie gasped, "Don't kill them, Lew. They've done you no harm!"

I wasn't so sure. My ribs still ached from the weight of somebody's boots. "I can do better than killing them," I said, cradling the matrix between my palms. Swiftly, incisively, I drew into the minds of the drugged men. *Sleep*, I commanded, *sleep long and well, sleep till the rising sun wakes you. Marjorie never came here, you drank no wine, drugged or wholesome.*

The poor devils would have to answer to Beltran for sleeping at their post. But I'd done what I could.

I tiptoed down the corridor, Marjorie hugging the wall behind me. Outside the great guest suite were two more drugged guards; Marjorie had been thorough. I stooped over them, sent them, too, more deeply into their dreams.

My hands are strong. I made shorter work of the bolts than Marjorie had done. Briefly I wondered at the kind of hospitality that puts a bolt on the outside of a guest room door for any contingency. As I stepped inside, Danilo quickly stepped between me and Regis. Then he recognized me and fell back.

Regis said, "I thought they'd killed you—" His eyes fell on my face. "It looks as if they'd tried! How did you get out?"

"Never mind," I said. "Get on your riding-things, unless you love Aldaran's hospitality too well to leave it!"

Regis said, "They came and took away my sword, and Danilo's dagger." For some reason the loss of the dagger seemed to grieve him most. I had no time to wonder why. I went and hauled at the senseless guardsmen's sword-belts, gave one to Regis, belted the other around my own waist. It was too long for me, but better than nothing. I gave the daggers to Marjorie and Danilo. "I have repaid my kinsman's theft," I said, "now let's get out of here."

"Where shall we go?"

I had made my decision swiftly. "I'll take Marjorie to Arilinn," I said. "You two just get away as fast and far as you can, before all hell breaks loose."

Regis nodded. "We'll take the straight road to Thendara, and get the word to Comyn."

Danilo said, "Shouldn't we all stay together?"

"No, Dani. One of us may get through if the others are recaptured, and the Comyn must be warned, whatever happens. There is an out-of-control, unmonitored matrix being used here. Tell them that, if I cannot!" Then I hesitated. "Regis, don't take the straight road! It's suicide! It's the first place they'll look!"

"Then maybe I can draw pursuit away from you," he said. "Anyway, it's you and Marjorie they'll be after. Danilo and I are nothing to them."

I wasn't so sure. Then I saw what I could not mistake. I said, "No. We cannot separate while I send you on the route of danger. You are ill." Threshold sickness, I finally realized. "I cannot send the heir to Hastur into such danger!"

"Lew, we *must* separate." He looked straight up into my eyes. "Someone *must* get through to warn the Comyn."

What he said was true and I knew it. "Can you endure the journey?" I asked.

Danilo said, "I'll look after him, and anyway he's better off on the road than in Beltran's hands, especially once you've escaped." This was true also and I knew it. Danilo was quickly separating the contents of Regis' saddlebags, discarding nearly everything. "We've got to travel light. There's food here from Regis' journey north . . ." He quickly divided it, rolling meat and fruit, hard bread, into two small parcels. He handed the larger one to me and said, "You'll be on the back roads, further away from villages."

I stuffed it into the inside pocket of my riding cloak and looked at Marjorie. "Can we get out unseen?"

"That's easy enough, word won't have reached the stables. We'll get horses, too."

Marjorie led us out a small side door near the stables. Most of the stablemen were sleeping; she roused one old man who knew her as Kermiac's ward. It was eccentric, perhaps, for her to set forth at nightfall with some of Beltran's honored guests, but it wasn't for an old horse-keeper to question. Most of them had seen me with her and had heard the castle gossip that a marriage was being arranged. If he had heard of the quarrel, this would have accounted for it in his mind, that Marjorie and I had run away to marry against Beltran's will. I'm sure this accounted for the looks of sympathy the old groom gave us. He found mounts for us all. I thought tardily of the escort from Comyn, who had come here with me.

I could order them to go with Regis and Danilo, protect them. But that would make a stir. Marjorie said softly, "If they don't know where you've gone, they cannot be made to tell," and that decided me.

If we rode hard till morning, and Beltran's guards slept as I had insured they would, we might be beyond pursuit. We led our horses toward the gates; the groom let us out. I lifted Marjorie to her saddle, readied myself to mount. She looked back with a faint sadness but, seeing me watching, she smiled bravely and turned her face to the road.

I turned to Regis, holding him for a moment in a kinsman's embrace. Would I ever see him again? I thought I had turned my back on Comyn, yet the tie was stronger than I knew. I had thought him a child, easily flattered, easily swayed. No. Less so than I was myself. I told myself firmly not to be morbid, and kissed him on the cheek, letting him go. "The Gods ride with you, *bredu*," I said, turning away. His hand clung to my arm for a moment, and in a split second I saw, for the last time, the frightened child I had taken into the fire-lines; he remembered, too, but the very memory of conquered fear strengthened us both. Still, I could not forget that he had been placed in my charge. I said hesitantly, "I am not sure . . . I do not like letting you take the road of most danger, Regis."

He gripped my forearms with both hands and looked straight into my eyes. He said fiercely, "Lew, you too are the heir to your Domain! And I have an heir, you don't! If it comes to that, better me than you!" I was shocked speechless by the words. Yet they were true. My father was old and ill, Marcus, so far as we knew, was without *laran*.

I was the last male Alton. And it had taken Regis to remind me!"

This was a man, a Hastur. I bowed my head in acquiescence, knowing we stood at that moment before something older, more powerful than either of us. Regis drew a long breath, let go of my hands, and said, "We'll meet in Thendara, if the Gods will it, cousin."

I knew my voice was shaking. I said, "Take care of him, Dani."

He answered, "With my life, Dom Lewis," as they swung into their saddles. Without a backward glance, Regis rode away down the path, Danilo a pace behind him.

I mounted, taking the opposite fork of the road, Marjorie at my side. I thanked all the gods I had ever heard of, and all the rest I hadn't, for the time I had spent with maps on my northward journey. It was a long way to Arilinn, through some of the worst country on Darkover, and I wondered if Marjorie could endure it.

Overhead two of the moons swung, violet-blue, green-blue, shedding soft light on the snow-clad hills. We rode for hours in that soft night light. I was wholly aware of Marjorie: her grief and regret at leaving her childhood home, the desperation which had driven her to this. She must never regret it! I pledged my own life she should not regret.

The green face of Idriel sank behind the crest of the pass; above us was a bank of cold fog, stained blood color with the coming sunrise. We must begin to look somewhere for shelter; I was sure the hunt would be up soon after daylight. I was enough in contact with Marjorie to know when her weariness became almost unendurable. But when I spoke of it, she said, "Another mile or so. On the slope of the next hill, far back from the roadway, is a summer pasture. The herd-women have probably taken their beasts down into the valleys, so it will be empty."

The herdwomen's hut was concealed within a grove of nut trees. As we drew near my heart sank, for I could hear the soft lowing of herd aminals, and as we dismounted I saw one of the women, barefoot in the melting snow, her hair long and tangled around her face, clad in a ragged leather skirt. Marjorie, however, seemed pleased.

"We're in luck, Lew. Her mother was one of *my* mother's people." She called softly, Mhari!"

The woman turned, her face lighting up. *"Domna Marguerida!"* She spoke a dialect too ancient for me to follow; Marjorie answered her softly in the same patois. Mhari grinned widely and led us into the hut.

Most of the inside was taken up with a couple of dirty straw pallets on which an older woman lay, entangled with half a dozen small children and a few puppies. The only furniture was a wooden bench. Mhari gestured to us to sit on it, and ladled us out bowls of hot, coarse, nut-porridge. Marjorie almost collapsed on the bench; Mhari came to draw off her riding-boots.

"What did she say to you, Marjorie? What did you tell her?"

"The truth. That Kermiac was dead, that on his deathbed he had promised me to you, and that you and Beltran had quarreled, so we are going into the lowlands to marry. She has promised that neither she nor her friend, nor any of the children, will say a word of our being here." Marjorie took another spoonful of the porridge. She was almost too weary to lift her spoon to her mouth. I was glad to down my portion, to put aside my sword and haul off my boots and later, when the conglomeration of babies and puppies had vacated the mattress, to lie down there in my clothes beside Marjorie.

"They should have gone, days ago," Marjorie said, "but Caillean's husband has not come for them. She says they'll be out all day with the beasts and we can sleep safely here." And indeed, very shortly the clamoring crew of babies and puppies had been fed on the rest of the porridge and hustled outside. I drew Marjorie into the circle of my arm, then realized that in spite of the noise made by children and dogs she was already deeply asleep. The straw smelled of dogs and dirt, but I was too tired to be critical. Marjorie lying in the curve of my arm, I slept too.

The next thing I knew it was late evening, the room was full of puppies and children again, and we rose and ate big hot bowlfuls of vegetable soup that had been simmering over the fire all day. Then it was time to pull on our boots and go. The women, from their vantage point high on the slopes, had seen no riders, so we were not pursued yet. Marjorie kissed Mhari and the smallest of the babies, and warned me not to offer them money. Mhari and her friend insisted that we take bags of nuts and a loaf or two of the hard-baked bread, telling us they had too much to load on their pack animals on the way down into the valley for winter. I didn't believe a word of it, but we could not refuse.

The next two or three nights of travel were duplicates of that one. We were blessed with good weather and there was no sign of pursuit. We slept by day, concealed in herd-huts, but these were deserted. We had food enough, although we were almost always cold. Marjorie never complained, but I was desperately concerned about her. I could not imagine any woman I had ever known enduring such a journey. When I said so to Marjorie, she laughed.

"I am no pampered lowland lady, Lew, I am used to hard weather, and I can travel whenever I must, even in dead winter. Thyra would be a better companion, perhaps, she is hardened to long journeys with Bob, in and out of season . . ." She fell silent, and quickly turned her face away. I kept silent. I knew how close she had been to her sister and how she felt about this parting. It was the first time she spoke of her life at Castle Aldaran. It was also the last.

On the fourth or fifth morning we had to ride far into daylight to find any shelter at all. We were now in the wildest part of the mountains, and the roads had dwindled away to mere trails. Marjorie was dropping with weariness; I had half resolved that for once we must find a sheltered place in the woods and sleep in the open, when suddenly, riding into a small clearing, we came on a deserted farmstead.

I wondered how anyone had ever managed to farm these bleak hills, but there were outbuildings and a small stone house, a yard which had once been fenced, a well with wooden piping still splashing water into a broken stone trough in the year—all wholly deserted. I feared it had become the haunt of birds or bats, but when I forced the door open it was weathertight and almost clean.

The sun was high and warm. While I unsaddled Marjorie had taken off her cloak and boots and was splashing her hands in the stone trough. She said, "I am past my first sleepiness, and I have not had my clothes off since we set out. I am going to wash; I think it will refresh me better than sleep." She was suiting action to words, pulling off her riding-skirt and fur-lined tunic, standing before me in her long heavy shift and petticoat. I came and joined her. The water was icy cold, coming straight down from a mountain spring above us, but it was marvelously refreshing. I marveled how Marjorie could stand barefoot in the last melting runnels of the last night's snowfall, but she seemed not as cold as I was. We sat in the growing warmth of the sun afterward, eating the last of the herdwomen's coarse bread. I found a tree in the yard where the former owners had farmed mushrooms, an intricate system of small wooden pipes directing water down the trunk. Most of the mushrooms were hard and woody, but I found a few small new ones high up, and we

ate them at the end of our meal, savoring their sweet fresh-
ness.

She stretched a little, sleepily. "I would like to sleep here
in the sun," she said. "I am beginning to feel like some
night-bird, never coming out into the light of day."

"But I am not hardened to your mountain weather," I
said, "and we may have to sleep in the open, soon enough."

She made a mock-serious face. "Poor Lew, are you cold?
Yes, I suppose we must go inside to sleep." She gathered up
our heavy outer clothes and carried them. She spread them
out on an old, abandoned pallet in the farmhouse, wrinkling
a fastidious nose at the musty smell. I said, "It is better than
dog," and she giggled and sat down on the heap of clothing.

She had on a thick woolen shift, knee-length and with long
sleeves; I had seen her far more lightly clothed at Aldaran,
but there was something about being here like this that roused
an awareness that fear and weariness had almost smothered.
All during this trip she had slept within the circle of my
arm, but innocently. Perhaps because I was still recovering
from the effects of Kadarin's brutal beating. Now, all at
once, I was aware again of her physical presence. She felt
it—we were lightly in rapport all the time now—and turned
her face a little away, color rising along her cheekbones.
There was a hint of defiance as she said, "Just the same, I
am going to take down my hair and comb and braid it properly, before it gets tangled like Mhari's and I have to cut it
off!" She raised her arms, pulled out the butterfly-shaped
clasp that held her braids pinned at the nape of her neck, and
began to unravel the long plaits.

I felt the hot flush of embarrassment. In the lowlands a sister who was already a woman would not have done this even
before a grown brother. I had not seen Linnell's hair loose
like this since we were little children, although when we were
small I had sometimes helped her comb it. Did customs really differ so much? I sat and watched her move the ivory
comb slowly through her long copper hair; it was perfectly
straight, only waved a little from the braiding, and very fine,
and the sun, coming in cracks through the heavy wooden
shutters, set it all ablaze with the glint of the precious metal.
I said at last, hoarsely, "Don't tease me, Marjorie. I'm not
sure I can bear it."

She did not look up. She only said softly, "Why should
you? I am here."

I reached out and took the comb away from her, turning her face up to meet my eyes. "I cannot take you lightly, beloved. I would give you all honor and all ceremony."

"You cannot," she said, with the shadow of a small smile, "because I no longer ..." the words were coming slowly now, as if it were painful to speak them. "—no longer acknowledge Beltran's right to give me in marriage. My foster-father meant to give me to you. That is ceremony enough." Suddenly she spoke in a rush. "And I am not a Keeper now! I have renounced that, I will not keep myself separate from you, I will not, *I will not!*"

She was sobbing now. I flung the comb away and drew her into my arms, holding her to me with sudden violence.

"Keeper? No, no, never again," I whispered against her mouth. "Never, never again—"

What can I say? We were together. And we were in love.

Afterward I braided her hair for her. It seemed almost as intimate as lying down together, my hands trembling as they touched the silken strands, as they had when I first touched her. We did not sleep for a long time.

When we woke it was late and already snowing heavily. When I went to saddle the horses, the wind was whipping the snow in wild stinging needles across the yard. We could not ride in this. When I came inside again, Marjorie looked at me in guilty dismay.

"I delayed us. I'm sorry—"

"I think we are beyond pursuit now, *preciosa*. But we would only have had to turn back; we cannot ride in this. I'll put the horses into the outbuilding and give them some fodder."

"Let me come and help—"

"Don't go out in the snow, beloved. I'll attend to the horses."

When I came in, Marjorie had kindled a fire on the long-dead hearth and, finding an old battered stone kettle discarded in a corner, had washed it, filled it at the well and put some of our dried meat to stew with the mushrooms. When I scolded her for going into the yard—in these snow-squalls men have been lost and frozen between their own barnyard and doorway—she said shyly, "I wanted us to have a fireside. And a ... a wedding-feast."

I hugged her close and said, "The minute he sees you my father will be delighted to arrange all that."

"I know," she said, "but I'd rather have it here."

The thought warmed me more than the fire.

We ate the hot soup before the fire. We had to share one spoon and eat it straight from the old kettle. We had little fuel and the fire burned down quickly, but as it sank into darkness Marjorie whispered, "Our first fireside."

I knew what she meant. It was not the formal ceremony, *di catenas*, the elaborate wedding-feast for my kin, her proclamation before Comyn Council, that would make her my wife. Everywhere in the hills, where ceremonies are few and witnesses sparse, the purposeful sharing of "a bed, a meal, a fireside" acknowledges the legal status of a marriage, and I knew why Marjorie had risked losing her way in the snow to kindle a fire and cook us up some soup. By the simple laws of the hills, we were wedded, not in our own eyes alone, but in a ceremony that would stand in the eyes of all men.

I was glad she had been sure enough of me to do this without asking. I was glad the weather kept us here for another night. But something was troubling me. I said, "Regis and Danilo are nearer to Thendara now than we are to Arilinn, unless they have been recaptured. But neither of them is a skilled telepath, and I doubt if a message has gone through. I should send a message, either to Arilinn or to my father. I should have done it before."

She caught my hand as I pulled the matrix from its resting place. "Lew, is it really safe?"

"I must, love, safe or not. I should have done it the moment I had my matrix back. We must face the possibility that they will try again. Beltran won't abandon his aims so quickly, and I fear Kadarin is unscrupulous." I backed off from speaking the name of Sharra aloud, but it was there between us and we both knew it.

And if they did try again, without my knowledge or control, without Marjorie for Keeper, what then? Playing with forest fire would be child's play, next to the risk of waking that thing without a trained Keeper! I had to warn the towers.

She said hesitantly, "We were all in rapport. If you ... use your matrix ... can they *feel* it, trail us that way?"

That was a possibility, but whatever happened to us, Sharra must be controlled and contained, or none of us would ever be safe again. And in all these days I had sensed no touch, no seeking mind.

I drew out the matrix and uncovered it. To my dismay, I felt a faint, twisting tinge of sickness as I gazed into the blue depths. That was a danger signal. Perhaps during the days I had been separated from it, I had become somewhat unkeyed. I focused on it, steadying my mind to the delicate task of establishing rapport again with the starstone; again and again I was forced to turn my eyes away by the pain, the blurring of vision.

"Leave it, Lew, leave it, you're too tired—"

"I cannot." If I delayed, I would lose mastery of the matrix, be forced to begin again with another stone. I fought the matrix for nearly an hour, struggling with my inability to focus it. I looked at Marjorie with regret, knowing that I was draining my strength with this telepathic struggle. I cursed the fate that had made me a telepath and a matrix mechanic, but it never occurred to me that I should abandon the struggle unfinished.

If this had—unimaginably—happened in Arilinn, I would have been given *kirian* or one of the other psi-activator drugs and helped by a psi monitor and my own Keeper. Now I had to master it alone. I myself had made it impossible and dangerous for Marjorie to help me.

At last, my head splitting, I managed to focus the lights in the stone. Quickly, while I still had the strength, I reached out through the gray and formless spaces that we call the underworld, looking for the light-landmark that was the relay-circle at Arilinn.

For a moment I had it. Then, within the stone, there was a wild flaring flame, a rush of savage awareness, a too-familiar surge of fiery violence . . . flames rising, the great form of fire blotting out consciousness . . . a woman, dark and vital, bearing a living flame, a great circle of faces pouring out raw emotion. . . .

I heard Marjorie gasp, fought to break the rapport. *Sharra! Sharra! We had been sealed to it, we were caught and drawn to the fires of destruction. . . .*

"No! *No!*" Marjorie cried aloud, and I saw the fires thin out and vanish. They had never been there. They were reflected in the dying coals of our ritual marriage-fire; the eerie edge of light around Marjorie's face was only the last firelight there. She whispered, trembling, "Lew, what was it?"

"You know," I hesitated to say the name aloud, "Kadarin. And Thyra. Working directly with the sword. Zandru's hells,

Marjorie, they are trying to use it the old way, not with a Keeper-controlled circle of telepaths in an orderly energon ring—and it's uncontrollable even that way, as we found out—but with a single telepath, focusing raw emotion from a group of untrained followers."

"Isn't that terribly dangerous?"

"Dangerous! The word's inadequate! Would you kindle a forest fire to cook your supper? Would you chain a dragon-fire to roast your chops or dry your boots? I wish I thought they would only kill *themselves*!"

I strode up and down by the dead fire, restlessly listening to the battering of the storm outside. "And I can't even warn them at Arilinn!"

"Why not, Lew?"

"So close to—to Sharra—my own matrix won't work," I said, and tried to explain how Sharra evidently blanked out smaller matrices.

"How far will that effect reach, Lew?"

"Who knows? Planet-wide, maybe. I've never worked with anything that strong. There aren't any precedents."

"Then, if it reached all the way to Arilinn, won't the telepaths there know that *something* is wrong?"

I brightened. That might be our only hope. I staggered suddenly and she caught at my arm.

"Lew! You're worn out. Rest here by me, darling." I flung myself down at her side, dizzy and despairing. I had not even spoken of my other fears, that if I used my personal matrix, I, who had been sealed to Sharra, might be drawn back into that vortex, that savage fire, that corner of hell. . . .

She knew, without my saying it. She whispered, "I can feel it reaching for us. . . . Can it draw us back, back into itself?" She clung to me in terror; I rolled over and took her to me, holding her with savage strength, fighting an almost uncontrollable desire. And that frightened hell out of me. I should be drained, spent, exhausted, incapable of the slightest sexual impulse. That was frustrating, but it was normal, and I had long since come to terms with it.

But this wild lust—and it was pure lust, a hateful dark animal thing with no hint of love or warmth—set my pulses racing, made me gasp and fight against it. It was too strong; I let it surge up and overwhelm me, feeling the fire burn up in my veins as if some scalding ichor had replaced the blood in my body. I smothered her mouth under mine, felt her weakly struggling to fight me away. Then the fire took us both.

It is the one memory I have of Marjorie which is not all joy. I took her savagely, without tenderness, trying to slake the burning need in me. She met me with equal violence, hating it equally, both of us gripped with that uncontrollable savage desperation. It was fierce and animal—no! Not animal! Animals meet cleanly, driven only by the life-force in them, knowing nothing of this kind of dark lust. There was no innocence in this, no love, only raw violence, insatiable, a bottomless pit of hell. It *was* hell, all the hell either of us would ever need to know. I heard her sobbing helplessly and knew I was weeping, too, with shame and self-hatred. Afterward we did not sleep.

Chapter TWENTY-ONE

Even at Nevarsin, Regis thought, it had never snowed so hard, or so persistently. His pony picked its way deliberately along, following in the steps of Danilo's mount, as mountain horses were trained to do. It was snowing again.

He wouldn't mind any of it, he thought, the riding, the cold or the lack of sleep, if he could see properly, or keep the world straight under him.

The threshold sickness had continued off and on, more on than off in the last day or so. He tried to ignore Danilo's anxious looks, his concern for him. There wasn't anything Danilo could do for him, so the less said about it, the better.

But it was intensely unpleasant. The world kept thinning away at irregular intervals and dissolving. He had had no attacks as bad as the one he'd had at Thendara or on the way north, but he seemed to live in mild chronic disorientation all the time. He didn't know which was worse, but suspected it was whichever form he happened to have at the time.

Danilo waited for him to draw even on the path. "Snowing already, and it's hardly midafternoon. At this rate it will take us a full twelve days to reach Thendara, and we'll lose the long start we had."

The more quickly they reached Thendara, the better. He knew a message *must* get through, even if Lew and Marjorie were recaptured. So far there was no sign of pursuit. But Regis knew, cursing his own weakness, that he could not take much more of the constant exertion, the long hours in the saddle and the constant sickness.

Earlier that day they had passed through a small village, where they had bought food and grain for the horses. Perhaps they could risk a fire tonight—if they could find a place to build it!

"Anything but a hay-barn," Danilo agreed. The last night they had slept in a barn, sharing warmth with several cows

and horses and plenty of dry hay. The animals had made it a
warm place to sleep, but they could not risk a fire or even a
light, with the tinder-dry hay, so they had eaten nothing but
hard strips of cured meat and a handful of nuts.

"We're in luck," Danilo said, pointing. Away to the side of
the road was one of the travel-shelters built generations ago,
when Aldaran had been the seventh Domain and this road
had been regularly traveled in all seasons. The inns had all
been abandoned, but the travel-shelters, built to stand for
centuries, were still habitable, small stone cabins with attached sheds for horses and proper amenities for travelers.

They dismounted and stabled their horses, hardly speaking,
Regis from weariness, Danilo from reluctance to intrude on
him. Dani thought he was angry, Regis sensed; he knew he
should tell his friend he was not angry, just tired. But he was
reluctant to show weakness. He was Hastur: it was for him
to lead, to take responsibility. So he drove himself re-
lentlessly, the effort making his words few and sharp, his
voice harsh. It only made it worse to know that if he had
given Danilo the slightest encouragement, Dani would have
waited on him hand and foot and done it with pleasure. He
wasn't going to take advantage of Danilo's hero-worship.

The Comyn had done too much of that. . . .

The horses settled for the night, Danilo carried the saddlebags inside. Pausing on the threshold, he said, "This is the interesting time, every night. When we see what the years have
left of whatever place we've found to stay."

"It's interesting, all right," Regis said dryly. "We never
know what we'll find, or who'll share our beds with us." One
night they had had to sleep in the stables, because a nest of
deadly scorpion-ants had invaded the shelter itself.

"Um, yes, a scorpion-ant is a lower form of life than I
care to go to bed with," Danilo said lightly, "but tonight we
seem to be in luck." The interior was bare and smelled dusty
and unaired, but there was an intact fireplace, a pair of
benches to sit on and a heavy shelf built into the wall so they
need not sleep on the floor at the mercy of spiders or ro-
dents. Danilo dumped the saddlebags on a bench. "I saw
some dead branches in the lee of the stable. The snow won't
have soaked them through yet. There may not be enough to
keep a fire all night, but we can certainly cook some hot
food."

Regis sighed. "I'll come and help you get them in." He

opened the door again on the snow-swept twilight; the world toppled dizzily around him and he clung to the door.

"Regis, let me go, you're ill again."

"I can manage."

"Damn it!" Suddenly Danilo was angry. "Will you stop pretending and playing hero with me? How the hell will I manage if you fall down and can't get up again? It's a lot easier to drag a couple of armfuls of dry branches in, than try to carry *you* through the snow! Just stay in here, will you?"

Pretending. Playing hero. Was that how Danilo saw his attempt to carry his own weight? Regis said stiffly, "I wouldn't want to make things harder for you. Go ahead."

Danilo started to speak but didn't. He set his chin and strode, stiff-necked into the snowy darkness. Regis started to unload the saddlebags but became so violently dizzy that he had to sit down on one of the stone benches, holding on with both hands.

He was a dead weight on Danilo, he thought. Good for nothing but to hold him back. He wondered how Lew was faring in the mountains. He'd hoped to draw pursuit away from him, that hadn't worked either. He felt like huddling on the bench, giving way to the surges of sickness, but remembered Javanne's advice: move around, fight it. He hauled himself to his feet, got his flint-and-steel and the wisps of dry hay they had kept for tinder, and knelt before the fireplace, clearing away the remnants of the last travelers' fire. How many years ago was that one built? he wondered.

Wind, and cold slashes of snow blew through the open doorway; Danilo, laden with branches, staggered inside, shoved them near the fireplace, went quickly out again. Regis tried to separate the driest branches to lay a fire, but could not steady his hands enough to manipulate the small mechanical flint-and-steel, fed with resinous oil, which kept the spark alive. He laid the device on the bench and sat with his head in his hands, feeling completely useless, until Danilo, bent under another load of branches, came in and kicked the door shut behind him.

"My father calls that a lazy man's load," he said cheerfully, "carrying too much because you're too lazy to go back for another. It ought to keep the cold out awhile. Anyway, I'd rather be cold here than warm in Aldaran's royal suite, damn him." He strode to where Regis had laid the fire, kneeling to spark it alight with Regis's lighter. "Bless the man who invented this gadget. Lucky you have one."

It had been part of Gabriel's camping-kit that Javanne had given him, along with the small cooking pots they carried. Dani looked at Regis, huddled motionless and shivering on the bench. He said, "Are you very angry with me?"

Silently, Regis shook his head.

Danilo said haltingly, "I don't want to ... to offend you. But I'm your paxman and I have to do what's best for you. Even if it's not always what you want."

"It's all right, Dani. I was wrong and you were right," Regis said. "I couldn't even light the fire."

"Well, I don't mind lighting it. Certainly not with that gadget of yours. There's water piped in the corner, there, if the pipes aren't frozen. If they are, we'll have to melt snow. Now, what shall we cook?"

The last thing Regis cared about at that moment was food, but he forced himself to join in a discussion about whether soup made from dried meat and beans, or crushed-grain porridge, would be better. When it was bubbling over the fire, Danilo came and sat beside him. He said, "Regis, I don't want to make you angry again. But we've got to have this out. You're no better. Do you think I can't see that you can hardly ride?"

"What do you want me to say to you, Dani? I'm doing the best I can."

"You're doing *more* than you can," said Danilo. The light of the blazing fire made him look very young and very troubled. "Do you think I'm blaming you? But you must let me help you more." Suddenly he flared out, "What am I to say to them in Thendara, if the heir to Hastur dies in my hands?"

"You're making too much of this," Regis said. "I never heard that anyone died of threshold sickness."

Yet Javanne had looked genuinely frightened ...

"Maybe not," Danilo said skeptically, "but if you cannot sit your horse, and fall and break your skull, that's fatal, too. Or if you exhaust yourself and take a chill, and die of it. And you are the last Hastur."

"No I'm not," Regis said, at the end of endurance. "Didn't you hear me tell Lew? I have an heir. Before I ever came on this trip I faced the fact that I might die, so I named one of my sister's sons as my heir. Legally." Danilo sat back on his heels, stunned, wide open, and his thought was as clear as if he had spoken aloud, *For my sake?* Regis forcibly stopped himself from saying anything more. He could not face the naked emotion in Danilo's eyes. This was the time of danger, the forced intimacy of these evenings, when he must barricade himself continually against revealing what he felt. It would be all too easy to cling to Danilo for strength, to take advantage of Danilo's emotional response to him.

Danilo was saying angrily, "Even so, I won't have your death on my head! The Hasturs need you for *yourself*, Regis, not just for your blood or your heir!"

"What do you suggest I do about it?" Regis did not know, himself, whether it was an honest question or a sarcastic challenge.

"We are not pursued. We must rest here till you are well again."

"I don't think I shall ever be well again until I have a chance to go to one of the towers and learn to control this." *Laran?* Gift? Curse, he thought. In his blood, in his brain. But that was not the only thing making him ill, he knew. It was the constant need to barrier himself against his feelings, against his own unwelcome thoughts and desires. And for that there was no help, he decided. Even in the towers they could not make him other than he was. They might teach him to conceal it, though, live with it.

Danilo laid his hand on Regis' shoulder. "You must let me look after you. It is my duty." He added after a moment, "And my pleasure."

By an effort that literally made his head spin, Regis remained motionless under the touch. Rigidly, refusing the proffered rapport, he said, "Your porridge is burning. If you're so eager to do something, attend to what you're supposed to be doing. The damned stuff is inedible even when properly cooked."

Danilo stiffened as if the words had been a blow. He went to the fire and took off the boiling concoction. Regis did not look at him or care that he had hurt him. He was beyond thinking about anything, except his own attempt *not* to think.

He felt a violent anger with Danilo for forcing this intimate confrontation on him. Suddenly he recalled the fight Danilo had picked in the barracks; a fight which, had it not been for Hjalmar's intervention, might have gone far beyond a single blow. He wanted to lash out at Danilo now, flay him with cruel words. He felt a need to put distance between them, break up this unendurable closeness, keep Dani from looking at him with so much love. If they fought, perhaps Regis would no longer have to be constantly on guard, afraid of doing and saying what he could not even endure to think. . . .

Danilo came with porridge in a small pannikin. He said tentatively, "I don't think this is burned . . ."

"Oh, stop being so damned *attentive!*" Regis flung at him. "Eat your supper and let me alone, damn you, just stop hovering over me! What must I do to make you realize I don't want you, I don't need you? *Just let me alone!*"

Danilo's face went white. He went and sat on the other bench, his head bent over his own porridge. His back to Regis, he said coldly, "Yours is there when you want it, my lord."

Regis could see clearly, as if time had slid out of focus, that searing moment in the barracks, when Danilo had flung him off with an insult. It was clear in Danilo's mind, too: *He has done to me, knowing, what I did to him, unknowing.*

By main force Regis held himself back from immediate apology. The smell of the porridge made him feel violently sick. He went to the stone shelf and laid himself down, wrapping himself in his riding-cloak and trying to suppress the racking shudders that shook his whole body. It seemed to him that he could hear Danilo crying, as he had done so often in the barracks, but Danilo was sitting on the bench, quietly eating his supper. Regis lay looking at the fire, until it began to flare up, flame—hallucination. Not forest fire, not Sharry. Just hallucination again. Psi out of control.

Still, it seemed that he could see Lew's face, vividly, by firelight. Suppose, Regis thought, when I reached up toward him, drew him down beside me, he had flung me off, slapped me? Suppose he had thought the comfort I offered him a thing too shameful to endure or acknowledge?

I was only a child. I didn't know what I was doing.

He wasn't a child. And he knew.

Unable to endure this train of thought, he let the swaying sickness take him again. It was almost a relief to let the world slide away, go dim and thin out to nothing. Time vanished. He heard Danilo's voice after a time, but the words no longer made sense; they were just vibration, sound without sense or relevance. He knew with the last breath of sanity that his only hope of saving himself now was to cry out, get up and move around, call out to Danilo, hang on to him as an anchor in this deadly nowhere—

He could *not*. He could not surrender to this; he would rather die . . . and he heard some curious remote little voice in his mind say *Die, then, if it is so important to you*. And he felt something like a giant swing to take him, toss him high, further out into nowhere with every swooping breath, seeing stars, atoms, strange vibrations, the very rhythm of the universe—or was it his own brain cells vibrating, madly out of control?

He'd done this to himself, he knew. He'd let it happen, too much of a coward to face himself.

Call out to Dani, that inner voice said. *He'll help you, even now, if you ask him. But you'll have to ask, you've made it impossible for him to come to you again unless you call him. Call quickly, quickly, while you still can.*

I can't—

He felt his breathing begin to come in gasps, as if he hung somewhere in the far spaces which were all he could see now, with every breath coming for an instant back to that struggling, dimming body lying inert on the shelf. *Quickly! Cry out now for help or you will die, here and now with everything left undone because of your pride . . .*

With the last of his strength Regis fought for enough voice to shout, call aloud. It came out as the faintest of stifled whispers.

"Dani . . . help me . . ."

Too late, he thought, and felt himself slide off into nothingness. He wondered, with desperate regret, if he was dying . . . because he could not bear to be honest with himself, with his friend. . . .

He swung in darkness, immobile, numb, paralyzed. He felt Danilo, only a dim blue haze through his closed eyes, bending over him, fumbling at his tunic-laces. He could not even feel Danilo's hands except that they were at his throat. He thought insanely, Is he going to kill me?

Without warning his body convulsed in a spasm of the most hideous pain he had ever known. He was *there* again, Danilo's face visible through a reddish blood-colored mist, standing over him, his hand just touching the matrix around Regis' neck. Regis said hoarsely, "No. Not again—" and felt the bone-cracking spasm return. Danilo dropped the matrix as if it burned him and the hellish pain subsided. Regis lay gasping. It felt as if he had fallen into the fire.

Danilo gasped, "Forgive me—I thought you were dying! I knew no other way to reach your mind. . . ." Carefully, without touching it, Danilo covered the matrix again. He dropped down on the stone bed beside Regis, as if his knees were too weak to hold him upright.

"Regis, Regis, I thought you were dying—"

Regis whispered, "I thought so too."

"I told myself, if I let you die because I could not forgive a harsh word, then I was a disgrace to my father and all those who had served Hastur. I am a catalyst telepath, there had to be *something* I could do to reach you—I shouted and you didn't hear, I slapped and pinched you, I thought you were dead already, but I could *feel* you calling me. . . ." He was entirely unstrung. Regis whispered, "What was it that you did? I felt you—"

"I touched the matrix—nothing else seemed to reach you, I was so sure you were dying—" He broke down and sobbed. "I could have killed you! I could have killed you!"

Regis drew Danilo down beside him, holding him tight in his arms. *"Bredu,* don't cry," he whispered. "See, I'm not dead." He felt suddenly shy again. Danilo's face, wet with tears, was pressed against his cheek. Regis patted it clumsily. "Don't cry any more."

"But I hurt you so—I can't bear to hurt you," Danilo said wildly.

"I don't think anything less would have brought me back," Regis said. "It's my life I owe you this time, *bredu.*" He was still dizzy and aching with the aftermath of what he now knew must have been a convulsion. Later he was to learn that this last-resort heroic treatment, gripping a matrix, was used only at the point of death; when stronger telepaths determined that without it, the sufferer might wander endlessly in the corridors of his own brain, cutting off all outside stimuli, until he died. Danilo had done it by pure instinct. Now Regis remembered what Javanne had said. "I've got to get up and move around or it may come back. But you'll have to help me, Dani, I'm too weak to walk alone."

Danilo helped him upright. By the last light of the dying fire Regis could see the tears on his face. He kept his arm around Regis, steadying him. "I should never have quarreled with you when you were sick."

"It was I who picked the quarrel, Dani. Can you forgive me?"

He was cruel to Dani out of fear, Regis knew, fear of what he was himself. Perhaps Dyan, too, turned to cruelty out of fear and came at last to prefer cruelty to fear—or to shame—at knowing himself too well.

Laran was terrible. But they had no choice, only to meet it with honor.

Danilo said shyly, "I kept your porridge hot for you. Can you try to eat it now?"

Regis took the hot pottery pannikin, burning his fingers a little on the edges. The thought of food made him feel sick, but obediently he chewed a few mouthfuls and discovered that he was actually very hungry. He ate the hot unsweetened stuff, saying after a time, "Well, it's no worse than what we got in barracks. If you ever find yourself a masterless man, Dani, we'll get you a job as an army cook."

"God forbid I should be a masterless man while you live, Regis."

Regis reached for Danilo's hand, holding it tight. He felt exhausted and aching, but at peace. He finished the porridge and Danilo took the bowl away to rinse it out. Regis lay down on the shelf again. The fire was dying down and it was cold. Danilo came and spread out his own cloak and blanket beside Regis, sat beside him, pulling off his boots.

"I wish I knew more about threshold sickness."

"Be damn glad you don't," Regis said harshly, "it's hell. I hope you never have it."

"Oh, I *had* it," Dani said. "I know now that's what it must have been when I began . . . reading minds. There was no one to tell me what it was, and I never had it so seriously. The trouble is, I don't know what to do about it. Or I could help you." He looked at Regis hestitantly in the dim light and said, "We're still in rapport a little. Let me try."

"Do what you want to," Regis said, "I won't drive you away again. Only be careful. Your last experiment was painful."

"I did find out one thing," Danilo said. "I could see and feel things. There's a kind of . . . of *energy*. Look." He bent over Regis, running his fingertips lightly above his body, not touching him. "I can feel it this way, without touching you, and certain places it's strong, and others I feel it ought to be and isn't. . . . I don't know how to explain it. Do you feel it?"

Regis remembered the very little the *leronis* had told him when she tested him, unsuccessfully, for *laran*. "There are certain ... energy centers in the body, which waken with the wakening of *laran*. Everybody has them, but in a telepath they're stronger and more ... perceptible. If that's true, you should have them, too." He reached out toward Danilo, running his hands over his face, feeling the definite, tangible flow of power. "Yes, it's like an ... an extra pulsebeat here, just above your brow." He had once been shown a drawing of these currents, but at that time he had no reason to believe it applied to him. Now he struggled to remember, sensing it must be important. "There's one at the base of the throat."

"Yes, I can see it," Danilo said, touching it lightly with a fingertip. The touch was not painful, but Regis felt it like a faint, definite electric shock. Yet once he was fully aware of the pulse, his perceptions cleared and the dizziness which had been with him for weeks now seemed to clear and shift somehow. He felt that he had discovered something very important, but he didn't know what. Danilo went on, trying to trace out the flows of power with his fingertips. "I don't really have to touch you to feel them. I seem to know—"

"Probably because you've got them yourself," Regis said. "Matrix work needs training, but it must be possible to learn to control *laran*, or the techniques couldn't have evolved. Unless you want to believe all those old stories about gods and demigods coming down to teach the Comyn how to use them, and I don't." It was very dark, but he could see Danilo clearly, as if his body were outlined with the pale, pulsing energy flows. Danilo said, "Then maybe we can find out how to keep you from going into that kind of ... of crisis again."

Regis said, "I seem to be in your hands, Dani. Quite literally. I don't know if I could live through another attack like that one." He knew that the physical shock Danilo had given him by touching his matrix had revived him, but that he was drained, dangerously weak. "You had threshold sickness? And got over it?"

"Yes. Though, as I say, I had no idea what it was. But finding out about these energy currents helped. I could make them flow smoothly, most of the time, and it seemed that I could *use* that energy. I'm not saying this very well, am I? I don't know the right words."

Regis smiled ruefully and said, "Maybe there aren't any." He lay watching the energy flows in Danilo's body and had the strange sensation that, although they were both heavily clothed against the cold, they were both, somehow, naked, a different kind of naked. Maybe this is what Lew meant: living with your skin off. He could feel the energy flows in Danilo, too, pulsing, moving smoothly and steadily with the forces of life. Danilo went on, gently searching out the flows, not touching him; even so, the touch that was not a touch stirred physical awareness again. Regis had not heard Lew explain how the same currents carried telepathic force and sexual energy, but he sensed just enough to be self-conscious about it. He gently reached out and held Danilo's hand away from him.

"No," he said, not angry now, but honestly, facing it—they could not lie to each other now. "You don't want to stir *that* up, do you, Dani?"

There was a frozen instant while Danilo almost stopped breathing. Then he said, in a smothered whisper, "I didn't think you knew."

"So when you called me names—you were nearer right than you knew yourself, Dani. I didn't know it then, either. But I would rather not . . . approach you as Dyan did. So take care, Dani."

He was not touching Danilo now, but just the same he felt the steady currents of energy in Danilo begin to halt, the pulse go ragged and uneven, like an eddy and whirlpool in a smooth-running river. He didn't know what it meant, but he sensed without knowing why that it was important, that he had discovered something else that he really needed to know, something on which his very life might depend.

Danilo said hoarsely, "You? Like Dyan? *Never!*"

Regis fought to steady his own voice, but he was aware of the energy currents now. The steady pulsing which had eased and cleared his perceptions was beginning to back up, eddy and move unevenly. He said, fighting for control, "Not in any way that . . . that you have to fear. I swear it. But it's true. Do you hate me, then, or despise me for it?"

Danilo's voice was rough. "Don't you think I can tell the difference? I will not speak your name in the same breath—"

"I am very sorry to disillusion you, Dani," Regis said very quietly, "but it would be worse to lie to you now. That's what went wrong before. I think it was trying so hard to . . . to keep it from you, to keep it from *myself*, even, that has been making me so sick. I knew about your fears; you have good reason for them. I tried very hard to keep you from knowing: I almost died rather than let you think of me like Dyan. I know you are a *cristoforo*, and I know your customs are different."

He should know, after three years in one of their monasteries. And now Regis knew what cut off his *laran*: the two things coming together, the emotional response, wakening that time with Lew, and the telepathic awareness, *laran*. And for three years, the years when they should have been wakening and strengthening, every time he had felt any kind of emotional or physical impulse, he had cut it off again; and every time there was the slightest, faintest telepathic response, he had smothered it. To keep from rousing, again, all the longing and pain and memory. . . .

Saint-Valentine-of-the-Snows, saint or no, had nearly destroyed Regis. Perhaps, if he had been less obedient, less scrupulous . . .

He said, "Just the same, I must speak the truth to you, Dani. I am sorry if it hurts you, but I cannot hurt myself again by lying, to you or myself. I *am* like Dyan. Now, at least. I will not do what he has done, but I feel as he felt, and I think I must have known it for a long time. If you cannot accept this, you need not call me lord or even friend, but please believe I did not know it myself."

"But I know you've been honest with me," Danilo gasped. "*I* tried to keep it from *you*—I was so ashamed—I wanted to die for you, it would have been easier. Don't you think I can tell the difference?" he demanded. Tears were streaming down his face. "Like Dyan? *You?* Dyan, who cared nothing for me, who found his pleasure in tormenting me and drank in my fear and loathing as his own joy—" He drew a deep, gasping breath, as if there were not enough air anywhere to breathe. "And you. You've gone on like this, day after day, torturing yourself, letting yourself come almost to the edge of death, just to keep from *frightening* me—do you think I am *afraid* of you? Of anything you could say or . . . or do?" The lines of light around him were blazing now, and Regis wondered if Danilo, in the surge of emotion blurring them both, really knew what he was saying.

He stretched both hands to Danilo and said, very gently, "Part of the sickness, I think, was trying to hide from each other. We've come close to destroying each other because of it. It's simpler than that. We don't have to talk about it and try to find words. Dani—*bredu*—will you speak to me, now, in the way we cannot misunderstand?"

Danilo hesitated for a moment and Regis, frightened with the old agonizing fear of a rebuff, felt as if he could not breathe. Then, although Regis could feel the last aching instant of fear, reluctance, shame as if it were in himself, Danilo reached out his hands and laid them, palm to palm, guided by a sure instinct, against Regis' own hands. He said, "I will, *bredu*."

The touch was that small but definite electric shock. Regis felt the energy pulses blazing up in him like live lightning for an instant. He felt the current, then, running through them both, from Danilo into him, into his whole body—the centers in the head, the base of the throat, beneath the heart, down deep inside his whole body—and back again through Danilo. The muddied, swirling eddies in the currents began to clear, to run like a smooth pulse, a swift current. For the first time in months, it seemed, he could see clearly, without the crawling sickness and dizziness, as the energy channels began to flow in a straightforward circuit. For a moment this shared life energy was all either of them could feel and, under the relief of it, Regis drew what seemed his first clear breath in a long time.

Then, very slowly, his thoughts began to merge with Danilo's. Clear, together, as if they were a single mind, a single being, joined in an ineffable warmth and closeness.

This was the real need. To reach out to someone, this way, to feel this togetherness, this blending. Living with your skin off. This is what laran *is.*

In the peace and comfort of that magical blending, Regis was still aware of the tension and clawing need in his body, but that was less important. *But why should either of us be afraid of that now?*

This, Regis knew, was what had twisted his vital forces into knots, blockading the vital energy flows until he was near death. Sexuality was only part of it; the real trouble was the unwillingness to face and acknowledge what was within him. He knew without words that the clearing of these channels had freed him to be what he was, and what he would be.

Some day he would know the trick of directing those currents without making them flow through his body. But now this is what he needed, and only someone who could accept him entirely, all of him, mind and body and emotions, could have given it to him. And it was a closer brotherhood than blood. Living with your skin off.

And suddenly he knew that he need not go to a tower. What he had learned now was a simpler way of what he would have been taught there. He knew he could use *laran* now, any way he needed to. He could use his matrix without getting sick again, he could reach anyone he needed to reach, send the message that had to be sent.

Chapter TWENTY-TWO

(Lew Alton's narrative)

For the ninth or tenth time in an hour I tiptoed to the door, unfastened the leather latch and peered out. The outside world was nothing but swirling, murky grayness. I backed away from it, wiping snow from my eyes, then saw in the dim light that Marjorie was awake. She sat up and wiped the rest of the snow from my face with her silk kerchief.

"It's early in the season for so heavy a storm."

"We have a saying in the hills, darling. Put no faith in a drunkard's prophecy, another man's dog, or the weather at any season."

"Just the same," she said, struggling to put my own thoughts into words, "I *know* these mountains. There's something in this storm that frightens me. The wind doesn't rage as it should. The snow is too wet for this season. It's *wrong* somehow. Storms, yes. But not like this."

"Wrong or right, I only wish it would stop." But for the moment we were helpless against it. We might as well enjoy what small good there was in being snowbound together. I buried my face in her breast; she said, laughing, "You are not at all sorry to be here with me."

"I would rather be with you at Arilinn," I said. "We would have a finer bridal chamber."

She put her arms around me. It was so dark we could not see one another's faces, but we needed no light. She whispered, "I am happy with you wherever we are."

We were exaggeratedly gentle with one another now. I hoped a time might come, some day, when we could come into one another's arms without fear. I knew I would never forget, not while I lived, that terrifying madness that had gripped us both, nor those dreadful hours, after Marjorie had cried herself into a stunned, exhausted sleep, while I lay restless, aching with the fear she might never trust or love me again.

That fear had vanished a few hours later, when she opened her eyes, still dark and bruised in her tear-stained face, and impulsively reached for me, with a caress that healed my fears. But one fear remained: could it seize us again? Could anyone, ever, be sane, after the touch of Sharra?

But for now we were without fear. Later Marjorie slept; I hoped this prolonged rest would help her recover her strength after long traveling. I moved restlessly away, peering into the storm again. Later, I knew, I must brave the outdoors to give the last of our grain and fodder to the horses.

There was something very wrong with the storm. It made me think of Thyra's trick with the waterfall. No, that was foolish. No sane person would meddle with the weather for some private end.

But I had said it myself: Could anyone be sane, after the touch of Sharra?

I dared not even look into my matrix, check what, if anything, was behind the undiminished strangeness of the storm. While Sharra was out and raging, seeking to draw us back, my matrix was useless—worse than useless, dangerous, deadly.

I fed the horses, came back inside to find Marjorie still sleeping and knelt to kindle a fire with a little of our remaining wood supply. Food was running low, but a few days of fasting would not hurt us. Worse was the shortage of fodder for the horses. As I put some grain to cook for porridge, I wondered if I had yet made Marjorie pregnant. I hoped so, of course, then caught myself with a breath of consternation. Evanda and Avarra, not yet, not yet! This journey was hard enough on her already. I felt torn, ambivalent. With a deep instinct I hoped she was already bearing my child, yet I was afraid of what I most desired.

I knew what to do, of course. Celibacy is impossible in the tower circles, except for the Keepers, and it takes an unimaginable toll of them. Yet pregnancy is dangerous for the women working in the relays, and we cannot risk interruption of their term. I suspected Marjorie would be shocked and indignant if I tried to protect her this way. I would not have had her feel otherwise. But what were we to do? At least we should talk about it, honestly and openly. It would have to be her own choice, either way.

Behind me Marjorie stirred restlessly in her sleep, cried out "No! No! Thyra, no—" and sat bolt upright, holding her hands to her head as if in wild terror. I ran to her. She was sobbing with fright, but when I got her fully awake she could not tell me what she had seen or dreamed.

Was Thyra doing this to her? I didn't doubt she was capable of it, and now I had no faith in her scruples. Nor in Kadarin's. I braced myself against the hurt of that. We had been friends. What had changed them?

Sharra? If the fires of Sharra could break through the discipline of years at Arilinn, what would it do to a wild telepath without it?

Marjorie said, a little wistfully, "You were a little in love with Thyra, weren't you?"

"I desired her," I said quietly, facing it. "That kind of thing is unavoidable in a close circle of that sort. It might have happened with any woman who could reach my mind. But she did not want it; she tried to fight against it. I, at least, knew it could happen. Thyra was trying very hard not to be aware of it."

How much had that battle with herself damaged and disrupted her? Had I failed Thyra, too? I should have tried harder to help her confront it, face it in full awareness. I should have made us all—*all*—be honest with one another, as my training demanded, especially when I saw where our undisciplined emotions were leading us—to rage and violence and hate.

We could never have controlled Sharra. But if I had known sooner what was happening among us all, I might have seen the way we were being warped, distorted.

I had failed them all, my kinsmen, my friends, by loving them too much, not wanting to hurt them with what they were.

The experiment, noble as Beltran's dream had been, lay in ruins. Now, whatever the cost, the Sharra matrix must be monitored, then destroyed. But again, what of those who had been sealed to Sharra?

The snow continued to fall all that day and night, and was still falling when we woke the next morning, drifting high around the stone buildings. I felt we should try to pass on, nevertheless, but knew it was insanity. The horses could never force their way through those drifts. Yet if we were trapped here much longer, without food for them, they would not be able to travel.

It must have been the next afternoon—events of that time are blurred in my mind—when I roused from sleep to hear Marjorie cry out in fear. The door burst inward and Kadarin stood in the doorway, half a dozen of Beltran's guards crowding behind him.

I snatched up my sword but within seconds I was hopelessly outmatched, and with a horrible sense of infinite repetition, stood struggling, helplessly pinioned between the guards. Marjorie had drawn back into a corner. As Kadarin went toward her I told myself that if he handled her roughly I would kill him, but he only lifted her gently to her feet and draped his own cloak over her shoulders. He said, "Foolish child, didn't you know we couldn't let you go like that?" He thrust her into the arms of two of the guards and said, "Take her outside. Don't hurt her, treat her gently, but don't let her go or I'll have your heads!"

"Do you make war on women? Can't you settle it with me, man to man?"

He was still holding my sword; he shrugged, flung it into a corner. "So much for your lowland toys. I learned long ago to fight my battles with sounder weapons. If you think I'd hurt Marjorie, you're more of a fool than I ever believed you. We need you both."

"Do you think I'll ever work with you again? No, damn you, I'll die first."

"Yes, you will," he said in an almost amiable tone. "There isn't the slightest use in your heroics, dear boy."

"What did you do, find you couldn't handle Sharra alone? How much did you destroy before you found it out?"

"I don't have to account to *you*," he said with sudden brutality. I fought momentarily against the men holding me and at the same time lashed out with a murderous mental assault. I had always been told that the unleashed rage of an Alton can kill, had been disciplined never, *never* to let my anger wholly free. Yet now ...

I let my rage go, visualizing hands at Kadarin's throat, my mind raining hatred and fury on him ... I felt him wince under the onslaught, saw him go white, sag to his knees ...

"Quick," he gasped in a strangled voice, "knock him—out—"

A fist connected with my jawbone, darkness crashed

through my mind. I felt myself go limp, hang helpless between my captors. Kadarin came and took over the beating himself, his ring-laden hands slashing hard at my face, blow after blow until I went down into a blurred, red-shot darkness. Then I realized they were hauling me out into the snowstorm; the cold sleet on my face revived me a little. Kadarin's face hung in a red mist before my eyes.

"I don't want to kill you, Lew. Come quietly now."

I said thickly, through my torn and bleeding mouth, "Better kill me . . . brave man, who beats a man held helpless by . . . a couple of others. . . . Give me two men to hold you and I'll beat you half dead too . . . dishonored . . ."

"Oh, save your Domain cant," he said. "I went beyond all that jabber of honor and dishonor long ago. I've no use for you dead. You are coming with me, so choose if you will come quietly, like the sensible lad you always were and will be again, or whether you will be carried, after these fellows beat you senseless? They don't like beating helpless men, either. Or shall I make it easy and immobilize you?" His hand went out toward the matrix on my neck.

No! No! Not again! I screamed, a frenzied cry which actually made him step back a pace. Then quietly—there had never been anything in the world as terrible as his low, even voice—he said, "You can't endure that again, can you? I'll do it if I must. But why not spare us both the pain?"

"Better . . . kill me . . . instead." I spat out the blood filling my mouth. It struck him in the face. Unhurriedly, he wiped it away. His eyes glinted like some bird of prey, mad and inhuman. He said, "I hoped you'd save me the worst threat. Nascar, go and get the girl. Get her matrix stone off of her. She carries it in—"

I cursed him, straining. "You devil, you fiend from hell! Do what you damn please with me, but let her alone!"

"Will you come, then, with no more of this?"

Slowly, defeated, I nodded. He smiled, a silky, triumphant smile, and jerked his head at the men to bring me along. I went between them, not protesting. If I, a strong man, could not endure that torment, how could I let them inflict it on Marjorie?

The men shoved us along through the blinding snow. A couple of hundred feet from the house, past the wall of trees, the snow stopped as if a water faucet had been turned off; the woodland road lay green before us. I stared, unbelieving.

Kadarin nodded. "Thyra has always wanted to experiment with storms," he said, "and it kept you in one place until we were ready for you."

My instinct had been right. We should have pressed through it. I should have known. Despair took me. A helicopter was waiting for us; they lifted me into one seat, set Marjorie in another. They had tied her wrists with her silk scarf, but had not otherwise harmed her. I reached out to touch her hand. Kadarin, swiftly coming between us, gripped my wrist with fingers of steel.

I jerked away from him as if he had been a cold corpse. I tried to meet Marjorie's eyes. Together we might master him . . .

"It's no use, Lew. I cannot fight you and keep threatening you all the way to Aldaran," Kadarin said tonelessly. He reached into a pocket, brought out a small red vial, uncapped it. "Drink this. And don't waste time."

"No—"

"I said drink it. Quickly. If you contrive to spill it, I shall have no recourse except to tear off your matrices; first Marjorie's, then yours. I shall not threaten again."

Glancing at those inhuman eyes—Gods! This man had been my friend! Did he even know what he had become?—I knew we were both defenseless in his hands. Defeated, I raised the flask to my lips and swallowed the red liquid.

The helicopter, the world slid away.

And did not return.

I did not know then, what drug he had given me. I am still not entirely sure. Nor have I ever known how much of what I remember from the next few days is dream and how much is underlaid by some curious core of reality.

For a long time I saw nothing but fire. Forest fire raging in the hills beyond Armida; fire raining down on Caer Donn; the great form of fire, stretching out irresistible arms and breaking the walls of Storn Castle as if they had been made of dough. Fire burning in my own veins, raging in my very blood.

I stood, once, on the highest point of Castle Aldaran and looked down on a hundred assembled men and felt the fire blazing behind me, sweeping through me with its wild lust and terror. I felt the men's raw emotions surging up to where

I stood, the Sharra sword between my hands, feeding my nerves with crude fear, lust, greed. . . .

Again, a terrified child, I stood between my father's hands, docilely awaiting the touch that could give me my heritage or my death. I felt the fury rising in me, raving in me, and I let the fire take him. He went up in flames, burning, burning. . . .

I saw Regis Hastur, lying in a small dark hut somewhere on the road between Aldaran and Thendara, and knew he had failed. He lay there dying, his body torn with the last dying convulsions, unable to cross that dark threshold, failed, dying, burning. . . .

I felt Dyan Ardais seize me from behind, felt my arm snap in his hands, felt through his touch the combined cruelty and lust. I turned on him and rained hatred and violence on him, too, and saw him go up under the flame of my hatred, burning, burning. . . .

Once I heard Marjorie crying helplessly and fought up to consciousness again, and then I was in my room in Castle Aldaran, but I was tied down with enormous weights. Someone wedged my jaws open and poured down another dose of the pungent red drug, and I began to lose myself again in the dreams that were not dreams.

I stood atop a great flight of stairs, leading down and down and down forever into a great burning pit of hell, and Marjorie stood before me with the Sharra matrix between her hands and her face white and empty, and the matrix gripped in my hands burned me like fire, burned through my hand. Down below, the faces of the men, upturned to me, poured wave upon wave of raw emotion through me again, so that I burned endlessly in a hell-fire of fury and lust, burning, burning. . . .

Once I heard Thyra crying out "No, no, I can't, I won't," and a terrible sound of weeping. Even at the deathbed of her father she had not wept like this. . . .

And then without transition Marjorie was there in my arms and I threw myself on her as I had done before. I covered her with frenzied and despairing kisses; I plunged gratefully into her warmth, my body and the very blood in my veins, burning, burning, trying in a single act to slake the frenzy of rage and lust which had tormented me, helpless, for days, months, years, eternities. . . . I tried to stop myself, feeling that there was some dimension of *reality* to this which had not been in most of the other dreams or illusions. I tried to

cry out, it was happening again, the thing I feared and I
hated, the thing I desired ... the thing I dared not see—I
was responsible, personally responsible for all this cruelty and
violence! It was my own hate, never acknowledged, never admitted, which they were using, channeling through me! I was
powerless to stop myself now; a world of frenzy was shaking
me, endlessly tearing at me with great claws. Marjorie was
crying helplessly, hopelessly, and I could feel her fear and
pain burning in me, burning, burning.... Lightning ripped
through my body, thunder crashing inside and out, a world of
lust and fury was pouring through my loins ... burning, burning. ...

I was alone. I lay spent, drained, still confused with the
dreams. I was alone. Where was Marjorie? Not here, thanks
to all the Gods, not here, not here! None of it had been real.

My mind and body at peace, I slept, but far away in the
blackness, someone was crying. ...

Chapter
TWENTY-THREE

"It's not threshold sickness this time, *bredu*," Regis said, raising his head from the matrix. "This time I'm doing it right, but I can't see anything but the . . . the image that struck me down on the northward road. The fire and the golden image. *Sharra*."

Danilo said, shuddering, "I know. I saw it too."

"At least it didn't strike me senseless this time." Regis covered the matrix. It roused no sickness in him now, just an overwhelming sense of heightened perception. He should have been able to reach Kennard, or someone at Arilinn, but there was nothing—nothing but the great, burning, chained image he knew to be Sharra.

Yes, something terrible was happening in the hills.

Danilo said, "I'd think every telepath on Darkover must know it by now, Regis. Don't they keep a lookout for such things in the towers? No need for you to feel guilty because you can't do it alone, without training."

"I don't feel exactly guilty, but I am dreadfully worried. I tried to reach Lew, too. And couldn't."

"Maybe he's safe at Arilinn, behind their force-field."

Regis wished he could think so. His head was clear and he knew the sickness would not return, but the reappearance of the image of Sharra troubled him deeply. He had heard stories of out-of-control matrices, most of them from the Ages of Chaos, but some more recent. A cloud covered the sun and he shivered with cold.

Danilo said, "I think we should ride on, if you've finished."

"Finished? I didn't even start," he said ruefully, tucking the matrix into his pocket again. "We'll go on, but let me eat something first." He accepted the chunk of dried meat Danilo handed him and sat chewing it. They were sitting side by side

345

on a fallen tree, their horses cropping grass nearby through the melting snow. "How long have we been on the road, Dani? I lost count while I was sick."

"Six days, I think. We aren't more than a few days from Thendara. Perhaps tonight we'll be within the outskirts of the Armida lands and I can send word somehow to my father. Lew told Beltran's men to send word, but I don't trust him to have done it."

"Grandfather always regarded Lord Kermiac as an honorable man. Beltran is a strange cub to come from such a den."

"He may have been decent enough until he fell into the hands of Sharra," Danilo said. "Or perhaps Kermiac ruled too long. I've heard that the land which lives too long under the rule of old men grows desperate for change at any cost."

Regis wondered what would happen in the Domains when his grandfather's regency ended, when Prince Derik Elhalyn took his crown. Would his people have grown desperate for change at any cost? He was remembering the Comyn Council where he and Danilo had stood watching the struggle for power. They would not be watching, then, they would be part of it. Was power always evil, always corrupt?

Dani said, as though he knew Regis' thoughts, "But Beltran didn't just want power to change things, he wanted a whole world to play with."

Regis was startled at the clarity of that and pleased again to think that, if the fate of their world ever depended on the Hasturs, he would have someone like Dani to help him with decisions! He reached out, gave Danilo's hand a brief, strong squeeze. All he said was, "Let's get the horses saddled, then. Maybe we can help make sure he doesn't get it to play with."

They were about to mount when they heard a faint droning, which grew to a sky-filling roar. Danilo glanced up; without a word, he and Regis drew and the horses under the cover of the trees. But the helicopter, moving steadily overhead, paid no attention to them.

"Nothing to do with us," said Danilo when it was out of sight, "probably some business of the Terrans." He let out his breath and laughed, almost in apology. "I shall never hear one again without fear!"

"Just the same, a day will come when we'll have to use them too," Regis said slowly. "Maybe the Aldaran lands and the Domains would understand each other better if it were not ten days' ride from Thendara to Caer Donn."

"Maybe." But Regis felt Danilo withdraw, and he said no more. As they rode on, he thought that, like it or not, the Terrans were here and nothing could ever be as it was before they came. What Beltran wanted was not wrong, Regis felt. Only the way he chose to get it. He himself would find a safer way.

He realized, with astonishment and self-disgust, the direction his thoughts were taking. What had he to do with all that?

He had ridden this road from Nevarsin less than a year ago, believing then that he was without *laran* and free to shrug his heritage aside and go out into space, follow the Terran starships to the far ends of the Empire. He looked up at the face of Liriel, pale-violet in the noonday sky, and thought how no Darkovan had ever set foot even on any of their own moons. His grandfather had pledged to help him go, if Regis still wanted to. He would not break his word.

Two years more, given to the cadets and the Comyn. Then he would be free. Yet an invisible weight seemed to press him down, even as he made plans for freedom.

Danilo drew his horse suddenly to a stop.

"Riders, Lord Regis. On the road ahead."

Regis drew even with him, letting his reins lie loose on his pony's neck. "Should we get off the road?"

"I think not. We are well within the Domains by now; here you are safe, Lord Regis."

Regis lifted his eyebrows at the formal tone, suddenly realizing its import. In the isolation of the last days, in stress and extremity, all man-made barriers had fallen; they were two boys the same age, friends, *bredin*. Now, in the Domains and before outsiders once again, he was the heir to Hastur, Danilo his paxman. He smiled a little ruefully, accepting the necessity of this, and let Danilo ride a few paces ahead. Looking at his friend's back, he thought with a strange shiver that it was literally true, not just a word: Dani would die for him.

It was a terrifying thought, though it should not have been so strange. He knew perfectly well that any one of the Guardsmen who had escorted him here and there when he was only a sickly little boy, or ridden with him to and from Nevarsin, were sworn by many oaths to protect him with their lives. But it had never been entirely real to him until Danilo, of his free will and from love, had given him that pledge. He rode steadily, with the trained control he had been taught, but his back was alive with prickles and he felt the very hairs rise on his forearms. Was this what it meant, to be Hastur?

He could see the riders now. The first few wore the green-and-black uniform he had worn himself in the past summer. Comyn Guardsmen! And a whole group of others, not in uniform. But there were no banners, no displays. This was a party of war. Or, at least, one prepared to fight!

Ordinary travelers would have drawn off the road, letting the Guardsmen pass. Instead Regis and Danilo rode straight toward them at a steady pace. The head Guardsman—Regis recognized him now, the young officer Hjalmar—lowered his pike and gave formal challenge.

"Who rides in the Domains—" He broke off, forgetting the proper words. "Lord Regis!"

Gabriel Lanart-Hastur rode quickly past him, bringing his horse up beside Regis. He reached both hands to him. "Praise to the Lord of Light, you are safe! Javanne has been mad with fear for you!"

Regis realized that Gabriel would have been blamed for letting him ride off alone. He owed him an apology. There was no time for it now. The riders surrounded them and he noted many members of the Comyn Council among Guardsmen and others he did not recognize. At the head of them, on a great gray horse, rode Dyan Ardais. His stern, proud face relaxed a little as he saw Regis, and he said in his harsh but musical voice, "You have given us all a fright, kinsman. We feared you dead or prisoner somewhere in the hills." His eyes fell on Danilo and his face stiffened, but he said steadily, "Dom Syrtis, word came from Thendara, sent by the Terrans and brought to us; a message was sent to your father, sir, that you were alive and well."

Danilo inclined his head, saying with frigid formality, "I am grateful, Lord Ardais." Regis could tell how hard the civil words came. He looked at Dyan with faint curiosity, surprised at the prompt delivery of the reassuring message, wondering why, at least, Dyan had not left it to a subordinate to give. Then he knew the answer. Dyan was in charge of this mission, and would consider it his duty.

Whatever his personal faults and struggles, Regis knew, Dyan's allegiance to Comyn came first. Whatever he did, everything was subordinate to that. It had probably never occurred to Dyan that his private life could affect the honor of the Comyn. It was an unwelcome thought and Regis tried to reject it, but it was there nevertheless. And, even more disquieting, the thought that if Danilo had been a private citizen and not a cadet, it genuinely would *not* have mattered how Dyan treated or mistreated him.

Dyan was evidently waiting for some explanation; Regis said, "Danilo and I were held prisoner at Aldaran. We were freed by Dom Lewis Alton." Lew's formal title had a strange sound in his ears. He did not remember using it before.

Dyan turned his head, and Regis saw the horse-litter at the center of the column. His grandfather? Traveling at this season? Then, with the curiously extended senses he was just beginning to learn how to use, he knew it was Kennard, even before Dyan spoke.

"Your son is safe, Kennard. A traitor, perhaps, but safe."

"He is no traitor," Regis protested. "He too was held a prisoner. He freed us in his own escape." He held back the knowledge that Lew had been tortured, but Kennard knew it anyway: Regis could not yet barricade himself properly.

Kennard put aside the leather curtains. He said, "Word came from Arilinn—you know what is going on at Aldaran? The raising of Sharra?"

Regis saw that Kennard's hands were still swollen, his body bent and bowed. He said, "I am sorry to see you too ill to ride, Uncle." In his mind, the sharpest of pains, was the memory of Kennard as he had been during those early years at Armida, as Regis had seen him in the gray world. Tall and straight and strong, breaking his own horses for the pleasure of it, directing the men on the fire-lines with the wisdom of the best of commanders and working as hard as any of them. Unshed tears stung Regis' eyes for the man who was closest to a father to him. His emotions were swimming near the surface these days, and he wanted to weep for Kennard's suffering. But he controlled himself, bowing from his horse over his kinsman's crippled hand.

Kennard said, "Lew and I parted with harsh words, but I could not believe him traitor. I do not want war with Lord Kermiac—"

"Lord Kermiac is dead, Uncle. Lew was an honored guest to him. After his death, though, Beltran and Lew quarreled. Lew refused . . ." Quietly, riding beside Kennard's litter, Regis told him everything he knew of Sharra, up to the moment when Lew had pleaded with Beltran to renounce his intention, and promising to enlist the help of Comyn Council ... and how Beltran had treated them all afterward. Kennard's eyes closed in pain when Regis told of how Kadarin had brutally beaten his son, but it would not have occurred to Regis to spare him. Kennard was a telepath, too.

When he ended, telling Kennard how Lew had freed them with Marjorie's aid, Kennard nodded grimly. "We had hoped Sharra was laid forever in the keeping of the forge-folk. While it was safely at rest, we would not deprive them of their goddess."

"A piece of sentiment likely to cost us dear," Dyan said. "The boy seems to have behaved with more courage than I had believed he had. Now the question is, what's to be done?"

"You said that word came from Arilinn, Uncle. Lew is safe there, then?"

"He is not at Arilinn, and the Keeper there, seeking, could not find him. I fear he has been recaptured. Word came, saying only that Sharra had been raised and was raging in the Hellers. We gathered every telepath we could find outside the towers, in the hope that somehow we could control it. Nothing less could have brought me out now," he added, with a detached glance at his crippled hands and feet, "but I am tower-trained and probably know more of matrix work than anyone not actually inside a tower."

Regis, riding at his side, wondered if Kennard was strong enough. Could he actually face Sharra?

Kennard answered his unspoken words. "I don't know, son," he said aloud, "but I'm going to have to try. I only hope I need not face Lew, if he has been forced into Sharra again. He is my son, and I do not want to face him as an enemy." His face hardened with determination and grief. "But I will if I must." And Regis heard the unspoken part of that, too: *Even if I must kill him this time.*

Chapter
TWENTY-FOUR

(Lew Alton's narrative concluded)

To this day I have never known or been able to guess how long I was kept under the drug Kadarin had forced on me. There was no period of transition, no time of incomplete focus. One day my head suddenly cleared and I found myself sitting in a chair in the guest suite at Aldaran, calmly putting on my boots. One boot was on and one was off, but I had no memory of having put on the first, or what I had been doing before that.

I raised my hands slowly to my face. The last clear memory I had was of swallowing the drug Kadarin had given me. Everything after that had been dreamlike, hallucinatory quasi-memories of hatred and lust, fire and frenzy. I knew time had elapsed but I had no idea how much. When I swallowed the drug, my face had been bleeding after Kadarin had ripped it to ribbons with his heavy fists. Now my face was tender, with raised welts still sore and painful, but all the wounds were closed and healing. A sharp pain in my right hand, where I bore the long-healed matrix burn from my first year at Arilinn, made me flinch and turn the hand over. I looked, without understanding, at the palm. For three years and more, it had been a coin-sized white scar, a small ugly puckered patch with a couple of scarred seams at either side. That was what it *had* been.

Now—I stared, absolutely without comprehension. The white patch was gone, or rather, it had been replaced by a raw, red, festering burn half the breadth of my palm. It hurt like hell.

What had I been doing with it? At the back of my mind I was absolutely certain that I had been lying here, hallucinating, during all that time. Instead I was up and half dressed. What in the hell was going on?

I went into the bath and stared into a large cracked mirror.

The face which looked out at me was not mine.

My mind reeled for a moment, teetering at the edge of madness. Then I slowly realized that the eyes, the hair, the familiar brows and chin were there. But the face itself was a ghastly network of intersection scars, flaming red weals, blackened bluish welts and ridges. One lip had been twisted up and healed, puckered and drawn, giving me a hideous permanent sneer. There were stray threads of gray in my hair; I looked years older. I wondered, suddenly, in insane panic, if they had kept me here drugged while I grew old. . . .

I calmed the sudden surge of panic. I was wearing the same clothes I had worn when I was captured. They were crushed and dirty, but not frayed or threadbare. Only long enough for my wounds from the beating to heal, then, and for me to acquire some new ones somehow, and that atrocious burn on my hand. I turned away from the mirror with a last rueful glance at the ruin of my face. Whatever pretensions to good looks I might ever have had, they were gone forever. A lot of those scars had healed, which meant they'd never look any better than they did now.

My matrix was back in its bag around my neck, though the thong Kadarin had cut had been replaced with a narrow red silk cord. I fumbled to take it out. Before I had the stone bared, the image flared, golden, burning . . . *Sharra!* With a shudder of horror, I thrust it away again.

What had happened? Where was Marjorie?

Either the thought had called her to me or had been summoned by her approaching presence. I heard the creaking of the door-bolts again and she came into the room and stopped, staring at me with a strange fear. My heart sank down into my boot soles. Had that dream, of all the dreams, been true? For an aching moment I wished we had both died together in the forests. Worse than torture, worse than death, to see Marjorie look at me with fear. . . .

Then she said, "Thank God! You're awake this time and you know me!" and ran straight into my arms. I strained her to me. I wanted never to let her go again. She was sobbing. "It's really you again! All this time, you've never looked at me, not once, only at the matrix. . . ."

Cold horror flooded me. Then some of it had been true.

I said, "I don't remember anything, Marjorie, nothing at all since Kadarin drugged me. For all I know, I have been in this room all that time. What do you mean?"

I felt her trembling. "You don't remember *any* of it? Not the forge-folk, not even the fire at Caer Donn?"

My knees began to collapse under me; I sank on the bed and heard my voice cracking as I said, "I remember nothing, nothing, only terrible ghastly dreams...." The implications of Marjorie's words turned me sick. With a fierce effort I controlled the interior heaving and managed to whisper, "I swear, I remember nothing, nothing. Whatever I may have done . . . Tell me, in Zandru's name, did I hurt you, mishandle you?"

She put her arms around me again and said, "You haven't even *looked* at me. Far less touched me. That was why I said I couldn't go on." Her voice died. She put her hand on mine. I cried out with the pain and she quickly caught it up, saying tenderly, "Your poor hand!" She looked at it carefully. "It's better, though, it's much better."

I didn't like to think what it must have been, if this was *better*. No wonder fire had flamed, burned, raged through all my nightmares! But how, in the name of all the devils in all the hells, had I done this?

There was only one answer. Sharra. Kadarin had somehow forced me back into the service of Sharra. But how, *how?* How could he use the skills of my brain while my conscious mind was elsewhere? I'd have sworn it was impossible. Matrix work takes deliberate, conscious concentration. . . . My fists clenched. At the searing pain in my palm I unclenched them again, slowly.

He dared! He dared to steal my mind, my consciousness . . . But how? *How?*

There was only one answer, only one thing he could have done; use all the free-floating rage, hatred, compulsion in my mind, when my conscious control was gone—and take all that and channel it through *Sharra!* All my burning hatred, all the frenzies of my unconscious, freed of the discipline I kept on them, fed through that vicious thing.

He had done that to me, while my own conscious mind was in abeyance. Next to that, Dyan's crime was a boy's prank. The ruin of my face, the burn of my hand, these were nothing, nothing. He had stolen my conscious mind, he had

used my unconscious, uncontrolled, repressed passions. . . .
Horrible!

I asked Marjorie, "Did they force you, too, into Sharra?"

She shivered. "I don't want to talk about it, Lew," she
said, whimpering like a hurt puppy. "Please, no, no. Just . . .
just let's be together for now."

I drew her down on the bed beside me, held her gently in
the circle of my arms. My thoughts were grim. She stroked
her light fingers across my battered face and I could feel her
horror at the touch of the scars. I said, my voice thick in my
throat, "Is my face so . . . so repulsive to you?"

She bent down and laid her lips against the scars. She said
with that simplicity which, more than anything else, meant
Marjorie to me, "You could never be horrible to me, Lew. I
was only thinking of the pain you have suffered, my darling."

"Fortunately I don't remember much of it," I said. How
long would we be here uninterrupted? I knew without asking
that we were both prisoners now, that there was no hope of
any such trick as we had managed before. It was hopeless.
Kadarin, it seemed, could force us to do anything. *Anything!*

I held her tight, with a helpless anguish. I think it was then
that I knew, for the first time, what impotence meant, the
chilling, total helplessness of true impotence.

I had never wanted personal power. Even when it was
thrust on me, I had tried to renounce it. And now I could
not even protect this girl, my wife, from whatever tortures,
mental or physical, Kadarin wanted to inflict on her.

All my life I had been submissive, willing to be ruled,
willing to discipline my anger, to accept continence at the
peak of early manhood, bending my head to whatever lawful
yoke was placed on it.

And now I was helpless, bound hand and foot. What they
had done they could do again. . . . And now, when I needed
strength, I was trully impotent. . . .

I said, "Beloved, I'd rather die than hurt you, but I *must*
know what has been going on." I did not ask about Sharra.
Her trembling was answer enough. "How did he happen to
let you come to me now, after so long?"

She controlled her sobs and said, "I told him—and he
knew I meant it—that unless he freed your mind, and let us
be together, I would kill myself. I can still do that and he
cannot prevent me."

I felt myself shudder. It went all the way to the bone. She

went on, keeping her voice quiet and matter-of-fact, and only I, who knew what discipline had made her a Keeper, could have guessed what it cost her. "He can't control the ... the matrix, the *thing*, without me. And under drugs I can't do it at all. He tried, but it didn't work. So I have that last hold over him. He will do almost anything to keep me from killing myself. I know I should have done it. But I had to"—her voice finally cracked, just a little—"to see you again when you knew me, ask you ..."

I was more desperately frightened than ever. I asked, "Does Kadarin know that we have lain together?"

She shook her head. "I tried to tell him. I think he hears only what he wants to hear now. He is quite mad, you know. It would not matter to him anyway, he thinks it is only Comyn superstition." She bit her lip and said, "And it cannot be as dangerous as you think. I am still alive, and well."

Not well, I thought, looking at her pallor, the faint bluish lines around her mouth. Alive, yes. But how long could she endure this? Would Kadarin spare her, or would he use her all the more ruthlessly to achieve his aims—whatever, in his madness, they were now—before her frail body gave way?

Did he even know he was killing her? Had he even bothered to have her monitored?

"You spoke of a fire at Caer Donn . . . ?"

"But you were there, Lew. You really don't remember?"

"I don't. Only fragments of dreams. Terrible nightmares."

She lightly touched the horrible burn on my hand. "You got this there. "Beltran made an ultimatum. It was not his own will—he has tried to get away—but I think he is helpless in Kadarin's hands now too. He made threats and the Terrans refused, and Kadarin took us up to the highest part of the city, where you can look straight down into the city, and—oh, God, Lew, it was terrible, terrible, the fire striking into the heart of the city, the flames rising everywhere, screams ..." She rolled over, hiding her head in the pillow. She said, muffled, "I can't. I can't tell you. Sharra is horrible enough, but this, the fire . . . I never dreamed, never imagined. . . . And he said next time it would be the spaceport and the ships!"

Caer Donn. Our magical dream city. The city I had seen transformed by a synthesis of Terran science and Darkovan psi powers. Shattered, burned. Lying in ruins.

Like our lives, like our lives. . . . And Marjorie and I had done it.

Marjorie was sobbing uncontrollably. "I should have died first. I will die before I use that—that destruction again!"

I lay holding her close. I could see the seal of Comyn, deeply marked in my wrist a few inches above the dreadful flaming burn. There was no hope for me now. I was traitor, doubly condemned and traitor.

For a moment, time reeling in my mind, I knelt before the Keeper at Arilinn and heard my own words: ". . . swear upon my life that what powers I may attain shall be used only for the good of my caste and my people, never for personal gain or personal ends . . ."

I was forsworn, doubly forsworn. I had used my inborn talents, my tower-trained skills, to bring ruin, destruction on those I was doubly sworn, as Comyn, as tower telepath, to safeguard and protect.

Marjorie and I were deeply in rapport. She looked at me, her eyes wide in horror and protest. "You did not do it willingly," she whispered. "You were forced, drugged, tortured—"

"That makes no difference." It was my own rage, my own hate, they had used. "Even to save my life, even to save *yours,* I should never have let them bring us back. I should have made him kill us both."

There was no hope for either of us now, no escape. Kadarin could drug me again, force me again, and there was no way to resist him. My own unknown hatred had set me at his mercy and there was no escape.

No escape except death.

Marjorie—I looked at her, wrung with anguish. There was no escape for her either. I should have made Kadarin kill her quickly, there in the stone hut. Then she would have died clean, not like this, slowly, forced to kill.

She fumbled at the waist of her dress, and brought out a small, sharp dagger. She said quietly, "I think they forgot I still have this. Is it sharp enough, Lew? Will it do for both of us, do you think?"

That was when I broke down and sobbed, helplessly, against her. There was no hope for either of us. I knew that. But that it should come like this, with Marjorie speaking as calmly of a knife to kill us both as she would have asked if her embroidery-threads were the right color—that I could not bear, that was beyond all endurance.

When at last I had quieted a little, I rose from her side, going to the door. I said aloud, "We will lock it from the inside this time. Death, at least, is a private affair." I drew the bolt. I had no hope that it would hold for long when they came for us, but by that time we would no longer care.

I came back to the bed, hauled off the boots I had found myself putting on for some unknown purpose. I knelt before Marjorie, drawing off her light sandals. I drew the clasps from her hair, laid her in my bed.

I thought I had left the Comyn. And now I was dying in order to leave Darkover in the hands of the Comyn, the only hands that could safeguard our world. I drew Marjorie for a moment into my arms.

I was ready to die. But could I force myself to kill her?

"You must," she whispered, "or you know what they will make me do. And what the Terrans will do to all our people after that."

She had never looked so beautiful to me. Her bright flame-colored hair was streaming over her shoulders, faintly edged with light. She broke down then, sobbing. I held her against me, straining her so tightly in my arms I must have been hurting her terribly. She held me with all her strength and whispered, "It's the only way, Lew. The only way. But I didn't want to die, Lew, I wanted to live with you, to go with you to the lowlands, I wanted . . . I wanted to have your children."

I knew no pain in my life, nothing that would ever equal the agony of that moment, with Marjorie sobbing in my arms, saying she wanted to have my children. I was glad I would not live long to remember this; I hoped the dead did not remember. . . .

Our deaths were all that stood between our world and terrible destruction. I took up the knife. Touching my finger to the edge left a stain of blood, and I was insanely glad to feel its razor sharpness.

I bent down to give her a long, last kiss on the lips. I said in a whisper, "I'll try not to . . . to hurt you, my darling. . . ." She closed her eyes and smiled and whispered, "I'm not afraid."

I paused a moment to steady my hand so that I could do it in a single, swift, painless stroke. I could see the small vein

throbbing at the base of her throat. In a few moments we
would both be at peace. Then let Kadarin do his worst. . . .

A spasm of horror convulsed me. When we were dead, the
last vestige of control was gone from the matrix. Kadarin
would die, of course, in the fires of Sharra. But the fires
would never die. Sharra, roused and ravening, would rage on,
consume our people, our world, all of Darkover. . . .

What would we care for that? The dead are at peace!

And for a painless death for ourselves, would we let our
world be destroyed in the fires of Sharra?

The dagger dropped from my hand. It lay on the sheets
beside us, but for me it was as far away as if it were on one
of the moons. I regretted bitterly that I could not give Marjorie, at least, that swift and painless death. She had suffered
enough. It was right that I should live long enough to expiate
my treason in suffering. It was cruel, unfair, to make Marjorie share that suffering. Yet, without her Keeper's training,
I would not live long enough to do what I must.

She opened her eyes and said tremulously, "Don't wait,
Lew. Do it now."

Slowly, I shook my head.

"We cannot take such an easy way, beloved. Oh, we will
die. But we must *use* our deaths. We must close the gateway
into Sharra before we die and destroy the matrix if we can.
We have to go into it. There's no chance—you know there's
no chance at all—that we will live through it. But there *is* a
chance that we will live long enough to close the gateway
and save our world from being ravaged by Sharra's fire."

She lay looking at me, her eyes wide with shock and
dread. She said in a whisper, "I would rather die."

"So would I," I said, "but such an easy way is not for us,
my precious."

We had sacrificed that right. I looked with longing at the
little dagger and its razor sharpness. Slowly, Marjorie nodded
in agreement. She picked up the little dagger, looked at it regretfully, then rose from the bed, went to the window and
flung it through the narrow window-slit. She came back,
slipped down beside me. She said, trying to steady her voice,
"Now I cannot lose my courage again." Then, though her
eyes were still wet, her voice held just a hint of the old
laughter. "At least we will spend one night together in a
proper bed."

Can a night last a lifetime?

Perhaps. If you know your lifetime is measured in a single night.

I said hoarsely, drawing her into my arms again, "Let's not waste any of it."

Neither of us was strong enough for much physical love-making. Most of that night we spent resting in each other's arms, sometimes talking a little, more often caressing one another in silence. From long training at disciplining unwelcome or dangerous thoughts, I was able to put away almost completely all thought of what awaited us tomorrow. Strangely enough, my worst regret was not for death, but for the long, quiet years of living together which we would never know, for the poignant knowledge that Marjorie would never know the hills near Armida, that she would never come there as a bride. Toward morning Marjorie cried a little for the child she would not live long enough to bear. Finally, cradled in my arms, she fell into a restless sleep. I lay awake, thinking of my father and of my unborn son, that too-fragile spark of life, barely kindled and already extinguished. I wished Marjorie had been spared that knowledge, at least. No, it was right that someone should weep for it, and I was beyond tears.

Another death to my account . . .

At last, when the rising sun was already staining the distant peaks with crimson, I slept too. It was like a final grace of some unknown goddess that there were no evil dreams, no nightmares of fire, only a merciful darkness, the dark robe of Avarra covering our sleep.

I woke still clasped in Marjorie's arms. The room was full of sunlight; her golden eyes were wide, staring at me with fear.

"They will come for us soon," she said.

I kissed her, slowly, deliberately, before I rose. "So much the less time of waiting," I said, and went to draw back the bolt. I dressed myself in my best, defiantly digging from my packs my finest silk under-tunic, a jerkin and breeches of gold-colored dyed leather. A Comyn heir did not go to his death like a common criminal being hanged! Some such emotion must have been in Marjorie yesterday, for she had evidently put on her finest gown, pale-blue, woven of spider-silk and cut low across the breasts. Instead of her usual plaits, she coiled her hair high atop her head with a ribbon. She looked beautiful and proud. Keeper, *comynara*.

Servants brought us some breakfast. I was grateful that she could smile proudly, thanking them in her usual gracious manner. There were no traces in her face of the tears and terror of yesterday; we held our heads high and smiled into each other's eyes. Neither of us dared speak.

As I had known he would, Kadarin came in as we were silently sharing the last of the fruits on the tray. I did not know how my body could contain such hate. I was physically sick with the lust to kill him, to feel my fingers meeting in the flesh of his throat.

And yet—how can I say this?—there was nothing left there to hate. I looked up just once and quickly looked away. He was not even a man any more, but something else. A demon? Sharra walking like a man? The real man Kadarin was not there any more. Killing him would not stop the thing that used him.

Another score against Sharra: this man had been my friend. The destruction of Sharra would not only kill him, it would avenge him, too.

He said, "Have you managed to make him see sense, Marjorie? Or must I drug him again?"

Her fingertips touched mine out of his sight. I knew he did not see, though he would always have noticed before. I said, "I will do what you ask me." I could not bring myself to call him Bob or even Kadarin. He was too far from what I had known.

As we walked through the corridors, I looked sidewise at Marjorie. She was very pale; I felt the life in her flaring fitfully. Sharra had drained her, sapped her life-forces nearly to the death. One more reason not to go on living. Strange, I was thinking as if I had a choice.

We stepped out onto the high balcony overlooking Caer Donn and the Terran airfield. On a lower level I saw them all assembled, the faces I had seen in my ... what? Dream, drugged nightmare? Or had that part been real? It seemed I knew the faces. Some ragged, some in rich garments, some knowing and sophisticated, some dulled and ignorant, some not even entirely human. But one and all, their eyes gleamed with the same glassy intensity.

Sharra! Their eagerness burned at me, tearing, ravaging.

I looked down at Caer Donn. My breath stuck in my throat. Marjorie had told me, but no words could have prepared me for this kind of destruction, ruin, desolation.

Only after the great forest fire that had ravaged the Kilghard Hills near Armida had I seen anything like this. The city lay blackened; for wide areas not one stone remained upon another. All the old city lay blasted, wasted, the damage spreading far into the Terran Zone.

And I had played a part in this!

I had thought I knew how dangerous the great matrices could be. Looking down on this wasteland which had been a beautiful city, I knew I had never known anything at all. And all these deaths were on my single account. I could never expiate or atone. But perhaps, perhaps, I might live long enough to end the damage.

Beltran stood on the heights. He looked like death. Rafe was nowhere to be seen. I did not think Kadarin would have hesitated to destroy him now, but I hoped, with a deep-lying pain, that the boy was alive and safe somewhere well away from this. But I had no hope. If the Sharra matrix was actually smashed, no one who had been sealed into it was likely to live.

Kadarin was unwrapping the long, bundled length of the sword which contained the Sharra matrix. Beyond him I saw Thyra, her eyes burning into mine with an ineradicable hatred. I had hurt her beyond bearing, too. And, unlike Marjorie, she had not even consented to her death. I had loved her, and she would never know.

Kadarin placed the sword in my hand. The matrix, throbbing with power at the junction of hilt and blade, made my burned hand stab blindly with a pain that reached all the way up my arm, made me feel sick. But I must be in physical contact with it, not mental touch alone. I took it from the sword, held it in my hand. I knew my hand would never be usable again after this, but what matter? What did a dead man care for a hand burned from his corpse? I had been trained to endure even such terrible pain, and it could not last long. If I could endure just long enough for what I had to do . . .

We know what you are trying to do, Lew. Stand firm and we will help.

I felt my whole body twitch. It was my father's voice!

It was cruel, a stabbing hope. He must be very near or he could never have reached us through the enormous blanking-out field of the Sharra matrix.

Father! Father! It was a great surge of gratitude. Even if

we all died, perhaps his strength added to mine could help us
live long enough to destroy this thing. I locked firmly with
Marjorie, made contact through the Sharra matrix, felt the
old rapport flame into life: Kadarin's enormous sustaining
strength, Thyra like a savage beast, giving the linkage claws,
savagery, a wild prowling frenzy. And it all flooded through
me. . . .

It was not the way we had used it before, the closed circle
of power. As I raised the matrix this time I felt a mighty
river of energy flooding through Kadarin, the vast floods of
raw emotion from the men standing below: worship, rage,
anger, lust, hatred, destruction, the savage power of fire,
burning, burning . . .

This was what I had felt before, the dream, the nightmare.

Marjorie was already etched in the aureole of light. Slowly,
as the power grew, pouring into my mind through the linked
focus, then channeling through me into Marjorie, I saw her
begin to change, take on power and height and majesty. The
fragile girl in the blue dress merged, moment by moment,
into the great looming goddess, arms tossed to the sky, flames
shaking exultantly like tossed tresses, a great fountain of
flame . . .

*Lew, hold steady for me. I cannot do this without your full
cooperation. It will hurt, you know it may kill you, but you
know what hangs on this, my son. . . .*

My father's touch, more familiar than his voice. And almost the same words he had spoken before.

I knew perfectly well where I was, standing in the matrix
circle of Sharra on the heights of Castle Aldaran, the great
form of fire towering over me. Marjorie, her identity lost,
dissolved in the fire and yet controlling it like a torch-dancer
with her torches in her hands, swooped down to touch the
old spaceport with a fingertip of fire. Far below us there was
a vast booming explosion; one of the starships shattered like
a child's toy, vanishing skyward in flames. And yet, though
all of me was here, now, still I stood again in my father's
room at Armida, waiting, sick with that terrible fear—and
elation! I reached for him with a wild and reckless confidence. *Go on! Do it! Finish what you started! Better at your
hands than Sharra's!*

I felt it then, the deep Alton focused rapport, blazing alive
in me, spreading into every corner of my brain and being, filling my veins. It was such agony as I had never known, the

fierce, violent traumatic *tearing* rapport, a ripping open of every last fiber of my brain. Yet this time I was in control. I was the focus of all this power and I reached out, twisting it life a steel rope in my hand, a blazing rope of fire. The hand was searing with flame but I barely felt it. Kadarin was motionless, arched backward, accepting the stream of emotions from the men below, transforming them into energons, focusing them through me and into Sharra. Marjorie ... Marjorie was there somewhere in the midst of the great fire, but I could see her face, confident, unafraid, laughing. I looked at her for a brief instant, wishing in anguish that I could bring her, even for a fraction of a second, out and free from Sharra, see her again—no time. No time for that. I saw the goddess pause to strike. I must act now, quickly, before I too was caught up in that mindless fire, that rage for violence and destruction. I looked for a last instant of anguish and atonement into my father's loving eyes.

I braced myself against the terrible throbbing agony in the hand that held the matrix. *Just a little more. Just a moment more,* I spoke to the screaming agony as if it were a separate living entity, *you can bear it just an instant more.* I focused on the black and wavering darkness behind the form of fire where, instead of the parapets and towers of Castle Aldaran, a blurring darkness grew, out of focus, a monstrous doorway, a gate of fire, a gate of power, where *something* hovered, swayed, bulged as if trying to break through that gateway. I gathered all the power of the focused minds, all of them, my father's strength, my own, Kadarin's and all the hundred or so mindless, focused believers behind him pouring out all their raw lust and emotion and strength. . . .

I held all that power, fused like a rope of fire, a twisted cable of force. I focused it all on the matrix in my hand. I smelled burning flesh and knew it was my own hand burning and blackening, as the matrix glowed, flared, flamed, ravened, a fire that filled all the worlds, the gateway between the worlds, the reeling and crashing universes. . . .

I smashed the gateway, pouring all that fire back into it. The form of fire shrank, died, scattered and dimmed. I saw Marjorie, reeling, collapse forward; I leaped to snatch her within the circle of my arm, clinging to the matrix still. I heard her screaming as the fires turned back, flaring, blazing up in her very flesh. I caught her fainting body in my arms and with a final, great thrust of power, hurled myself between space, into the gray world, *elsewhere.*

Space reeled under me; the world disappeared. In the formless gray spaces we were bodiless, painless. Was this death? Marjorie's body was still warm in my arms, but she was unconscious. I knew we could remain between worlds only an instant. All the forces of balance tore at me, pulling me back, back to that holocaust and the rain of fire and the ruin at Castle Aldaran, where the men who had spent their powers collapsed and died, blackened and burned, as the fires burned out. Back there, back there to ruin and death? No! *No!* Some last struggle, some last vitality in me cried out *No!* and in a great final thrust of focused power, draining myself ruthlessly, I pushed Marjorie and myself through the closing gates and *escaped.* . . .

My feet struck the floor. It was cool daylight in a curtained, sunlit room; there was hellish pain in my hand, and Marjorie, hanging between my arms, was moaning senselessly. The matrix was still clutched in the blackened, crisped ruin that had been a hand. I knew where I was: in the highest room of the Arilinn Tower, within the safety-field. A girl in the white draperies of a psi-monitor was staring at me, her eyes wide. I knew her; she had been in her first year at Arilinn, my last year there. I gasped "Lori! Quick, the Keeper—"

She vanished from the room and I gratefully let myself fall to the floor, half senseless, next to Marjorie's moaning body.

We were here at Arilinn. Safe. And alive!

I had never been able to teleport before, but for Marjorie's sake I had done it.

Consciousness came and went, wavering like a gray curtain. I saw Callina Aillard looking down at me, her gray eyes reflecting pain and pity. She said softly, "I am Keeper here now, Lew. I will do what I can." Her hand insulated in the gray silk veil, she reached out to take the matrix, thrusting it quickly within the field of a damper. The cessation of the vibration behind the matrix was a moment of almost heavenly comfort, but it also turned off the near-anesthesia of deep focused effort. I had felt hellish pain in my hand before, but now it felt flayed and dipped anew in molten lead. I don't know how I kept from screaming.

I dragged myself to Marjorie's side. Her face was contorted, but even as I looked, it went slack and peaceful. She had fainted and I was glad. The fires that had burned my hand to a sickening, charred ruin had struck inward, through her, as the fire of Sharra withdrew back through that opened gateway. I dared not let myself think what she must have suffered, what she must still suffer if she lived. I looked up at Callina with terrible appeal and read there what Callina had been too gentle to tell me in words.

Callina knelt beside us, saying with a gentleness I had never heard in any woman's voice, "We will try to save her for you, Lew." But I could see the faint, blue-lighted currents of energy pulsing dimmer and dimmer. Callina lifted Marjorie in her arms, kneeling, held her head against her breast. Marjorie's features flickered for a moment in renewed consciousness and renewed pain; then her eyes blazed into mine, golden, triumphant, proud. She smiled, whispered my name, rested her head peacefully on Callina's breast and closed her eyes. Callina bent her head, weeping, and her long dark hair fell like a mourning veil across Marjorie's stilled face.

I let consciousness slip away, let the fire in my hand take my whole body. Maybe I could die too.

But there was not even that much mercy anywhere in the universe.

Epilogue

The Crystal Chamber, high in Comyn Castle, was the most formal of all the meeting places for Comyn Council. An even blue light spilled through the walls; flashes of green, crimson, violet struck through, reflected from the prisms everywhere in the glass. It was like meeting at the heart of a rainbow, Regis thought, wondering if this was in honor of the Terran Legate. Certainly the Legate looked suitably impressed. Not many Terrans had ever been allowed to see the Crystal Chamber.

". . . in conclusion, my lords, I am prepared to explain to you what provisions have been made for enforcing the Compact on a planet-wide basis," the Legate said, and Regis waited while the interpreter repeated his words in *casta* for the benefit of the Comyn and assembled nobles. Regis, who understood Terran Standard and had heard it the first time around, sat thinking about the young interpreter, Dan Lawton, the redheaded half-Darkovan whom he had met at the spaceport.

Lawton could have been on the other side of the railing, listening to this speech, not interpreting it for the Terrans. Regis wondered if he regretted his choice. It was easy enough to guess: no choice ever went wholly unregretted. Regis was mostly thinking of his own.

There was still time. His grandfather had made him promise three years. But he knew that for him, time had run out on his choices.

Dan Lawton was finishing up the Legate's speech.

". . . every individual landing at any Trade City, whether at Thendara, Port Chicago or Caer Donn, when Caer Donn can be returned to operation as a Trade City, will be required to sign a formal declaration that there is no contraband in his possession, or to leave all such weapons under bond in the Terran Zone. Furthermore, all weapons imported

366

to this planet for legal use by Terrans shall be treated with a small and ineradicable mark of a radioactive substance, so that the whereabouts of such weapons can be traced and they can be recalled."

Regis gave a faint, wry smile. How quickly the Terrans had come around, when they discovered the Compact was not designed to eliminate Terran weapons but the great and dangerous Darkovan ones. They had had enough of Darkovan ones on the night when Caer Donn burned. Now they were all too eager to honor the Compact, in return for a Darkovan pledge to continue to do so.

So Kadarin accomplished something. And for the Comyn. What irony!

A brief recess was called after the Legate's speech and Regis, going to stretch his legs in the corridor, met Dan Lawton briefly face to face.

"I didn't recognize you," the young Terran said. "I didn't know you'd taken a seat in Council, Lord Regis."

Regis said, "I'm anticipating the fact by about half an hour, actually."

"This doesn't mean your grandfather is going to retire?"

"Not for a great many years, I hope."

"I heard a rumor—" Lawton hesitated. "I'm not sure it's proper to be talking like this outside of diplomatic channels . . ."

Regis laughed and said, "Let's say I'm not tied down to diplomatic channels for half an hour yet. One of the things I hope to see altered between Terran and Darkovan is this business of doing everything through diplomatic channels. It's your custom, not ours."

"I'm enough of a Darkovan to resent it sometimes. I heard a rumor that there would be war with Aldaran. Any truth to it?"

"None whatever, I'm glad to say. Beltran has enough trouble. The fire at Caer Donn destroyed nearly eighty years of loyalty to Aldaran among the mountain people—and eighty years of good relations between Aldaran and the Terrans. The last thing he wants is to fight the Domains."

"Rumor for rumor," Lawton said. "The man Kadarin seems to have vanished into thin air. He'd been seen in the Dry Towns, but he's gone again. We've had a price on his head since he quit Terran intelligence thirty years ago—"

Regis blinked. He had seen Kadarin only once, but he would have sworn the man was no more than thirty.

"We're watching the ports, and if he tries to leave Darkover we'll take him. Personally I'd say good riddance. More likely he'll hide out in the Hellers for the rest of his natural life. If there's anything natural about it, that is."

The recess was over and they began to return to the Crystal Chamber. Regis found himself face to face with Dyan Ardais. Dyan was dressed, not in his Domain colors, but in the drab black of ritual mourning.

"Lord Dyan—no, Lord Ardais, may I express my condolences."

"They are wasted," Dyan said briefly. "My father has not been in his right senses for years before you were born, Regis. What mourning I made for him was so long ago I have even forgotten what grief I felt. He has been dead more than half of my life; the burial was unduly delayed, that was all." Briefly, grimly, he smiled.

"But formality for formality, Lord Regis. My congratulations." His eyes held a hint of bleak amusement. "I suspect those are wasted too. I know you well enough to know you have no particular delight in taking a seat in Council. But of course we are both too well trained in Comyn formalities to say so." He bowed to Regis and went into the Crystal Chamber.

Perhaps these formalities were a good thing, Regis thought. How could Dyan and he ever exchange a civil word without them? He felt a great sadness, as if he had lost a friend without ever knowing him at all.

The honor guard, commanded today by Gabriel Lanart-Hastur, was directing the reseating of the Comyn; as the doors were closed, the Regent called them all to order.

"The next business of this assembly," he said, "is to settle certain heirships within the Comyn. Lord Dyan Ardais, please come forward."

Dyan, in his somber mourning, came and stood at the center of the rainbow lights.

"On the death of your father, Kyril-Valentine Ardais of Ardais, I call upon you, Dyan-Gabriel Ardais, to relinquish the state of Regent-heir to the Ardais Domain and assume that of Lord Ardais, with wardship and sovereignty over the Domain of Ardais and all those who owe them loyalty and allegiance. Are you prepared to assume wardship over your people?"

"I am prepared."

"Do you solemnly declare that to your knowledge you are fit to assume this responsibility? Is there any man who will challenge your right to this solemn wardship of the people of your Domain, the people of all the Domains, the people of all Darkover?"

How many of them could truly declare themselves fit for that? Regis wondered. Dyan gave the proper answer.

"I will abide the challenge."

Gabriel, as commander of the Honor Guard, strode to his side and drew Dyan's sword. He called in a loud voice, "Is there any to challenge the worth and rightful wardship of Dyan-Gabriel, Lord of Ardais?"

There was a long silence. Hypocrisy, Regis thought. Meaningless formality. That challenge was not answered twice in a score of years, and even then it had nothing to do with fitness but with disputed inheritance! How long had it been since anyone seriously answered that challenge?

"I challenge the wardship of Ardais," said a harsh and strident old voice from the ranks of the lesser peers. Dom Felix Syrtis rose and slowly made his way toward the center of the room. He took the sword from Gabriel's hand.

Dyan's calm pallor did not alter, but Regis saw that his breathing had quickened. Gabriel said steadily, "Upon what grounds, Dom Felix?"

Regis looked around quickly. As his sworn paxman and bodyguard, Danilo was seated just beside him. Danilo did not meet Regis' eyes, but Regis could see that his fists were clenched. This was what Danilo had feared, if it came to his father's knowledge.

"I challenge him as unfit," Dom Felix said, "on the grounds that he contrived unjustly the disgrace and dishonor of my son, while my son was a cadet in the Castle Guard. I declare blood-feud and call formal challenge upon him."

Everyone sat silent and stunned. Regis picked up Gabriel Lanart-Hastur's scornful thought, unguarded, that if Dyan had to fight a duel over every episode of that sort he'd be here fighting until the sun came up tomorrow, lucky for him he was the best swordsman in the Domains. But aloud Gabriel only said, "You have heard the challenge, Dyan Ardais, and you must accept it or refuse. Do you wish to consult with anyone before making your decision?"

"I refuse the challenge," Dyan said steadily.

Unprecedented as the challenge itself had been, the refusal was even more unprecedented. Hastur leaned forward and said, "You must state your grounds for refusing a formal challenge, Lord Dyan."

"I do so," Dyan said, "on the grounds that the charge is justified."

An audible gasp went around the room. A Comyn lord did not admit that sort of thing! Everyone in that room, Regis believed, must know the charge was justified. But everyone also knew that Dyan's next act was to accept the challenge, quickly kill the old man and go on from there.

Dyan had paused only briefly. "The charge is just," he repeated, "and there is no honor to be gained from the legal murder of an old man. And murder it would be. Whether his cause is just or unjust, a man of Dom Felix' years would have no equitable chance to prove it against my swordsmanship. And finally I state that it is not for him to challenge me. The son on whose behalf he makes this challenge is a man, not a minor child, and it is he, not his father, who should rightly challenge me in this cause. Does he stand ready to do it?" And he swung around to face Danilo where he sat beside Regis.

Regis heard himself gasp aloud.

Gabriel, too, looked shaken. But, as protocol demanded, he had to ask:

"Dom Danilo Syrtis. Do you stand ready to challenge Lord Dyan Ardais in this cause?"

Dom Felix said harshly, "He does or I will disown him!"

Gabriel rebuked gently, "Your son is a man, Dom Felix, not a child in your keeping. He must answer for himself."

Danilo stepped into the center of the room. He said, "I am sworn paxman to Lord Regis Hastur. My Lord, have I your leave to make the challenge?" He was as white as a sheet. Regis thought desperately that the damned fool was no match for Dyan. He couldn't just sit there and watch Dyan murder him to settle this grudge once and for all.

All his love for Danilo rebelled against this, but before his friend's leveled eyes he knew he had no choice. He could not protect Dani. He said, "You have my leave to do whatever honor demands of you, kinsman. But there is no compulsion to do so. You are sworn to my service and by law that service takes precedence, so you have also my leave to refuse the challenge with no stain upon your honor."

Regis was giving Dani an honorable escape if he wanted it. He could not, by Comyn immunity, fight Dyan in his place. But he could do this much.

Danilo made Regis a formal bow. He avoided his eyes. He went directly to Dyan, faced him and said, "I call challenge upon you, Lord Dyan."

Dyan drew a deep breath. He was as pale as Danilo himself. He said, "I accept the challenge. But by law, a challenge of this nature may be resolved, at the option of the one challenged, by the offer of honorable amends. Is that not so, my lord Hastur?"

Regis could feel his grandfather's confusion like his own, as the old Regent said slowly, "The law does indeed give you this option, Lord Dyan."

Regis, watching him closely, could see the almost-involuntary motion of Dyan's hand toward the hilt of his sword. This was the way Dyan had always settled all challenges before. But he steadied his hands, clasping them quietly before him. Regis could feel, like a bitter pain, Dyan's grief and humiliation, but the older man said, in a harsh, steady voice, "Then, Danilo-Felix Syrtis, I offer you here before my peers and my kinsmen a public apology for the wrong done you, in that I did unjustly and wrongfully contrive your disgrace, by provoking you willfully into a breach of cadet rules and by a misuse of *laran;* and I offer you any honorable amends in my power. Will this settle the challenge and the blood-feud, sir?"

Danilo stood as if turned to stone. His face looked completely stunned.

Why did Dyan do it? Regis wondered. Dyan could have killed him now with impunity, legally, and the matter could never be raised against him again!

And suddenly, whether or not he received the answer directly from Dyan, or his own intuition, he knew: they had all had a lesson in what could happen when Comyn misused their powers. There was disaffection among the subjects and even among themselves, in their own ranks, their own sons turned against them. It was not only to their subjects that they must restore public trust in the integrity of the Comyn. If their own kinsmen lost faith in them they had lost all. And then, as for an instant Dyan looked directly at him, Regis knew the rest, right from Dyan's mind:

I have no son. I thought it did not matter, then, whether I passed on an unsullied name. My father did not care what his son thought of him and I had no son to care.

Danilo was still standing motionless and Regis could feel his thoughts, too, troubled, uncertain: I have wanted for so long to kill him. It would be worth dying. But I am sworn to Regis Hastur, and sworn through him to the good of the Comyn. Dani drew a long breath and wet his lips before he could speak. Then he said, "I accept your honorable amends, Lord Dyan. And for myself and my house, I declare no feud remains and the challenge withdrawn—" Quickly he corrected himself: "The challenge settled."

Dyan's pallor was gradually replaced by a deep, crimson flush. He spoke almost breathlessly. "What amends will you ask, sir? Is it necessary to explain here, before all men, the nature of the injustice and the apology? It is your right . . ."

Regis thought that Dani could make him crawl. He could have his revenge, after all.

Danilo said quietly, "It is not necessary, Lord Ardais. I have accepted your apology; I leave the amends to your honor."

He turned quietly and returned to his place beside Regis. His hands were shaking. More advantages to the custom of formality, Regis thought wryly. Everyone knew, or guessed, and most of them probably guessed wrong. But now it need never be spoken.

Hastur spoke the formal words which confirmed Dyan's legal status as Lord Ardais and warder of the Ardais Domain. He added: "It is required, Lord Ardais, that you designate an heir. Have you a son?"

Regis could feel, through the very air, his grandfather's regret at the inflexibility of this ritual, which must only inflict more pain on Dyan. Dyan's grief and pain, too, was a knife-edge to everyone there with *laran.* He said harshly, "The only son of my body, my legitimate heir, was killed four years ago in a rockslide at Nevarsin."

"By the laws of the Comyn," Hastur instructed him needlessly, "You must then name your choice of near kinsmen as heir-designate. If you later father a son, that choice may be amended."

Regis was remembering their long talk in the tavern and

Dyan's flippancy about his lack of an heir. He was not flippant now. His face had paled to its former impassivity. He said, "My nearest kinsman sits among the Terrans. I must first ask if he is prepared to renounce that allegiance. Daniel Lawton, you are the only son of the eldest of my father's *nedesto* daughters, Rayna di Asturien, who married the Terran David Daniel Lawton. Are you prepared to renounce your Empire citizenship and swear allegiance to Comyn?"

Dan Lawton blinked in amazement. He did not answer immediately, but Regis sensed—and knew, when he spoke a minute later—that the hesitation had been only a form of courtesy. "No, Lord Ardais," he said in *casta*, "I have given my loyalty and will not now renounce it. Nor would you wish it so; the man who is false to his first allegiance will be false to his second."

Dyan bowed and said, with a note of respect, "I honor your choice, kinsman. I ask the Council to bear witness that my nearest kinsman has renounced all claim upon me and mine."

There was a brief murmur of assent.

"Then I turn to my privileged choice," Dyan said. His voice was hard and unyielding. "Second among my near kinsmen was another *nedestro* daughter of my father; her son has been confirmed by the Keeper at Neskaya to be one who holds the Adrais gift. His mother was Melora Castamir and his father Felix-Rafael Syrtis, who is of Alton blood. Danilo-Felix Syrtis," Dyan said, "upon the grounds of Comyn blood and Ardais gift, I call upon you to swear allegiance to Comyn as heir to the Ardais Domain; and I am prepared to defend my choice against any man who cares to challenge me." His eyes moved defiantly against them all.

It was like a thunderclap. So these were Dyan's honorable amends! Regis could not tell whether the thought was his own or Danilo's, as Danilo, dazed, moved toward Dyan.

Regis remembered how he'd thought Dani should have a seat on Comyn Council! But like this? Did Kennard engineer this?

Dyan said formally, "Do you accept the claim, Danilo?"

Danilo was shaking, though he tried to control his voice. "It is ... my duty to accept it, Lord Ardais."

"Then kneel, Danilo, and answer me. Will you swear allegiance to Comyn and this Council, and pledge your life to serve it? Will you swear to defend the honor of Comyn in all just causes, and to amend all evil ones?" Dyan's speaking voice was rich, strong and musical, but now he hesitated, his voice breaking. "Will you grant to me ... a son's duty ... until such time as a son of my body may replace you?"

Regis thought, suddenly wrung by Dyan's torment, who has taken revenge on whom? He could see that Danilo was crying silently as Dyan's wavering voice went out: "Will you swear to be a ... a loyal son to me, until such time as I yield my Domain through age, unfitness or infirmity, and then serve as my regent under this Council?"

Dani was silent for a moment and Regis, close in rapport with him, knew he was trying to steady his voice. At last, shaking, his voice almost inaudible, he whispered, "I will swear it."

Dyan bent and raised him to his feet. He said steadily, "Bear witness that this is my *nedestro* heir; that none shall take precedence from him; and that this claim"—his voice broke again—"may never be renounced by me nor in my name by any of my descendants."

Briefly, and with extreme formality, he embraced him. He said quietly, but Regis heard, "You may return for the time to your sworn service, my son. Only in my absence or illness need you take a place among the Ardais. You must attend this Council and all its affairs must be known to you, however, since you may need to assume my place unexpectedly."

As if he were walking in his sleep, Danilo returned to his place beside Regis. Bearing himself with steady pride, he slid into the seat beside him. Then he broke and laid his head on the table before them, his head in his arms, crying. Regis reached his hand to Danilo, clasped his arm above the elbow, but he did not speak or reach out with his thoughts. Some things were too painful even for a sworn brother's touch. He did think, with a curious pain, that Dyan had made them equals. Dani was heir to a Domain; he need be no man's paxman nor vassal, nor seek Regis' protection now. And no one could ever again speak of disgrace or dishonor.

He knew he should rejoice for Danilo, he did rejoice for him. But his friend was no longer dependent on him and he felt unsure and strange.

"Regis-Rafael Hastur, Regent-heir of Hastur," Danvan Hastur said. In the shock of Dyan's act, Regis had wholly forgotten that he, too, was to speak before the Council. Danilo lifted his head, nudged him gently and whispered, in a voice that could be heard two feet away, "That's *you*, block-head!"

For a moment Regis thought he would break into hysterical giggles at this reminder. Lord of Light, he could not! Not at a formal ceremony! He bit his lip hard and would not meet Danilo's eyes, but as he rose and went forward he was no longer worried about what their relationship might become after this. He had been a fool to worry at all.

"Regis-Rafael," his grandfather said, "vows were made in your name when you were six months old, as heir-designate of Hastur. Now that you have reached the age of manhood, it is for you to affirm them or reject them, in full knowledge of what they entail. You have been affirmed by the Keeper of Neskaya Tower as possessing full *laran*, and you are therefore capable of receiving the Hastur gift at the proper time. Have you an heir?" He hesitated, then said kindly, "The law provides that until your twenty-fourth year you need not repeat formal vows of allegiance nor name an heir-designate. And you cannot be legally compelled to marry until that time."

He said quietly, "I have a designated heir." He beckoned to Gabriel Lanart-Hastur, who stepped into the hallway, taking from a nurse's arms the small plump body of Mikhail. Gabriel carried him to Regis, and Regis set the child down in the center of the rainbow lights. He said, "Bear witness that this is my *nedestro* heir, a child of Hastur blood, known to me. He is the son of my sister Javanne Hastur, who is the daughter of my mother and of my father, and of her lawful consort *di catenas*, Gabriel Lanart-Hastur. I have given him the name of Danilo Lanart Hastur. Because of his tender years, it is not yet lawful to ask him for any formal oath. I will ask him only, as it is my duty to do: Danilo Lanart Hastur, will you be a good son to me?"

The child had been carefully coached for the ceremony but for a moment he did not answer and Regis wondered if he had forgotten. Then he smiled and said, "Yes, I promise."

Regis lifted him and kissed his chubby cheek; the little boy flung his arms around Regis' neck and kissed him heartily. Regis could not help smiling as he handed him back to his father, saying quietly, "Gabriel, will you pledge to foster and rear him as my son and not your own?"

Gabriel's face was solemn. He said, "I swear it on my life and my honor, kinsman."

"Then take him, and rear him as befits the heir to Hastur, and the Gods deal with you as you with my son."

He watched Gabriel carry the child away, thinking soberly that his own life would have been happier if his grandfather had given him entirely up to Kennard to foster, or to some other kinsman with sons and daughters. Regis vowed not to make that mistake with Mikhail.

And yet he knew his grandfather's distant affection, and the harsh discipline at Nevarsin, too, had contributed to what he had become. Kennard was fond of saying, "The world will go as it will, not as you or I would have it." And for all Regis' struggles to escape from the road laid out before birth for the Hastur heir, it had brought him here, at the appointed time. He turned to the Regent, thinking with pain that he did not have to do this. He was still free. He had promised three years. But after this he would never again be wholly free.

He met Danilo's eyes, felt that somehow their steady, affectionate gaze gave him strength.

He said, "I am ready to repeat my oath, Lord Hastur."

Hastur's old face was drawn, tense with emotion. Regis felt his thoughts, unbarriered, but Hastur said, with the control of fifty years in public life, "You have arrived at years of manhood; if it is your free choice, none can deny you that right."

"It is my free choice," Regis said.

Not his wish. But his will, his choice. His fate.

The old Regent left his place, then, came to the center of the prismed lights. "Kneel, then Regis-Rafael."

Regis knelt. He knew he was shaking.

"Regis-Rafael Hastur, will you swear allegiance to Comyn and this Council, pledge your life to serve it? Will you ..." He went on. Regis heard the words through a wavering mist of pain: never to be free. Never to look at the great ships bound outward to the stars and know that one day he would follow them to those distant worlds.

Never to dream again. . . .

". . . pledge yourself to be a loyal son to me until I yield my place through age, unfitness or infirmity, and then to serve as Regent-heir subject to the will of this Council?"

Regis thought, for a moment, that he would break into weeping as Danilo had done. He waited, summoning all his control, until he could lift his head and say, in a clear, ringing voice, "I swear it on my life and honor."

The old man bent, raised Regis, clasped him in his arms

and kissed him on either cheek. His hands were trembling with emotion, his eyes filled with tears that ran, unheeded, down his face. And Regis knew that for the first time in his life, his grandfather saw him, him alone. No ghost, no shadow of his dead son, stood between them. Not Rafael. Regis, himself.

He felt suddenly, immensely lonely. He wished this council were over. He walked back to his seat. Danilo respected his silence and did not speak or look at him. But he knew Danilo was there and it warmed, a little, the cold shaking loneliness inside him.

Hastur had mastered his emotion. He said, "Kennard, Lord Alton."

Kennard still limped heavily, and he looked weary and worn, but Regis was glad to see him on his feet again. He said, "My lords, I bring you news from Arilinn. It has been determined there that the Sharra matrix can neither be monitored nor destroyed at present. Until such time as a means of completely inactivating it can be devised, it has been decided to send it offworld, where it cannot fall into the wrong hands and cannot raise again its own specific dangers."

Dyan said, "Isn't that dangerous, too, Kennard? If the power of Sharra is raised elsewhere—"

"After long discussion, we have determined that this is the safest course. It is our opinion that there are no telepaths anywhere in the Empire who are capable of using it. And at interstellar distances, it cannot draw upon the activated spots near Aldaran, which is always a risk while it remains on Darkover. Even the forge-folk could not hold it inactive now. Offworld, it will probably be dormant until a means of destroying it can be devised."

"It's a risk," Dyan said.

"*Everything* is a risk, while anything of such power remains active in the universe anywhere," Kennard said. "We can only do the best we can with the tools and techniques we have."

Hastur said, "You are going to take it offworld yourself, then? What of your son? He was at least partly responsible for its use—"

"No," said Danilo suddenly, and Regis realized that Danilo now had as much right as anyone there to speak in Council, "he refused to have any part in its misuse, and endured torture to try to prevent it!"

"And," Kennard said, "he risked his life and came near to losing it, to bring it to Arilinn and break the circle of destruction. If he and his wife had not risked their lives—and if the girl had not sacrificed her own—Sharra would still be raging in the hills and none of us would sit here peacefully deciding who is to sit in Council after us!" Suddenly the Alton rage flared out, lashing them all. "Do you know the price he paid for you Comyn, who had despised him and treated him with contempt, and not one of you, not a damned one of you, have so much as asked whether he will live or die?"

Regis felt flayed raw by Kennard's pain. He was sent to Neskaya, but he knew he should somehow have contrived to send a message.

Kennard said harshly, "I came to ask leave to take him to Terra, where he may regain his health, and perhaps save his reason."

"Kennard, by the laws of the Comyn, you and your heir may not both go offworld at once."

Kennard looked at Hastur in open contempt and said, "The laws of the Comyn be damned! What have I gained for keeping them, what have my ten years in Council gained me? Try to stop me, damn you. I have another son, but I'm not going through all that rigamarole again. You accepted Lew, and look what it's done for him!" Without the slightest vestige of formal leave-taking, he turned his back on them all and strode out of the Crystal Chamber.

Regis got hurriedly to his feet and went after him; he knew Danilo followed noiselessly at his heels. He caught up with Kennard in the corridor. Kennard whirled, still hostile, and said, "What the hell—"

"Uncle, what of Lew? How is he? I have been in Neskaya, I could not—don't damn me with them, Uncle."

"How would you expect him to be?" Kennard demanded, still truculent, then his face softened. "Not very well, Regis. You haven't seen him since we brought him from Arilinn?"

"I didn't know he was well enough to travel."

"He isn't. We brought him in a Terran plane from Arilinn. Maybe they can save his hand. It's still not certain."

"You're going to Terra?"

"Yes, we leave within the hour. I haven't time to argue with your damned Council and I won't have Lew badgered."

Angry as he sounded, Regis knew it was despair, not hostility, behind Kennard's harsh voice. He tried to barricade himself against the despairing grief. At Neskaya he had been taught the basic techniques of closing out the worst of it; he no longer felt wholly naked, wholly stripped. He could face Dyan now, and even with Danilo they need not lower their barriers unless they both wished it.

"Uncle, Lew and I have been friends since I was only a little boy. I—I would like to see him to say farewell."

Kennard regarded him with hostility for some seconds, at last saying, "Come along, then. But don't blame me if he won't speak to you." His voice was not steady either.

Regis could not help recalling the last time he had stood here in the great hall of the Alton rooms, before Kennard and his grandfather. And the time before that. Lew was sitting on a bench before the fireplace. Exactly where he was sitting that night when Regis appealed to him to waken his *laran.*

Kennard asked gently, "Lew, will you speak to Regis? He came to bid you farewell."

Lew's barriers were down and Regis felt the naked surge of pain, rejection: *I don't want anyone, I don't want anyone to see me now.* It was like a blow, sending Regis reeling. But he braced himself against it, saying very softly, *"Bredu—"*

Lew turned and Regis shrank, almost with horror, from the first sight of that hideously altered face. Lew had aged twenty years in the few short weeks since they had parted. His face was a terrible network of healed and half-healed scars. Pain had furrowed deep lines there, and the expression in his eyes was of someone who has looked on horrors past endurance. One hand was bundled in clumsy bandages and braced in a sling. He tried to smile but it was only a grimace.

"Sorry. I keep forgetting, I'm a sight to frighten children into fits."

Regis said, "But I'm not a child, Lew." He managed to block out the other man's pain and misery and said as calmly as he could manage, "I suppose the worst of the scars will heal."

Lew shrugged, as if that was a matter of deadly indifference. Regis still looked uneasily at him; now that they were together he was uncertain why he had come. Lew had gone dead to all human contact and wanted it that way. Any closer contact between them, any attempt to reach him with *laran,* to revive their old closeness, would simply breach that merciful numbness and revive Lew's active suffering. The quicker he said goodbye and went away again, the better it would be.

He made a formal bow, resolving to keep it that way, and said, "A good journey, then, cousin, and a safe return." He started to move backward. He bumped into Danilo in his retreat, and Danilo's hand closed over his wrist, the touch opening a blaze of rapport between them. As clearly as if Danilo had spoken aloud, Regis felt the intense surge of his distress:

No, Regis! Don't shut it all out, don't withdraw from him! Can't you see he's dying inside there, locked away from everyone he loves? He's got to know that you know what he's suffering, that you don't shrink from him! I can't reach him, but you can because you've loved him, and you must, before he slams down the last barrier and locks everyone out forever. It's his reason at stake, maybe his life!

Regis recoiled. Then, torn, agonized, he realized that this, too, was the burden of his heritage: to accept that nothing, nothing in the human mind, was too fearful to face, that what one person could suffer, another could share. He had known that when he was only a child, before his *laran* was fully awake. He hadn't been afraid then, or ashamed, because he wasn't thinking of himself then at all, but only of Lew, because he was afraid and in pain.

He let go of Danilo's hand and took a step toward Lew. One day—it flashed through his mind at random and, it seemed, irrelevantly—as the telepathic men of his caste had always done, he would go down, with the woman bearing his child, into the depths of agony and the edge of his death, and he would be able, for love, to face it. And for love he could face this, too. He went to Lew. Lew had lowered his head again. Regis said, "Bredu," and stood on tiptoe, embracing his kinsman, and deliberately laying himself open to all of Lew's torment, taking the full shock of rapport between them.

Grief. Bereavement. Guilt. The shock of loss, of mutilation. The memory of torture and terror. And above all, guilt, terrible guilt even at being alive, alive when those he had loved were dead. . . .

For a moment Lew fought to shut away Regis' awareness, to block him out, too. Then he drew a long, shaking breath, raised his uninjured arm and pressed Regis close.

... you remember now. I know, I know, you love me, and you have never betrayed that love ...

"Goodbye, *bredu*," he said, in a sharp aching voice which somehow hurt Regis far less than the calm controlled formality, and kissed Regis on the cheek. "If the Gods will, we shall meet again. And if not, may they be with you always." He let Regis go, and Regis knew he could not heal him, nor help him much, not now. No one could. But perhaps, Regis thought, perhaps, he had kept a crack open, just enough to let Lew remember that beside grief and guilt and loss and pain, there was love in the world, too.

And then, out of his own forfeited dreams and hope, out of the renunciation he had made, still raw in his mind, he offered the only comfort he could, laying it like a gift before his friend:

"But you have another world, Lew. And you are free to see the stars."

Presenting JACK VANCE in DAW editions:

The "Demon Princes" Novels
STAR KING #UE1402—$1.75
THE KILLING MACHINE #UE1409—$1.75
THE PALACE OF LOVE #UE1442—$1.75
THE FACE #UJ1498—$1.95
THE BOOK OF DREAMS #UE1587—$2.25

The "Tschai" Novels
CITY OF THE CHASCH #UE1461—$1.75
SERVANTS OF THE WANKH #UE1467—$1.75
THE DIRDIR #UE1478—$1.75
THE PNUME #UE1484—$1.75

The "Alastor" Trilogy
TRULLION: ALASTOR 2262 #UE1590—$2.25
MARUNE: ALASTOR 933 #UE1591—$2.25
WYST: ALASTOR 1716 #UE1593—$2.25

Others
EMPHYRIO #UE1504—$2.25
THE FIVE GOLD BANDS #UJ1518—$1.95
THE MANY WORLDS OF
  MAGNUS RIDOLPH #UE1531—$1.75
THE LANGUAGES OF PAO #UE1541—$1.75
NOPALGARTH #UE1563—$2.25
DUST OF FAR SUNS #UE1588—$1.75
SHOWBOAT WORLD #UE1660—$2.25

A note from the publisher concerning:

THE FRIENDS OF DARKOVER

So popular have been the novels of the planet Darkover that an organization of readers and fans has come into being, virtually spontaneously. Several meetings have been held at major science fiction conventions, and more recently specially organized around the various "councils" of the Friends of Darkover, as the organization is now known.

The Friends of Darkover is purely an amateur and voluntary group. It has no paid officers and has not established any formal membership dues. What it does have is an offset journal called *Darkover Newsletter*, published from four to six times a year which carries information on meetings, correspondence concerning the aspects and problems raised in the Darkover works, and news of future Darkover novels and critical commentaries.

Contact may be made by writing to the Friends of Darkover, Thendara Council, Box 72, Berkeley, CA 94701, and enclosing a dollar for a trial subscription.

DAW presents TANITH LEE

"A brilliant supernova in the firmament of SF"—Progressef

10th Year as the SF Leader!
Outstanding science fiction

DAW PRESENTS MARION ZIMMER BRADLEY

☐ **SHARRA'S EXILE**
The newest Darkover book tells how the Sharra Matrix returned from the stars to threaten the whole of Darkover's
domains.   (#UE1659—$2.95)

☐ **STORMQUEEN!**
"A novel of the planet Darkover set in the Ages of Chaos
. . . this is richly textured, well-thought-out and involving."
—**Publishers Weekly.**   (#UE1629—$2.50)

☐ **THE SHATTERED CHAIN**
"Primarily concerned with the role of women in the Darkover
society . . . Bradley's gift is provocative, a top-notch blend
of sword-and-sorcery and the finest speculative fiction."—
Wilson Library Bulletin.   (#UE1683—$2.50)

☐ **THE FORBIDDEN TOWER**
"Blood feuds, medieval pageantry, treachery, tyranny, and
true love combine to make another colorful swatch in the
compelling continuing tapestry of Darkover."—**Publishers
Weekly.**   (#UE1599—$2.25)

☐ **DARKOVER LANDFALL**
"Both literate and exciting, with much of that searching
fable quality that made **Lord of the Flies** so provocative."
—**New York Times.** The novel of Darkover's origin.
                                            (#UJ1684—$1.95)

☐ **TWO TO CONQUER**
A novel of the last days of the Age of Chaos and the ultimate conflict.   (#UE1651—$2.50)

☐ **THE KEEPER'S PRICE**
New stories of all the ages of Darkover written by MZB and
members of the Friends of Darkover.   (#UE1517—$2.25)
